BEDSIDE MANNERS

A MEDICAL THRILLER

Baerly

— Hope

you.

enjoy

BEDSIDE MANNERS

A MEDICAL THRILLER

BY

ALAN S. MAISEL, M.D.

1stBooks – rev. 4/11/2001

ABOUT THE BOOK

During Danny Raskin's graduation speech, he exposes the Dean of his medical school for his racist admission policies. Danny leaves his home in Michigan a hero, knowing full well of the rigorous year of internship ahead. Danny doesn't know the half of it. Patients, Danny's patient's in particular, are found dead, and Danny is accused of negligence. Yet there is something deeper, more desperate going on. Danny is stabbed while attending a Nazi protest rally, and though he survives, mysterious people are suddenly demanding a file missing from the ex-Dean's office. The ex-Dean is found dead, a victim of suicide. Danny suspects murder and is suddenly flung head-first into the middle of a master plot by a master race, whose goal is to erase the ugliest chapter of the 20th century. A host of eccentric characters weave a web of intrigue and danger: Danny's best friend, Alex, is a self-acclaimed Zionist who doesn't believe Danny's allegations of conspiracy, yet has secrets of his own. Maxine Chu, Danny's beautiful patient who wants to experience physical love before being overtaken by a deadly disease, is targeted for murder. Rasta Jimmi, a dread-locked orderly, runs his own drug store in the hospital basement and knows only too well the drugs that will get you high and the one drug that will instantly kill you. Danny ultimately believes that the Vice-President of the United States, the first Jewish Vice-President, will be in mortal danger if he visits Danny's hospital. But the "coming out" party of a vicious, secretive organization has already been planned. Only Danny Raskin stands in their way. The stakes are high and treachery lurks in unlikely places. Who are Danny's friends? Who are his enemies?

PROLOGUE

Every night I have the same dream. I'm standing at the podium, velvet pleats of my ceremonial gown wafting in the steamy breeze, facing classmates, family and the powers that be at the medical school. They're all waiting for the 'here's to the future' speech.

But this particular day, on the brink of medical adulthood, something happens. I suddenly abandon my prepared remarks, shredding them right there, and Charles Cantrell, Dean of the Medical School admissions committee becomes the new subject of my graduation speech. In a calm voice filled with resolve, I expose the deceptive admission policies of Dean Cantrell, detailing the methods he used to keep blacks and other minorities out of Arbor Hills Medical School. Dean Cantrell rises from his chair, fingers rubbing together like Captain Queeg, in an attempt to stifle this damning diatribe. Hands on either side of him pull him back into his seat.

Having served on that admissions committee, I had confronted Dean Cantrell previously with my suspicions, only to be rebuffed to the point of being threatened with dismissal. So I did what I had to do. I removed Dean Cantrell's personal files from a locked cabinet in his office in order to find proof for my accusations.

When, on that hot spring day, I conclude by waving one of those files over my head, I am fanning a fire, one whose flames spread rapidly across the entire graduation ceremony like a match set to every diploma. Dean Cantrell is led from the stage amid a barrage of cat calls and insults, triangular black caps with blue and gold tassels flying at him like a swarm of frisbees.

The rest of the dream seems even more real-- a blurred apparition of Charles Cantrell floating above me, waving his arms and yelling, "You killed me, you sonofabitch! You killed me!" Cantrell reaches back and extracts a twelve inch knife from just below his scapula. A bloody aorta is sausaged to the tip of the blade. As blood showers my body I taste the salt of an angry ocean.

"You're dead too," he says, breaking into a ghoulish laugh. "You may have killed me, but you've also killed yourself."

I look down as my belly begins to unzip itself. I watch one abdominal organ after another sever itself from its pulsating stalk and fall to the floor at my feet: liver, spleen, one kidney then the other. Each organ is tagged with identification, just as it was on the cadaver back in anatomy class.

"You are the cadaver," he laughs. "You should have minded your own fucking business." He dissipates into nothingness.

Usually I wake at this point, sitting up in bed and shaking so hard that beads of sweat fly off my body as if from a sprinkler. I look down at my hairless belly, and though satisfied that nothing has been removed, I cannot go back to sleep.

A week after graduation, I leave Arbor Hills for Chicago to begin a year of internship.

The dreams stop.

The real nightmare begins.

PART ONE:

SUMMER

MOMMA WARNED ME NOT TO COME

"Momma told me not to come...
That ain't the way to have fun son,
That ain't the way to have fun."

Three Dog Night, 1976

Chapter 1
Into Chicago

Maybe I should have listened to Mom about staying in Michigan for my internship. She was seated next to me playing Captain Radio, twiddling the dial.

"Hey, slow down. Don't you see the sign?"

Of course I saw the sign: 'Welcome to Illinois.' Years before on a family trip I would have plunged my hand as far forward in the car as possible, taunting my brother, whose right foot would have been sticking straight out the window in a last ditch attempt to beat me. "I got there first." He who gets there first lays claim to the state. This time I was first. The city was mine.

I rolled down the window of my Pontiac and inhaled the inaugural smells of Chicago, my new home, which reeked of steel and hot rubber. A new beginning with two stand-up letters at the end of my name: Daniel Raskin M.D. I had been daydreaming all the way from Detroit. Daydreaming was my minor in college.

"You're going ninety miles an hour and that's the eighth peanut butter cup you've eaten."

The sweeping horizon of Lake Michigan would have been much more exhilarating without Mom sitting beside me. Fiddling with the radio, supervising first my driving and now my diet.

"Eighty's too fast," she said, tuning in a news station.

"A neo-Nazi group has scheduled a rally in downtown Chicago...The National Guard is on alert."

"Turn that up, Mom."

"When you slow down."

Mom increased the volume. "Vice President Harold Barrish, a native Chicagoan who is himself Jewish, denounced the planned gathering as hateful and called it a disservice to the city and the country."

Mom shut off the radio. "Don't even think about it."

"I've only got three days to get settled. No time for rallies."

Mom shifted in her seat. Since she was saddled with a son who chased after causes the way an entomologist chases butterflies, she made it her calling to rescue me from any complications that resulted. As a teen, I was arrested for picketing with farm workers in northern Michigan, and she tried bailing me out of jail by telling authorities that I was allergic to grapes. Then there was the summer during college when I aided Greenpeace in cutting tuna nets that were inadvertently trapping thousands of dolphins. Mom told the authorities: "That couldn't have been my son, not the one who used to root against Flipper!"

She must have read my mind. "I won't be there to help you out, Daniel."

"Don't worry, mom." I meant it. Internship was going to be the roughest year of my life. No time for causes, girlfriends, nothing but the monastic study of internal medicine.

A siren behind us made me squint into the rear-view mirror. "Shit."

Mom folded her arms in an "I told you so" position. I pulled off the highway, heart pulsing in my throat. Ten minutes past the state line and my dad's parting words had come to pass: "Don't get stopped by a Chicago cop."

Rolling down the window, I fumbled for my wallet.

"I'm a doctor now. I can handle this, mom."

"You have peanut butter on your nose." I reached over to the glove compartment for some tissue.

"Hold it right there."

The man loomed before me: black helmet, boots to the knee, leather jacket. Plastic eyes of a shark. "Michigan plates, huh?" he said, grinning like a sadistic executioner. He demanded my license, insurance, even stuck his head inside the car and took a long, deep whiff, as if Mom and I had been smoking Marijuana the whole way down. "How about a urine sample?" I muttered under my breath.

He began scribbling on his pad. "Seventy five in a fifty five zone." He shook his head.

Mom leaned forward. "Excuse me, officer."

"Mom!"

She brushed her hair to one side. "My son just graduated from Arbor Hills Medical School. He's an M.D.," she beamed. "He exposed a corrupt Dean right in the middle of his graduation speech."

"Mom!"

Mom handed me a tissue. "Peanut butter," she whispered. "I'll take care of this." She turned back to the policeman.

"We're not just visiting Chicago, sir. My son Danny is starting internship at Richard Meese. He's going to be a Cardiologist."

The writing stopped. He looked up. "Richard Meese?"

Like school kids, we nodded. As I glanced down at his holster, my mind began firing--he probably hates that place.

"Step outside, please."

Oh God, he's going to shoot me. Ten minutes in Chicago and I'm smoke. I took a deep breath and got out of the car. In my bravest voice I said: "Stay here, Mom." She followed me out of the car.

The patrolman held the ticket up, loosening his helmet strap. "Good place, Richard Meese Hospital. That's where they take cops if we get hurt." Removing his helmet, two beefy cheeks and a double chin spilled out. "If I get shot tonight, the last thing I want to see under the emergency room lights is the face of a doctor I just gave a ticket to. Capisce?" He ripped the ticket into shreds.

I nodded, transfixed by his face. His eyes were no longer aggressive, his double chin circled his collar like a scarf. We chatted for several minutes, and in the process he loosened his belt, which disappeared under a jelly roll of flesh. "See you in the coffee room down in the ER," he said, shaking hands.

"What?"

"I'm assigned there three shifts a week. Mulroney's the name."

As he walked back to his car I shouted: "Hey, what's the deal with the neo-Nazi rally?"

Mulroney turned and raised his hand. "It's trouble, doc. Stay away."

After pulling back onto the highway, I looked at Mom. Her jaw was tensed. She picked at her cuticles.

"You never listen," she snapped.

"Nothing happened."

Taking temporary solace in the radio, mom turned away. Frank Sinatra seemed to be singing *My Way* just to her, filling her with fresh resolve. "Five minutes into Illinois and trouble starts. If only you didn't stick your nose where it doesn't belong. You should have stayed at Arbor Hills rather than come out here to... " She paused.

"Say it mom. A second rate program."

"I didn't say that."

"That's what you meant."

She might have been right. Though Richard Meese Hospital by all accounts had the number one internal medicine program in Chicago, it was still considered a notch below Mass General and Hopkins, programs to which I had been actively recruited. But rather than heading east, I was drawn to Richard Meese, a large hospital in Chicago. One of the oldest hospitals in the state, it was situated one block away from Hyde Park Medical School and was considered a pillar of support to both the Jewish and black communities of the city.

I turned onto Lake Shore Drive, heading south. On my right, colorful skyscrapers with more glass than The Emerald City glistened in the afternoon sun. On my left, sailboats tacked in the Lake Michigan breeze, while on shore kids sculpted sand castles and old men moved pawns on cement chess boards alongside the lakeshore walkway. The neo-Nazi rally was no longer center stage on the airwaves. A Chicago alderman under indictment. There had been two shootings at Cabrini Green housing project. The Cubs had lost. My kind of town, I thought, turning into the parking lot of an apartment complex directly across from the hospital. Prairie Dog Towers, my burrow for this year, at least. I stuffed peanut butter cup number nine into my mouth.

"Why the name, Prairie Dog?" asked Mom, not trying to hide her distaste for the concrete monstrosity before her.

I shrugged, avoiding the fact that cockroaches on the south side got so large they were often referred to as prairie dogs.

While we unloaded my car, Mom commented on how my belongings had been thrown into the trunk without the slightest regard for organization.

"It's her fault, isn't it?" She accented 'her' like she was cursing.

"Whose fault?"

"That girl you told me about. That blond *shiksa* you met after graduation. The one who kept you in Arbor Hills two days after you were supposed to be home with us. The one who made my eldest son miss his going away dinner." Mom looked skyward. "Lamb chops and blueberry pie. His favorite."

Linda Johnson was a student moving into my apartment building just as I was moving out. She needed a mattress, I was throwing one away. She asked me to bring it up to her place. I did, and we tried it out. For two days. Which is why mom was so upset. Besides not having her son home for a final two days of coddling, her time with me in Chicago was also limited. Tomorrow she had to catch a flight back to Detroit and get my little sister safely off to summer camp.

After settling into my eighth floor apartment, Mom took me shopping for food and a few appliances, and made me a farewell spaghetti dinner. Before leaving early the next morning she extracted a promise from me to stay away from trouble. I knew that she specifically meant neo-Nazi demonstrations. It was a promise I expected to keep. I was, after all, here for another reason.

Sitting in a parked Mercedes outside Danny Raskin's apartment complex, a man gazed through a pair of binoculars at the silhouette of the young man and his mother some eight floors up. On orders, he had driven all the way to Michigan, for the sole reason of following the two as they made their way to the Windy city. Why his bosses were so paranoid, he had no idea. Raskin wasn't going to make contact with anyone during the trip. Hell, he was just a kid. He didn't even realize what he had done. But orders were orders, and he was trained to carry them out without question. He glanced down at his Nikon. He had one picture left, having shot the entire roll as Raskin unpacked

7

the trunk of his car. The man hoped his telephoto lens had found what his bosses were looking for. He aimed the camera eight floors up at the shadow of mom and son. "Welcome to Chicago, Raskin, you sonofabitch."

Chapter 2 the rally

For the next two days I immersed myself in Chicago. I toured glitzy Michigan Avenue, sampled the Frango mints at Marshall Fields, watched the shoppers through the glass elevators at Water Tower Place. I wandered among the north side cafes and jazz bars, even jogged in Lincoln Park, absorbing the scent of oak trees and suntan oil. At night I hit Rush Street-- the after-hours playground for the hormonally supercharged.

It was my final day before internship orientation, and as I left the Whitman Gallery, in the heart of the downtown business district, I was lured to a food cart by the fragrance of real Polish sausage. "Can I have mine topped with spaghetti sauce?" I asked politely when my turn came. The vendor wiped his greasy hands on his apron.

"I got mustard, I got onions, I got relish," he said. "You want pizza sauce? Go to Giordanos on State."

As I spread out the dollop of mustard that had been slapped atop my hot dog, a moving figure caught my eye. As he got closer he appeared to be a teenager, dressed in a leather jacket, hair slicked back, arms flailing, chest heaving. Spotting me, he stopped just a foot away. "They're marching!" he shouted. "They're marching!"

"Who's marching?" I wiped my mustardy fingers on a napkin. The boy's rapid breaths came through parched lips, his sunken eyes focused on my drink. I offered the cup, which he grabbed eagerly.

"The Nazis!" he said, gulping it down. "The Nazis are at Daley Plaza, and they're going to march!" He handed me the empty cup. "Thanks," he paused a moment, then snatched my Polish sausage and took off.

"Hey!" I yelled, but Paul Revere had galloped away, broadcasting the Nazi arrival. I shrugged. Who cared? This was my last free day. There was a Renoir exhibit at the Art Institute, a mock coal mine at the Museum of Science and Industry. Besides, I had promised Mom I'd steer clear of trouble.

As I turned the corner, the scene suddenly changed. A flood of pedestrians came rushing past, heading toward the plaza.

"I vill make these meshuganah goyim pay for vat happened," I heard an elderly man in a wheelchair say.

"Treblinka," a man pushing the chair shouted, holding up a tattooed arm: "Remember Treblinka."

My parents had lost family to Hitler's ovens a long time ago. But these guys weren't real Nazis, just a bunch of misplaced wierdos. I turned right at the next corner. More people, rushing in my direction like water from a broken dam. Swimming against the crowd was impossible, so I turned. *Why fight it?* You don't get to see a real live neo-Nazi protest rally every day. At the very least, it promised to be good theater.

Tension gripped the crowd gathered at the Plaza. Curious onlookers carried cameras; others clutched baseball bats or posters with slogans like: "Never Again." Old, young, black, white. As I wove forward, the aroma of tobacco, marijuana, and Afro Sheen filled my lungs. I shivered when I spotted them. Ten mannequins poised in salute, wearing those little toilet bowl hats I used to see on Hogan's Heroes. Nazis!

Moving closer, I saw the police barricade themselves between the growing swarm of angry people and the Nazis. Fright filled the eyes of the two youngest Nazis; hate in the eyes of the others.

A flash bulb popped like a firecracker in front of me, and I jumped. To my left a group of older people were singing in Hebrew. To my right a black man was telling his story to an ABC TV reporter. "Black and Jew--we must join hands as brothers." Supporters shouted their approval.

Screams filled the Plaza.

"What's happening?" I yelled, straining on my toes to see. A hand touched my shoulder.

"They're moving, my friend. Get ready."

I turned. The voice belonged to a confident looking white man around my age, wearing an NYU sweatshirt, faded blue jeans, with the handsome face of a Greek olive grower. In each hand he gripped a rock. The crowd surged forward. I sensed a riot and wanted out, but the crowd trapped me in its forward thrust. I inhaled to make sure I wouldn't suffocate.

"Look at those bastards!" my rock-toting colleague seethed. Jumping up to see over the crowd, I caught a glimpse of the goose-step routine.

"Kill the Nazis!" somebody screamed. "Kill the Nazis!"

"Here, have a rock."

"No thanks. That ain't my style."

"You Jewish?"

That question always made me uneasy. "Like I said, throwing rocks ain't my style."

"What is your style? Letting people shit on you?"

Anger pressed the crowd forward. "Come on," he nudged. "Kill the Nazis. Kill the Nazis!"

I was dizzy. What did he mean, letting people shit on me? Old images broke free--flooded my mind--elementary school-(*Second grade*: *"Where are your horns? My father said all Jewish people have horns"*). Bastards.

And then I was whispering it: "Kill the Nazis. Kill the Nazis.

The crowd surged forward. My friend launched a rock that narrowly missed the leader's head.

I couldn't breathe--*Third grade*: *"Danny, you must sing the word, 'Christ', like all the other children.."*

"Good shot," I blurted. My God, I couldn't believe I'd said that.

"Have a rock, man!" he said, pulling two more out of a Marshall Field's shopping bag. He handed one to me and threw the other. What the hell was I doing?

The noise around me was deafening. Lifting their shields, the police tightened their barricade.

"Kill the Nazis! Kill the Nazis!"

High school: "Sorry, Raskin, no matter how good he is a Jew just wouldn't fit on our wrestling team."

I said it softly to myself: "Kill the Nazis!" It felt right. My knuckles whitened around the rock. I bit my lip. The ABC news reporter, now finished with the black leader, motioned to his camera man. One of the Nazis picked up a rock and heaved it.

Enraged, the crowd retaliated, throwing rocks, sticks, signs. This was war.

"You going to use that as a paperweight?" It was my colleague.

The reporter, seeing my tee-shirt, cupped the microphone: "Here we have someone who has apparently come all the way from Michigan. Sir. Are you here to fight the neo-Nazis?"

I couldn't answer. My adrenalin was too high. "Kill the Nazis!" I yelled, trying to push past the camera to the front. "Kill the Bastards!"

"Sir!" the reporter yelled, grabbing me by the shoulders.

"Hey, watch it," I snapped. "Out of my way, dammit!"

Another tap on my shoulder. "What are you going to do with that rock?"

"What do you think?" I yelled. I reached back and launched it as far as I could. It landed fifty feet beyond the marchers.

"You came all the way from Michigan to smash some heads and kill some Nazis?"

The cloud of hysteria lifted, bringing me back to reality. This newsman was for real. I'd seen him and his silver hairpiece on TV. My voice softened. "Oh no...you see... I'm a doctor. You know, doctor...I ..uh ..heal people."

....Silence.

Shit, I just threw a rock at some crazy kids. What the hell had I done?

I looked over at my friend. At that instant a sharp pain ripped into my lower back.

"Oww!" I yelled, turning. In the distance I thought I saw someone looking my way as he rapidly disappeared into the crowd. My hand went to my back, settling on something wet just above my waist. I brought my hand to my face. Blood. I looked down at the pavement. A small red pool formed at my feet. "What the hell?"

My friend lifted my shirt. "Jesus H. Christ! You must have gotten hit by a hunk of glass."

"I think I was stabbed." My knees wanted to buckle. Tightness gripped my chest.

"Take it easy," he said, putting pressure on my back. "It's only a small puncture wound. No big deal. Must have been glass."

More screaming. I was oblivious to the riot, weak on my feet. In the distance I heard shrill police sirens.

"You OK?"

"I swear I felt a hand back there; I saw someone running. He turned twice in my direction."

"Somebody probably threw a bottle."

I didn't see any glass remnants on the concrete. Then again, it took at least ten minutes before I could focus my eyes or my thoughts on anything. In that time, the riot had died off. Police escorted the Nazi marchers into the safety of their vans and issued warnings through bullhorns for the crowd to disperse or face a night in jail. I watched people pick up their belongings and walk away.

"That was something, huh?" I said, putting pressure on the wound.

"Hope those bastards get a ride to the lockup on the same kind of train our relatives rode to the gas chambers."

I smiled. "If we're lucky it'll break down on the south side."

My new friend examined my back. "Looks okay, now. Maybe someone accidentally cut you as he passed by." He held out his hand. "Name's Rosen, Alex Rosen." His grip made me feel like I'd lost more blood than I thought.

"Daniel Raskin. You really know your way around a wound. You a doctor?"

He nodded. "You too, I gather from what you said to the reporter."

"Intern. Richard Meese hospital."

"You're bullshitting!"

"It's a good program," I said defensively. Alex smiled again. Anger had given way to a smooth, baby-face.

"I didn't mean it wasn't," he said. "It's just that I'm starting there too!"

"Hey, don't bullshit a bullshitter."

"No kidding, man. Graduated N.Y.U."

We both stood there, incredulous.

13

"Look what this hospital has to look forward to," Alex finally said. "A couple of rock-throwing Zionists."

That was the first time I was ever called a Zionist. "I don't go much for the religious stuff."

Alex laughed. "Before you know it, we'll be throwing IV bottles at those pig-headed attending physicians. Is Richard Meese in trouble, or what?" We laughed. "What do you say we grab a beer? Riots make me thirsty."

"Let's grab a couple," I replied-- "I need to dilute what's left of my blood volume."

Alex pulled up my shirt one more time and anchored a handful of tissues to my belt and covered my wound.

"Let's detour by the hospital. Make sure there's no glass in there."

"It wasn't glass, Alex."

"Well the least we can do is sterilize the damn thing with a tetanus shot."

I smiled. "Let's start with alcohol. Works just as well."

Our conversation at Mulligan's Pub went down as easily as our first two pitchers of Guiness. We had bonded against a common enemy, one not so easily eradicated by bed rest, fluids, and antibiotics. I listened as Alex detailed the vagaries of growing up on the streets of Brooklyn, constantly defending himself and his religion to his Puerto Rican neighbors. His father had been killed in a subway mishap the week before he started college, forcing him to work full time while carrying a full premed course load. Even during medical school, he worked the graveyard shift at the medical library just to make ends meet. After residency, Alex planned on moving to Israel, maybe becoming a physician in the Israeli Air Force. When I told him of my plans to specialize in Cardiology, he suggested I first consider a year of research at the Weitzman Institute.

While we were talking, I noticed several women looking in our direction. Since any second look I had ever received usually meant I had part of my lunch splattered on my shirt, I could only assume they were looking at Alex. His body of a wolf and face of a lamb was a lethal combination. Suddenly I wasn't so sure I wanted Alex around the whole year.

I took a breath. "You married?"

"Nope."

"Engaged?"

"Nope."

"Girl back home?"

"Nope."

Damn. One last try.

"Gay?"

"Nope."

"Man, I need another beer!"

That evening, I found that Alex and I had more in common than just throwing rocks. We both had left cities we had grown up in, neither of us knowing a soul in Chicago. Both had left relationships: mine two years, his two months.

The beer flowed freely. By ten o'clock the blood oozing from my back had taken on a frothy consistency, and when I pulled out the Kleenex and showed Alex its pinkish tint, he laughed and said: "It worked. The beer diluted your blood."

I signaled the waiter. "A glass of your darkest Cabernet, please."

We called it quits shortly after midnight, and agreed to meet for breakfast in the hospital coffee shop at 6:45 the next morning, the start of orientation.

"Can you spot me the tab, Danny?" Alex asked sheepishly. "Barely had enough for gas money to make it down here."

"Lose a bet?"

Alex's jet black eyebrows lifted. "Matter of fact, bet my last six months of rent on the Superbowl. Ended up sleeping on a friend's couch."

I laid down a twenty.

Alex glanced to his left as we stood up. "See that blonde standing at the bar? She's been downing Kamikazes like they were Kool-Aid."

"What about her?"

"Bet you five bucks she hits on me on the way out."

"You're drunk."

15

Alex flashed a youthful grin. "Yeah, you're right. Let's take off." Alex had drunk twice as much as I did, yet seemed in complete control. I almost fell over backward trying to keep up with him. A cool breeze lightly slapped us at the door. Our exit was blocked.

"Leaving so soon?" It was the Kamikaze woman, and her face was within an inch of Alex's.

Alex shrugged his shoulders in mock modesty. "Another drink wouldn't hurt. Stick around, Danny, this is..."

"Sherry Martoris," she said, licking her vampish lips. I tried swallowing my pride, but it was stuck somewhere in the back of my throat along with a plate of stale guacamole.

"No thanks, gotta go."

Alex slithered up beside me and winked. "Just need a little mud for my turtle," he whispered. "If you know what I mean."

"See you at 6:45," I mumbled, staggering out the front door into the balmy night, jealousy filling my veins. "Have fun with Sherry what's her name....Majoris....Clitoris .... no, I mean..."

"Hey Danny." It was Alex. I turned around, almost falling. "About tomorrow...lets make it 7:30, okay?"

Chapter 3 orientation

Failing to set my alarm correctly, I awoke an hour later than I had intended, too late to meet Alex for coffee, much less make the start of our orientation breakfast. When I opened the glass door and stepped into the Department of Medicine Conference room some thirty minutes late, the speaker's voice halted in mid-sentence and everyone's eyes turned toward me. I, too, stopped and looked around. The room overflowed with lox, cream cheese, and new interns chewing on old bagels.

"Nice of you to grace us with your presence this morning, Dr. Raskin."

I looked into the eyes of Sol Goldman, chief of medicine, understudy to God himself. I was frozen by his glare, and no one dared to breathe. I watched as his dark eyes fell trance-like to my lower back. I could have sworn he was staring at the place where I was stabbed yesterday. That was impossible. He couldn't have known about that. Though it turned out to be a fairly superficial wound, the damn thing was still sore, worse when I bent over. Sol Goldman's eyes remained fixed as I began to spread peanut butter on an onion bagel and finally walked toward a seat, I sat next to Alex Rosen, who was slumped into a chair in the corner. He was wearing the same disheveled street clothes he'd had on at the neo-Nazi riot.

Dr. Goldman frowned and ran his hands through the wispy waves of hair anchored across his partially balding head. He stood six feet tall, yet at the time of my interview six months before he'd seemed more like seven. Especially with regards to his reputation. During my visit I was told to get on his good side. If he likes you, you're one of his boys. If not... well, nobody showing us around wanted to get into that.

Dr. Goldman leaned over and whispered something to his chief resident, his glasses teetering on the bridge of his nose.

"As I was saying, we....." he paused, seemingly distracted. "I was about to tell you...." he stopped again, studied his notes, then took a long sip from his Yale coffee mug. Next to me, Alex's head was yo-yo-ing against his chest. Goldman's chief resident whispered something back and he nodded. "Thank you. I was about to tell you that in the tradition of Richard Meese's excellence in patient care, next spring we are having a ground breaking ceremony for a state of the art, five million dollar Cardiac Center." A thin smile decorated his lips. "Vice President Harold Barrish, who, as many of you know, was born at Richard Meese Medical Center fifty-two years ago, will be doing the honors." A few heads nodded, some mumbling. I noticed that the intern sitting across from me, reddish curls and freckles, lifted her finger in the air and waved it in a circular, whoopee motion. I smiled.

"There will be quite a fanfare," he continued, "enough so our institution will be under a microscope for the entire country to observe. I want everything in this hospital working at maximum capability. I am asking you and the residents to work hard. I won't tolerate anyone who isn't excellent in every respect."

Dr. Goldman picked up a second manila folder and studied it.

Alex Rosen's eyes opened and he hit me on the shoulder. "Hey, buddy."

I whispered: "Rough night?"

Alex grinned. "Think I look bad? Sherry couldn't even walk this morning."

"Did you get her number?"

"Not my style. No time for a steady."

"Not for you, stupid, for me." We giggled.

Goldman looked up. "Here at Richard Meese, we attract the best students from the best medical schools. You'll be taking care of patients with difficult problems. You'll take care of indigent patients who have no other access to the medical system. This combination, along with the best second year residents anywhere in the country for guidance, will allow you to expand your knowledge of internal medicine greatly ."

Dr. Goldman picked a piece of lox off his bagel and dabbed at his tongue like he had a sodium deficiency. "Our medical library has the New England Journal of Medicine, JAMA, and the Annals. For now, that should be enough."

A hand shot up. Dr. Goldman lifted his glasses.

"Dr. Malcolm Spool, I presume."

Malcolm Spool and I both interviewed at Meese on the same day. Johns Hopkins' wonder boy. Perfect board scores, a dozen published papers, highly recruited, or so he had told me at lunch. Too much anal sphincter tone for my liking.

Malcolm's face was chiseled from granite, his voice a monotone: "I already subscribe to those journals."

"Your residents are your teachers. When it comes to patient care, they have more knowledge than any twelve journals."

"What if we disagree with their approach?"

"Malcolm, your residents have more experience in patient care than you have, and I...."

"That's not what I asked." Malcolm's eyes were dark marbles of contempt. Chief resident Mike Brenlow, seated next to Dr. Goldman, looked fearful. Sol's outbursts were legendary. Cross him, and you were history.

Dr. Goldman weighed his response. "Your residents are your liaisons. If there's any disagreements over how to handle a case, let them fight the battle, not you." He paused and straightened his body. "The only battles you fight are on the front lines of patient care. This is internship, gentlemen. You're the ones in the trenches."

Who did he think he was, General Patton?

A glass door in back of the room banged open. The person entering had wet stringy blond hair that danced off his shoulders. His bare feet slipped on the tile and he crashed head first into the deli table. In one hand he held what appeared to be a wet suit. His hairless chest was partially covered by his white coat, which looked as if he had worn it while taking a stroll through a car wash.

Sol Goldman stood and glared. "Dr. Brian Picolli," he thundered. "What the hell are you doing?"

Stacking his plate with bagels, Brian turned around. He had blood-shot baby blue eyes and a sandy-white smile with a chipped front tooth. He bit into a bagel and said: "surfin." Brian walked toward a vacant seat flicking water from his head like a spaniel.

"Dr. Picolli, don't bother sitting down. I don't give a damn that you were magna cum laude at UCLA. Get your wet ass out of here. You come to this hospital, you look presentable--shoes, shirt, tie..."

Brian seemed confounded by Sol's anger. "What's the big deal, Sol? I'll change right after the meeting."

"Do not call me Sol!" he said, pounding his fist on the table. "Call me by my first name again, you'll be doing rectal exams down in the morgue. Now get out. I'll see you when you're more appropriately attired."

Brian winced, then shook his head as he walked to the door. At the last moment he turned back to the deli table and grabbed up a tin of cream cheese and a handful of lox.

"Out, dammit!"

Sol Goldman straightened his unfashionably loud tie. "Anybody else here doesn't think I run a tight ship, let him speak now."

Alex leaned over and whispered: "Aye, aye, Captain Ahab."

"We're under tremendous pressure to get this hospital functioning at its highest capacity." He pounded his fist on the table again. "I want no mistakes, no screw-ups and no unexpected deaths. I have no tolerance for that, not this year, not any year."

Dr. Goldman finished by giving us our schedules, talking about call nights, and then one final pep talk. "You have a busy day," he concluded. "Laboratory orientation, beeper instructions, the X-ray department. There's a lot to learn."

I helped Alex from his chair. "I gotta pee," he announced, and made a beeline for the men's room. I headed toward my mailbox in the Department office. Sol Goldman seemed to be waiting for me.

"Doctor Raskin."

I turned and nodded. This time his eyes were focused darts.

"Your reputation precedes your arrival here."

I waited. Dr. Goldman looked hard. For the first time I noticed aging lines in his cheeks and forehead. "You planning on giving any speeches while you're here?"

I looked away. How the hell did he know about that?

"The Detroit Free Press. New doctor unseats racist dean. You were a hero."

"I'd rather not talk about it." I paused a moment. "Not the speech, not sleeze bag Charles Cantrell."

He turned red again. "I knew that sleeze bag," he said. "Quite well as a matter of fact."

Shit. Way to go, Raskin. First day and you've already alienated the Chief. Things were getting tougher by the minute.

"No screw ups, Raskin. It's a long year and I'm going to watch you very closely."

As I turned to leave, Goldman said: "You okay?"

I stopped.

"The way you're walking looks like you hurt your back." His face was solemn. Real concern.

"Cut it," I said. "On a piece of glass."

Dazed, I traveled through orientation. We learned about blood smears in Hematology, learned how to do a proper urinalysis without having to taste the stuff in Chemistry. I was given half a dozen white coats in laundry and got a dirty look when I asked how to remove peanut butter stains. I could barely concentrate. What was it with Goldman? Why was he on my case?

After Laundry we went to the Security office, where we were photographed and given ID badges. Alex stole a look at the hospital's photographic roster, scribbling down the names of several beauty queens before having his hand slapped by the pencil pusher in charge. At the switchboard office, we were given a lecture on use of the paging system, stuff like don't drop the beepers in the toilet or put them in the microwave. We were then herded to the administration building where Wanda Bylevin, secretary to the Chief of Administrative Services, gave us a talk on chart dictation and how to use the computer system to retrieve patient information from past hospital admissions. Her emerald green eyes seemed to fix on Alex while she spoke.

"She's checking us out, Danny," whispered Alex.

"She's checking you out, Alex," which really pissed me off despite that fact that I had planned to avoid any personal entanglements, at least for the year.

Alex and I stayed on for the hospital historical tour, given by Dr. Emile Horner, one of the elder statesmen of the hospital. He showed us the first dialysis machine used in Chicago and the first mechanical ventilator, both, according to Horner, bought and paid for by the philanthropic Jewish community of Chicago. Every machine, every pavilion, was named after a hospital benefactor. The Ida Gardner House Pavilion, the Rosenblum CAT scanner. Even many of the patient rooms had plaques outside their doors. "Look," said Alex. "Here's one that says: 'In memory of Seymour Hershowitz.' How would you like to be a patient staying in old Seymour's room? He probably died in that room."

"Hope they changed the sheets," I added.

I asked Emile Horner the reason for the overwhelming number of philanthropic gestures.

"Back in the thirties, when the Christian church-run hospitals turned a cold shoulder to the plight of the European Jewish immigrants, Richard Meese Hospital kept its doors opened. The Jews never forgot. They continue to be born here, and they will continue to die here."

The intern with the red hair said: "Fine, but please, not on my shift." Her name tag read Gail Peterson. She looked serious.

Alex removed a bottle of vitamin C from his pants pocket and launched several to the back of his throat. "Besides supplying care to the Jews who have long since moved up north, Richard Meese Hospital continues to make free medical care available to the indigent of South Hyde Park. That's part of the reason I came here."

Emile Horner, a man who seemingly shrunk in his old age to a paltry five foot, nodded and smiled at Alex. "Yes, my friend. This is one of the few remaining hospitals whose sole purpose is not the almighty dollar."

Alex and I parted company at the edge of the parking lot. As I turned toward my apartment complex, a warm breeze fanned my forehead. It was the first time I'd realized that

Richard Meese Hospital was more than just a place to train doctors, more than just a care-giver to the disenfranchised people of the south side. Richard Meese was a symbol to the Jewish people, a foundation of support, security. I thought back to the neo-Nazi rally. Just the thing a bunch of goons like that would want to destroy.

Chapter 4 the e.r.

"Well, if it isn't Lead Foot, the medical school savior."

I looked up to see Officer James Mulroney reclining on one of the couches in the ER coffee room. A plate containing two slices of anchovy pizza, a double cheeseburger and a sugar-glazed donut sat anchored on Officer Mulroney's lap. He slugged down his coffee and cracked a wicked smile. "What brings you down here at three in the morning? Don't tell me, let me guess. You're still running from that guy whose rib cage you busted the other night." Mulroney turned to his two comrades in blue, both smiling their approval.

"You heard?" Then again, half the hospital heard about my first call night. Awakened at 4 a.m. and told that a patient was having chest pain, I was panic stricken and ran to his room. Upon seeing a motionless body looking to all the world like he was dead, my fist went crashing down onto his chest. Last time I checked, dead men don't jump up and yell: "What the fuck?" His sound sleep had earned him three cracked ribs, and me a threatened malpractice suit.

"Heard you told the man you were only a medical student." Mulroney and his accomplices laughed. It was a real rookie mistake and who better to rub it in my face than captain Ahab himself? Sol Goldman suggested I spend a week in the morgue learning the subtle differences between death and sleep, starting, he said, with how to take a pulse. Not the way I had hoped to start the year. Bad reputations were difficult to shake. I couldn't afford another screw up. For the remainder of the week, I worked harder, staying longer than any other intern.

"Forget the speeding ticket I tore up on your way into Chicago. I ought to write you up for assault and battery." Mulroney's cadre of blue-suited pals laughed on cue. Mulroney folded his donut in half and shoved it in his mouth. "I also heard you disregarded my advice and went to the neo-Nazi rally."

"Who told you that?"

"Jeb Stuart, ABC News. Danny boy, you were on national TV--plain as the mole on my chin."

I wanted to ask him which of his three chins he was referring to. I only hoped mom hadn't been watching the evening news.

Mulroney stood and lumbered over to the late night buffet table, prepared by the midnight shift. "Who you coming for?" he asked, heaping a large portion of lasagna on top of his cheeseburger.

I checked my clipboard. "Randy Jordan is one."

Mulroney nodded. "Ahh, good old Randy. A regular around here. Gets high on Drano and then tries running down rival gang members with stolen cars. Surprised they haven't cut his liver out by now."

I looked over my notes. Car accident, driving under the influence. Rule out overdose and renal contusion. "Sounds like the same guy. How about Frank Tannenbaum, here for possible peptic ulcer disease?"

Mulroney rubbed his chins. "Doesn't ring a bell. But doc, you don't need me. Your bedside manner speaks for itself." Mulroney lifted his fist in the air. "A good whack in the chest'll take care of business."

Randy Jordan tried focusing through bloodshot eyes as I stood over his restrained body. When I lifted the sheet covering his abdomen, he let out a siren-like scream. "Shee...it! No white man gonna put his hands on this black body."

Growing up in Detroit, I had seen my share of racial outbursts and could usually take them for what they were. But it was three in the morning for God's sake. I hadn't had so much as a five minute nap. My last meal had been fourteen hours before when I sucked up a jar of Ragu through a straw while checking over the day's lab values. The three volumes of Randy's old records sat like cement blocks on top of the desk. I'd be lucky to get through them and get him worked up in time for morning rounds, which meant no sleep for the night. Ignoring Randy's racial incantations, I fought back a yawn and perused the first of his voluminous charts. One of seven children, moved to Chicago from Detroit after his father ran off, lived in the worst projects in the city. *Wait a minute.* I looked up. Randy was pounding out Hendrix's <u>Purple Haze</u> on the tissue paper covering the gurney.

"You got an older brother?"

Randy looked up through a purple haze of his own. "What you say?"

"A brother. Johnny Jordan. McKenzie High in Detroit?"

Randy's fingers stopped. He tried to sit up. "You knew Johnny?"

I smiled. "We wrestled on the same team, Randy. The McKenzie High Spartans. Man, oh man. Could Johnny do a guillotine. Took runner-up at the state meet."

Randy's voice sobered. "No shit, doc, you and Johnny? Pals?"

"Ran up and down the bleachers together three times every day after practice. Worked on take-downs two evenings a week."

Randy had the same jaw configuration and hazel eyes as his brother. Good old Johnny. I hadn't thought about him in years. Knew he went to Michigan State on a wrestling scholarship, then gave it up to be with his family in Chicago, finally settling on Illinois State, where last I heard he had become captain of the varsity team. "How's the old Gumby doing?" I asked, moving closer. That was the nick-name we'd given him. His legs were so flexible he often pinned his opponent without even using his hands.

"Johnny died," said Randy, bloodshot eyes watering. "He died saving Momma. She was being raped in our stairwell. Got himself shot in the head."

My throat tightened. "Jeez, Randy, I didn't know...."

"Untie me, doc. Let me out of these restraints."

"I would if I could ..... "

"Shit, doc, I mean you no harm. You a friend of Johnny, then you a friend of Randy."

"Aren't you under some sort of arrest?"

"Oh come on, doc. I ain't runnin' nowhere."

"Tell you what. Let me talk to a police officer I know."

I suddenly felt awake, didn't even care that I'd be up the rest of the night. Johnny had been my friend, and now his brother

27

needed my help. I had to talk to Mulroney. As I stepped out of Randy's room, the next door opened.

"Doctor Raskin, could I have a word with you?"

I squinted at the name on the door plate. 'Tannenbaum,' my other admission. But how did he know who I was?

"I'll be with you shortly," I said, continuing to walk.

"Please. One minute. It's important."

I stepped into the room and Frank Tannenbaum shut the door behind us. He was middle-aged, nearly six foot, and sported a well-groomed beard and mustache. He wore heavy glasses that covered most of his upper face. A designer sweatshirt hung loosely over knit pants. For three in the morning, he looked better than I did. The smell of bratwurst filled my nostrils, making me gag. "Isn't it a little late to be eating that stuff?"

Mr. Tannenbaum sat himself down on the corner of the bed.

"I was waiting for you."

"I'm sorry, I've been running all night. I have one more patient to finish seeing..."

"Randy Jordan."

"How did you know that?"

"You don't recognize me, do you?"

I looked him over. I sensed a certain familiarity. His eyes were of interest, but then I've always noticed peoples' eyes. A fluffy yellow haze outlined the upper part of his pupils, like a popping flash bulb.

A smile peeked out through his mustache. "Surprised the Cubs didn't call you for spring training," he said. "You're not too bad with rocks."

The rally? I thought back, but still no memory. Except for the occasional wincing pain in my lower back I had forgotten about the whole thing. "How did you know who I was?"

"I make it my business."

Everybody seems to be making everything their business. "Well, how did you happen to come in when I'm on call?"

"Luck, I guess."

It didn't strike me as luck. An ulcer at this time of night? Except for the slight tremor in his hands he looked perfectly healthy. Why not take two antacids and call me in the morning?

28

My watch said three thirty. What the hell, I thought, sitting down on a stool opposite him. Randy Jordan could wait a minute. "What's with the ulcer?"

"I saw the guy who stabbed you."

An icy chill filled my chest. "What?"

He repeated himself.

I took a deep breath. "I got hit by glass." As I spoke, I relived the moment, felt the tearing pain in my back, smelled the warm blood.

Mr. Tannenbaum folded his arms across his chest, outlining his taught upper body musculature. "Saw the whole thing. Some guy stalking you, then pulling out a metal object. Next thing you know he's running. Only question is why?"

My instincts told me to get the hell out of the room. "I really have to go."

A firm hand was on my shoulder easing me back in my seat. I looked up. His eyes had narrowed; the furrows above his lids made him look old and didn't match the rest of his face. A one inch shiny scar under his right eyebrow seemed to have been buffed with car wax.

"Maybe he was trying to send you a message. Give you a warning."

"Look Mr. Tannenbaum, this is neither the time nor...."

"Maybe you did something mean-spirited?"

"Like what? Throwing rocks? Everyone was throwing rocks."

"Something else, perhaps?"

"Mister Tannenbaum," I said sternly, beginning to stand. "I do not have the time to..."

This time both his hands put force on my shoulders. I didn't resist.

"You got Dean Charles Cantrell fired from your medical school by slandering him in your graduation speech."

"Who the hell are you?"

Tannenbaum remained calm. "Don't kill the messenger, Daniel. It's my job to make a few discreet inquiries. I simply want to know where you got your damaging information about him."

Keep calm, Raskin, I told myself. ,

"Well, did you?" His arms were folded, his jaw taut.

"Did I what?"

"Take Dr. Cantrell's private files?"

I wanted to say none of your god-damn business, wanted to take him by the shirt and throw his ass out of there. But I wasn't stupid. I knew how to lie through a smile, how to keep my pupils from giving me away. "Of course not. What do you think I am, a thief?" My denial caught him by surprise. I leapt off the stool and opened the door. "Listen, I have to go. I'll be back in fifteen minutes."

"Sure, Dr. Raskin. Hope you're not upset with me. Like I said, I'm only the messenger. Say hello to Randy Jordan for me."

Officer Mulroney belched as I walked in. "Pretty quick for your second week."

"Haven't even started," I snarled.

"Too busy with old Randy, huh?"

I took a deep breath, then tried exhaling the vision of Tannenbaum. "Actually, Randy was no problem at all. In fact his brother and I wrestled together in high school." I paused. "He died. And so will Randy if he doesn't get out of that gang. I think I can help. Got a minute?"

Mulroney handed me a package of Reese's peanut butter cups. "Eat this first."

"I love these. How did you know?"

"The wrappers were all over the floor of your car that day on the freeway. Besides, you need some energy."

"I need some sleep."

Mulroney laughed. "Get used to it, son."

We sat together a few minutes, eating peanut butter cups, talking about James Mulroney. I discovered that he used to be a big honcho in homicide division, headed up the ladder--a shoo-in for chief, a possible candidate for the FBI. Then the scandal hit. Cops taking kickbacks, a drug laundering scheme gone bad. Mulroney was one of the few not kicked out or jailed, but he was demoted back to the streets. Mulroney claimed innocence and I believed him. Lost his wife over it, began drinking. Got some help, then turned to eating. That, he said, was his real calling.   While listening to Mulroney I also thought about what I could do to help out Randy Jordan. When he finished, I asked whether he could get the charges against Randy dropped.

"Won't do any good."

"Give me a chance. Please."

Mulroney shook his head. "He'll be back inside a week."

"One chance, Mulroney. That's all I'm asking."

Mulroney waved his hands in the air. "You new interns. Always think you can change the world."

"Not the world. Just one kid. Besides you owe me."

"What?"

"Back there on the freeway. I saved you from writer's cramp."

Mulroney managed a smile. "Okay, kid, but it won't do you any good."

"Thanks. In fact, I'd be willing to trade you perps. You can handcuff that other patient of mine, Frank Tannenbaum." Momentarily I felt an involuntary spasm of fear rack my body. "That guy gives me the creeps. Says he saw me at the neo-Nazi rally I attended."

Mulroney waved me off. "The ER is filled with nut cases this time of night."

"He sure seemed to know a hell of a lot about me."

"Hey, it's a full moon, Danny. Last night we had a broad in here who thought she was having a baby. Got up in the stirrups screaming bloody murder, pushing like it was on its way out. Turned out she wasn't even pregnant. Only thing she pushed out was a six pound turd."

"Thanks for the enlightening story, Mulroney," I said leaving the room.

"Hey doc," he yelled down the hallway. "You want to hear what we named it?"

The back corridor of the ER was eerily quiet, especially for a south side ER in the middle of the night. An ambulance sounded in the distance. I passed two surgeons discussing a possible appendectomy. I calculated that I could probably get Randy Jordan plugged into treatment within an hour. There would be plenty of time in the next few weeks to talk him into rehab, start inching him away from his gang. And as for Tannenbaum, I decided I'd do a quick workup, then send him home with a referral to GI clinic.

Tannenbaum's door was open. Randy's was closed, the reverse of how I had left it. Tannenbaum's room was empty. He was gone. Fine by me, I thought. Save me an hour. The possibility of sleep loomed closer.

I opened Randy's door. The room was dark. A suspicious odor filled my nostrils. "Randy, you sleeping?" I took a step, feet sliding in something wet. I flipped the light switch. It didn't hit me at first. Randy was lying peacefully, covered up to his eyes by the sheet. His stare. So blank. I leaped forward, pulling the sheet off him. His neck was slit from one end to the other. Blisters of blood dribbled onto the floor. I wanted to scream, but nothing came out. Above him, on the wall, painted in blood, was a large dripping swastika.

Chapter 5 gone fishing

I struggled through work the next day, then went home and slept until the following afternoon. I woke up feeling like I had a hangover. It was Saturday, and Alex and I had plans to go fishing. I rolled my aching body out of bed and dressed it. Alex handled the specifics: poles, worms, beer, and me, and as we headed north on Lake Shore Drive, was nice enough not to mention the previous night. Instead he told me about Sheila, a radiology tech with an unusual hobby: intercourse in the workplace. "Took two x-rays of us doing the horizontal mambo," he said with a wicked grin. "One with me on top, one with her. Needed documentation for the Guiness Book of Records. Most fucks on an x-ray table."

I wasn't really listening. My nose was glued to the window, watching the sun cast flickering shadows through the park, eying the kids who were tossing frisbees, watching young lovers play tongue hockey under the sloping oaks.

The corner of the termite-infested pier jutted out into a small marina which emptied into Lake Michigan. We popped two beers and baited our hooks, then in silence fished for half an hour. I was thankful that Alex didn't push me to talk right away. The sun began melting away the tension that iced my body. It was then that I told him what had happened--Tannenbaum, Randy Jordan, the swastika on the wall. My chagrin at how the cops refused to believe that Tannenbaum was involved in Randy's murder.

"Mulroney said it was gang retaliation. That Randy had it coming."

Alex nodded. "Cops know what they're talking about, Danny. The South Side is filled with gang stuff."

"Then why cover everything up so quickly?" In thirty minutes, the police had cordoned off the area, removed Randy's body, and scrubbed the room clean. Half the ER staff didn't even know what had happened. Why hush up a gang murder? Those things happened at County Hospital all the time.

Alex played with the radio until he hit a sports show highlighting the box scores.

"Like sports?" I asked.

Alex shook his head. "Not particularly. I'm trying to catch the over-under on today's Cubs game."

"You bet?"

Alex laughed. "Actually my bookie places the bets. Looking for some action?"

I shook my head. The last bet I won was back in summer camp as a teenager. Someone bet me ten dollars I couldn't get my hand inside of Cindy Minkowitz's brassiere. I won only because she went fifty-fifty. It was downhill after that.

Feeling kinship with the wriggling worm, I baited my hook. "Tannenbaum was at the rally. He saw me get stabbed. He knew me, Alex."

I described Tannenbaum to Alex, but he could only shake his head. He then pulled out a pack of Marlboros and struck a match. "Don't freak out, Danny. I only smoke on two occasions, sex and fishing."

If Mulligan's bar or the Radiology suite were any indication, I figured Alex must be up to ten packs a day. A cool lake breeze carried off Alex's exhalation. Two dirty seagulls swooped down onto the water.

"Why would Tannenbaum knock off Randy Jordan?"

"He said he was a messenger, Alex."

Alex reeled in his line. "Hell of a message, Danny."

"What about the swastika?"

"Neo-Nazi, Danny. White gangs worship anything fascist."

I felt a tug on my line. When it turned out to be a piece of algae-covered plywood I breathed relief. I wouldn't know what to do if I caught a fish, especially from this swamp.

I felt myself begin to relax. Maybe Alex and Mulroney were right. I looked at Alex who was scanning the box scores in the paper.

"But why was Tannenbaum asking questions about Charles Cantrell?"

Alex popped the cap off his second Budweiser. "Who is this Cantrell, anyway?"

I looked out at the harbor, saw the wind lifting the masts of the sailboats that dotted the lake. "Charles Cantrell was Dean of Admissions at Arbor Hills Medical School." I took a deep inhalation of lake breeze. "He was a liar and a racist and a god damn cheat."

A smile filled Alex's face. "Don't mince any words, Danny boy."

Chapter 6 charles cantrell and the admission committee

Charles Francis Cantrell's pinstriped suit was just dark enough to hide the stains of deceit that followed him from Yale to Arbor Hills Medical School, where his solid reputation as an advocate of disadvantaged minorities made him the obvious choice as Dean of Admissions. Keeping true to his reputation, he offered acceptances to at least forty minority applicants every year, though for reasons I didn't understand at first, only a fraction ever matriculated.

As student rep to the medical school admissions committee, an elected position, I interviewed prospective students, attended meetings, and had the same voting power as the faculty members. In September of my junior year, I interviewed a black premed student from the east side of Detroit named John Lewis. Living with his mother and seven siblings, John somehow had managed to steer clear of drugs and gang violence so common to his city. He earned a scholarship to Wayne State University where, in addition to taking a full college curriculum, he worked forty hours a week to help support his family. His 3.2 grade point average and his above average Medical College admission scores were better than those of many other applicants of similar backgrounds.

John's dedication and compassion overflowed during the interview, and I spent an hour showing him around the campus. A week later I received a letter from John telling me that even though he had been accepted at Columbia, Arbor Hills was still his first choice. Our committee offered unanimous approval and an acceptance letter was to be sent the following day.

That was October. The following August, two weeks before the new academic year, I noticed that John Lewis was not on the list of incoming students. Even worse, I counted only six minority students out of a class of 210, less than three percent of the class.

I asked Dean Cantrell for an explanation.

"Beats me, Raskin. We offered forty-five acceptances this year. Just can't force them to take something they don't want."

The word 'them' struck a sour note. I decided to call John at home.

"I was looking forward to seeing you this year at Arbor Hills," I said.

He remembered who I was, but sounded ill-at-ease. "I'm going to Columbia."

I told him how the committee enthusiastically voted him in. "I thought it was your first choice. What made you change your mind?"

There was a pause. "If you were so enthusiastic, why did you wait until yesterday to send me a letter of acceptance?"

"Yesterday? We accepted you back in October."

"Nobody told me," he said. "Besides, I'm settled in New York; got my financial aid rolling, have a place to live, even started talking to some of the Profs about research opportunities."

The idea of Cantrell claiming to be recruiting minorities, when, in fact, he appeared to be doing just the opposite, left me seething. The man was a closet racist far as I could tell, a man who while extolling the virtues of diversity among the new generation of physicians, in reality acted upon his deep-seated bigoted notion that our nations icon for physicians should continue to sit on a pedestal molded of alabaster white. The following morning I stormed into his office, presented my findings and accused him of perpetrating a fraud.

"Read the figures, Daniel," he countered. "I offer more acceptances to minorities than any other medical school, even Harvard."

"Bullshit!" I said, surprised at my choice of words. "You hold onto those letters until you're sure they're going somewhere else."

Cantrell remained calm, assuring me that my information was incorrect, that John Lewis's case had been an administrative error. That everything was on the level. He then added that his power at Arbor Hills reached far beyond the admissions committee and that if I wanted a chance at a decent residency, I'd better mind my own business.

"Is that a threat?"

Dr. Cantrell shrugged his shoulders. "I don't have time for parasites like you. Why don't you and the rest of your kind just get the hell out?"

Rest of my kind? What did that mean?

Cantrell recovered quickly. "You would-be detectives. Take it somewhere else."

Alex let out a huge belch. "Great story, Danny. Why didn't you nail him right then?"

"Surgery rotation started the next day and I don't think I made it back to my apartment twice in the next two months. By the time I was finished, I had already put the whole mess behind me."

"But you got him at your graduation."

I had briefly told Alex what Sol Goldman had heard about my graduation day. That my speech was responsible for getting Cantrell fired. It was over. He couldn't hurt me anymore. Could he?

"What about those files Tannenbaum asked about?" wondered Alex.

"There were two. I ended up only opening one. It gave me all the information I needed to nail his ass."

"What happened to the other?"

"Who knows? Maybe it's in one of the boxes in my apartment. Except for clothes, I haven't even unpacked yet."

Alex slapped me on the back. "Water under the bridge, Danny. How about we pack up and head over to Jose's? I'm dying for a burrito."

The next few days passed without incident, and Randy Jordan's death rapidly became old news. I was glad Sol Goldman was still out of town. When I went down to the ER on my next call night, I stopped outside the room where Randy had been murdered. The room was clean and sterile, the bloody swastika peroxided into oblivion. *It's over, time to move on.* I headed over to the room of my new admission, pausing outside her door. I looked at the name on top of the chart.

Maxine Chu.

Chapter 7 maxine chu

When I first laid eyes on Maxine Chu I thought I had entered the wrong room. If not for the hem of a folded hospital gown which peeked out from her leather coat, she might have sprung from the pages of the Vogue magazine resting in her lap.

As I came in, she lifted her head from the gurney. A wave of glistening black hair swept high in the air and then dropped behind her head in a single symphonic movement. She managed a smile but the pallor of her lips eluded her Revlon disguise. I paused as our eyes met, and suddenly felt vulnerable. Though she had a veneer of composure, I felt her eyes probing the innermost recesses of my brain. There was an intensity in her eyes, some yet-to-be-discovered planet locked tight in a solar system of fear.

One of her hands gripped the arm of a scrawny young Chinese man. He glanced at me and then peeled back a grin from crooked teeth. He turned possessively toward the patient, doting on her every movement as she vigorously chomped on her chewing gum.

I was so taken with her appearance, that I anticipated her first words to be couched in some ancient Chinese riddle--a mystical proverb posed as a question, passed down from a timeworn eastern ancestry.

"Hey Doc, how 'bout some left-over shrimp fried rice?"

So much for the Chu dynasty, I thought, extending my hand and introducing myself.

The heels of her high black boots dug into the paper gurney cover as she continued her incessant chewing.

I studied her chart. "Is that Maxine Chu, like in shoe?" I asked.

Her companion spoke up. "It's like a big sneeze, Doc--Ahhh Chu.

Maxine shot a glance his way. "Excuse the rudeness of my boyfriend, Lo. He manages Moon Palace restaurant in China Town. That's the only reason I date him!" This time they both laughed. Maxine's laugh was short, easy, and free spirited.

"Well, Ms. Chu, ..."

"Maxine... or better yet Max."

Lo interrupted. "Tell him my pet name for you."

Maxine blushed. "Why I agreed to marry him, I'll never know," she said. "I should have held out for someone handsome, with a future..." She threw a coy pout toward Lo. "Instead, look what I get stuck with-- Lo man on the totem pole!"

They laughed hysterically. Opposites attract, I thought smiling, like sweet and sour. Lo put his arm around Maxine. "Okay, my little Mandarin fur ball!"

"Lo Wong Sien!" Maxine blushed and pushed him full force off the gurney, then tossed her magazine at him. "Please excuse Lo, Doctor Raskin. It's all that MSG he eats." She turned to Lo. "You want me to tell Dr. Raskin *your* nickname?" Lo retreated quietly.

I studied the chart for a moment. "Ms. Chu, I mean Maxine. It says here that you came to the ER because of weight loss and a fever?"

"I came here because he made me," she said, staring at Lo. "It's like I was telling Dr. Klein. If you ate the food that Lo cooked up every night, you'd drop a few pounds, too, spending half your life in the bathroom, for God's sake. Look, if I promise to watch what I eat, will you let me go home?"

"How much is a few pounds, Maxine?"

Maxine shrugged her shoulders and reached for a nail file resting on a tray table next to the bed.

"Max drop fifteen pound in two months," volunteered Lo.

Maxine flung the nail file at Lo. "A gentleman never gives away a woman's weight, Lo. Or didn't your grandma teach you that little proverb?" She smiled at me. "Like I said, Lo's cooking sucks."

"It more than just weight loss," Lo continued. "Tell Dr. Raskin how you wake up in middle of night with sweat all over." Lo waved his hands in the air. "It like monsoon season in bed. Bed sheet all wet."

"Lo Wong Sien," Maxine declared. "Don't you dare talk about my bed sheets. Not until you've slept in them."

The color drained from Lo's face. His eyes were moist. Maxine took a brush from her table and pulled several tangles from its bristles. "Sorry, Doc. Lo comes from a traditional Chinese family. He's saving himself for marriage." She wrapped a strand of hair around her finger. "Can I go now? I swear there's nothing else wrong with me. I'm in the middle of summer quarter at De Paul. I have exams to study for."

"She so tired," said Lo, "that she fall sleep the minute she come home. Very bad, Doctor, very bad."

Lo covered his face as Maxine pretended to throw the brush at him.

"Maxine, before we come to a decision on whether you should stay or go, I need to examine you."

"I've never been so much in demand," she said. "Two other doctors have already examined me."

After explaining how we're all supposed to perform our own examination, I ushered Lo out to the waiting area. When I returned, Maxine's head was buried in her magazine.

At her bedside, I looked her over carefully. There seemed to be a certain sallowness in her complexion, despite an attempt to cover it with makeup. Everything else seemed normal-at least until I pulled her gown from her shoulders and began palpating her neck. Her carotids were normal as was her thyroid gland. But as my hands ran up and down the sides of her neck, I found a palpable chain of nodules extending from just below the jaw all the way down to the clavicle. As I palpated deeper, they rolled back and forth under my fingertips, like partially fused rubber marbles. Maxine jumped when I squeezed a little too hard.

"Yow!"

"Sorry. I guess I don't need to ask if these things hurt."

"What things?"

"These little cervical lymph nodes that you have running down both sides of your neck."

"Oh those," she said, nonchalantly, turning the page of her magazine. "They don't hurt. You just pinched me."

"How long have they been there?"

43

"Oh, I don't know," she answered, fidgeting. "Had a strep infection a while back. Went to student health at De Paul and the doctor told me it was nothing to worry about--said they would go away in a short time."

"How long ago was that, Maxine?"

Maxine paused. "About eight weeks," she finally said without looking up.

Eight weeks was a long time for a bacterial infection to be draining.

Maxine looked up. "They're okay, aren't they?" Her voice was steady, but slightly softer now. She set her magazine down on her lap. It was then that I noticed the red blotches on her arms.

"What's under this makeup?" I asked, tearing open an alcohol pad.

Maxine looked at me suspiciously. "They're just blemishes. You can't expect me to go to class with blemishes."

When I had succeeded in removing most of her makeup, I examined the red blotches in more detail. This was clearly no rash; these were broken blood vessels, most likely secondary to an abnormality of her platelets. But why? I began to search for other areas of vascular fragility. "Have you noticed that you bruise more easily than usual?"

"Why? You going to punch me or something?" She laughed. "How do you like that. First you remove my makeup and now you're going to punch me. Is that any way to treat a lady?"

She had half a dozen more splotches on her legs.

"Now that you mention it," Maxine said sheepishly, "I guess I have noticed an extra black and blue mark or two."

I felt an abrupt tug at my breath. "Hasn't your boyfriend said anything about them?"

Maxine waved me off. "Lo? You've got to be kidding. When he saves himself for marriage, he means it."

Her heart and lungs were normal, and her breasts were small enough that I was confident that nothing of significance could have escaped my detection.

"It seems so natural that a doctor is able to touch a woman's breast with total impartiality," said Maxine, watching as I

44

palpated each of the four quadrants of mammary tissue. "Lo thinks touching my breasts violates the sanctity of marriage," she said with exasperation. "I have to force him to feel me up. And when he does, afterwards he washes his hands for thirty minutes!"

I had no comment, so I turned my attention to her abdomen, placing my right hand lightly on top of my left and then palpating each of the four quadrants of her belly. Her skin was soft, almost doughy in texture, and my fingers easily kneaded their way through the skin folds covering her visceral organs.

"Take a deep breath." As she did my fingers burrowed deep into the recesses of her belly. "Hold it there." I pushed further, deeper under her rib cage. And then I felt it. My breath stopped in mid-inspiration. Don't get excited. You'll scare her. Be calm. That's it. Keep the patient relaxed.

"What's wrong?" Maxine asked. *So much for bedside manner.*

"Maxine, I'm going to press a little bit deeper. Let me know if I'm hurting you."

While I carefully delineated the extent of the mass, I wondered why no one else had felt it. Maybe I knew what I was doing, after all. "Does it hurt when I press here?"

Maxine shook her head, but she was quietly biting her lip.

I practically ran to the nurse's station where my resident, Dave, was talking to the ER resident. In his hand he held a large sterile package along with several needles.

I tapped him on the shoulder. "You gotta feel the mass I found in Maxine Chu's abdomen!"

Dave smiled at the ER resident. "You mean the enlarged spleen?" he asked.

"Uh, yeah, I guess it was the spleen tip," I replied.

"Tip? That spleen fills the whole abdomen!" exclaimed Dave. "It's the largest spleen I ever felt!"

"How about the liver?" asked the ER resident. "The liver's enlarged to almost twice it's normal size. Did you feel that?"

An embarrassing warmth filled my cheeks.

Dave slapped me on the shoulder. "Come on, we've got a bone marrow biopsy to do."

"On Maxine?"

"Who else?"

"But Dave," I pleaded, quickly forgetting my bruised ego. "A bone marrow biopsy down here in the ER? Now? Why don't we wait until we get to the floor?"

"The bed's not ready," he answered.

Dave turned to say something to the ER resident. Why do a bone marrow biopsy now, I wondered. Especially since Maxine thinks she's going home. Couldn't we at least wait until morning? You know, let her get used to the idea. Besides, some of the blood tests would be back. "We can rule out something like Strep or Mono."

"I saw the blood smear," he said shaking his head. "She has nasty looking lymphocytes, and I can't find a trace of platelets."

Damn. That was bad. "What do you think?"

"Lymphoma," he said. "If we do the marrow now, we can get the results by tomorrow afternoon."

"Maxine thinks she's going home tonight."

Dave saw the concern in my eyes.

"Tell you what," he said, handing me the bone marrow tray and syringes. "You go in and set up. Make her understand. This young woman may have a long and difficult road ahead of her."

Maxine was standing in her underwear pulling her tee-shirt over the top of her head when I entered.

"Where you going?"

"Home," she replied. "You probably need the bed."

"We have one reserved for you upstairs."

Maxine stood still, staring. "What's all that stuff for?" she asked as I began unwrapping the bone marrow kit. Her eyes fixated on the long spinal needle.

I took a deep breath. "Look Maxine, we found some abnormalities. It might be nothing but we have to do more tests."

"Fine," she said, straightening her tee-shirt. "I'll come back after exams. Art History is going to be a bitch."

46

"It's not that simple. We need to admit you to the hospital to run those tests." I held up the needle. "One of them involves taking a small piece of bone marrow from your hip."

Maxine was quiet. "Fine," she finally said with resolution. Without pausing, she removed her tee-shirt and unfastened the front hook on her black lace bra. She then slid her matching panties down, letting them drop to the floor. Her eyes remained glued to mine.

I turned my back, fumbling with the equipment setup. I was finding it extremely difficult to swallow. Maxine covered herself in a hospital gown, then picked up her magazine. After a minute, she cleared her throat. "So, what do you think we'll find?"

"I'm only an intern, Maxine, so I don't have that much experience."

Maxine lay on the gurney face down, legs kicking up in back, head immersed in her magazine. She winced as I swabbed the cold, dark Betadine over a large circular area on her lower back and buttocks. "Off hand, I might say mononucleosis, hepatitis, or something like that."

"How about Hodgkins Lymphoma?"

Thank God Maxine couldn't see my eyes.

"Who said anything about Hodgkins Lymphoma?"

Maxine squirmed. "That stuff sure is cold on the tush. I heard Dr. Klein talking to another doctor about a sick Chinese girl," she said. "'The one with the spleen that ate Chicago!'"

I finished the antiseptic preparation of Maxine's iliac crest and began opening the needles and syringes onto a sterile sheet.

"Where do you stand on all this?" she asked.

"Like I said, Maxine, I'm just the intern." Maxine's gaze locked onto mine from over her shoulder: She didn't move.

"Look Maxine, I don't know exactly what's going on, but I promise you I won't keep anything from you and..."

"And what?"

I swallowed hard. "And whatever it turns out to be, we'll fix it." Maxine rested her head on the bed.

"I trust you," she said gently.

The cortical bone of Maxine's hip seemed just as impenetrable to the biopsy needle as it had been to the anesthetic. Dave's face was bright red as he leaned over Maxine, pushing and twisting the long needle with all his weight. It was like trying to jam a nail into a piece of wood without a hammer and Dave was failing miserably. In an attempt to keep from screaming, Maxine clutched my hand-squeezing it so hard that it lost all sensation. My other hand was also busy, wiping away the tears that rolled down Maxine's face. And mine.

Lo stood in the background, his hands cupped over his mouth, looking like a ghost who had bumped into his own shadow. How he and Maxine had gotten together was not readily apparent.

Dave pushed harder, Maxine just barely containing her sobs. I squinted through misty eyes at the clock. Nine p.m. There were other admissions waiting to be worked up, orders to write, tests to check. I could hardly believe there was still ten hours of call left. And Sol Goldman was due back into town sometime tonight. He was sure to check his messages and find out what had happened down in the ER.

Dave pushed harder onto the needle and finally, as he seemed on the verge of giving up, a loud 'pop' filled the room.

"Pay dirt!" he yelled, steadying the needle with one hand, and wiping his forehead with the other. Maxine's grip loosened, and I dabbed her eyes. Dave removed the stylet from the aspiration needle and attached a syringe. "Hold still, Maxine. We're just about done," and pulled back on the syringe ever so slowly. We watched as a dark viscous substance bubbled into the syringe.

"Look at that," yelled Lo, who had moved closer once Maxine seemed more comfortable.

"Oil," said Dave, dispensing a sigh of relief. "Black gold."

"Texas tea," whispered Maxine weakly from underneath the sheet.

When the first syringe was full, Dave removed it and held it in the air. The black spicules glistened in the dim fluorescence of the ceiling lights.

"Marrow," he said, showing his fortune to Maxine. "The original primordial broth--the stock which forms the basis for all our blood elements."

"Yech," I said under my breath, remembering how my father used to suck that stuff from discarded soup bones before tossing them under the table to our gluttonous mutt, Noodles.

Dave left to send the marrow to the lab, and I finished dressing Maxine's wound. Maxine stretched her back as she sat up, wincing slightly.

"So, Dr. Raskin," she said matter of fact. "What do we do if it's cancer?"

Lo jumped forward. "Maxine, it not cancer!"

"Settle down, Chopstick Dick," she said. "Like Dr. Raskin said earlier, let's just wait. Besides, no matter what it is, Dr. Raskin will fix it."

There was no sense in telling Maxine Intern Rule Number 7: If tumor's the rumor, then cancer's the answer. I put my hand on her shoulder. "I'll see you upstairs in a little while," I said with feigned lack of emotion. "Anything I can get for you?"

Maxine looked at Lo. "Yeah, a new boyfriend." Lo shrank back demurely. "I knew we should have done it last night, Lo" she scolded. "God only knows when I'll be getting out of this place. I may never lose my virginity!"

Lo's face was covered with tears. He ran up and flung his arms around me. "You fix her, Doctor, won't you? You fix my little fur ball?"

I held Lo for a moment until he regained his composure, whereupon he stepped back. I nodded, then looked at Maxine. In a mere two hours we had bonded with each other. She was part of my life now, and for better or worse, I was part of hers.

Chapter 8 up all night

Leaning back in an easy chair opposite the nursing station, I gazed out the window toward Lake Michigan where the sun was making its ascent above the horizon. Below, a battalion of lilacs presented arms to the morning warmth, while junipers swayed gracefully in the summer breeze. If only for an hour, I needed to escape my chains.

Sleep was now a stranger who'd last appeared thirty hours ago. A shower had done little to jump-start my adrenalin. "Why'd you bother shaving?" asked Dave, as we waited for the rest of the team to show up for morning rounds. "You deserve to look like hell. It's a vaccination. Keeps you immune from the more malignant attendings."

Maxine was sitting in bed reading Mademoiselle and sipping tea when we walked in. Chewed up Dentyne lay on a crumpled piece of Kleenex. She was freshly showered with damp, shiny hair and was wrapped in a silk-lined bathrobe. I was now glad I, too, had showered. Maxine offered up a smile.

"Here I am," she said. Dave introduced Gail Peterson, the other intern. Two medical students eagerly eyed Maxine.

"You guys are just in time for the early bird special," said Maxine. "Twenty five cents and you too can examine the spleen that ate Chicago." Dave blushed. After the students and Gail finished their examination, Dave sat down on Maxine's bed and explained that we would wait until late afternoon when the bone marrow biopsy results were back before ordering further tests. "Make sure Dr. Raskin comes with you," she said.

Dave smiled. "Don't worry. Besides, it will take both of us to control the circus around here once I present your case at our morning conference. Not many doctors have ever felt a spleen that big."

Gail Peterson stepped forward. "Don't worry, Maxine. If you want, we can post a 'no visitors' sign. Nobody will bother you if you don't want them to." Dave flashed Gail a withering look.

Maxine waved them off. "My price just rose to fifty cents." One of the medical students giggled. Maxine drew me into her sights. "As long as I know I'm going to recover, you and your students can probe all you want."

We paused outside of Maxine's room. "Get used to the attention," Dave said. "Everybody is going to want to see her. There will be conferences, papers passed around. We're going to be the most popular team in the hospital."

Gail Peterson slammed down a chart onto the chart rack. "I don't believe you guys."

"This is a great case," said Dave.

"Oh yeah," she retorted, "a real mortality conference special." She shook her head. "Did you look at her?"

I stood frozen.

"She's doing okay," said Dave. The students nodded.

Gail said: "She was scared to death. That's what I hate about great cases. The person with the disease gets trampled on."

Gail was right on the mark. Later I went over and thanked her, told her I thought she said the right thing, even though it pissed off our resident. Gail smiled, one of her front teeth slightly in front of the other. "If I came on a bit strong, it's because I have a cousin with Hodgkin's."

"You were right, Gail. I felt like slapping myself."

"You were up all night. Besides, you have other things on your mind. Like what happened down in the ER."

"You heard?"

"Not really. But I'd love to. Time for coffee?"

In fifteen minutes I recapped everything--meeting Mulroney on the freeway, the Nazi rally, the incident in the ER with Tannenbaum and Randy Jordan. Even told her about my infamous dean at Arbor Hills. It poured out so easily with Gail. Or maybe I just needed to talk to keep the anxiety away. When I was finished, she was smiling.

"What?"

"Your coffee's cold."

I felt myself blush. "Sorry. You're either a great listener or I was talking so fast you couldn't get a word in."

"Some of both," she said, brushing a sausage of red curls off her eyebrow. Gail slid her chair back. "Lot to do before attending rounds," she said. She pulled out three dollars worth of meal tickets and dropped them on the table.

"Wait." My decibel level was a give away. "Hey, how about finishing this up later? Want to meet at Mr. Gee's after work?" Mr. Gee's was the local pub, a watering hole for off-duty hospital staff, graduate students, and the occasional patient who might slip away for a glass of Mr. Gee's house wine, a barely palatable cross between chablis and vinegar.

"Another time," said Gail. "You haven't had any sleep."

"How about lunch?" I held up my meal tickets. "My treat."

Gail shook her head. "Got some patients' families coming in. Some other time."

She got up to leave.

"Wait."

"Yes?"

"I'm just embarrassed, Gail. I told you all this stuff about me. You didn't tell me anything about yourself."

"Not much to tell. Top of my class at Colorado. I'm a firm believer that patient care comes first. And..." she touched my hand: "I don't date doctors."

The rest of the morning was spent writing my daily patient progress notes, exchanging information with private physicians, and worrying about Maxine. Alex met me twice for coffee. He was as tired as I was, though he hadn't been on call. He had spent the entire night getting his own private respiratory treatments from a therapist he had met in the hallway.

That afternoon in clinic, I dozed off while a patient was giving me his history. I also checked off the wrong box on the radiology request form, ordering a barium enema instead of a chest x-ray. Fortunately, the clinic nurse caught my mistake. At one point I heard Sol Goldman walking down the clinic hallway, and I ducked for cover behind the examining table just as he poked his head in the door. I didn't want to talk to him about the ER, or anything else. I stared at my watch, wondering when

Dave was going to call with the bone marrow results. I jumped when my beeper finally sounded.

"The hematologists are about to read it," he said.

My pulse quickened. "One more patient. Be there in fifteen minutes."

"Afraid not, Danny. Just got a call from Sol Goldman's office. He wants to see you as soon you're done with clinic."

My heart hammered at my throat. "But Dave...Maxine... her marrow."

"Believe me, I told him you'd been up all night. His secretary said it was urgent."

I slammed down the receiver. What could be more urgent than Maxine?

Chapter 9--Sol Goldman

Just who did he think he was, calling me in at five o'clock in the evening after a night with no sleep?

Between the indignant steps I took to his office, I realized exactly who he was. Chief of Medicine for fifteen years, Sol Goldman had single-handely turned the internal medicine residency program into the best Chicago had to offer. His reputation was international. Prestigious eastern medical schools lusted after his services. Pharmaceutical companies offered him lucrative salaries to run their clinical trials. Sol used those offers in negotiating with the Meese administration, bolstering his position as the most powerful man at the medical center. Sol Goldman got what he wanted, when he wanted it. Apparently that included me.

Dr. Goldman remained seated as I entered his office, waving me toward a leather chair with polished oak arm rests. I sat across from him at a large oak desk, staring at the bookshelves and oak-framed diplomas that graced his walls. It was a damned oak forest in here.

As if on cue, his secretary came in and set down two cups of coffee. She paused, then walked from one corner of the office to the other, sniffing the air like an Irish setter tracking an animal.

"What's the matter, Sandy?" Sol scolded. "Been that long since you caught the scent of an intern after a night on call?" Sol laughed as Sandy excused herself and retreated to the outer foyer.

"You need a shower, doctor."

"Took one this morning."

"Take two from now on."

"Yes, sir."

Sol Goldman look his time stirring in a teaspoon of sugar. "So, what do you think of Richard Meese?"

I wanted to get the hell out of there and find out about Maxine's biopsy. "Fine, I guess."

Dr. Goldman opened a folder sitting on his desk. "I was looking over the police report on last week's incident." Sol pulled his wire-rimmed glasses an inch lower on the bridge of his nose so that we made eye contact. "You do know the incident I am referring to?"

I nodded.

"Gangs. When they import their business into our emergency room, that's going too far." Sol turned the pages. "You told the police that a man named Frank Tannenbaum asked about your dean."

"Former dean," I corrected.

Sol cleared his voice. "Why would a stranger ask you about Dr. Cantrell?"

The coffee had cleared my nasal passages, giving me some appreciation of Sandy's sense of smell. Maybe that's why Gail Peterson didn't date interns.

"Well?"

"I have no idea, Dr. Goldman. He claimed he saw me at that neo-Nazi protest."

"I'm familiar with the report. Was there anything else? Anything you forgot to tell the police?"

I looked deeply into his eyes. Composure 101, here we go again. "That's it. I really have a lot to do before .... "

"That's not it," he said, slapping the file closed. He dabbed a bushy eyebrow with his napkin.

"I want to hear about you and Cantrell."

Oh, God, not again. "Could we possibly do it another time? I really..."

"I want to hear it now. I don't care if you've been up for a week." His cheeks were flushed and sweat filled in the recesses in his cheeks. He reached into his desk drawer and pulled out a small pill bottle, throwing two caplets into his mouth.

"Heart problem?"

Sol snarled. "No, dammit, an intern problem."

"Look, Dr. Goldman. If Dr. Cantrell is some sort of friend of yours..." I paused. "I really don't want to offend you."

"I'm already offended, Raskin. Besides, I didn't know him really. Just sat on a few committees together. A long time ago. Now talk, or you'll be taking call every night for a month."

It took me half an hour just to give him the lowdown on Cantrell as I knew it.

"Probably saw himself as the last bastion of white knighthood," said Sol when I finished talking. "Bigots don't need an excuse to do what they do. Crazy as it sounds, I'm sure Cantrell felt that keeping blacks out of medical school made him some sort of hero."

"Yeah, protecting the interests of a racially pure America." I stood up to leave. "Where are you going?"

"That's all there is."

"Sit down."

Shit. I would never get out of here. I hadn't seen Maxine Chu since morning. She would probably never talk to me again. I took my seat. "There's really nothing else to say. If you want I can tell you how I nailed him at graduation."

"The files."

"What files?"

"Don't be a funny guy. The police report concerning the ER incident talked about some files of Dr. Cantrell's that you supposedly took."

"How come people keep asking me about those files?"

Sol relaxed a little. "Look, I'm just following up on something. There's a reason for asking. I'll tell you when you're done." His eyes demanded my cooperation.

I looked up at the ceiling. "All right, where do you want me to begin?"

Sol slid his chair over to the intercom, pressed a button and said: "Hold my calls for the next hour, Sandy."

An hour? My God, it was after six already.

Sol swiveled around. "Why don't you start by telling me what made you go into his personal files in the first place?"

I thought for a moment. "Bob Calpern. I held Charles Cantrell personally responsible for what happened to Bob Calpern."

"I'm all ears," said Sol.

57

Chapter 10--bob calpern and friends of tomorrow

Bob Calpern never should have been admitted to Arbor Hills Medical School, or for that matter any medical school. "Hit me five, Broooo!" he would yell in a deeply drawn out nasal voice as his six foot nine frame tripped over size 12 Reeboks into a seat in the middle of a row, disrupting the entire class. He took notes that were third-grade quality, fifteen words to a page, upper case, using a heavy pen that resembled a Crayola crayon.

Sol Goldman shouted into his intercom for more coffee, then turned back to me. "How did he pass the first two years? All that book work and all."

"I think he had a photographic memory. One of those idiot savants you read about."

"What about his clinical rotations?" Sol cleared his throat. "You can't fake bedside manner. How did he survive third year?"

"He didn't."

Dr. Goldman waited while Sandy poured the coffee, which wasn't long since she was holding her breath the entire time. After she left, I took a long drink and told Sol Goldman about Bob's third year clinical rotations. His first was internal medicine, where his atrocious communication skills were surpassed only by a new low in the physical exam. He was removed from the medicine service after fracturing someone's knee cap with his reflex hammer.

It was felt he would do better in pediatrics, where communication skills were not essential and the smell of dirty diapers would overcome Bob's own body odor. On his third day, the pediatric chief resident found Bob carrying a newborn to the nursery tucked in his backpack between his class notes and a peanut butter sandwich. He was quickly transferred to the surgical service.

Here, it was felt, Bob would flourish. After all, on surgery, expertise in histories and physicals, along with bedside manner, were considered of secondary importance. He could carry all the excised gall bladders he desired in his backpack and no one would blink.

On his first day in the operating room, he was ordered to stand silently over the sterile field, holding a retractor while the Chief of Surgery performed a pancreatic resection. Several hours into the operation, Bob, a foot taller than anyone else in the OR, leaned over the sterile drapes to get a better look into the exposed surgical field. Without warning, his black horn-rimmed glasses fell from his face and plunged into the open abdominal cavity, instantly turning the sterile field into the Florida Everglades. The surgeon, veins bulging from his forehead, barely mustered enough control to say: "You may as well have shit into that wound!"

Bob Calpern lasted exactly four hours on the surgical service.

Two months into his clinical clerkships, Bob was admitted to the Psychiatry service for severe depression. The administration felt he should be hospitalized at his own institution rather than be farmed out someplace where people might ask questions.

After two weeks of suffering the humiliation of having his fellow classmates make rounds on him, Bob Calpern inflated a blood pressure cuff around his neck, and deflated his life.

I looked up at Dr. Goldman. He nodded for me to continue. "As the student representative to the admissions committee, I felt it was my responsibility to figure out how this poor guy had ever been offered a spot in our class in the first place."

"Why didn't you go through proper channels?"

"I did. Sort of."

It was true. I began by asking some of the senior faculty. Nobody wanted to talk about it. I then went through Bob's file. Everything seemed to be in order. 'A' average at Yale undergraduate, almost perfect Medical College Admission Test scores. I was about to close the file when I noticed something missing. Where were the interview reports from the faculty? I checked again; missing. A chill settled over me. First, minority students; now this. Something was wrong.

"Did you ask Dr. Cantrell about it?" Sol was sitting up straight, concern in his eyes.

"He told me they were misplaced. When I asked him who the faculty members were, he told me to mind my own business."

Sol Goldman managed a weak smile. "Which you didn't, of course."

"I waited until he was out of town. I got his office key from his secretary."

"Just like that?"

"Remember, I was a bonafide member of the admissions committee. I told her I had some after hours work to do on the minority recruitment files."

"So?" Sol's eyes brightened.

"Inside the drawer were two metal files, one locked, the other not. The unlocked one contained a number of manila folders, one of which had the name 'Bob Calpern' stamped across the top."

Sol sat motionless while I described what I found: letters from both interviewers stating that under no circumstance should Bob Calpern be allowed to matriculate at Arbor Hills. Yet he had been admitted anyway. It was clear that Cantrell had admitted a student who wasn't qualified.

"Why?" asked Sol.

"Would a million bucks make a difference?"

Sol leaned forward.

"There was a check made out for one million dollars, from Dr. Raymond Calpern, Bob's father, payable to Friends of Tomorrow."

Goldman's eyes literally jumped. He took a breath and in a noncommittal tone asked: "Who are Friends of Tomorrow?"

His eyes betrayed him. This was not the first time he had heard the name, Friends of Tomorrow. "The way I figured, it was probably some dummy corporation that Cantrell used to funnel the bribe money into."

"So you're telling me that this student's parents paid a million dollars to get him into medical school?"

61

"He wasn't the only one who got in like that."

Goldman was up from his chair, leaning across his table as if he wanted to grab me by my coat. "What the hell do you mean?"

"I'm not sure, really, but that file also contained a ledger book. Looked like the parents of a few of my classmates also donated to Friends of Tomorrow. Not a million bucks, from what I remembered, but it wasn't chump change either. The funny thing was, from what I recalled, those other students were damn good. I'm sure they were good enough to get in on their own merits."

"What are you saying?"

"That my beloved Dean of admissions was on the take. Pressuring families who really wanted their kids to go to Arbor Hills to make a donation to his own favorite charity--himself."

Sol Goldman looked spent. I wondered why he was so interested in Charles Cantrell. Where the hell was that guy, anyway?

"This ledger," Goldman finally said, folding his hands on the table top, "is there anything else you can tell me?"

"Just that there was also a debit side."

"How so?"

"A list of checks made out to people, some of them medical students."

Goldman nodded. "Maybe Friends of Tomorrow was a philanthropic organization. They took from those who could give and gave to those who needed it."

"Tuition at Arbor Hills was twelve K a year. Some of those checks were six figures."

Sol looked away. "Remember any names?"

I shook my head. Who the hell cared? The point was the Charles Cantrell seemed to be the George Steinbrenner of my medical school. A hand-picked team. He wanted somebody, he got them.

"Why?" Goldman wanted to know.

That was the part I had never figured out. Why would you pay someone to go to your medical school? Arbor Hills attracted some of the best candidates in the country.

After a minute, Sol spoke. "What about the other file, the locked one?"

It was my turn to lie. "Beats me. I wasn't about to steal the thing."

"But you told police that this man Tannenbaum was asking about two files. You took two of them."

"I think he was referring to the information I stole, not the file itself." I flashed Sol a smile. No sense in telling him I had taken that locked file but never opened it. But then again, what was the big deal? I had found all the damaging information I needed in the first file. Cantrell was gone, fired because of that information. What more was needed?

I waited while Sol scribbled a few notes on a pad, thinking as soon as I found the time I better unpack my boxes and see what exactly was in that file.

Sol finished writing, closed the folder and then stared hard. "That's quite a story, young man. Were you a fiction writer in college?"

"Huh?"

"First you have Dr. Cantrell involved in a plot to keep minorities out of medical school. Then you have him taking a million dollar bribe to take in a student who is two SAT points short of a turnip. And finally you tell me he's taking that money and using it to hand-pick his own medical students. You don't expect me to believe all this?" His voice had risen, there was a look of anger and fear in his eyes. He was suddenly different, suddenly distant.

I scooted my chair away from the table. "Look, if you don't want to believe me, fine. Somebody did. He got fired, you know."

"Thanks to you and your graduation speech. That bit of news traveled far. I can't wait to hear about that."

"He got what was coming to him. It wasn't my fault he was fired. If I ever see him again, I'll tell him. By the way, what ever happened to the bastard?"

Sol Goldman stood up and gathered his papers. "Last night, Charles Cantrell, was found dead."

Chapter 11 - maxine

Gail Peterson pleaded with me to sign out and go home. "I'll finish up whatever you want."

It was nine p.m. I hadn't slept in thirty six hours and I still had hours of work ahead of me. "Thanks for the offer, Gail, but I have to check Maxine Chu's biopsy results."

Gail looked down. "You haven't heard."

My heart raced.

"I thought everyone in the hospital knew by now. Maxine Chu has advanced stage 4 B disseminated Hodgkins disease. I'm sorry, Daniel. The slides are classic."

I fought for breath. "Does she know?"

Gail shook her head. "Dave thought you might want to talk to her first. He's waiting for you."

I found Dave in the resident's dictation room. He told me about the lymphangiogram, already scheduled for tomorrow. Dye injected into both feet and taken up into lymph tissue as it spread upward into the abdomen. "It will help the surgeons to determine the extent of the laparotomy."

"Laparotomy?"

"That's the easy part. The radiation and chemo afterward is the bitch. Given all that, her chance of survival is still only twenty five percent."

The number stuck in my throat. I remembered misbehaving as a youngster and my father quoting me those same odds on whether or not I'd be receiving my allowance that week. Twenty five percent.

Dave thought I should break the news to Maxine. "This is the kind of thing interns have to learn how to do," he said.

Maxine was sitting up in bed, chewing gum and solving the Tribune crossword puzzle. She greeted me with a half-smile. "Thought you forgot about me."

I checked her temperature chart. Maxine had spiked a high fever twice during the day. I placed my palm on her forehead.

"Stir fry some veggies up there," she murmured, placing her hand on top of mine. It was warm and soft. My heart raced. "Lo just went back to his restaurant. He left enough food for an army. What'll it be-- ribs or moo shoo?"

I sat down on the edge of the bed, kicked off my shoes and yawned. Fatigue had me bleary eyed. I rested my head in my hands, hoping to make the fog disappear. "How about sweet and sour pillow?"

Maxine lifted my chin and looked into my eyes. "Dr. Raskin, did you get any sleep last night?"

"Would a 'no' rob you of your confidence in me?"

"Yes!"

"No, I didn't."

Maxine smiled, setting her pencil down on the puzzle. "I'm sorry you don't feel well."

"Maxine, I'm supposed to ask how *you* feel."

Maxine pointed to the door. "Ask the twenty people who have already been here."

"Damn. I knew the place was going to be a zoo. We should have closed the room to visitors."

"That's okay. They've got to learn what a spleen feels like, don't they?"

"Well, then you should have charged them."

"By the pound?"

I laughed, but only for a moment.

"They acted like they knew what they were doing, all except for one fourth-year surgery student--the guy was sweaty, and he stuttered like a fiend. He was even wearing a bow tie," she exclaimed. "First he feels my spleen, then he moves up the belly to the chest, copping a little feel of my boobs. So I said: 'Hey, the action is down here. Both my boobs put together don't come close to the size of my spleen.' Must have been the first time he got to second base with a Chinese woman!" She winked and could no longer suppress a smile. "Must have heard about our sultry reputations." With a quick flick of her head, her hair danced to one side.

"Nobody should be doing that to you, Maxine. I should report him."

"Don't you dare. I haven't had a man drool over me in I don't know how long."

She paused. "Lo... he just drools, period."

"Maxine, we have to talk."

"Let's eat first."

"I don't know."

"Come on. Eat."

"You sound like my mother."

Maxine smiled. "I grew up in Skokie. Put in twenty hours a week at Kaufman's Deli. When it wasn't Cantonese, it was cream cheese. When it wasn't chow mien, it was chopped herring. I'm also engaged to the mother of all Jewish mothers, poor old Lo. So eat!"

The only calories I had ingested the past twelve hours consisted of a three-day-old bagel, half of which felt like an undigested paperweight in my stomach. Maxine served up a plate of delicious egg rolls, fried rice and ribs.

Maxine was silent as I ate, filing her nails and looking out the window, watching the evening gracefully darken the lake. I had to find just the right moment to break the news. And I had to break it in exactly the right way.

When I finished eating, I looked at her and noticed that her smile had faded with the light of day. I wiped my mouth with my coat sleeve and scratched my forehead with one of the chopsticks.

"Great table manners," she said.

"I was raised by wolves."

"Still hungry, Dr. Wolf?"

"Yes, do you have a spare rib?"

Maxine looked me in the eye. "Only if you have a spare spleen. I'll be needing one after the surgery."

I coughed so hard I nearly lacerated my soft palate with the chopsticks.

"Maxine, why didn't you tell..."

"Why didn't you tell me? Why did I have to hear it from some resident I'd never met? He just barged in here, poked around for forty five painful minutes, and then proceeded to tell me everything I didn't want to know about disseminated Hodgkin's disease. He even drew pictures!"

"Who?"

"He said he's a friend of yours," she said. "Dr. Spool."

"That son of a bitch!"

Maxine put her hand on my shoulder. "Hey, where did you pick up language like that?"

I wanted to blurt out the nickname Alex had given to Malcolm Spool. Malformed Stool. Instead, I breathed deeply, hoping to exorcise Malcolm's image from my mind.

Maxine shifted her file to the other hand. "Besides," she continued. "I'm the one who should be venting my spleen--while I still have one."

A single tear rolled down her face, landing two down and four across on her crossword puzzle.

"I'm sorry, Max. I've been in clinic all day and ..."

"Don't," she said, dabbing at her face. "Just tell me that a laparotomy is no big deal."

I explained it the best I could-- the general anesthesia, the removal of the spleen along with any abnormal looking lymph tissue they might find while there.

"Why do they have to take out the spleen?" she asked.

"Makes it easier to tolerate the radiation and the ...rest of the treatment."

"Chemotherapy?"

"Sorry. I didn't want to burden you with too much all at once."

"Tell that to Dr. Spool."

I took a breath. "It's Dr. Stool, Maxine. And you can count on it."

I looked out Maxine's window at the grey-blue skyline. My body craved sleep and if I didn't leave soon, I wouldn't even have the energy necessary to cross the street to my apartment. "I have to go, Maxine. The cockroaches in my apartment haven't been fed in two days."

Maxine handed me a fortune cookie. "Lo's cookies are filled with Chinese proverbs. Let's see what you got."

"Maxine, I really need..."

"Come on," she urged. "These cookies never lie. Open it."

Maxine and I cracked our cookies at the same time, sealing our fortunes together. I read mine first. "Distance tests the endurance of a horse; time reveals a man's character."

We both paused momentarily. Maxine then nodded her head. "I knew it. Just like I said, it fits."

"Let's hear yours."

Maxine unfolded the crumpled paper.

"A good friend is like a genie--three wishes will be granted you." She paused, then looked in my eyes. "Three wishes," she mused. "Three wishes from my physician-friend with Chinese food all over his coat."

Self-consciously I ran my hand across my chest.

Maxine moved closer. "First, I want to know the whole truth--and I don't want Lo to know any of the gory details."

"Done."

"Second, if you would be so kind as to come to my laparotomy."

"I'm no surgeon, Maxine."

"Neither is that fourth year medical student who thought my breasts were Playdoh. God only knows what he'll be fondling in the operating room." Her eyebrows rose in expectation. "I feel safe when you're around."

"Granted," I sighed. "And the final wish from her majesty is..."

Maxine took a deep breath.

"Cure me."

Chapter 12 the swimming pool

The laparotomy proved to be a long one, both for Maxine and me. Besides the spleen removal, there were lymph nodes to flush out of hidden places, like behind her abdominal aorta, where one slip of the knife meant perforation and death. Standing next to the anesthesiologist on a perch behind the surgical field, I heard my heart race watching the meticulous work of the surgeons, and occasionally peaking beneath the sterile drapes at Maxine's face. It was as if she had fallen asleep while reading her fashion magazine. Maybe she was dreaming that this ordeal was just a nightmare from which she would awaken.

For three hours I watched the tedious dissection, the sections trimmed and dropped into bubbling liquid nitrogen, then rushed off to pathology. The dismantling and rearranging of Maxine Chu. And when it was over I did something I hadn't done during my entire four years of medical school: I sat in the bathroom stall in the surgical locker room and sobbed. It took twenty minutes to clear my eyes of the redness. As I exited the locker room, Sol Goldman was waiting.

"You look terrible," he said, touching my sweat-soaked scrubs.

Suddenly I was glad I had gotten it all out of my system. To break down in front of the Chief would have been a sign that I was incapable of acting in a professional manner. Sol wanted professionals around, not cry-babies. Sol Goldman's hand remained on my shoulder. "Sorry I was so hard on you the other day." I looked up, for the first time seeing tenderness in his eyes. "I probably deserved it."

"I haven't seen you since our little chat. After what you told me, I was sure that Charles Cantrell's death was due to foul play. I only just found out, it was ruled a suicide."

If Sol said that to relieve me of any guilt, it didn't work. In fact, it now seemed that his death was my fault, seeing as I was the one who got him fired.

Sol Goldman read my thoughts. "Don't blame yourself," he said softly. "Besides, you have enough on your mind. I heard about your patient, Maxine Chu. How is she?"

"Have to wait and see," I answered.

"Been to the pool yet? It's down in the basement."

I shook my head. "I think I'll wait until Maxine wakes up. I'd like to be there."

"A swim will do you good. Maxine won't be awake for several hours."

"But Dr. Goldman, I have other things to do."

"Call me Sol. Look, Daniel.."

"Call me Danny, please."

Sol smiled. "I'll have your resident paged. He'll cover for you."

"That wouldn't be fair."

"Believe me. He won't complain if it comes from my mouth."

The swimming pool at Richard Meese hospital was situated in what appeared to be an old auditorium in the basement, just outside the nursing student living quarters. Though it was closed at eight p.m., a properly inserted credit card was all it took to gain entrance.

The pool was eerily deserted, making me wonder what motivated Alex to want to party here. He had been invited for a late-night swim by two dietitians. He refused to comment other than to say that by the time he was done the pool was in dire need of chlorine.

I gazed upward at the rafters and their patina of ancient graffiti. Reflections from the water shimmered against spider webs dangling from the wooden ceiling. I imagined I could hear a winged creature flap its way across the windowless expanse of the room.

I kicked off the edge of the pool, gliding through the water like a dolphin who'd been land-locked. Sol was right. The pool was a release, physically and spiritually. I hadn't felt so good since coming to Chicago. Internship wasn't so bad after all; the rally, the ER, all that was behind me--there were only good things to come. Somehow I would pull Maxine Chu through her ordeal.

I soon lost count of my laps and found myself off the coast of San Diego, rocking in the waves under a midday sun.

As I dove under water to make my turn, I kicked against the side of the pool a little harder than usual, holding my breath under water for half the length of the pool. When I surfaced there was darkness.

I stood up, rubbing my eyes; pitch black. A power outage?

It wasn't me, was it? I'd read about air embolisms causing acute blindness. But that was in sixty feet of water, not in a swimming pool.

Then I heard footsteps---distant but heavy. Boots--metal on the bottom--security--that's it! Security must have shut the lights off thinking no one was here.

"Hey. It's me! Dr. Raskin. I'm in the pool. Turn on the lights!"

Except for the echo of my voice, there was silence. I shivered. I heard them again, closer this time.

"Enough already--I can't see a damn thing."

Darkness. Silence. My heart raced.

"Okay, the joke's over! Turn on the damn lights!" More footsteps, racing with my pulse. I squinted in the shadows-- somebody wearing a white coat- carrying something ---a bag?

The door to the locker area suddenly opened and I could hear someone running. The ceiling lights burst on like at a night game at Comisky Park as the large iron door swung shut behind the disappearing figure. I squinted until I regained vision.

There, emblazing the door, was a blood red swastika.

Chapter 13 maxine

When Maxine awoke from surgery, I expected her to ask me a million questions about what they'd found.

She didn't.

Or about her prognosis and future treatment plan.

She didn't.

Or at the very least about the eight pounds of spleen removed by the surgeons.

She didn't.

Instead, as soon as Maxine opened her eyes and saw me standing there, she winced in pain, weakly lifted her gown, and in a soft but concerned voice asked: "Did they get rid of the chicken fat around my thighs?"

Over the next three days, Maxine refused to take any pain medications, opting instead for my hand, which I offered liberally. She gripped it like a lifeline, often until she slipped peacefully off to sleep.

When her strength and appetite returned, she held court in the large chair in the corner of her room. I talked about the upcoming treatment plan--the radiation, the chemo, all the follow-up tests she would need, but she only halfheartedly listened, her eyes usually closely focused on one of her glamor magazines.

Finally, one morning a week after the operation, she asked me to close the door, and then asked: "So, just how much is this radiation going to hurt?"

"It doesn't Max. I've told you a hundred times."

"What about Hiroshima?"

I explained for the fifth time that all we were doing was trying to shrink the tumor bulk. That the chemotherapy would then do the rest.

"Will I be able to have kids?"

"You're not even married. One thing at a time."

Maxine smiled, propping herself up in bed. "The hell with this save yourself until marriage stuff. As soon as I get my strength back, I'm losing my virginity." She held up a copy of

Mademoiselle. "I bet there isn't a single virgin in this whole magazine," she said. "I'm as modern as they are. If Lo wants to keep his fossilized penis in the Ming dynasty, let him."

I stifled an urge to laugh, then winced as my beeper sounded. I said good-bye to Maxine and went to the nurse's station where I phoned the page operator.

"Long distance holding," she said. "Just a moment please."

My heart pounded. Unexpected long distance phone calls, especially during the day, often signaled trouble.

Mom's voice came through hoarsely. "Danny?"

"What's wrong, Mom? Somebody sick?"

"No, nothing like that."

I took a deep breath. "Why are you calling? It's the middle of the day?"

She paused. "We were robbed last night."

My chest thumped. "Everybody okay?"

"We weren't home, thank God."

"What did they take?"

"Nothing."

"What do you mean, nothing?" I heard the receiver drop and a moment later my dad spoke. "Danny, I have a question for you and I want a straight answer." He cleared his throat. "Do you use drugs?"

"What?"

"Answer the question."

"No, dad, but why in God's name are you..."

"Other than the garage, the only place that was ransacked was your bedroom."

I gasped. "My coin collection. Is it still there?"

"Untouched."

I quickly went through a list of my other childhood treasures, none of which should be of the slightest interest to burglars: autographed picture of Alan Trammel, Eagle Scout badge, wrestling and track medals. Everything was present and accounted for.

"So you have no idea why someone would take your room apart? Nothing specific to look for?"

I assured Dad that whatever had held the perpetrator's interest, it wasn't drugs, and that other than caffeine and an occasional beer, I was drug free. His relief was obvious as we hung up the phone.

I forgot about the burglary for the rest of that very busy day. It wasn't until I headed home at nine thirty that evening, as I was crossing the unlit parking lot, that the memory of our phone conversation returned. My father's assumption that the break was targeted at my bedroom was crazy. My bedroom was closest to the garage, surely the first room the intruder came to. He was probably rifling through my old baseball card collection when he heard a car pull up in the driveway. Whatever the case, I was thankful nobody was hurt.

As I unlocked and opened the door to my apartment, the light from the hallway sent several insects scrambling for cover. "Sorry guys," I muttered, stepping into the dark living room. "Hope I didn't disturb a cockroach orgy or something." I turned on the light. For a moment I thought I was somewhere else. The living room looked like a hurricane had passed through. Couches overturned, lamps dismantled, bookshelves spilled of their contents. The kitchen was worse. The items from every cabinet had been swept onto the tile floor. The contents of ten jars of spaghetti sauce, my entire cache, covered the floor like a pizza with broken glass topping. In the bathroom, deodorant, cologne, and shaving supplies had all been swept from the cabinet. My bedroom was unrecognizable. Bed sheets strewn over the floor, my mattress upended and leaning against the window. Every box pulled out of my closet, turned upside down, their contents scattered across the room. Everything I had brought with me from Arbor Hills that I was meaning to unpack, but hadn't found the time, had now been unpacked for me. Sol Goldman's words suddenly hit me: *What happened to Cantrell's file?*

Officer James Mulroney arrived five minutes after I called. He and his partner carefully surveyed each room, jotting notes onto a pad and then spraying something that was supposed to bring out fingerprints. Mulroney never had believed my story about Randy Jordan's death, and I doubted he'd believe someone broke into my apartment just to steal a file from me that I had stolen from somebody else. When he finished, he spit out a wad of tobacco as large as a cupcake. "Doesn't look like they took anything."

I threw my hands in the air. "What's there to take, Mulroney? I'm an intern. No money, no possessions, I don't even have any cold beer."

While his partner watched, Mulroney dusted the door for prints, then carefully examined the metal bolt and its surrounding wooden encasement. "No sign of forced entry," he announced. "You have to be more careful about leaving your door unlocked."

"I didn't."

"You must have. Either that or someone used a key. And I'm sure your front office is not in the habit of giving room keys out to drug addicts from the Washington Street projects."

I asked how he could be so sure of that.

"Happens all the time. Kids sneak past security and then wander the hallways looking for unlocked doors. That's why you're not missing anything. They were just looking for some quick cash to pocket."

As they were leaving, I touched Mulroney's shoulder and thanked him. "I have a favor to ask. Can you..well sort of ... not write this incident up?

Mulroney glared.

"It's just that if my Chief finds out..you know, I've been getting myself in enough trouble already."

Mulroney smiled, his brown teeth stained from tobacco. "Don't want to draw any more attention to yourself, huh?" He ripped up his notes. "Just like the ticket I gave you," he said. "But if I were you, the next time I chose to leave without locking the door, I'd leave a sign posted: 'Intern lives here.' Poor bastard probably spent the better part of an hour looking for money. If he knew you were an intern, he wouldn't have wasted his time."

After Mulroney left, I drank a beer, then got down on my knees, sorting through every item on my bedroom floor. Books, class notes, drug company paraphernalia.

The file I had taken from Charles Cantrell, now deceased, was not there.

Chapter 14 recovery

By the time I cleaned up my apartment, it was three a.m. I slept fitfully, twice awakening to imaginary noises, and come morning, stared in the bathroom mirror at the dark and sagging skin folds under my lids. Intern eyes, I thought, and I hadn't even been on call. After a shower, during which I envisioned Anthony Perkins stabbing me repeatedly, I dressed and sprinted across the street where I grabbed a Spanish omelet in the Richard Meese cafeteria. While it quenched my hunger, it did little to assuage my rising feeling of inadequacy and vulnerability. On morning rounds I was incapable of making any sound decisions. It seemed as though my confidence had been gouged out with the same instrument used to inexplicably open my apartment door. Half-way through our patients, Dave turned and asked; "What's wrong Danny? Been burning the candle at both ends?" With that he winked, as if he could imagine the sordid trouble I must have gotten into the night before-chief donor at the city sperm bank or something. I let it pass. After rounds, Gail Petersen came up and handed me one of the order sheets I had filled out. "I don't think this will help Rose Kaplan's stomach, Danny." I glanced at my writing: "Take two teaspoons of Milk of Amnesia."

Over a cheeseburger at lunch and I told Alex about the apartment break in. The funny thing about it was that I had sensed something was wrong even before I got there.

"A real clairvoyant," said Alex, smiling pleasantly at every waitress who passed. Alex was so smooth that they fought over who would clear his dirty dishes.

"I don't think it's that, Alex. It's just that earlier in the day, my parents' house in Detroit had been robbed. It must have been in the back of my mind."

Alex's eyes bulged as I told him what had happened. How my father assumed that since it had been my bedroom that took the only hit during the robbery, that I must have been the kingpin for the entire Colombian cocaine cartel.

"Don't you get it?" he asked incredulously.

"Get what?"

Alex stopped to compliment the waitress on her impeccable service. "The two robberies are related."

"To what?"

"To that file, Campell's missing file that Tannenbaum asked you about in the emergency room."

"They would go all the way to Michigan looking for that file?"

"Information, Danny. Something about Cantrell, something that he might actually have killed himself over."

The juice running down the side of my cheeseburger reminded me of Randy Jordan's blood. I pushed the plate away. "That's over, Alex. I made that information public in my graduation speech. I exposed Cantrell and he was fired."

"But you said there was another file. One you hadn't opened."

"Same stuff, Alex."

"How do you know?"

I shrugged my shoulders. "What else could it be?"

"Well, where is it?"

"It's gone."

Alex looked perturbed. "They stole it?"

"Must have. I was sure it was in one of the boxes I brought to Chicago and never bothered to unpack. Whoever broke into my apartment likely got what they came for."

"Let's hope so for your sake, Danny boy. They might not be so friendly the next time around."

As we got up from the table, Alex handed me his check. "You mind? I'm in a bit of a money crunch."

I took his check. "No problem."

"Thanks, Danny." He had a boyish smile. "Tell you the truth, I'm actually short on this month's rent."

"More bad luck?"

Alex rested his hand on my shoulder. "Temporary set back, that's all. Went too far with a bad tip."

"Cubs?"

"Horses. Del Mar. Off-track stuff."

On the way home from work, I stopped at a newly-opened Montgomery Ward's and picked up a pair of running shoes. Swimming wouldn't cut it after my last experience, and besides, I had achieved a regular jogging schedule during my first two years of medical school. No reason I couldn't take it up again in Chicago.

When I got home, I rechecked each thing I had brought with me from Arbor Hills. Everything I had repacked last night, I now unpacked, looking for Cantrell's file. It wasn't large, just a legal-size metal file with a lock on top. It could have been missed in my exhausted state.

It wasn't there. Had it ever been? I thought back to those last days at Arbor Hills, when I had either thrown away or packed up everything in my apartment. I remembered seeing that file, and set it aside to return it unopened to the admission's office. I ended up getting side tracked by Linda Johnson, leaving her place two days late, and dumping everything in the trunk of my car. The file had to have been with me.

Was it possible that someone wanted that unopened file enough to have killed Randy Jordan? Just to send me a message? A coldness flooded through my body and and I hopped into bed, pulling the covers over my shoulders. The flashing red light of an ambulance reflected off my window as it turned into the ER across the street. It seemed they were sending me multiple messages. It didn't take a surgeon to find someone's aorta with a knife. If they'd wanted to kill me they certainly could have. And then the swastika on the swimming pool wall. Maybe I should have told Mulroney about the swastika, as well as the stabbing. But they didn't seem connected back then, and now with Mulroney pegging me as paranoid conspiracy nut, it was probably too late to convince him of my new theories. Besides I thought, maybe I was a little off the deep end. Maybe the pressures of internship had taken their toll. Maybe it was time to put it all behind me.

Tomorrow was a new day. No rally, no swimming pool, no files. I turned over in bed and thrust the covers over my head, drowning out the nighttime noises of South Side Chicago and fell asleep.

The man hung up the phone and cursed. How could they have said those things to him? Questioned his competence, his loyalty? Nobody in the organization was more loyal than he. Hadn't he proved it over and over again? It was that bastard, Raskin, dammit. He was the one causing the unnecessary publicity. He was the one acting like an uncooperative pain in the ass. Perhaps it was time for another communication, this time more direct and to the point. He smiled, then saluted at the picture hanging from his wall. The Fuhrer saluted back.

Chapter 15 running

Later, when people asked why I didn't notice the footsteps behind me, I lied. Told them I was too busy trying to plant my Adidas between the rocks and broken glass which lay like land mines on the lakeside trail. I was on a seven minute pace with two miles to go--my best since coming to Chicago for internship. Or perhaps it was the sound of the oldies station blaring from my head phones that masked the danger:

"Momma told me not to come...
That ain't the way to have fun son,
That ain't the way to have fun."

No reason to tell the truth, that thinking about women is what kept me from noticing someone behind me. Women are life's one distraction for me, have been ever since wide-eyed Mimi Kirschbaum looked up the leg of my gym shorts as I climbed the rope in Phys Ed class. The unusual tingling between my legs and my memorable first orgasm ended with a fifteen foot fall to the floor in front of the entire seventh grade.

But at the lakefront on the south side of Chicago, where I had no business jogging at seven P.M. when darkness ushered in a dangerous new ecosystem, I heard footsteps, behind me; someone in a hurry. Don't turn around, I told myself. Don't give them the edge to pass you.

I glanced at my watch. Those Chicago runners were competitive sons of bitches. All right, Mister, let's pick up the pace, take it to a six-minute mile. I whipped myself harder, the resounding music piercing my cortex.

"Momma told me not to come ..."

The footsteps faded. I breathed relief. My first run in three weeks rescued me from ruin. I sucked in a breath of twilight.

The footsteps were back. Those shoes were hard bottomed. Who the hell can run a six minute mile in street shoes? I thought of turning around. No, let's take it up another notch. Two hundred yards ahead I could see a shed outlined against the darkness. The finish line. Go for it. Fly, every muscle, every joint working overtime. Five minute mile, asshole. Beat that.

I was running as fast as I could, my legs pumping as if my feet weren't even touching the ground, but I could hear the boots closing fast and turned just in time to see the broad end of a baseball bat swinging towards me. I threw my arms up to protect my face, but not in time. A meteor of pain exploded in my skull. The sky became a mass of laser lights, arrows of perfect pain. My mouth filled with blood. *Play dead, Danny, for Christ's sake, don't be an asshole.*

I saw the spurred black boots. I tried to make out his face, saw the sudden movement of the boot as it delivered an excruciating thwack to my crotch.

"I want that file."

I'd heard the voice before but my mind wasn't working. I hurt too much to think anything but *lie there, Danny boy, play dead.*

"Okay, Jewboy, where's the file?"

That got me to my knees. "Fuck you!" I bellowed just as the Louisville Slugger struck my head, pitching me backward into a dark empty space.

End of part 1

PART II

Autumn

Hatred or oppression toward any member of society is hatred against society itself. If we are to survive into the next century we must meet the purveyors of hate head on and beat their message into the ground so that all people may walk the earth in peace.

Vice-President Harold J. Barrish -speech given at annual meeting of NAACP

Chapter 16 back to work

It was a welcome back lunch of sorts. Alex Rosen and Gail Peterson, treating me to my first meal of solid food in two weeks. We were joined by Brian Picolli, the Southern California surfing champ turned intern, who had been on duty in the ER the day the ambulance brought me in.

"Believe me, you look a whole lot better now," said Brian, sucking a chocolate milkshake through the chewed end of a straw. "I thought you were one dead dude."

One dead dude was close to the truth. A mass of bloody pulp piled on a pair of shoulders, was how they described it to me when I awoke. I couldn't remember the particulars, of course. A baseball bat had permanently knocked that bit of memory out of my cerebral ball park.

"The first thing I recall was this beam of light piercing one eye and then the other and somebody asking me to name the president."

"You said Grover Cleveland," said Brian.

Alex leaned forward. "What did you expect with sixty IQ points worth of brains splattered on the sidewalk?"

I shrugged my shoulders. "How about a surgical residency?"

The three of them laughed loudly. I only wished I could open my mouth that wide. As it was, I was having a terrible time trying to negotiate a hamburger past my lower lip.

"You were a maniac, Danny," offered up Brian. "Pulling on your IV's, screaming at the top of your lungs. Man, you were psycho. Thank God for Thorazine."

"Slept for two days," added Gail.

"Which is too bad," said Alex, saluting me with his eyebrows. "That was a mighty sexy nursing student who shoved that Foley catheter up your shlong."

The Foley catheter is placed into the bladder by way of the penis in any obtunded or critically ill patient in order to monitor urine output. Sexy or not, whoever had passed mine had never learned the proper insertion technique. For weeks after, it stung like hell when I peed. I glanced at Gail, who turned sheepishly away.

"Who was it?" I asked Alex.

"Tall blond with a southern accent."

"The babe just jumped right in," said Brian.

"Took her time, too," added Alex. "She held that pink pencil of yours like it was an old friend." Alex slapped my shoulder.

We ordered coffee refills and apple pie, which was almost impossible to slide past my bruised jaw. Apple sauce was more my speed.

It had been two weeks of hell. Three days in intensive care unit, mom at my side, trying to convince the doctors that I'd be better in no time if only they'd pour her chicken noodle soup into the nasogastric tube leading to my stomach. Then four more days in a private room on 6-Gardner House, then home, where every day for a week I sipped a nutritional supplement composed of Ensure blended with peanut butter cups, watched three hours of Gilligan's Island reruns, and slept in stretches of up to fourteen hours. I was glad to be back, but still not as strong as I should be. My legs wobbled if I stood for too long, and my head throbbed after ten minutes of concentration.

Alex asked me if I had seen Sol Goldman.

"This was supposed to be a pleasant meal." Sol Goldman was the last person I wanted to see. I remembered waking up in the ER to his voice telling me the whole escapade was my fault. That I had no business jogging south in this part of the city. Goldman was convinced that the two black kids picked up near the lake were the perpetrators. He claimed their fingerprints were on the baseball bat.

I pushed the plate of pie over to Brian Picolli. "Those kids are innocent. The person chasing me was older and wore tall boots."

Alex picked at the pie crust. "I thought you ran track in high school."

I nodded. I had placed second in the mile my senior year of high school.

"Well then how the hell did someone wearing boots...?"

"Damn if I know, Alex."

"When you came to," added Picolli, "you were mumbling some gnarly stuff. Nazis. Stabbings. Spooked the hell out of me."

"First thing I heard when I got down there," said Alex, "was Goldman and Mulroney arguing. Mulroney didn't think it was those kids, either. Said that gash was too big a job for a twelve year old."

I sat in silence the remainder of the meal. Goldman was hiding something. He had to have some reason for putting me on the defensive. According to him, everything was my fault--the baseball bat, the fact that my patient had his throat slit; something told me he even blamed me for the death of Charles Cantrell. Why? I intended to find out.

Chapter 17 emile horner

Beyer House Pavilion was two buildings south of Gardner House and was connected to it by a second floor corridor as well as a basement tunnel. It was the second oldest building on the medical campus. The low-lying ceilings took angled turns around dimly lit corridors, making hurried passage dangerous. The wrought iron doors on the elevator clanged ominously and the visitor's lounge had all the ambience of a Route 66 truck stop.

The only things older than the building itself were the physicians admitting patients there. They were the last remnants of the eager young doctors who first put Richard Meese on the medical map; some in research; others as respected clinical specialists. One by one most of them had died, and the dozen or so remaining were in their eighties and practiced a form of medicine popular over twenty years before. Though many hospital officials recommended that their hospital privileges be revoked, Sol Goldman revered these men for their pioneering accomplishments, and rather than putting them out to pasture, herded them into 3-Meyer House where they were allowed to graze to their hearts' content.

My favorite of these aged attendings was Emile Horner. The oldest doctor on staff, he nonetheless came to work dressed as if he were forty-five; well-tailored black suit, crisp white shirt and polished wing-tips. Burying clothes, some whispered. And they weren't joking. The white satin scarf that hugged his thin neck was no fashion statement--it helped keep in valuable body heat. His skin stretched tightly over a bony face with the texture of petrified wood, eighty five furrows in all. Nature had treated his hair more kindly, leaving him a full complement of thick, bristly gray waves parted perfectly on the left and coated generously with Vitalis. He hunched over an olive wood cane, and when he stopped to talk, his hazel eyes were always searching. An aura of sour cream and herring clung to him like a bad cold.

Dr. Horner had survived Auschwitz not because he was an honored Viennese physician, but because had been a virtuoso violinist in the Vienna Symphony. Soon after Austria was annexed, Emile Horner was betrayed by jealous colleagues and eventually sent to Auschwitz, where he was placed in the concentration camp orchestra. It was a time he refused to talk about.

After the war, he moved to Chicago, retrained in medicine, and at the age of forty, became one of the pioneers of Richard Meese. Until five years ago he sat in regularly with the Chicago Symphony Orchestra. At one point he had composed a requiem to the Holocaust which was conducted by Leonard Bernstein and televised across the country.

The patients Emile Horner admitted to the hospital were little old ladies and men complaining that something was sore. A diagnosis was rarely made, but most recovered after two weeks, regardless of the treatment. A few died, also regardless of the treatment. I respected the fragility of his patients; so did Gail Peterson, who was once again on the same service as I was. We, too, realized that even a procedure as benign as a barium enema could cause a bowel perforation, and that in the elderly predisposed patient, a single dose of Tylenol could lead to intractable liver failure.

The third intern on the service was not as agreeable. Kurt Mallincroft had garnered a reputation for refusing to take care of patients he felt were inappropriately admitted. "Especially the gomers," Kurt would announce. Gomer was an acronym for 'Get Out of My Emergency Room' and was usually attributed to the less than wholesome patient. "Horner's a gomer, his patients are gomers, and I don't know if I can take many more of these admissions." This I heard him say after he found one of his patients brushing his teeth with Preparation-H.

"Look on the bright side," I injected. "It shrinks the gums."

I adored the soft-spoken and gentle way Emile Horner would sit at his patients' bedsides, cuddling their hands in his own. I also liked the way he let me run the cases, allowing me to make the decisions without compromising his self-esteem.

"Well, Dr. Raskin," he would say in a delicate Austrian accent. "What do you think we should do about Mr. Schwartzman's lower back problem?"

I answered with deference. "I think for starters, some simple rest, heat, and analgesia, followed by range-of-motion treatment. If he doesn't feel better in two weeks, we can order some spine films and a bone scan."

Dr. Horner rested his hand on my shoulder. "My thoughts, exactly," he replied. "And don't forget to make sure they have a bowel movement every day."

That's the way it went for most of his patients. One bowel movement and they were happy as second graders at a birthday party. Morning rounds featured the prune juice sonata: "Good morning, Mrs. Pincus. Did your bowels move? Oh, very good. See you later." "Good Morning, Mrs. Finenagel. Aren't we all nice and pretty today. Guess that old mineral oil did the trick."

As was to be expected on a medical floor filled with feeble octogenarians, death also found its way to 3-Meyer House. When I lost two patients my first week there, both of whom died in their sleep, nobody blinked.

Nobody, that is, except for Sol Goldman.

Chapter 18 Sol Goldman

"Getting used to my office?"

It was another call day and I had just been paged about a seizing patient who was being admitted to my service. My head had been aching almost continuously since the accident, and I still had intermittent bouts of blurred vision. I was just trying to make it through the day the best I could, an hour at a time. The last thing I needed was an intrusion by Sol Goldman.

He waited patiently at his desk until Sandy entered with a tray of coffee and bagels. Upon seeing me, she immediately sniffed, then smiled politely.

"The man finally discovered soap," Sol said as she set down the tray. On his desk were two charts. I recognized the names of my two deceased patients. "What are you trying to do?" he asked after taking a few sips, "single-handely decrease Chicago's Jewish population?"

"They were both in their eighties, Dr. Goldman. Nursing home residents."

"One of them didn't particularly like you, it seems. I hope that didn't interfere with the care you gave her," he said, brushing back his hair and squinting over his glasses. "The night nurses noted that you inflicted unnecessary pain. I'd like to hear your side of it."

Poor, demented Mrs. Dombrowsky. I remember being called at three in the morning to restart the IV she had pulled out. The veins in her arms seemed to panic at the touch of my needle, rolling under her pleats of doughy skin at the last second.

"Oy, Oy Oy Oy," she screamed. She kept it going for ninety minutes.

"Please Mrs. Dombrowsky," I remember pleading, tears in my eyes, scrub shirt heavy with sweat, fatigue loosening my grip on reality. "Hold still."

"Vhy are you hoiting me?"

Don't get unnerved, Danny, I told myself. Just keep going. I felt a pop as the needle entered the vein. Blood seeped out around the end of the catheter.

"Okay, Mrs. Dombrowsky. I'm in the vein. All that remains is for me to pass the IV over the needle." I carefully slid the outer portion of the tubing over the metal tip that was now presumably resting in the vein.

"Oops!" A large ugly swelling suddenly appeared in her arm. I quickly loosened the tourniquet and put pressure over the site to ebb the flow of blood from the torn vessel. Add one more bruise to the list.

"Vhat do you mean, 'Oops'?" she asked indignantly. "Vhat are you, a meshuganah medical student? Vhy are you killing me? Vhy must I suffer? You should live this long to know the suffering I am going through. Treblinka was nothing compared to this."

"Mrs. Dombrowsky. I'm sorry, the vein just popped open. It's no one's fault. I don't like this any more than you do." I told myself never to say 'Oops' in front of a patient again unless he or she was safely under general anesthesia.

The veins on the other arm were in no better shape, but I went after a small one at the base of the wrist. Although I couldn't visualize it through the film of fatigue that glossed over my eyes, I was able to palpate it under my fingers. It was worth a try.

"Oy, Oy, Oy, Oy," she screamed again. "You're killing me! Can't this vait?" Tears led to sobs and more tears.

My body tightened, fighting to keep control. It was four in the morning. The only thing standing between me and two hours of sleep was that damn IV. After ten sticks I got the vein, the last visible one. As I threaded the catheter through the introducer, Mrs. Dombrowsky jerked her arm, dislodging the entire apparatus.

"Dammit to hell," I said, startling her. Her sobs turned into deep heavy wails that took away any sense of self-respect I had. Is this the kind of doctor I turned out to be? Is this what lack of sleep does? Shouldn't they have screened me out for such behavior during the medical school interview?

"I'm sorry, Mrs. Dombrowsky. I've been up all night. I apologize for taking it out on you. It wasn't your fault. The IV came out. Let's just work together to get this done."

"Two deaths in twenty-four hours," Sol announced after I finished. "Makes me wonder whether that hit over the head you got knocked loose your last two years of medical school."

"They were old, Sol. Mrs. Dombrowsky had ovarian cancer. Mr. Schwartz had renal failure. At least they died in their sleep."

Sol leaned forward. "They both had heart attacks."

I caught my breath. "Heart attacks? How do you know?"

"Autopsy."

An autopsy on an eighty year old? It didn't make sense. The pathology report sailed like a frisbee across the desk.

"Take a look."

I couldn't believe it. Necrotic cardiac tissue on gross exam. Myocyte destruction on microscopic.

"Convinced?"

"What did the coronary arteries look like?"

"What are you, a pathologist?" Sol asked, his tone changing. "What do you think they looked like? With infarcts that size, they had to be occluded."

It didn't seem possible. I had taken careful histories; neither patient had symptoms of angina. Their ECG's were normal.

An attitude crept into Goldman's face. "My boy, older people rarely have classic signs of a heart attack. As physicians, we must learn to pick up on the more subtle nuances."

"Like screaming while I'm putting in an IV?"

Sol paused. "You put her through a hell of a lot of stress."

I sought to control the anger burning inside me. "I suppose you think I was responsible for Randy Jordan getting killed in the ER?"

"Trouble does have a way of following you around." He folded his arms slowly, as if he had just stated the truism of the year.

"You've been on my case from the beginning."

"With good reason." Sol leaned closer. "First, you tell me about this mystery man following you around, slitting throats.

99

Then you get your head bashed in for running the wrong way at the lake." Sol paused and chewed a piece of bagel. "It wasn't easy getting coverage for you for those two weeks. And now this."

"This? What are you saying?"

"I'm watching you Raskin. Every move from here on out. I won't have any slackers in my Department. Not when the Vice President of the United States is coming."

His words stung. I felt a surge of strength. Suddenly I was back on the pavement at Lake Michigan, shouting 'fuck you' instead of playing dead. "At least I'm not a bullshitter."

Goldman stiffened and barked: "What did you say?"

"You lied to me, Dr. Goldman. More than once. The baseball bat by the lake. You say the cops caught two little black kids, fingerprints on the bat. Said it was an open-and-shut case."

I looked deep into his poker eyes. He was good, that was damn clear. "You're lying. Officer Mulroney told me those kids were cleared. Said there was a witness who saw a man, an adult running from the scene. I remember an older man standing over me." I paused.

"So what?"

"He asked me about Cantrell's file before he hit me!"

"Mulroney had no right to talk to you about police business."

"Why lie, Sol? What are you covering up?"

"Not a damn thing, doctor. I had no idea those boys were cleared."

"I have a right to know if someone's trying to hurt me."

"No one's out to hurt you."

"Tell that to the guy at Daley Plaza who tried to shiskabob my liver."

Sol paused, trying out his best look of surprise. We both knew it failed. I was right. Sol knew about the stabbing at the Nazi rally. That first day of orientation--the way he looked at me, eyes fixated on my lower back. Who the hell would have told him?

For a moment Sol's shoulders slumped in defeat, his bushy eyebrows drooping. "I didn't know a thing about it, Daniel.

Why didn't you tell me? One of my interns gets hurt, I'm supposed to know. What happened?

"I'm not going to talk about it."

"You'd better."

"Not until you answer a few questions."

"Like?"

"The swimming pool in the nurse's residence. You insisted I go for a swim a few weeks ago."

Sol nodded. "You needed it."

"Just like I needed my head clubbed in."

"What are you getting at?"

"Someone was there Sol. At the pool. Whoever it was painted a swastika on the wall."

Sol held his breath a moment. "So? Another practical joke."

"It was the same guy who hit me at the lake."

"Nonsense."

"You lied before Sol. How do I know you're not lying now?"

"Young man, I won't take that from you."

"I have to go, Sol. I've got a seizing patient downstairs." I stood up and walked to the door. As I opened it, Sol's fist pounded his desk.

"Look, Raskin. If I were you, I'd concentrate on taking care of your patients. If they don't survive, neither do you."

Chapter 19 eddie ingraham

Eddie Ingraham lay motionless on the ER gurney, a flaccid mass of flesh, temporarily neutralized by his grand mal seizures. They found him seizing in the waiting room nearly an hour before, his only I.D. an unrecognizable picture and a beat up insurance card. Medical Records ran his name through the computer but came up empty.

"It wasn't my idea," scowled Kurt Mallincroft. He sneered at our resident, Bruce Creagen. "If it was up to me I would have shipped this gomer over to County." Kurt ran his finger across Eddie's forehead, then wafted his sooty appendage in the air. "This guy's the world's biggest dirt bag. Track marks over every vein, scars running across his chest and abdomen." He lifted the side of Eddie's dark, stringy hair and pointed to the rough edged dents in his scalp, burr holes drilled by neurosurgeons to relieve buildup of intracranial pressure, most often seen in drunks and drug addicts. "Looks like he fell asleep in a nest of woodpeckers."

Bruce turned to Gail. "Care to offer up a differential diagnosis?"

Kurt stepped forward. "Let's play Jeopardy. How about 'dirt bags' for' one hundred?"

Bruce shot Kurt a look. "Let's start with the obvious. Do we know whether these seizures are new or old?"

"Old," Gail said quickly. "Either from multiple head traumas or running out of medications."

Bruce nodded approvingly.

"Drugs, maybe," I added.

"There's hope for you guys." Gail and I exchanged sheepish smiles.

"I'm not working him up," said Kurt. "I saw enough of these dirt bags on 6-Meese last month. If I were you, I'd turf his sorry ass to County."

Gail shook her head. "There was an insurance card in his pocket."

"Five bucks says it's a forgery," said Kurt.

Gail stayed to watch while Bruce and I worked up the patient. Part way through our exam, Eddie opened his eyes and stared into space, his eyes fixed on an imaginary object.

"Eddie, can you hear me? Are you awake?"

He muttered something that resembled 'chilly.'

"Are you cold?" I asked.

"Chilly," he repeated. His voice was deep and guttural. The furrows under his eyes blended into scars.

"You want a blanket?"

"Torture, torture," he mumbled.

"No, Eddie," said Gail, lightly grabbing his shoulders. "No one is trying to torture you."

"Jim," he said, a little more clearly. "Ask Jim."

"Who's Jim?"

Eddie tried to sit up. A large cockroach scampered for cover. Gail bit down on her lip. "Phone number. Note pad," he said, sounding more awake.

"What note pad, Eddie?" Gail asked. Edward made a motion toward his left boot. Gail reached in and pulled out a small notebook. On the inside, a phone number was scrawled next to the name, 'Jim'. Gail took it and ran to the phone, while Bruce and I finished our examination. We found Eddie Ingraham's body to be a road map of scarification; neck, chest, abdomen, legs, buttocks--each connected by a defaced and disfigured interstate of fibrous blemishes. I wondered what horrific life experiences accounted for his drug addiction and violent life-style. Yet despite his forehead full of scars and divers, Eddie had some handsome features. Smooth face flowing into a sculptured chin, large toffee-colored eyes with long lashes. A boyish appearance to his body.

I was about to ask Bruce why Eddie's reflexes were normal, not limp like they should be after a seizure, when a wounded mongrel sound erupted from deep inside Eddie. His body straightened and thick, frothy sputum sputtered from his mouth. His teeth clenched down on a protective mouthpiece. His arms and legs executed rhythmic, synchronous arpeggios while his eyes deviated to the far right corner of their sockets.

Bruce barked orders for Valium and phenobarbital, and when those failed, alerted Anesthesia for possible intubation and induction of barbiturate coma. Bruce appeared confident, his knowledge of medicine all encompassing. Yet, behind those collegiate good looks I sensed a modicum of worry.

"Those seizures should have stopped by now," he said. "Maybe something else is going on."

"Like what?" I asked, as I pushed the final one hundred milligrams of Dilantin into Eddie's vein.

"He's a dirt-bag gomer," yelled Kurt, who came over to look. "He's probably resistant to every drug ever synthesized."

Just then Gail Peterson ran into the room, two shades whiter than when she had left. "Just got off the phone with Mr. Ingraham's friend, Jim," she panted. "He's an airborne reservist. Ed moved in with him only two weeks ago." Gail took several deep breaths.

Kurt folded his arms. "What did he have to say, that Eddie was out trying to score some China gold?"

Gail's lips curled downward. "Your so called dirt bag is a pilot in the armed forces. And he's a medical student! She stared at the helpless figure seizing on the bed. "Oh God," she cried. "He postponed his final year of medical school to do Peace Corps work in Chile."

That was what he'd meant by the word 'Chile.' His group was ambushed by guerrillas. Captured and tortured. They brainwashed him. Multiple intravenous injections, beat him over the head with rifles. He's no more an alcoholic or drug addict than you or I!"

What had we said? I felt more like a criminal than a doctor.

Gail sniffed back angry tears. "He was the only one to escape. Everyone else was killed!" Bruce handed her a tissue. "He's here in Chicago to finish medical school."

We watched in numb silence as his seizure ground to a halt. I followed Bruce outside where he began pacing the hall. In two weeks together, this was the first time he had misjudged a patient.

"You okay?"

Bruce looked up. "Yeah, sure. What did Goldman want?"

"What else? Ragging me out about those two patients who died."

Bruce shook his head. "What is it with you two? He's been snooping around the floor, checking your charts, looking at your orders. I told him you had nothing to do with those deaths, that I hadn't picked up on any heart problems, either."

"We both missed it, Bruce. Coronary artery occlusion."

Bruce shook his head. "Their coronary arteries were normal. Looked at them myself. Those patients had Syndrome X: Myocardial infarctions with normal coronary arteries."

I felt weak. Sol Goldman had been explicit. The heart attacks had been caused by blockages in the coronary arteries. Why would he lie about that? As I reentered Eddie's room, he began moaning. Gail rushed to his bedside.

"We understand," she cried. "We know what those bastards did to you!"

Edward turned over and in an eerily coherent voice asked, "You talked to Jim?"

"Yes! Yes, we know everything!"

"Torture, torture! Cattle prods," he said covering his genitals with his hands. "Chains. Needles!"

"It's okay Edward," Gail comforted. "You're safe here."

Hah, I thought. The way we treated you, you'd probably be better off taking your chances in the jungle.

Kurt Mallincroft walked in with a handful of books. "Found these in the waiting room," he said apologetically. "Medical texts. Here's one on epilepsy."

"I'm hungry," Edward moaned. "Haven't eaten in days!"

"Don't worry," said Gail. "As soon as you're able, we'll get you whatever you want."

"Spaghetti," he mumbled. "Haven't had spaghetti in months."

I felt like running back across the street and bringing him my entire cache of Ragu.

"Let's call Channel 8," said Kurt. "This is a great story."

Eddie's previously flaccid arms rose in protest. "No media. Strictly classified." He tried sitting up. "Word gets out, government won't pay for school."

"Tough case, Bruce," I said, following him to the nurses' station.

"Tougher than you think," he answered. Bruce asked the head nurse to let him know the moment the security check was finished on Edward. He then retraced his steps to Edward's room and asked Gail to phone Edward's roommate, Jim. "I need to talk to him in person."

"Why?"

"Just do it!" he snapped. That tone was rare for Bruce. Edward started seizing again.

"He needs the I.C.U.," said Gail.

"No!" barked Bruce. "We can handle it. Let's just get him up to the floor, stat! Private room." He turned and walked out, feet heavy on the tile floor. I chased after him.

"What gives, Bruce?"

Bruce continued his rapid pace. "There's more to this case."

"What are you talking about?"

"A few things about our war hero's story don't fit."

"I thought everything fit --his history..."

"Given by someone else."

"Why would he lie?"

"Maybe he's repeating what he was told."

"He can't fake seizures."

"No? He had a book on epilepsy with him."

My pulse quickened. "What are you getting at?"

"Did you notice how quickly he became alert after that last seizure?"

"So?"

"After a seizure, you're out of it for an hour, easy. As soon as Gail told him she'd reached his roommate, Eddie was wide awake."

"His deep-tendon reflexes recovered faster than normal."

"Just my point," he exclaimed, waving his finger. We pondered the implications of our words. "Come on," said Bruce. "Let's go back and examine our war hero one more time."

Edward began seizing the moment we entered the room. Bruce went to the bedside and lifted one of Edward's eyelids. He rapidly brought his open hand down to within an inch of Eddie's face. Edward didn't wince.

"Hard to fake," I whispered.

"Unless you're a pro." Bruce's word's were audible enough for Eddie to have heard, if indeed he was feigning his seizures.

Gail returned to report that Eddie's roommate, Jim, would stop by the hospital on his way to his base. Bruce nodded. "Well," he said placing Edward's index finger between his thumb and first finger, "let's see if Mr. Ingraham really is seizing, shall we?" He began squeezing. Edward seemed unaffected by the pain. Bruce pointed to his right cheek. Was that the beginning of a slight twitch? It was hard to tell. Bruce pressed harder, until Eddie's finger was a dark shade of purple.

"What in God's name are you doing?" screamed Gail. "He's had enough torture. Leave him alone!" I held Gail back as she started toward Bruce.

"Go with it, Gail. Just for a minute." Bruce squeezed harder. Eddie's finger was white down to the second knuckle. Bruce pointed to his eyes. "There it is again," he whispered. "That little change." I shook my head. I wasn't really sure. He stuck his head a mere inch from the patient's face. "Edward!" he yelled. "Do you hear me? I don't think you're having real seizures. I think you're faking it!"

Edward kept right on seizing.

"You guys are as bad as those terrorists!" Gail yelled, her freckles a steamy orange. "Why can't doctors admit when they fuck up?"

Gail was right. Those scars and burr holes corroborated Jim's story. Eddie wasn't faking.

Bruce signaled me to step outside. "You and Gail move Edward to the floor," he whispered. "As soon as he stops seizing, get an arterial blood gas and let me know what the pH is, I mean stat! I'm going up to medical records."

"What's up?"

"Following a hunch, that's all."

For the remainder of the morning, Eddie continued to have intermittent seizures, allowing me ample opportunities to obtain a blood sample from his radial artery. Yet each time my needle touched his skin, another seizure commenced, thereby aborting my attempt.

At 11:15, Bruce called from medical records. "Did you get the blood?"

"Every time I get ready to stick him, he seizes. He could lose his radial artery if I keep it up." I paused. "You don't think a needle stick can trigger a seizure, do you?"

"Wise up, Daniel. He's seizing on purpose, and as soon as Officer Mulroney gets here, I'll prove it. Anyone who's seizing as much as Eddie should be markedly acidotic. The blood pH should be very low. If this guy is who and what I think he is, the pH of his blood will be normal."

"Another thing," Bruce said, his breathing heavy. "I've checked with the Registrar's office at the medical school. They have no record of a fourth year transfer named Edward Ingraham."

"I'll be a ..."

"Guess what else? Eddie's roommate, Jim? Hardly even knows Eddie. Met him at the reservist center. Not only is he unable to substantiate any of Eddies heroic efforts in Chile, but yesterday he saw Eddie standing in front of his mirror flailing his arms back and forth and spitting all over the floor. You ever see a patient having a seizure while standing?"

"You think he was practicing?"

"We'll find out soon enough. By the way," Bruce said, "the next time Mr. Ingraham wakes tell him we may need to do some very invasive procedures on him. You know... spinal tap, maybe another burr hole in his head."

"What the hell for?"

"Bet you your stethoscope he'll go along with anything you suggest."

"Bruce."

"I'm not saying another word."

"Come on."

"One hint, or rather one word--Munchausen's!"

"My God!"

"Just get me that blood gas!"

"He won't let me."

"Use your imagination!"

I didn't know much about Munchausen's disease, only that it was a disorder where people intentionally inflicted pain upon themselves. Lots of it. There would be plenty of time to learn about it later. In the meantime, I spent the better part of an hour convincing Gail Peterson that Bruce's hypothesis was valid, or at least reasonable enough to test it in the way he planned.

At 12:05 p.m. Gail entered Edward's room. I was already there. "Bad news, Dr. Raskin," she began on cue. "The lab called and said the blood we sent from the ER clotted. They need another tube."

"Jeez, Gail," I said, scouting Edward's arms. "He doesn't have any more veins. We'll have to cancel the tests."

"You can't. Bruce says Eddie may need an operation. They need a type and cross for possible transfusion."

"Damn," I said, throwing in an extra measure of irritation for Eddie's benefit.

"Edward, can you hear me? This is Dr. Raskin. You might have to go to the O.R. I need some blood and all your veins are shot."

Edward rolled over, his black, wavy hair matted down with grease and sweat. "Use the femoral vein," he said. "But be careful, it sits right next to the femoral artery."

Damn right it did. He had taken the bait. Gail attached a long needle to the syringe, while I prepped the area of the groin where the femoral artery and vein course as partners across the inguinal ligament. I was taken aback by Bruce's idea of Munchausen's disease. I couldn't believe Eddie or anyone could wish for an operation. Bruce had to be wrong. I'd prove it. "Hey, Ed. I've got some bad news. Fluid has re-accumulated inside your head. The neurosurgeons may have to drill a few more holes."

I couldn't believe what I'd said. After all I'd learned in school about ethical treatment of patients, I'd just told an

110

enormous lie. Bruce was wrong. Eddie would decompensate and it would be my fault. I'd end up doing a pathology residency where you can say anything you want. The patients don't talk back.

Eddie managed a weak smile. "It's okay by me, Doc. Had 'em before. Can have 'em again."

I looked at Gail in disbelief. Not to be outdone, Gail touched Edward on his shoulder. "That's not the only bad news, Edward. You also have an infection in your abdomen. The surgeons may need to unzip your belly."

"Like I said, Doc, whatever it takes. I've already had two laparotomys. Three's the charm."

"Right you are, Ed." I said, swallowing my surprise.

"Okay, Ed. I'm going to stick your femoral vein. Here it goes." Instead of sticking the needle one finger breadth medial to the pulsation of the artery, where the vein is found, I went like a B-17 bomber straight for my real mission, the pulsating artery that would make or break Edward's story. A geyser of bright red arterial blood gushed into the syringe. "There we go Edward," I said, passing the syringe to Gail. "I'll just hold pressure here and Dr. Peterson will run this right over to the lab."

Five minutes later the blood gas results came back. Normal.

"Page Bruce, stat," I whispered excitedly to Gail.

"No need for that, Danny." Bruce was at the doorway. Standing next to him was Officer James Mulroney. He had a smile pasted across his cherubic face, a wad of chewing tobacco distorting his cheek.

"If it isn't my old friend, Eddie Ingraham," he said, walking over to Eddie's bed and throwing the handcuffs on like he were roping a steer. "Or is it David Smith? Maybe it's Phil Jackson. Whatever you're going by these days, I was proud to come in from home just to tell you that you're under arrest!"

Edward tried sitting up. "What are you talking about? I've been tortured. I barely escaped with my life!"

Bruce turned. "Last month this hero was caught impersonating a medical student. He entered the labor and delivery suites and was just about to deliver a baby."

"That time he escaped," added Mulroney.

"That's bullshit, Doc, and you know it! I'm a medical student! Check it out."

"We did Ed. And you're not. At least not here. And we checked with your so called best friend, Jim. Except for the cock-a-maimie stories you told him, he doesn't know a thing about you." Bruce looked at us and continued. "We cross-referenced his record with seven other hospitals. Seems Eddie is fond of manufacturing illnesses. Do you know what they call that, Ed? You must have read about it in your textbooks."

"Screw you!"

"Munchausen's, Ed." Bruce ripped away the bed sheet. "See these scars on his thighs? They're not from torture. They're remnants of an infection he got from injecting himself with his own saliva."

"You're full of shit, Doc."

"No, Edward. This time I am afraid you're the one who is full of shit. Which is why we're forced to keep you in the hospital rather than sending you someplace where the rooms have more padding." Bruce removed a syringe from his pocket, the stench of which left no doubt as to its contents. "We found this in a bathroom wastebasket near the waiting area. Eddie injected himself with his own feces. Within forty eight hours he'll come down with one hell of an infection."

Better his own feces than someone else's I wanted to say, but held my tongue. Bruce's eyes bulged as if he'd just exposed the devil himself. "Listen to this," he said, removing a three-by-five card from his pocket. "He can fake an acute myocardial infarction so well that he's had seven admissions at five different hospitals, and he's talked himself into coronary angiograms on four different occasions." He looked down at Eddie. "Good job, Ed. But until you learn how to lower your blood pH and dilate your pupils when you're faking a seizure, I suggest you stick to the second rate hospitals."

By now, Edward was struggling to sit up in bed. "I won't stand for this. My commanding officer will be here any minute. Get me out of these handcuffs!"

Gail turned to Bruce. "Is he dangerous?"

"Only to himself. When confronted with the truth, Munchausen patients often become combative to the point of bolting the hospital the minute they get the chance."

"Forget the handcuffs," said Eddie. "I won't hurt anybody."

"You may be septic, Eddie. If you leave, you could die."

"And there's the matter of impersonating a medical student," Mulroney added. "We have a warrant."

Eddie tried moving his arms. "Look, un-cuff me and I'll stay. Otherwise I'll sign one of those papers--you know--leave against medical advice. If I die, it will be your fault."

Bruce folded his arms. "Guess that means we'll have to get you committed to Psych."

"You can't do that!"

"No. But a shrink can!"

The word 'shrink' turned Eddie into a cornered fox. "I'm not seeing those guys. They're all crazy!"

Suddenly his masquerade dissolved and he pleaded like a small boy caught with his fist in the chocolate chips. "Can't we keep the shrinks out of this? Please?"

Bruce was firm. "That depends on you. If you behave, we might just settle for round the clock sitters. If not, it's off to La La land."

A few minutes later, I paged Alex and asked him to join Gail and me in the Kaplan Deli for celebratory chocolate milk shakes. Alex's eyes were wide as we told him how we had uncovered Eddie's charade. I tried imitating Eddie's seizures but couldn't come close.

"Unbelievable," said Gail. "I can't even fake an orgasm."

I spit out my milkshake, while Alex remained unaffected. "Come on over tonight and you won't have to."

"Alex," I said, feeling uncomfortable.

Gail straightened her shoulders. "Talk to Danny, Alex. He'll tell you. I don't date doctors."

Alex smiled. "Who said anything about a date?"

After lunch Alex walked us to the elevator. "Shoot," he said as the elevator opened. "I forgot to give this to you. I cut it out of the Tribune last night."

While the elevator door played ping-pong with my foot trying to close, I read, then re-read the article. When I finished, I jumped out, my face red with anger. "Gotta go."

"Where?" said Gail, as the door closed.

"See that bastard, Goldman."

Chapter 20 goldman

"Young man, I won't take that from you. I have not lied."

I was doing everything I could to aggravate Sol Goldman. I wanted to watch the blood drain from his face when I told him.

"How have I lied?"

"Dean Cantrell. You said his death was a suicide, that it was unrelated to anything."

"Far as I know, it was."

I reached into my white coat and fished out the crumpled newspaper clipping. I placed it in front of him, watching his eyes as he read.

Arbor Hills

Investigation into the mysterious death of Clarence Cantrell, former Dean of Arbor Hills Medical School, continues to baffle authorities. Police now admit that Cantrell was found slumped in his office chair, rope marks around both wrists. There appeared to be evidence of a struggle, and several files were missing when he was found.

The DA revealed that Cantrell was about to cooperate with authorities concerning his involvement with Friends of Tomorrow, a group which reportedly had ties to ultra-right-wing, terrorist organizations. Though the autopsy revealed a heart attack as the cause of death, Dr. Cantrell's personal physician stated that the former dean was in excellent health and had recently passed an exhaustive treadmill test.

"Who gave you this?"

"It was in the friggin' Tribune."

Sol picked up some Kleenex and mopped his forehead. He looked pale.

"Who killed Charles Cantrell, Sol? And why?"

Sol's jaw clenched. "You tell me, Raskin. You're the one that discovered the checks signed by Friends of Tomorrow. You sure you had no idea they were an ultra-right militant organization?"

I shook my head then asked: "What the hell does any of this have to do with me?"

"Who said it does?"

"Come on, Sol. Somebody seems very interested in that file of Cantrell's that I borrowed."

"Borrow is a little soft, wouldn't you say?"

Goldman's intercom buzzed. "I said I didn't want to be disturbed, dammit!"

Vicki's voice filled the room. "It's your daughter, Melissa. She's calling to remind you about her game tonight. What shall I tell her?"

Sol gave a startled look then looked at desk calender. "Shit," he winced. He glanced at his watch, then spoke into the intercom. "Don't I have a dinner meeting with the regents scheduled for tonight?"

"Preceded by a cocktail party at the Drake at six thirty."

"Cancel it. Call Regent Davidson and tell him something unexpected came up."

"And your daughter?"

Sol picked up the phone. "Hello Melissa...of course I'll be there tonight....wouldn't miss it for the world.. how's the old jump shot doing?.... Take you and Sheila for burgers afterwards."

Sol gently replaced the receiver, then looked up, seemingly surprised I was still there. "Sorry about that Raskin." A slight smile filled in the creases between his cheeks. "Melissa plays point guard for New Trier High School. She was all-state last year, and looks to be in the running for junior all-american. Last game a Stanford scout showed up. Just to watch my Melissa. She..." Sol's voice trailed off, and he shook his head as if awaking from a trance.

"Anyway, Raskin, where were we?"

"Your family's very important to you, isn't it?"

I couldn't believe I just had asked my Chief of Medicine and one of the most influential men in American medicine that question. Who did I think I was, some fucking psychoanalyst?

116

Sol picked up the news clipping. "If your question was meant to suggest that I might not be the bastard everybody thinks I am, you're wrong." As he re-read the piece, he brow furrowed. "Look Danny, whatever is going on here, it's none of your business."

"But something is going on, isn't it?"

Sol looked as though he might surrender something important, then caught himself. He stood up, picking up a file.

. "Let me worry about it, Raskin. You just worry about keeping your patients alive. So far, it's not been your strong suit."

Chapter 21 chinese food

That evening Maxine Chu invited me to her room for dinner. I was pleased she had extended the invitation to Gail as well. The two of them had become close during the past two weeks, Gail stopping by almost as often as I did. When Gail was on call, I knew Maxine was in excellent hands. Not only smart, Gail cared about her work more than any other intern. Maybe too much, I sometimes thought. She worried about too many things she had no control over. Like the time X-ray broke down and she stayed at the hospital until three in the morning just so she could get a chest film on one of her patients.

I looked over at Gail as we walked in silence towards Maxine's room. Prettier than some red heads, homelier than others, she had rusty freckles, amber hair, and a slightly pinched nose that seemed a perfect fit. When she spoke, her thick red eyelashes fluttered delicately and curls sprang from her soft shoulders like ballerinas on a trapeze, so easy, graceful, so beautiful. Her work attire was mostly whites; oversized scrubs, v-necks cut close to the neck, though after a call night, she sometimes dressed in wool blazers that had me itch just looking at them. I liked her better in scrubs, found myself mesmerized by the way her breasts gently bobbed as she walked.

Gail spoke little of her family, even less of her life outside the hospital. Whenever I mentioned the two of us getting together outside the hospital, she gave a forlorn look and pleaded fatigue, or begged off in order to write a long overdue letter to a cousin.

Maxine Chu stood in her doorway pouting. "I haven't seen you all day."

"You were down in Radiation when I came by earlier," I said entering the room, Gail falling in behind me.

"Darn right I was," she said, smiling. She flitted her arms like a fashion model. "Check out the radioactive glow."

Lo set out a spread that included shrimp with lobster sauce, moo goo gai pan, and sweet and sour pork. We ate for a while, making the usual small talk. Though I had no business telling Maxine about other patients, Eddie Ingraham's story was too fresh to resist. Her eyes were transfixed while I spoke. "Maybe I'll bring him over to visit sometime," I said in conclusion. "You ask him for a spare rib and he might just give it to you." Lo had a paroxysm of laughter.

Lo removed a package wrapped in newspaper. The odor of dead fish filled the room.

"What's that?" gasped Gail.

"Sushi," replied Maxine, holding her nose. "Goldfish sushi. He picks the damn stuff right out of the aquarium."

Lo swallowed an entire baby fish. "Make Chinese man virile."

"Make Jewish man puke," I said.

"Put that away, Lo, or you can take your hormones somewhere else, not that you'll ever use them." Lo obligingly rewrapped the fish, and Maxine opened the window a few inches.

"And I'm supposed to marry this fool? I may as well marry you, Doctor Raskin, that is if Dr. Peterson doesn't already have dibs."

Gail remained composed. "Doctor Raskin and I work too hard to be married. We'd never see each other."

My furtive glances at Gail had not gone unnoticed by Maxine. "No one in her right mind would marry Dr. Raskin, not unless they loved doing laundry." Maxine laughed at the plum sauce dripping down my scrub shirt. "You may be the world's greatest doctor, but you're also the world's biggest slob." Maxine pulled out a bag of fortune cookies and passed them around. "Go ahead," she said, cracking hers. She pretended to read. "Confucius says unwise to air dirty laundry in public."

It was one of the few times I had seen Gail laugh. I separated my cookie like a wish bone, ripping the fortune in half. I held the two ends together. 'Your request for no monosodium glutamate was ignored."

"Ha!" laughed Lo, "I save the MSG for your pal, Dr. Mallincroft. He always make me give him leftover food. Say otherwise no more visiting hours."

120

After dinner I perused Maxine's temperature chart. No one had bothered to tell me she'd had a slight fever earlier in the day, and I had been too busy with Edward Ingraham to check for myself. Hopefully it would turn out to be nothing serious, though in the back of my mind, I knew the potential side-effects from massive amounts of radiation.

I asked Maxine if I could listen to her lungs before I left.

"This is a social visit, Dr. Raskin."

I explained that it was routine considering her slight temperature--that I just wanted to make sure she wasn't hiding the beginnings of a pneumonia.

"I told you I was okay," she said after I gave her the all clear sign. "When in the company of hunks like you and Lo, my temperature naturally climbs a few degrees! Didn't you see the movie, Body Heat?"

As we walked down the hall, Gail's hand brushed a piece of rice from my chin. "Didn't think there were many concerned physicians left, Danny."

I wanted to put my arm around Gail, just hug her like a good friend. "Want to go hear some blues over on Clark Street Saturday? Etta James is going to shatter a few wine glasses."

Gail's head dropped. "No thanks," she said, and kept on walking.

Chapter 22 eddie ingraham

For two days, Edward Ingraham sat silently in his bed staring out his window into the garden of watercress and lilacs. He refused to talk, refused nutritional supplementation, save three glasses of tomato juice, and refused his medication. On the third day I found him standing in front of the mirror, dabbing himself with hospital deodorant. He was showered and smoothly shaven, and his glistening black hair was layered neatly atop his head. Eliminate the scar railroading across his forehead, and Eddie was an attractive young man.

When I asked what he was doing, he smiled and went back to his bed, where he picked up the last piece of bread from his tray and carefully examined it before eating it.

"Think it's poison?" I asked.

"Better than the earth worms and rat shit they fed me in Chile. "

"Come on, Eddie."

Eddie folded his arms across his chest. "Don't believe me, doc. I could care less."

"Where you from Ed? Before Chile."

Ed picked up a Popular Mechanics magazine. "Grew up outside of St Louis."

"Big family?"

"Brother."

"Close?"

"Haven't seen him in fifteen years. Can we change the subject?"

"Friends in this area?"

"I've been ordered to avoid contact with all but essential personnel."

"Got a job?"

Edward's eyes settled on the bed. "I'm at the library getting ready for medical school. Hey, can you tell me the symptoms of lung cancer?"

"Forget it, Eddie. You're too young for lung cancer. No one would buy it. Stick to seizures. You do a good seizure."

123

"What tests do they do?"

"Wouldn't it be easier to fake a heart attack?"

"Too easy."

"Tell that to my two patients who just crumped."

"Heart attacks?"

"Big ones."

Eddie smiled widely then clutched his fist to his chest. "Like this?" Before my eyes his face turned to granite. Sweat began pouring down his cheeks. His lips turned blue and his jaw clenched. "Feel my pulse," he gasped.

I counted twenty beats per minute. What the hell was going on?

Eddie released his breath. Color reentered his face. His pulse returned to seventy.

"How'd you do that?"

"Studied autonomic reflex control in a Buddhist monastery. I can also hold my breath for over two minutes."

"Too bad my patients didn't have those warning symptoms. I might have been able to help them."

Eddie leaned forward. "None?"

"Died in their sleep."

"That's strange," he said. "A couple of years ago, when I was in the hospital... registered under the name Jonathan Berlinger, I think... you know, under cover operation.. "

I looked at my watch wondering what the hell I was doing here wasting time with a psycho. "Get to the point, Eddie."

"A couple of other patients croaked in their sleep. Same thing. Big heart attacks.-No symptoms. Lot of rumors floating around."

My pulse raced. "Like what?"

Eddie shrugged. "Foul play."

"Why?"

"The patients had clean coronary arteries."

My two patients had clean coronary arteries. "Are you talking about my patients Eddie?"

He nodded.

"How did you find out?"

"Computers," Eddie said smiling. "I'm a whiz at computers."

"You seem to be a whiz at lots of things, Eddie. I'm almost impressed."

"I pulled up the pathology reports. Big heart attacks, no coronary occlusions."

''Anything else?''

Eddie paused, tapping his fingers on the table. "Not really."

"What's that supposed to mean?"

Eddie paused. "It pissed me off that I couldn't pull up the results of the toxicology studies."

"What?"

"Tox screens, Raskin. You know, looking for another cause of death."

"You think they were poisoned?"

"Somebody thought so," said Eddie.

"Who?"

"No name on the request."

"You couldn't get the results?" I felt irritable. "I thought you were a pro?"

"Believe me, if the results were there, I would have accessed them." Eddie fixed his gaze in my direction. "People murdering patients, hitting you over the head with baseball bats. You ought to be more careful of the company you keep."

I looked stiffly at Eddie, wondering how he knew so much.

"What's going on, Eddie? How did you know about the baseball bat?"

"Nothing I want to talk about. At least not right now." His voice was gruff. "Get out," he snapped, draping a blanket over his shoulders. "I'm tired."

"Speaking of helping ourselves, Eddie, what about you? How do we cure you?"

Edward pressed a button on his console and the TV came on. He turned up the volume. "You can't get cured when you're not sick. Now get out."

"Come on, Eddie."

"Get out!"

125

"Fine." I huffed away like I'd been stood up on a date. Halfway down the hall I stopped and turned. I marched back to his room, stood directly over him, and folded my arms. "Look, Ed. I know very little about this Munchausen's disease. I don't even know when you're bullshitting me and when you're not. But I do know one thing. You and I, we're almost the same age. In the big scheme of things I may not know exactly where I fit. But I'm trying, Ed. You only get one life. And if you want to inject and cut and hammer away at yours, so be it."

I turned to walk out. The TV volume suddenly diminished. "Hey doc," he called out, "Got a girlfriend?"

I turned around. "Nope. Sure wish I did sometimes. How 'bout you?"

Eddie's five foot, eight inch, one hundred and forty pound frame flipped back in bed. "Never did, Doc. Nobody ever had the time."

I walked out the door. My God, he had some insight. Progress. A small opening into his psyche.

Edward called out loudly. "Except for the six whores in Chile who tried to seduce information from me!"

Oh, Ed.

Chapter 23 maxine

If worrying about Maxine Chu was therapeutic, she would have been cured already. Instead, the day before her planned discharge, her temperature spiked to 103 and she began coughing up green sputum by the spoonful. Her dusky blue lips reflected a drop in her arterial oxygen saturation and her chest x-ray revealed bilateral interstitial infiltrates.

The very day Maxine got sick, I too, began to get symptoms, sympathetic empathy, I was told, but nevertheless very real to me. She coughed and an hour later so did I. That first day I chugged half a bottle of Robitussin. Then her temperature climbed and I found myself voraciously wiping perspiration from my forehead. I became convinced that anytime now, Hodgkins would strike me, too. A cancerous lymph node would rear its ugly pedicle.   I stared into the mirror--waiting. Stretching my neck, waiting. I demanded that Bruce examine my abdomen, and when he failed to detect the spleen that I knew to be enlarged, I asked Alex. I was absolutely convinced that the fullness I felt was a massively enlarged spleen. Sometimes I had symptoms even before Maxine, like the morning I walked into her room complaining of a severe case of stomach cramps. Maxine smiled, reaching back into her purse.

"Just as I suspected," she confessed after looking at her date book. "Today's the day."

"For what?"

Maxine held the calender. "Here," she said, pointing to today's date. "George."

"Who's George and what does he have to do with stomach cramps?"

Maxine shook her head. "Men," she said. "I'm due for my period today."

"Huh?"

"I thought the cramps I was having were a side effect of the radiation or something."

Maxine explained the designation of 'George' on her calender as a reminder of her period. I knew men had names for their private parts- Peter, Willie, my college roommate called his Bartholomew, stuff like that; but women having a code name for their period? It was a new one on me.

"You should have seen Lo," she exclaimed, fanning herself with her calender. "He was writing something in my date book for me one day and suddenly looked up with tears in his eyes, wanting to know why I hadn't told him about George."

I smiled. "One date a month--that's not too bad is it?"

Maxine waved her frail hand in the air. "It took him six months before he realized that there wasn't much chance I was sleeping with this guy. Every time this mysterious friend and I went out, I was having my period!"

Ten days later Maxine's condition changed. Her white count returned to normal, her appetite improved, and her lungs sounded as clear as the fall breeze off the lake. The oncologists ran another battery of tests which showed the radiation had reduced her tumor load more than expected. As a result, they opted for stronger chemo, a regimen that hopefully would cure Maxine.

My own constellation of symptoms abated soon after Maxine's chest X-ray cleared. My once rigid belly became butter soft. The imagined lymph nodes in my neck miraculously disappeared. And my appetite improved so much that I celebrated with a twelve pack of Reese's peanut butter cups. And finally, as a last measure of self-inflicted good will, I canceled the liver-spleen scan I was scheduled to undergo, a test I had ordered myself under an assumed name. Frank Tannenbaum. Just for the hell of it.

Chapter 24 eddie ingraham

There were enough bacteria in Edward Ingraham's blood to have killed Dracula himself, that is of course, if a vampire was dumb enough to suck the blood of a Munchausen patient. The organisms were a species normally found in the intestinal tract, proving that Edward had, as Bruce hypothesized, injected his own feces under his skin. Oddly, I was almost as happy as Eddie that he would be staying around for awhile. Deep down I believed that, given the chance, I might be able to reach his diseased mind. Maybe I could forge a link to his inner self, something that might actually allow therapy to take place successfully. And though ashamed to admit it, I was also interested in another aspect of Eddie, the one that dealt with his knowledge about heart attacks and toxicology screens, not to mention people swinging baseball bats on Lakeshore Drive.

When a team of psychiatrists came to talk to our group about Munchausen's disease, I had more questions than I had realized. Why, for instance, would someone risk his life just to get hospitalized? And how in God's name could someone thrive on self-mutilation? The underlying pathology of Munchausen's, they said, related to early parental abuse or abandonment, culminating in the inability to form close relationships. Eddie refused to talk about his youth and grew hostile when asked about his parents, his father in particular. He did tell us he was hospitalized for a month as a child. The shrinks claimed that Munchausen patients learn to relive their painful childhoods through multiple hospitalizations. Thus, hospital settings were perceived as sources of the love they never got. Why does he crave bodily harm, I wanted to know. It sounded as if he really got off by doing those things. In a way, I was right. Edward's stunts were attempts to relieve unconscious guilt, the shrinks told us, using typical cryptic shrink jargon.

It took a week, but I finally felt as if Eddie was beginning to trust me. He stopped talking about Chile and no longer discussed going to medical school. And without realizing it, I began confiding some of my own worries to him, especially those concerning the particulars of the two patients that died while he was in the hospital. I plugged him for names, dates, anything that might provide a link to their deaths under similar circumstances. But unlike the shrinks who slapped each other's backs in congratulations on their presumed breakthroughs, I was not ready to join the Eddie Ingraham fan club, not yet anyway.

The shrinks were so happy with Eddie's progress that they gave permission for Eddie to share a room with another patient, a patient with a disease Eddie might be tempted to imitate.

"We don't have a choice," said Bruce. "His room has the only other unoccupied male bed on the floor. There's a patient being admitted for hematuria."

I cringed. The workup for blood in the urine included inserting a long tube through the penis into the bladder.

"I doubt Eddie would go to that extreme," Bruce said. "Especially after the gains he's made in therapy."

It turned out that Bruce was right. Eddie got on splendidly with his roommate, Sam Jenkins. Eddie explained the procedure to him better than the urologists had. When Mr. Jenkins returned from the OR suite, Eddie chipped in every chance he could, including the cumbersome task of draining Mr. Jenkin's Foley catheter and recording hourly measurements of urine output. Though against hospital policy, the short-staffed nursing service appreciated his assistance. Eddie, so it seemed, was finally making good use of his stores of medical knowledge. I decided I'd been wrong about Eddie.

Of course, I was wrong about that, too.

Chapter 25 lunch with horner

Brian Picolli ran his hand gently over the frail, hairless arm of Dr. Emile Horner, as though he were trying to erase the tattooed numbers with his fingertips. Finally he took a breath and removed his hand. "Man, they branded you like a cow."

Dr. Horner collected the remaining morsels of cottage cheese and Jello from his plate with dainty strokes of his fork and placed them delicately on his tongue. He paused momentarily, as if watching it all for the very first time on the six o'clock news. "We were branded, Brian. Then led to slaughter like sheep. If I hadn't played violin, I would have gone to the crematorium like my mother and sister." The sauerkraut on my Reuben sandwich suddenly seemed too foreign for my liking. Brain Picolli pushed his peanut butter and jelly sandwich to the side.

Dr. Horner slid his plate just far enough out of the way to spread his arms in front of himself and dabbed gently at his lips with a cloth napkin. He always asked for a cloth napkin, even in the noisy confines of Kaplan Deli. His quiet words rang out with an understated eloquence. "Eat up, boys," Dr. Horner said. "One should never waste food."

Brian stared at Dr. Horner's arm. "I've never talked to anyone who'd been in a concentration camp. I thought most died."

"I was one of the lucky ones. After the war, it still wasn't easy. Few medical schools would accept Jews."

"Huh? Growing up, the only Jewish people I knew were doctors."

"That's now. There used to be quotas."

I tapped my fork on the table. "Is that why they started osteopathic schools?"

Emile Horner nodded. "The worst was Chicago. Obtaining admitting privileges was next to impossible. Most hospitals were run by the Catholic Church."

"What about Jewish patients?" I asked, taking another go at my now krautless Reuben sandwich.

131

Brian touched my hand, leaving a peanut butter fingerprint. "I can't believe they were happy at the Catholic hospitals."

"They had little choice. Thirty years ago I had a cousin who lay dying at St. Elizabeth's. When I got to his bedside, he was being given his last rites by a priest." Dr. Horner paused, a distant expression highlighting the furrowed corners of his mouth. He turned his head and cleared his throat.

"That's why we have Richard Meese Hospital," he said hoarsely. "Like Israel, it's the last refuge for the Jews. Why else would patients travel hours to get here? It's home. Find me a Jewish person over the age of twenty who wasn't born here. The Vice President of the United States was born here." Horner let out a long sigh, then picked up a toothpick. "Things aren't the same. Affluence changes things. People forget what being Jewish is all about."

"But you don't eat kosher food, do you, Dr. Horner?" Brian was trying to understand.

Emile Horner smiled and patted him on the hand, leaving the toothpick in the corner of his mouth. "I keep kosher at home, Brian. Here, I just make sure not to mix meat with dairy products." Dr. Horner dabbed at his lips with his napkin.

"Enough about me, Dr. Picolli. Let me ask you a question."

"Fire away."

"Tell me why in God's name a gentleman of your background, West Coast, beaches your whole life, sunny warm weather, chose to come here to Richard Meese?"

Brian ran his hands through his stringy hair. "Meese was my fourth choice. The other three ...well, they were here in Chicago but didn't take me."

It certainly wasn't for academic reasons, I thought. Brian was cum laude at Stanford, then graduated at the top of his medical school class at UCLA. One thing was for certain: Brian never majored in religion.

"But why Chicago, Brian? When we first met, you were wearing that water suit." Emile traced his body with his hands.

"Wet suit."

"Yes, one of those. You're a Californian, Brian. Why leave the West Coast?"

"My mother had a tumor of the facial nerve. Nobody wanted to touch it in California. Too great a chance for permanent damage. Dr. Sedawitz is a pioneering surgeon out of Pres. St. Lukes. He saved her. Got the whole thing out and left no residual defects. I figured I owed something to the city." Brian paused a moment. He actually seemed choked up. "The Lake Michigan waves are a disappointment though."

There was silence for the next few minutes. I wanted to ask Horner about Goldman. See if he knew any reason Goldman might hide the fact that both my patients with heart attacks had clean coronary arteries. See if he knew of any other cases like the ones Eddie Ingraham claimed to have heard about. And most importantly, to see if he knew how this might relate to my once having a file from a corrupt Dean with ties to a right wing organization. Where was that damn file, anyway? I assumed it had been stolen from my apartment. But if that were the case, why did the person who attacked me down at the lake ask me where it was? Was it possible they never found it? Or was more than one party interested in its contents?

Brian cleared his throat. "What would happen to the Jews if Meese closed down?"

"There are many fine hospitals in Chicago, Brian, though a good number are affiliated with churches."

"Instead of taking a history, you'd take a confession," said Brian.

The veins in Dr. Horner's forehead surfaced, intersecting the wrinkles like a railroad crossing. "Closing this hospital would do more to hurt the Jews of this city than a Nazi march on Skokie." Horner removed a folded handkerchief and wiped his bifocals. "This hospital is more important to the Jews in Chicago than a synagogue."

"I can dig it," said Brian. "I pray all the time." Brian folded his hands. "Please Lord, no more admissions. Please God, grant me some far out waves." He made the sign of the cross. There was no irreverence intended, just an incredible naivete.

"I suppose you're right, Brian. It is a place of worship, a Jewish stronghold on the south side. It subtly reminds me of the Warsaw ghetto."

"But then the Jews fought back for a reason," Brian said, pointing his finger in the air like he had just discovered the theory of relativity. "They had to do something to those Nazi goons. But nobody is hassling us now." He smiled when he said the word 'us.'

Brian continued but I barely heard him. Emile Horner and I were staring at each other, concern in our eyes.

I turned to Emile Horner. "Can I ask you a hypothetical question?"

Dr. Horner answered with a slight nod. His hands remained folded, his left shirt sleeve still rolled up.

"Suppose some neo-Nazi group realized how valuable this hospital was to the Jewish community." I paused, not sure if I should finish. Horner gently turned his hand over; the camp numbers distracted me. "Do you think they would ever target the hospital?"

Picolli swiped the chocolate speckles from his chin.

"You mean like bombing the place?"

I took a breath. "Like bumping off patients?"

Sitting between a surfer and a concentration camp survivor, talking conspiracy, seemed like a new personal best for outrageousness. I felt like a fool.

Brian's beeper sounded and he excused himself. When he was gone, Emile Horner scooted his chair around the side of our rectangular table, knocking a spoon to the floor as he reached to support himself.

"Why don't you tell me your story," he said quietly, putting his arm around my shoulder. "Tell me everything."

Chapter 26 mrs. garber

Mrs. Garber ruined what should have been a great day. Two of my favorite patients, Eddie Ingraham and Maxine Chu were finally going home. There was reason to celebrate.

Mrs. Garber was a diabetic admitted for a trivial insulin dose adjustment, a procedure that easily could have been done on an outpatient basis. When I came to see her that morning, she was wearing a violet Christian Dior nightgown with a frilly chiffon collar and a wide satin sash. Her makeup was caked on like mud. She was sipping tea while thumbing through her appointment book.

"Young man," she said, after I introduced myself. "If you would be so kind as to come back later. I'm in the middle of my tea." She continued sipping and thumbing.

"Mrs. Garber, I'll only be a few minutes. I know you were admitted electively and..."

"Electively?" she sounded as if I had just declared that her Mercedes had a steering defect. "You think my wide swings in blood sugar are trivial?"

I did in fact think that. I also thought I had a lot of work to do before the emergency admissions began rolling in.

"If I work you up now, Mrs. Garber, we can make the necessary changes in your afternoon dose of insulin. You can go home tomorrow."

Mrs. Garber looked up through a pair of rose tinted bifocals with pearls embedded in the frames. "You're kidding, of course. Have you spoken to my doctor?"

"Not yet."

"I can't go home before Tuesday," she protested. "I'm having my living room re-carpeted. A week from Friday I'm hosting a fundraiser. Oh, that reminds me, can you see if there's an alternate fish choice on the luncheon menu? Halibut wreaks havoc with my eczema. And do you mind putting a page in to Dr. Fisher, my plastic surgeon? I have a question for him."

Yeah, like how he botched the nose job, I wanted to say. She tossed her head to one side in mock aristocracy and looked at me like I was a gnat which had landed in her soup.

"Now, please leave me alone. I've known Sol Goldman for years." She picked at her fingernails. "He wouldn't want to hear that I was unhappy."

Under my breath: "Shit."

I watched from the doorway of Mr. Jenkin's room as Eddie Ingraham outlined the path the cylindrical tube had taken up through the penis, past the urethra and into the bladder. It was an artistic rendering worthy of Grant's Atlas. For a Munchausen's man, Eddie was pure Renaissance.

Eddie smiled when I walked in. I followed him over to his bed, resting my arm on his shoulder. "Want to have one more seizure, for old time's sake?"

Eddie smiled and patted a stack of books, all of which related to peptic ulcer disease. "I'm glad to be going home. I have enough studying to keep me busy for a month."

"Getting an ulcer?"

Eddie shook his head. "Going to lecture about it, though."

"To whom?"

"My secret for now," he said. "You worry about finding out why your patients are dying of heart attacks."

I shrugged my shoulders. "Too bad you're not sticking around, Eddie. The next attending assigned here is Maurice Berger."

Eddie's eyes widened. "*The* Maurice Berger? Pioneer of Histamine-2 blocker therapy for ulcers?"

Eddie had done his homework. For a split second I regretted telling him, though I wasn't exactly sure why.

When I returned to Mrs. Garber's room two hours later, she was coating her nails with red lacquer. The place smelled like an embalming parlor. As soon as I walked in, her interior decorator called and she immediately launched into a diatribe about her Berber rugs clashing with the teakwood coffee table. She acknowledged my presence with a salute of one eyebrow and kept on talking. I waited a minute, then two, then went to answer a page, and came back to find her still talking. I tried clearing my throat, tapping a pencil on my clipboard. It was only after I began blowing my nose that she finally hung up.

"The lunch was atrocious," she said. "The salmon was over-cooked, the lettuce was wilted, and for dessert they gave me green Jello with whipped cream." She stared at me. "I did not order green Jello, young man," she said tapping her nail on the menu.

Fine, don't leave a tip, I wanted to say.

Mrs. Garber reached into a drawer below her nightstand, and fumbled through its contents. "I've already put a call in to Sol."

She gave me the kind of smirk that made me want to order blood tests from ten different veins.

"You probably know him as Dr. Goldman. With all I do for this hospital, you think I'd get a little respect. Do you have any idea how much money I've donated for the new cardiac center?" When I didn't answer, she continued: "I'll be sitting on the same stage as Vice President Barrish when he makes his dedication speech."

I moved to the side of the bed. "I have to get my work done, Mrs. Garber."

"Goodbye."

"I mean here, with you. I have to do a history and a physical."

"I need to curl my hair. I'm expecting visitors later this afternoon." She looked into the mirror and dabbed at smudged lipstick.

Tension gripped my jaw, frustration flowing through my veins. What did she think I was, one of her servants? I removed the mirror from her hand and set it on her night stand. "Sorry, Mrs. Garber. But it's my responsibility to take care of you. To do that properly, I need to do a history and physical now. "

"Your bedside manner leaves something to be desired. I shall make a note of it."

"How long have you had diabetes, Mrs. Garber?"

"Oh, really, Dr. Rushkin!"

"That's Raskin, Ma'am."

137

She peered at my name badge. "Dr. Friedman has all my records. I'm sure he will make them available as..."

"The records are here. As a matter of policy, I am still required to take a history and physical on all patients. We never can tell when we're going to find something new."

"Young man," said Mrs. Garber, "when I had my gall bladder attack last year, not a single surgeon bothered me with taking a history!"

"Surgeons never take histories, Mrs. Garber. They just cut. In internal medicine, we rely heavily on the patient's clinical history."

Mrs. Garber brushed back her hair. "Take your history, then. But there will be no physical exam. Are we clear on that point?"

Under normal circumstances I would have given up. I had better things to do, not the least of which was spending some needed time with Maxine since she was going home prior to starting chemotherapy. It would have been easy to write orders on Mrs. Garber without examining her. But it was wrong, and besides, she had pissed me off in a big way.

"Sorry, ma'am. This is a teaching hospital. Being admitted here you have agreed to abide by the rules, which clearly state that the intern will perform a complete examination. I will be happy to call the hospital administrator if you wish to argue any longer." We exchanged looks. "Now, about that diabetes..."

Maxine Chu wore a black-satin chemise which dangled tauntingly from her frail shoulders and outlined her small, shapely breasts. A Victoria's Secret box lay in the wastebasket.

"From Lo?"

Maxine laughed. "You've got to be kidding. I ordered this myself."

Maxine set down her magazine and tilted her head of long, shiny black hair. "You going to miss me?" she asked.

"Hell, yes, Maxine. What am I going to do for dinner these next two weeks? Maybe I'll admit Lo to the hospital. At least I'll get a good meal."

I loved making Maxine laugh, mostly because no matter how hard she tried, she was unable to hold it to a mere giggle. When she laughed, dynasties of royalty laughed with her, and during those evanescent moments, she seemed a bubbling fountain of youth and innocence. I watched Maxine cover her mouth, unable to contain a child-like chuckle. The outlines of her breasts painted vertical strokes of black satin beneath her gown. She took pleasure in watching the general direction of my eyes. "Don't worry, Danny," she said, looking down at her chest. "I'm going to make good use of these when I get out of here. There are plenty of other guys out there if Lo wants to stay a prude."

Once again, she tilted her head, and flipped her hair back, where it momentarily hung above her head like the cover girl's on the magazine lying nearby. Maxine was no longer a patient, but a young, desirable, and sexually hungry woman. For a moment, I very much wanted to be the object of her desires.

"Hey," she said, waving her hand in front of my face.

I recoiled in embarrassment. Christ, what was I thinking? She's my patient. Why the hell did I carry the frontal lobe of my brain between my legs?

"Lo loves you, Maxine. He's a traditionalist who believes in the sanctity of marriage."

"If I wanted to lose my virginity, I could do it in one date." She made no move to pull up the chemise, even though the top of her nipples were showing.

"Yeah, with who?" I asked, upping the ante.

"Dr. Stool," she said, folding her cards on the table.

"That's Spool."

"I thought you said his named was Stool. Anyway, I don't really like the guy. I just want to lose my virginity. With Dr. Stool it would be all business. More of a procedure, like a bone marrow biopsy."

Stool would probably write it up that, too: 'Hymenectomy performed on sterile drapes, under local anesthesia. Estimated blood loss, one pint.'

Maxine set down her nail file and ran both hands through her hair. "I'm only kidding."

My chest filled with fresh oxygen.

"I want it to be romantic. Lots of hugs and kisses, real slow, all that sort of stuff." She pointed to an article in Cosmo: How to make love a seven course meal. She smiled. "Hopefully it will be more hot than sour."

This time I laughed.

"I'm hoping things will work out with Lo," she added on an upbeat note. "That's the reason for the nightie. I even brought some matching panties."

She lay back in bed and hiked her gown up to her chest. The French-cut bikini panties with the lace front were as sheer as sheer could be, gently tracing up her thighs making light, textured contact. "It shows off the best part of my butt," she murmured. Maxine turned over so gracefully that it seemed she was floating.

It felt like I swallowed a microphone.

"What about you, Danny? What's with you and Gail? She's really nice, and I don't think she has a boyfriend."

"Too many other things to worry about, Max."

"Like what?"

"Your up-coming chemo." I rested my hand on hers. "If you call me from the oncology clinic, I'll stop by."

"And if you don't, I'll quit, and I mean it!"

"I'll be there, Maxine," I said, squeezing her hand.

Maxine was suddenly laughing and crying at the same time. I put my arm around her. "It scares me, too, Max. Chemo scares the hell out of me."

She finally said: "I'll miss you."

"See you in two weeks, for God's sake."

"It won't be the same. I want you calling the shots."

"I'm only the intern, Max. I hardly ever call the shots."

"It won't be the same."

"Yes, it will, you old fur ball. You'll see."

We exchanged hugs. I knew, of course that she was right. It would never be the same.

Over dinner in the cafeteria, I spoke to Alex about my conversation with Emile Horner. Horner had listened as I told him what happened at the Nazi rally, followed by the disaster in the ER, the dismantling of my apartment, the baseball bat on Lake Shore Drive, and now the thing that bothered me the most, the unexplained and perhaps unnatural death of two of my patients. Horner said I was neither crazy nor paranoid.

"Internship is getting to you," laughed Alex over a plate of lasagna. "Look at who's been sucking you into these crazy theories. A gomer doctor who's half dead, and a patient who thinks having seizures is a fun way to spend an afternoon." Alex paused then said, "I think I know what your problem is. Terminal DSB."

"Huh?"

"Dreaded semen back-up syndrome. The chief cause of depressional delusions among male interns."

I felt myself redden. "I'm really okay, Alex. Just have a lot on my mind."

"You're not okay," said Alex, sipping his coffee. "Look at you. You're a mess. Been so long since you dipped that ballpoint of yours, you're backed all the way up into your spinal fluid. If I did a spinal tap on you, bet you ten bucks I'd find sperm in there. Your brain's probably swimming in it! As your friend, I strongly advise you to stay away from places where you might lose control." Alex paused. "Take the Lincoln Park Zoo, for instance. They have a petting area with a bunch of sheep."

Though I knew Alex was right, I laughed. It hurt not having someone to share my life with. The daily doses of sickness, sorrow, and insecurity I had endured during internship made the last two days in Arbor Hills with Linda Johnson seem like three years ago, not three months.

"One release is swimming, Alex. I'm going over to the pool to see if I can work that DSB out of my system."

"Thought you gave up swimming for jogging," Alex said with a grin.

We walked together through the tunnel toward the swimming pool. As we turned down the final corridor, I looked up to see Sol Goldman coming our way. I nudged Alex and said, "Turn around, quick." But it was too late. Goldman raised his hand and called my name.

141

"Been looking for you," he said when he caught up to us. "Mrs. Garber insisted on telling me everything in person."

That bitch. "Listen, Doctor Goldman, I hope you don't believe anything she told you. She's the most..."

"She's donated over two hundred thousand dollars for the new cardiac center. It's through her efforts that Vice President Barrish is coming here. She's entitled to a little respect."

"Which means I get treated like shit. And I'm not allowed to do my job."

Alex covered his mouth to keep from laughing.

"This is supposed to be a teaching institution, Sol. What are you teaching us, how to raise money for charity?"

Sol's face reddened. I really needed that swim.

"Look," Sol said, regaining his composure. "I took personal care of her father before he died. Ever hear of Isador Garber? One of the few survivors of the Warsaw Ghetto. He became a millionaire after the war, trading on Wall Street. Used his money to bring Nazi war criminals to justice, left the rest to his only daughter, Ida. When she dies, it all goes to Israel. Richard Meese gets its share only while she's alive."

"Good incentive to take care of her," Alex joined in.

"Damned right," said Sol. "And I expect her to receive everything she wants. Don't screw up," he said, pointing a finger.

Alex nodded, smiling.

"Speaking of screwing up, Dr. Rosen, a message came to me via the hospital's payroll department. They were alerted by your bank that your last paycheck was cashed by someone other than yourself."

The fact that news of that nature would get back to the Chief of Medicine only underscored how Sol's power and influence reached far into the workings of the hospital.

Alex's hands went to his pockets, his eyes toward the ceiling. "Guess I lost the damn thing."

"Don't think so, Dr. Rosen. You endorsed it over to Fred Edelman." Sol paused, watching Alex fidget. It was the first time I'd ever see Alex uncomfortable. "Want to talk about it?" he finally asked.

142

"Oh that," Alex said, his eyes stern for the first time. "Freddie's my cousin. He needed a loan. It was more convenient than writing him a separate check."

"You sure?"

Alex was suddenly smiles again. "Oh yeah."

"No cash flow problems?"

"Have a stock portfolio that would make most of your friends jealous."

"Okay," said Sol, turning. "As long as there's no funny stuff involved."

After he was out of ear shot, I lightly punched Alex's shoulder. "You don't have any cousins in Chicago."

Alex nonchalantly slapped my back. "Freddie's my bookie. And if those fucking White Sox don't start covering the spread, I'm going to have to play for them, myself."

Alex and I walked the rest of the way through the basement tunnel in silence. Screw Sol Goldman and Mrs. Garber. Let them raise the money, let me take care of patients.

As we reached the entrance to the pool, a group of nursing students passed by. Most were wearing jeans, a few were uniformed for evening duty. A tall woman held back.

"Swimming?" She looked familiar, long blond hair and a curvaceous figure hard for any intern to forget. She wore purple eyeliner and held up bright red fingernails.

"It's Christie," she said, smiling. "Remember me? Oh wait-- I think you were unconscious when we met."

"What?"

Alex stepped forward. "Weren't you the one who put Dr. Raskin's Foley catheter in that day in the E.R.?"

"Guilty as charged." Christie took measure of Alex and then returned her gaze to me, looking me over top to bottom, her eyes finally settling on the part of my anatomy she had recently cannulated. I felt a stirring, thanks in no small measure to the fact that her eyes stayed glued to my crotch, like she were a shaman watching my cobra dance to her flute.

My beeper sounded.

"Report to 4 Gardner House room 302, stat."

Shit, Eddie Ingraham's room. He was supposed to be leaving. I weighed the possibilities. Christie's eyes were lubricated. Her inquisitive tongue was stroking her lips in soft suggestive tones of wetness. I wanted to chuck the beeper in the pool. Screw Eddie Ingraham; screw everyone, present company included.

"Sorry Christie, I gotta go."

Christie blinked a message: big mistake, fella.

After walking fifty yards back toward Gardner House, I turned. Alex and Christie were talking. I panicked and called back to Alex. We met midway and I whispered: "Bet you five bucks you two end up in the sack inside an hour."

"Five bucks, huh?" said Alex, pensively.

"Yep."

"Make it ten."

"You're on."

Alex laughed. "Easiest bet I won all year. I wouldn't take any meat from your table, Danny. You know that."

Walking away, I congratulated myself on such an inexpensive insurance policy, just in case there was still a chance of seeing Christie later. Then again, I realized that I had used Alex's only known weakness against him. The man loved to bet. I wondered why.

Chapter 27 eddie

"You got to believe me, Danny. I had no idea this would happen. Honest!"

Eddie Ingraham was standing at the toilet's edge, pissing away his hospital discharge. Bright red blood mixed with urine; blood clots by the spoonful.

I shook my head. "I suppose that's the Red Sea in there?"

"I didn't do anything. Ask Mr. Jenkins."

"I don't have to Eddie. Your roommate had hematuria and now you do. What do you think, it's contagious? What did you do this time, Eddie, manufacture some chemical to make your bladder hemorrhage?"

I turned to the nurse. "Please call Dr. Creagan."

The nurse informed me that he had just been here. I asked her to type and cross Eddie for two units of blood.

"You got your wish. You won't be going home today."

"I swear I didn't do anything wrong. Just started peeing blood. God only knows all the kidney problems I had."

Why should I give that sleeze bag the benefit of the doubt? I wanted to strangle him.

Eddie cleaned himself and returned to bed. He looked so innocent sitting there, faded robe hanging loosely from a tattered body. His cheeks were more flushed than I'd ever seen. Maybe he was telling the truth. Maybe a school of bacteria swimming around his bloodstream had made an unscheduled docking in his kidneys.

"You think I like being afflicted with Munchausen's disease? I love you guys," said Eddie. "I've had a therapeutic breakthrough thanks to you. I wouldn't jeopardize that for anything."

Maybe this wasn't Eddie's fault. Not the disease, not the seizures, not the blood in the toilet.

"All right Eddie," I said, resting a hand on his shoulder. "This time I'll give you the benefit of the doubt."

"Thanks, Danny. Your trust means a lot to me."

A child-like vulnerability surfaced. His eyes were telling the truth. I knew eyes and I knew Eddie.

As I turned to leave, Eddie spoke: "If you see that ulcer expert, Berger, tell him I'd appreciate a few minutes of his time."

Any more patients like Edward, I decided, and I, too, would need an ulcer specialist. I went to the nurses' station where I re-wrote Eddie's orders. I then paged Bruce.

"You bought that crap?" he yelled over the phone. "He's a professional liar."

Bruce was wrong this time. I was sure of it. I signed Eddie's orders and handed them to the ward clerk. It was nine o'clock. My muscles ached. I needed that swim. I got up and ambled to the elevator. I wondered whether Christie was still around, wondered if Alex decided the hell with our ten dollar bet and was off with Christie dusting some corner of the basement tunnel.

I felt a hand on my shoulder. It was Bruce. He was carrying a package. "Thought you might want this," he said, smiling. I smiled back. He held out a long, thin parcel wrapped in yesterday's Chicago Tribune. My smile faded quickly when I saw the contents. A straightened wire hanger, one end covered with drying blood clots.

"Eddie's?" I asked.

Bruce nodded. "Right up the penis. Instant hematuria."

I shook my head, disgusted. I'd been had.

Chapter 28 swimming

The auditorium was bathed in darkness except for the flickering shadows of chlorine dancing on the vaulted ceiling and walls. I walked to the pool side and removed my scrubs. I turned my beeper volume up, but swore if I received one more page, I was tossing the damn thing in the deep end of the pool.

I looked over the side, watching as the glimmering turquoise ripples danced off my body.

From behind, a hand on my back. I jumped.

"Take it easy there, rookie." I turned. Christie. Wearing a hip high terry cloth robe. No makeup, hair was hanging past her shoulders. My BVD's tightened. I was at a loss for words.

"Y'all goin' swimmin' without me?"

I shrugged.

Her deep blue eyes were wide and devilish. "Don't you believe in the buddy system?" Her hands came down the front of my chest. She playfully twirled some curls of hair (*did she do that to spaghetti*?), then moved closer, and planted her lips on my chest. She let out a soft moan. My legs felt like Silly Putty. She slipped to her knees and ran her hand over the top of my underwear. "That night in the emergency room," she purred. "Seein' you on the stretcher, all cut up and bleedin', maybe dyin'. I never got to put a catheter up a doctor's penis before. It was somethin' I had to do."

A regular Florence Nightingale, I thought.

"I mean it was so limp, so needy." She pressed herself close and whispered. "I like a man who's needy one minute and strong the next."

Christie's robe gracefully fell away from her shoulders. She was poured into a black lace bra, the sheerness of which hardly hid her nipples. Her panties revealed an inviting triangle of fluffy darkness. She planted another kiss, then stood up and dove into the pool, an angelic temptress of human idolatry. I launched myself high into the air, with the hoped for grace of a swan or a gymnast, and landed in a perfect belly-flop. I heard a loud laugh.

149

"If you're not careful, you'll break that thing in half." Christie lay on her back, the masts of her breasts shimmering in the moist air as she backstroked in my direction. When me met, we filled our lungs with one another. Christie cooed softly as I unhooked her transparent top; her nipples, pink and hard as eraser tips, quickly nestled on my lips. From cooing came moans which rippled through the water like the mating call of some exotic bird. Her hand slipped beneath the waves and pressed against my underwear. I leaned back and rested on the flower bed of rippling water, floating rhythmically with her caresses. I remembered Alex's words about DSB disease, and momentarily envisioned myself exploding--leaving no evidence of my existence save a pair of shredded BVDs and an auditorium spray-painted with semen.

Christie removed her hand and our waists pressed against each other, gyrating with the imaginary surf. I could feel her pushing me, holding me, rubbing me up against a door that was working its way open, the 'entrance' sign posted on fingertips that pressed into my back. Seconds now. Just seconds. I took a breath.

The sound of the beeper exploded with orgasmic intensity.

Attention! Attention! I jerked upward, foggy, out of a misty cloud. Shit. My beeper couldn't be that loud. It was the loudspeaker. I didn't even know they had an overhead speaker in here.

"Code Blue- 4 Beyer House! Code Blue- 4 Beyer House!"

Oh my God no! Not now! I was the USS Arizona, ready to enter port. And now this: a surprise attack on Pearl Harbor?

"Tora! Tora! Tora!'

"Code Blue- 4 Beyer House! Code Blue- 4 Beyer House!"

We fell back in the water and listened in stunned silence, hoping it was a mistake. My floor? Can't be. Even so, my brain had already begun sending messages to my hormonal machinery: "Okay all you glands--listen up. Cease testosterone production at once." I could feel the breathing space in my bathing suit.

"Tora! Tora! Tora!

"Code Blue- 4 Beyer House!"

Code Blue, asshole! Code Blue, asshole!

150

Code blue balls was more like it. I jumped out of the pool, slipped back into my underwear, and realizing I was too wet to get dressed, grabbed Christie's robe. I turned to look at her. Her nipples were hard and turned up. Her mouth was soft and turned down.

"Gotta go, Christie."

"Save a life, big guy!"

I didn't stop to ask what she was referring to as 'big guy.' I turned and ran into the night.

Chapter 29 death

Damn it, I knew I shouldn't have tried this. Sex and call nights just didn't mix, I thought as I slip-slid my way through the quarter mile tunnel connecting the pool area to Meyer house, wearing only a robe and wet underwear.

"Code Blue- 4 Beyer House! Code Blue- 4 Beyer House!"

"All right already!" I screamed, rounding a corner. Considering the hour, I wondered who would be there. I pressed the elevator button repeatedly without response. Fear and hormones joined together in keeping me disoriented. I realized I'd left my sign-out sheets back at the pool. Still, I didn't remember anyone being particularly sick.

The wooden doors opened and I pushed the bars apart, closing them on my robe as I jumped in. Another ten raps on the button, and then three kicks before the ancient motor turned over. My sign-outs from Gail and Herb were simple. Most patients were recovering or admitted for some elective procedure. *My* patients were certainly stable, weren't they? "Let's go, dammit!" I yelled to no one.

Sol Goldman's words pierced my brain: *"Don't let anything happen to Mrs. Garber."*

"Shit!" But she wasn't even sick! But it was her, I knew it. Oh God, don't let it be her!

"Tora! Tora! Tora!
Code Blue- 4 Beyer House!
Tora! Tora! Tora!
Code Blue- 4 Beyer House!"

"Get me out of here!" I said banging on the boxcar from hell. The elevator stopped at three and a family wheeling an elderly man lumbered toward the entrance.

"No!" I shouted. "This is an emergency!" The family was too busy trying to get the wheels over the lip of the elevator to pay attention. Besides the wheel chair, they piled in two suitcases, three boxes, and a fold-out chair.

"I'm a doctor!" I yelled at the middle-aged daughter, and then for reasons I'll never understand, I opened my robe and gave a high pitched laugh. "Anyone got a bed pan?"

The family members looked at each other in shocked disbelief and then hurriedly retreated. God, I could be an asshole sometimes.

"Code Blue- 4 Beyer House! Code Blue- 4 Beyer House!"

I ran out and aimed for the room where the resuscitation equipment was parked. Inside a surgical intern was shouting orders to two nurses and an anesthesiologist, while a medical student was performing chest compressions.

Mrs. Garber lay stone cold dead.

Chapter 30 the aftermath

Bruce Creagan called the code blue to a halt forty minutes later. Despite his best efforts, Mrs. Garber never regained any semblance of a heart rhythm.

I stood there, numb by the end, my arms so heavy from performing continuous chest compressions, I could hardly lift them.

"I'll call her attending," volunteered Bruce, his scrub shirt sticking to his chest. "You better go get some dry clothes on."

"Goldman's going to kill me, Bruce. He warned me not to let anything happen to her."

"You didn't, Danny. Diabetics get heart attacks without any warning. She probably had a massive one. Nobody could have predicted it. Not me, not you, certainly not Goldman. We'll know more after the autopsy tomorrow."

I changed into a pair of dry scrubs, then retraced my wet footsteps over to the auditorium. Christie was gone, the pool was deserted. I might have tried calling her, but didn't think she was the type you used just for her shoulder, which is what I was badly in need of. I reclaimed my clothes and clipboard. I wondered where Gail was. I thought about calling her at home, then changed my mind. Instead, I sat on the edge of the pool and put my head in my hands. How could Mrs. Garber have died? Her labs were normal. Her ECG was pristine. I didn't get it. What did I miss? For a moment I imagined she died just to spite me.

After a while, I made my way back to Beyer House. First, I paused outside Maxine Chu's empty room. *At least she had a chance.* I then retraced my steps to Mrs. Garber's room. Her body was wrapped in two bed sheets, her foot tagged for identification. Her belongings lay in a bag at the foot of the bed. I looked inside, saw the curling iron, the makeup, her address book, items that just hours ago were such an integral part of her life. I stood there for several minutes, finally getting the nerve to lift the sheet from her head. Her eyes were vacuous containers of nothingness, her skin, white, her lips dark blue. I touched her

155

face, and my fingers recoiled against the cold, almost rubbery feeling. I gently closed her eyes.

As I pushed her bed to the side my foot kicked something that rolled further under the bed. Out of curiosity I knelt down. It was a small glass ampule that must have been missed when housekeeping cleaned the room. The ampule was open and only a small amount of silvery, pink liquid remained. I was about to drop it in the wastebasket, when I caught the aroma. A strong, oily, almond tincture burned my nose like horseradish. My eyes watered. I'd never smelled anything like that during a code blue before. I held the vial up to a desk lamp. Hospital policy demanded labels on all medications, especially those taken from the crash cart, but this had nothing.

I went to the central module and asked the nurses. They smelled it and shrugged their shoulders. Nothing familiar. I opened the medical drawer on the crash cart, looking to match it with other vials. Everything else was labeled. I examined the vial again. About an eye dropper's worth of liquid remained at the bottom. For reasons I'm not sure of, I taped the top closed then placed the vial inside an opened test tube, which I also closed. Just for safekeeping, I thought. Just for safekeeping.

Chapter 31 the autopsy

I hated autopsies. I shivered at the sight of a chest being cracked open, a knife slicing its way into a brain, or a body being deveined like a shrimp. I never ate before an autopsy, the smell of formaldehyde mixing with death reminding me of spoiled salad dressing, and I avoided food for at least twelve hours after. Which is why I regretted dragging Alex Rosen with me to the morgue. As we watched the pathologist dissect the heart from its pericardial nest, Alex munched shamelessly on a fatty corned beef sandwich. I wouldn't have been there if it hadn't been crucial to learn what, if anything, had killed Mrs. Garber. If it was a heart attack, there ought to be an occlusion of one of the coronary arteries that supplied her heart muscle, and if that was the case, then so be it, I'd have to accept responsibility. And if not... well I couldn't even think about that.

The pathologist made a last snip with his scissors and then yanked Mrs. Garber's heart out of her chest and held it like someone holds up a giant turnip they just pulled out of the ground. He rinsed it in a bucket of saline and laid it on a wooden cutting board. The acrid preservatives burned my eyes. With a serrated knife he made rapid transverse cuts through the muscle, slicing the left then the right ventricle like a chef at Benihana's. Alex smiled, gnawing away on his corned beef and formaldehyde sandwich.

"Look here," the pathologist said, running his knife over a large circumferential area in the left ventricle. "Look how pale this area is. Transmural necrosis. She had a heart attack all right. A whopper."

"Can you date it?" asked Alex, picking a piece of fat from between his teeth.

"Less than 48 hours old."

The door to the morgue opened, and Sol Goldman entered. He was accompanied by a tall man in a plain dark suit and Italian loafers. Neither wore a smile. As soon as Sol spotted me his teeth clenched. I stepped out of the way while he reviewed the pathologist's findings.

"Large myocardial infarction." Sol repeated the words over and over like a mantra, trying to steady himself. He then asked that the coronary arteries be sliced open.

"As soon as I finish dissecting out the aorta," the pathologist answered.

"Now," he said firmly.

We huddled around the pathologist as he probed the opening of the left main artery with an instrument that looked like something a dentist used. Small mounds of plaque became evident as he sliced transversely through the coronary ostium. "Just as I thought," said Sol to his colleague. "Acute closure of the coronary artery. We missed our chance."

The "we," of course, was aimed at me. I stepped forward and asked the pathologist whether or not it was common for diabetics to have atherosclerosis. When he nodded, I then asked if the blockages he saw were severe enough to cause a heart attack as large as the one Mrs. Garber had.

"Generally, I'd say no, but these things are hard to tell, you know. It's possible some of the plaques were disrupted during the attempted rescussitation."

"Looks pretty damn severe to me," said Sol, piqued at my challenge. "I want slides made and stained by tomorrow. That will give us a better idea."

I looked hard at Sol then turned to the pathologist. "How about the toxicology screen? When will that be ready?"

Sol bit down on his lip. "Who ordered a tox screen?" he asked. His gaze was hard, his cheeks red as harvested beets.

"Routine after a sudden death," I answered, as if he didn't know. I felt for the small vial in my pocket. I wanted to pull it out, thrust it in Goldman's face and say, Look Sol, maybe somebody poisoned your damn patient.

The man with Sol cleared his throat. "I'm Dr. Venier. With the Medical Board."

Sol looked at me. "He's here to talk about you."

Alex choked on his corned beef. I felt weak-kneed. The Medical Board?

Dr. Venier pulled at the top of his tie. "I've looked into circumstances surrounding the deaths of your patients," he said.

158

"This being the third. It appears negligence played a role in their demise."

"That's you, Raskin," added Sol.

"You can't believe I had anything to do with those deaths."

"They were your patients." Sol looked at Dr. Venier. "In the ten years I've been here, we've rarely had a totally unexpected death. Now, in two weeks, we've had three."

What were they saying? I thought there were others, I mean Eddie Ingraham, Emile Horner, both knew of other cases. Why the hell was Sol Goldman going after me?

I released my grip on the vial and it fell to the bottom of my pocket. Better not share this. Not now. Not with Goldman. And who the hell was this Dr. Venier? His suit looked expensive, more hip then I'd expect from a Medical Board Member. For that matter, he didn't even look like a doctor, not that I knew what a doctor was supposed to look like. He just seemed out of place, like he had no business in the middle of an autopsy. I thought I'd test his medical acumen just to see. "Dr. Venier, do you think it's possible that something was ingested which caused those blockages to become acutely worse? Enough to limit blood flow to the heart?"

Dr. Venier shifted from one foot to the other.

"Can you review the distinguishing pathological features separating a new from an old myocardial infarction?"

"Dr. Venier is not here to discuss subtle nuances of the case," Goldman snapped. "He is here to ask for my recommendation on what to do with you. He thinks your appointment at this hospital should be terminated."

Alex stopped eating, the pathologist stopped cutting.

I stopped breathing. "What?"

"Termination," repeated Sol. "El finito."

"I didn't do anything."

"Precisely the point. You did nothing. Three patients died as a result of your neglect. Things you should have picked up on."

"Me? What about the residents? What about the attendings? Jeez, Dr. Goldman, what about you? If you were so concerned about your rich little patient, why didn't you pick up on her disease? Why the hell shouldn't you be fired?"

For a split second Sol let down his facade. It was in his eyes, I saw it. Something else was going on. Sol knew this wasn't my fault, knew I hadn't killed those patients any more than he or Alex had. I did a quick calculation. If I was wrong, I would regret it the rest of my life.

"Okay, Dr. Goldman. I'll make it easy for you. I quit."

Chapter 32 on the lam

For two days, I moped around, refusing to answer phone calls or knocks at my door. I took long walks in Lincoln Park, kicking at the crisp fallen leaves, thinking, crying, needing to be alone. Since coming to Chicago, it had been one thing after another. Stabbed at Daley Plaza, clubbed over the head at Lake Michigan. Mysterious people asking about my ex-dean, who then dies mysteriously, people ransacking my apartment for a file, the contents of which I had never seen, a patient stabbed in the ER, a swastika in the pool. And now three dead patients. It couldn't be a coincidence. I knew it, and Sol Goldman knew it.

I answered my phone on the third day. Sol Goldman wanted to see me in his office. When I arrived, he apologized for having blown his cool, blaming his outburst on stress from the medical board's inquiry.   After considerable thought he was recommending probation rather than dismissal, provided that I agreed to keep things quiet. He had already done his part, he explained, having Alex Rosen pass the word that I was out sick. He wanted to squelch any notion that I was incompetent for fear it would hurt my credibility with my colleagues.

If Sol thought I was really guilty of negligence, he would have slammed bus fare into my hand and kicked my butt back to Detroit in a matter of seconds. So why would he threaten to kick me out if he knew I was innocent? Was he worried about my safety for some reason? Or was he worried I was learning a little too much for my own good?

Chapter 33 detective raskin

Identifying the liquid that I found in the glass vial under Mrs. Garber's bed was harder than I expected. I initially brought the vial down to the maze of Biochemistry laboratories, where the Chief of Toxicology sniffed, shook, and held it up to a fluorescent light with one eye closed. "My equipment is calibrated to analyze human serum," he said with a doubting glance. "Running a liquid through a machine calibrated for blood could easily give you a false result. Not to mention screw up the analyzer."

"Can you change the calibrations?" I asked.

"The bearded man with the balding forehead shook his head. "Would take a major overhaul." He thought a moment, then added: "Be happy to try. Only thing is I'd need to use the whole vial."

"Would I get it back?"

He shook his head. "It's a one-shot deal. The sample gets vaporized."

I decided to look for other, less permanent solutions. I took it to the pharmacy, then to the Anesthesia Department, then ran it by the Coronary Care unit staff. Nobody had the faintest notion what it was. Some thought it smelled like a fruity cough syrup, others, a piquant cologne they wouldn't be caught dead wearing. Or something edible like low calorie salad dressing. But for now I wouldn't accept that hypothesis, just as one wouldn't accept the diagnosis of a cold in a patient who presented with cough and loss of appetite, not until he ruled out more exotic diseases like tuberculosis or cancer. That's how I saw the vial. Exclude the more dangerous things before pouring it on top of a salad.

I also considered the possibility that the vial contained a narcotic or hallucinogen. I asked Brian Picolli's opinion, and he offered to smoke some in his water pipe.

"No thanks," I said. "If something happened, I'd be in bigger trouble than I am now."

"Give it to Rasta Jimmi," he said. "Short of a crime lab's analysis, he can identify just about anything--a real, live, walking spectrophotometer."

Jimmi Redding was an escort working the graveyard shift. I didn't even know they had a escort shift past midnight, since nobody ever answered any of my calls.

"They hang out in a dead end corner of the basement tunnel near the all-night coffee shop," offered Brian. "They often don't answer their pages, cause their Reggae music is too loud to hear them. If you want to find Rasta Jimmi just take a left at the coffee shop and follow the cloud of herbal smoke."

The next afternoon found Alex and me huddled in our parkas, dangling fishing lines into Fullerton harbor and talking about Mrs. Garber's death. Alex believed the vial probably belonged to Mrs. Garber, not a bad thought considering her suitcase full of cosmetic paraphernalia. Maybe it was a facial oil, or something she dipped her fingernails in to preserve the shine. But I still had to account for three dead patients, and the only lead I had so far was the vial.

"Tell me what the hell it means?" I asked, baiting my hook for the tenth time. The bait and tackle shop had closed for the season so we had settled for beef jerky.

Alex smiled. "It means you're ready for the loony bin."

We fished in silence for a few minutes, an icy wind tearing at my parka. A wind surfer wearing a wetsuit appeared in the distance. The clouds were a bilious gray.

Alex sipped a Stroh's. "If I were you, I'd worry more about where that file is."

"The file's gone, Alex. They ransacked my apartment."

"If they found it, why would they still be after you? Why did they crack your head with the baseball bat?"

It was the same question I'd been asking myself, with only one plausible explanation. "Revenge. For getting Cantrell fired." I swallowed. "Or killed."

"But the guy who hit you on the head specifically asked where that missing file was. Revenge notwithstanding, why would he ask you that if he already had it?"

"Got me."

"I bet there's two different groups out there looking for the same file. Maybe one of those groups is the Feds."

The fishing pole nearly slipped from my hands. "Come on, Alex. We know Cantrell was dirty. For God's sake, he was taking bribes through his dummy organization, Friends of Tomorrow

"Maybe they're not as dummy as you think. You read the article, saw those words--ultra-right-wing-militant---in my book that's neo-fascist."

The wind had picked up and the beef jerky cracked like a piece of frozen taffy as I tried to thread it. I didn't want to talk about Cantrell and his cohorts anymore. I was tired, cold and confused. I remembered the news article on Cantrell, plus several follow up pieces. There had been a definite struggle before his death. His office had been ransacked, files were missing. The sound and image beside the lake suddenly appeared... the taunting: *"Okay, jewboy, where's the file?"* That had awakened something in me, led me to rise up from the dead and yell: *"fuck you"* which nearly got me killed. I never understood why I responded like that, didn't realize I cared about stuff like that. *"Okay, jewboy."* I had heard that phrase a million times growing up. I thought I was inured.

"You don't think my apartment break in had anything to do with what happened to Cantrell, do you?" I asked Alex.

"Million dollar question, my friend." Alex cast his line some forty yards farther than my longest toss. The man was perfect in just about everything, which only depressed me more. Why couldn't someone chase him around with a baseball bat for a change? After all, he was the Jewish zealot, not me. He was the one going to live in Israel, probably turn out to be a national hero. Alex put his arm around me as we walked back to the car. "I am sure of one thing," he said as we packed the fishing tackle in the trunk. "Goldman may be a jerk, but he's no conspirator." He sucked on a piece of left-over jerky. "Mrs. Garber was a major contributor to the hospital. Her death cost him plenty."

"Did you see the way he looked at me in the morgue? I asked about the toxicology results on her blood and he practically threw an embolus."

"Wouldn't you?"

Ordering a tox screen means you suspect foul play. The post clearly showed she died of Syndrome X: Myocardial infarction with normal coronary arteries. "What if the vial contains some type of cardiac poison? Even if the lab can't analyze it without risk of losing it, they are set up to analyze Mrs. Garber's blood."

"But how could you order a blood test on her. She was already dead."

"Biochemistry lab had a sample they had run a fasting blood sugar on. They keep the serum around a few days for quality control reasons. I called and asked that the remaining serum be routed to Toxicology."

Alex's eyes brightened. "You never told me." He nodded approvingly. "Very wise, though I doubt Goldman would let anything happen to his star benefactor."

Alex started the car and pulled out onto Fullerton Avenue. "So what are the results of the tox screen?"

I shrugged. "Results should have been ready two days ago. The computer listed the test as completed, but gave no results. The Tox lab has no other records--says the results were inputted and there must be some sort of glitch."

"There goes the lead, Sherlock."

"Not necessarily. I'm going to see someone who's a computer expert. Remember that administrative assistant in charge of patient information retrieval? Wanda Bylevin?"

Alex frowned. "I wouldn't."

"Why not?"

Alex paused. "I'm not sure her expertise lies with computers." A smile crossed Alex's lips. "Unless you're talking about computer joysticks."

"You've been out with her?"

"Not in the strict sense, Danny. Suffice it to say that we never left her office."

Alex filled me in while he drove. He was in her office trying to locate an old volume of a patient's chart. At one point he pulled a piece of lint from her cheek. Wanda melted. "It was pure, unadulterated desk-top sex," he said nonchalantly.

The closest I'd ever come to unorthodox sex was coming down the Hyatt Regency elevator at two in the morning at our Senior Prom when Mindy Katz plunged her hand down to the depths of my tuxedo pants, only to be discovered by the elevator attendant, some pimply face college dropout who turned and sneered, "Ballroom anyone?"

I pasted my nose to the car window, watching two lovers arm in arm, kicking leaves into the wind. "I have to try someone, Alex. I need help and she's the expert."

"Guess it can't hurt, Danny. But do me a favor. If she asks about me, tell her I have a girlfriend or something."

"Why lie?"

"You'd think she'd be satisfied with a simple fuck and that would be the end of it. She hasn't stopped paging me since. I feel like getting an unlisted beeper number."

"She's like all the rest of them, Alex. Fell madly in love with you."

"This is worse. She thinks I'm the man she was intended to marry."

Chapter 34 the computer

Wanda Bylevin sat on top of her desk, seemingly not bothered by the fact that her skirt had worked its way up to the neck of her panty hose. Her hair was a pile of black curls pinned atop her head. Large green-tinted glasses in avocado frames matched her eyeliner.

I explained that I needed to locate a toxicology result that the computer had swallowed. Wanda looked at me suspiciously, then glanced at her watch. "I've got ten minutes tops. I've got to debug a program for the chief of OB by this afternoon." From the sitting position, she leaned over and punched something on her keyboard. "You're lucky you're a friend of Alex's. Otherwise I couldn't even spare you the ten minutes, not without an appointment. By the way, did Alex say anything to you about me?"

She eyed me suspiciously. What did she want me to say? That I knew she and Alex had done it on top of her desk in broad daylight, without even closing the curtains to the other offices? I gave her my sincerest look. "Alex said that you two hit it off."

Her eyelids fibrillated. "Does he talk about me at all? You're his best friend. You'd know."

I shook my head and she sullenly sat down at her computer desk. I gave her Mrs. Garber's ID number and then stood over her as she scrolled through the 'Gs' on her screen. She seemed bothered, in a hurry.

"Really don't have time for this today."

"Come on Wanda. You looked up somebody for Alex."

Wanda laughed. "The hell I did. He told you that?"

"Yep."

"Then you don't know your friend, after all. Alex was trying to get on line with a Vegas sports book."

"What?"

Wanda continued entering numbers. "You can get odds on everything: baseball, horses, boxing. Ahh, here we go. Garber. Vital statistics, insurance, list of hospitalizations, lab values from previous admissions." Even the incident report Garber had filed against me was there. "Great bedside manner, doctor," she said after reading how discourteous I had been. At least she was smiling.

"Did Alex find it?" I asked.

"No. Speaking of odds, what do you think the chances are Alex will ask me out again?" She stared at her screen longingly. "It's been two weeks."

"I'm not a betting man, Wanda." There was something sadly seductive about Wanda. So wounded. So fragile.

Wanda shook her head as she read Mrs. Garber's code blue report.

"You guys botched it up pretty good," she said with a smirk. "Must have been awful messy down there."

Awful messy up here the other day, I wanted to say, remembering how Alex had described her post-coital desk top as a hot-plate with juices simmering on top.

"Here are the autopsy findings," said Wanda, adjusting her glasses. "Large anterior myocardial infarction, twenty percent obstruction of left main coronary artery. Not enough to cause a heart attack, is it?"

"That's why we're here," I said with authority, hoping to convince her of the importance of this. Wanda continued scrolling, biting her lip.

"Now," she said, "let's see, toxicology." She scrolled several screens then paused a moment, punching in more numbers. Then some more. "It should be right here." She scrolled for two more minutes.

"What's wrong?"

She turned briefly, lipstick smudged on her front teeth. "Not sure. It's logged in the computer, just like you said. But the results have been transferred to another file. Let's see if I can access it." My breathing quickened as she punched her keyboard. Two more minutes went by. Wanda let out a long breath. "It's gone but I know it was here. If it weren't, it wouldn't have been logged in to begin with. I can't pull up the damn file. Let me check something." Five more minutes passed before she looked up. "Very strange. I cross-checked all the toxicology results ordered this past month. It wasn't in that file, either. Two others are missing." She typed some more.

"Ever hear of a Mrs. Dombrowsky?" she asked.

My little old oyy, oyy, oyy lady I couldn't for the life of me get an IV into.

"And Mrs. Silver?" she asked. "Both died of heart attacks. Both were your patients. Both had tox screens ordered." Wanda looked at me hard. "Their results are also missing."

I felt the panic fill my veins. Those toxicology screens were ordered before I ever met Mrs. Garber. Before that glass vial had aroused any suspicions.

"I never ordered toxicology screens on those two patients."

"Somebody did."

I took a breath. "Who?"

My eyes were blurred. My scrub shirt was soaked.

"Oh, oh," Wanda said. "You're in trouble now. Doesn't your own boss trust you with your patients?"

My chest tightened. "Goldman ordered the toxicology screens?"

Wanda nodded. "He or somebody using his physician access number." Wanda continued typing while I stood over her. All I could figure was that Goldman must have suspected that they had been poisoned. That meant there had to be other patients who also had died under dubious circumstances.

"You Jewish?" she asked without turning.

"What's that got to do with anything?"

"It looks like the three patients you knocked off were all Jewish."

"That isn't funny."

"Sorry."

"How do you know that?"

"Religious preference, right at the top of their admissions forms."

An idea struck. "Do me a favor, Wanda. Can you cross-reference toxicology with heart attacks?"

"I don't have time."

"Please," I pleaded. "I have to have that now."

"That macho shit won't get you anywhere."

171

"Come on, Wanda."

"No."

"Tell you what, Wanda. Help me out and I'll put in a good word to Alex."

I regretted my words even before her eyes teared up. "He's never going to call me again." She gazed upward. "The man of my dreams makes passionate love to me on this very desk, whispering all the while how beautiful I am and how we were meant for each other, and gives me the greatest climax of my life, and now..." she sniffed, "he won't have anything to do with me."

I cringed inside, remembering that Alex had described it more as a sperm-fest. I felt sorry for Wanda, had the urge to take her in my arms and tell her that just because a man was handsome, suave, hypnotic and probably hung like a horse, didn't necessarily make him a viable partner 'til death did you part.

Wanda regained her composure, then flipped her head back like a woman scorned. "Any kind words on my behalf would be appreciated," she said. "I can give you two more minutes. State your question."

"Did anybody else die of a heart attack while on the medical floor?"

"Instead of in the ICU?"

"Yes."

"Over what period of time?"

I told her a year. I just needed one other name. Just one and I could go to Goldman, hit him with the data. I counted the minutes. "No luck," she said. "Let's try the two previous years." Two more minutes. This was a waste. What the hell was I thinking of? I stood motionless as data continued to scroll on the monitor.

"I pulled up all hospital deaths in the past three years which occurred within the first twenty four hours of admission. I then cross-referenced those names with those taken off autopsy reports during the same time period whose cause of death was classified 'acute myocardial infarction.'"

"Did you find any matches?"

Wanda took a breath. "Try fifteen."

"What?" My heart was a jumping bean in my chest. "Fifteen patients died just like my patients did?"

Wanda nodded. " All fifteen died in a three year span that ended the year before you started here."

"Tox screen. Did any of those patients have tox screens ordered?" My head pounded. Elation and fear.

"Sure did. All of them."

"What did they show?"

"Same thing. Classified. Can't get to them."

So, this whole business didn't start with me. Whatever happened to my patients had happened to others as well, long before I ever got to Chicago. I took the paper and headed to the door. "Thanks Wanda, I owe you for this."

"Any help with you know who would be greatly appreciated."

I opened the door.

"Hey wait," she called. "One more thing I forgot to tell you."

"About Alex?"

"No, about those fifteen patients on that list."

"Yeah?"

"Their religious preference.... all Jewish."

End of part 2

PART 3

Winter Solstice

While the constitution of the United States guarantees every citizen the right to free speech, that right does not extend to promulgation of lies and hatred intended to gather the forces whose ultimate purpose is the destruction of a people or a race.

Vice President Harold J. Barrish--speech given at the National Meeting of the Anti- Defamation League

Chapter 35 maxine chu

Like leaves crumpled to the ground by the blustery November chill, so too did Maxine's silky hair fall to the earth in lifeless clumps, gutted at the roots by the cruel winds of chemotherapy.   I stood in the Oncology clinic bathroom, watching, as Maxine stared at the tufts of hair lining the basin. She held a brush in one hand, while the other traced newly found ridges on her scalp. Tears welled up as she tested the threshold of brush strokes which would leave her hair intact. In the mirror her eyes searched mine.

She forced a smile. "There goes my show-piece. Never had boobs worth a second look, legs are like chopsticks, and the belly scar you guys gave me was one helluvan eyesore." She ran her hand softly through her hair, in the process removing a sample large enough to cover a barber's floor. "Who knows? Maybe bathing caps will be back in style next summer. Maybe I'll try out for the De Paul production of The King and I. Just think--a female Yul Brenner."

I put my arm around her, flashing back to that first time I saw her in the ER, her magnificent flowing black hair a symphony of beauty.

Maxine backed off slightly.

"Don't worry about me, Danny. It's not that bad. Lets me know the chemo's working. That's what's important."

"It'll grow back, Max. Lo can help you through this." My words were artificial, intended to placate Maxine rather than understand her. For reasons I didn't know, Lo was nowhere to be seen, not at the clinic, not in the lobby. Whose idea, I wondered; his or hers?

Maxine stopped initiating contact with me after that. Maybe I held her hand too tightly during that visit. Or maybe it was the fear she saw in my own bloodshot eyes as I rocked her back and forth in my arms trying to stifle her waves of nausea. If we happened to run into each other when she was in for a treatment, I got a 'hi,' or maybe a two minute discourse about school. When I asked how the chemo was going, she'd just shrug. "No problem," she would say. "No more nausea, no pain." I went along with Maxine, allowing her to keep up appearances, even though when I kissed her hello I thought I smelled traces of vomit hiding beneath her minty mouthwash.

Two weeks later, Maxine's white blood cell count plummeted to dangerously low levels, and she spiked a fever, forcing her to be hospitalized again. Emile Horner agreed to be her attending physician, allowing me to bring her into 4 Beyer House where I could take charge of her care.

When I walked into her room, I immediately realized how much weight she'd lost since the beginning of the therapy. Her cheek bones were more prominent, and when I greeted her, her frail hand had seemed lost in my palm. Maxine sat up in bed and pushed her night stand to the side. She adjusted her hairpiece, repositioning the six or seven hairs that protruded. "How do you like it?" she asked.

On anybody else, it was okay. But on Maxine, it was equine-like, so different from the flowing black silk that had wafted into my dreams so often. I bit down on my lip.

"Just for that, I'm not going to show you my bald head."

"Just for what?" I couldn't hide anything from Maxine. She knew me too well.

"Since I'm only staying a day or two, I'll just keep you guessing."

Maxine knew she was here for at least a week, maybe longer.

"I haven't eaten a good Chinese meal in months. You don't think I'm going to send my meal ticket home that quickly. Besides, as your physician, it's my job to fatten you up."

Maxine grimaced. "I can't stand the smell of that stuff."

I frowned. "I thought the chemo was going okay, Max? I thought your appetite was fine."

For a fraction of a second our eyes met. Then, as if jolted back to reality, she waved a slender, shapely arm above her head.

"It's not the food, silly, it's...." Maxine looked toward the door. "It's the person making the food."

"Lo?"

"The chemo's nothing. He's the one making me sick to my stomach."

I studied Maxine carefully. Her almond-shaped eyes, though recessed deeper into the skin folds of her lids than usual, had lost none of their luminescence. What remained of her eyebrows were now tweezed to perfection and penciled. Her cheeks, once unwrinkled and glowing, were splotchy in parts and formed an oblique angle to well-shaped but over-rouged lips. I rested my hand on her shoulder.

"There's nothing to talk about," she said, her eyes staring off to one side. "He's not what the doctor ordered."

Though well-intentioned and fully devoted to Maxine, it was clear that Lo lacked the spiritual resolve to help Maxine's frantic struggle for life. Lo Wen Chien's traditional Chinese way could no longer cut it with Maxine.

"Give him a chance, furball."

Maxine winced at my reference. "A chance for what?"

"Support, Maxine. Emotional and physical support."

Maxine let out a high-pitched laugh, tossing her head back. Far from the grand, flowing movement of her natural hair, her inadequate hairpiece shifted slightly to one side.

"Lo is more scared of Hodgkins disease than I am, Danny. Do you know what he would do if he saw me get sick from the chemo?"

"Wait a minute, Max. You never told me you were getting sick."

"Well, if I was, it would be the end of him. Talk about coping with cancer? Lo's a zero."

"Max, it's not cancer, not per se. Hodgkin's disease is curable."

"Let's not get into this, okay?" she said, a gritty edge in her voice. "Even before all this, Lo held me at arm's length."

"He worships you, Maxine."

Maxine nodded. "You're right. Like a saint. Trouble is, I'd rather be treated like a whore once in a while." Maxine ran her hand across her head, forgetting the waves of hair were gone. "You think Dr. Stool would like to ravish me?"

"That's Spool, Maxine, and the answer is no. Don't give up on Lo. After you're married, there will be plenty of time for..."

"Plenty of time is something I can no longer count on, Danny."

"Well..." I stammered, trying to organize my thoughts. "You just have to make sure Lo realizes the immediacy of the situation."

"Hah! Do you think there's a snowball's chance in hell he'd go to bed with me now?"

For such a cool day my armpits were sticky. "Tell Lo that many people believe a nurturing, close relationship is associated with a faster recovery. Make him part of the recovery process."

"I tried. I told him the only thing that would make me better was a hot beef injection."

Maxine watched as my eyes bulged, and paused long enough to hear the sound of my jaw thump. "Where, in God's name did you hear that expression?"

Maxine tried stifling a giggle by holding her index finger over her lips. "You hear lots of things walking through the basement of this place." A flush of color filled out her cheeks. "Especially around the escort service office."

I didn't need an imagination to picture Maxine walking to the Oncology clinic via the basement tunnel-- the catcalls, the propositions--the drugs. I suggested she use the second floor walkway. She waved me off.

"I can take care of myself. Besides," she added, picking up a *Cosmopolitan* magazine, "a woman in my situation--you know-- a dud for a boyfriend and a hairpiece that makes me look like a Kewpie doll--I need all the positive reinforcement I can get!"

Maxine was extremely attentive while I performed a physical examination, her eyes following my every movement. I became so self-conscious that I listened to her heart with my stethoscope placed on top of her gown rather than inside. And when I finally spread her gown open to examine her breasts, I found myself staring off in the distance. When I was finished, I explained the plan for the next few days. Besides feeding her large quantities of intravenous fluids supplemented with vitamins, we would continue chemotherapy with a regimen that we hoped would be more gentle on her bone marrow. I also told her I had ordered extra-strong anti-nausea medication, but had bet the nurses she wouldn't even need it. "Things are going great," I concluded. "Your lymph nodes are smaller, your liver scan last week looked better. We can lick this thing."

"And don't forget the part about my being the perfect patient."

I replayed her words, scanning for any hint of cynicism. "Maxine, you are the perfect patient. What you put up with last time you were in the hospital was beyond belief."

"Like that perverted medical student with a breast obsession."

"You never complain, never ask for pain meds. You never even called me during your outpatient visits. You are one strong kid."

"Don't take it to the bank."

"Why not?"

Maxine shrugged her shoulders. "Don't worry, your best patient won't disappoint you."

Chapter 36 thinking

Reluctantly, Wanda Bylevin supplied me with the medical records I requested, two large crates worth, enough to ruin my first complete weekend off. But what choice did I have? For three weeks I had been paralyzed by the knowledge that fifteen patients had died unexpectedly from myocardial infarctions. Besides the vial of liquid, those records were all I had. And thus far, all I had been able to ascertain from Wanda was that they were all the same religion. If there were any more links, I had to find them.

And as for the vial... to tell the truth, I didn't even want to think about that damn vial anymore...not after I had made a terribly stupid mistake. Somehow, I had let Eddie Ingraham swindle me out of half its contents. It was painful to think about, even three weeks after it happened, the last time I had seen Eddie before his discharge. "I'm a brilliant chemist," he assured me. Implored me to ask him anything. I did, and he seemed to know his stuff, ranging from the number of sulfur molecules in a loop diuretic to the method of synthesizing adrenalin from extracts of sheep adrenal glands. I finally and reluctantly gave in, poured half the liquid, quarter of a teaspoon full, into a glass test tube for Eddie. He smiled, telling me how important it was for a physician to develop trust in a Munchausen patient. "You won't be sorry," he said as he left his medical floor. That was three weeks ago. I hadn't heard from him since. I tried to get his number, but there was no listing recorded.

I couldn't afford another mistake with the remaining liquid. Despite keeping it inside an air-tight test tube, its volume was diminishing by the day. I was loathe to send it to a city laboratory for fear of losing it. Even worse, if they found a deadly poison, they might turn it over to the police. I'd already thought about the police, hinting to Officer Mulroney about running a toxicology analysis on something I found. Mulroney seemed more suspicious of me with each passing day. He asked too many questions, tried to open doors I wanted to have stay closed.

The only other person whose suggestion I had yet to follow was Brian Picolli. He said I should take it to Rastafarian Jimmi Redding, the night shift escort supervisor. It made me laugh just to think who I was left to trust on this: a basement-dwelling, pot-smoking Rastafarian escort, and a crazed Munchausen patient who I'd probably never see again.

Chapter 37 sharing a drink

Two days later I was paged to the ER by Officer Mulroney.

"Guess who showed up last night?" he said from his perch in the coffee lounge, where he was knee-deep in lasagna. "Would have called you at home but Old Eddie went straight to the O.R."

I felt both anger as well as elation on hearing Eddie Ingraham had returned. "What happened?"

"You know Maurice Berger, don't you?" he asked, his mouth full. "Berger was about to give Medical Grand Rounds down at the University. He left to answer a page. Eddie handcuffed him, gagged him, and threw him into a janitor's closet."

Mulroney related how Eddie calmly walked into the auditorium and announced that he was a visiting professor from Edinburgh who would be substituting for Dr. Berger, who had taken ill. He delivered a forty five minute dissertation on peptic ulcer disease. "Perfect Scottish brogue so I've been told," Mulroney said. "That psychopath got a standing ovation."

It wasn't hard to picture, Eddie standing there on his pedestal, basking in applause. Probably signed a few autographs at the reception. I turned to Mulroney. "How did he end up in the OR? You know he has Munchausen's disease."

"Of course we know. He was in Cook County jail, awaiting arraignment when he developed acute appendicitis."

Eddie's seizures flashed in my mind. Those seemed real, too.

Mulroney saw the doubt in my eyes. "For Christ's sake, don't look at me like that. Looked real to the surgeon--said he ruptured his appendix. Took him right to the OR. The surgical chief resident, Winston Hacklethorpe III himself, was handling the situation. I mentioned the Munchausen's part."

"And?"

"Don't even think he knew what it was. If it ain't a gall bladder or pancreatitis, they don't give a shit. He said it was obviously ruptured appendicitis and I should stick to pedaling parking tickets."

Winston Hacklethorpe III was my idea of what was wrong with surgery. The guy was a legacy, son of the retired chief of surgery at Mass General. He assumed the genetic linkage conferred deity status and mandated that medical students and interns pay constant homage to him, less they forfeit any future aspirations to a surgical residency.

"What did they find in the OR?"

Mulroney wiped a noodle from his sleeve. "It's been twenty four hours. If it were anything but a rupture, we would have heard by now."

Under other circumstances, it might have been amusing. Tying up Berger, a famous man but one hell of a boring lecturer, then, when Eddie's about to go to jail he ends up talking the surgeons into taking him to the O.R. It might have been a good story but I wasn't laughing, not after Eddie had let me down. Taking my precious liquid under false pretenses had ruined any trust I had in him.

I headed back down the basement, following the tunnel toward the surgical pavilion. It gave me the creeps; dark, empty places always did. I could hear the insects crunching under my feet as I walked, the musty air burned my nostrils. The last time I took this route I was wearing wet underwear and a terry cloth robe, on my way to Mrs. Garber's death party. I felt the vial on the inside of my coat. *What the hell happened to you, Mrs. Garber?*

The lights noticeably dimmed against the pinging of low-hanging water pipes as I turned into the older section of the tunnel. I opened my mouth to yawn and nearly swallowed a spider web, cotton candy filaments pasting themselves to the roof of my mouth. Past the coffee shop, I headed down a dead end hallway toward the piquant smell of marijuana and the sound of reggae music. Four young men were passing around a cigar shaped joint. If not for their gray flannel escort service uniforms, I would have assumed I was walking into a Jamaican pot party. Bob Marley's staccato voice reverberated from a ghetto blaster as big as my sofa.

"Hey mon, how about some ganja?"

"No thanks," I replied, clearing a path through the thick cloud of herb. I banged a shoulder into a wall. "Work to do."

"So do we, mon," answered a man who then inhaled so deeply that I thought he would burst. "We be escorting your patients for you mon!"

My fingers gripped the glass vial, thinking about Brian Picolli's suggestion. "Any of you know a man named Jimmi Redding?"

A man stood up, caught his balance, then stepped forward. He was tall, with a beard that had more braids than his long, stringy hair. He wore dark glasses and held Dylan Thomas's Under Milkwood at his side.

"I be Rasta Jimmi Redding. Who be asking, mon?"

"I work with Brian Picolli."

A mouthful of white teeth opened. "Ahh, me buddy Picolli." Only man who can smoke me under the table." Trying to teach the dude a little poetry." Jimmi yanked a sheet off the top of one of the gurneys, uncovering what looked like a small missile launcher. The other escorts leaned forward and nodded approvingly. "It be a bong, Doc. Gonna celebrate our friendship with some hashish from Jamaica town." He removed a foil pack from his pocket, pulling out a dark rock.

"No thanks," I said.

Jimmi shrugged his shoulders, turning away. "So be it, mon." I studied Jimmi while he and his buddies took turns inhaling the vaporous smoke. Jimmi's skin was a lighter shade of black than his friends. Almost a dark, bronze tan, barely visible under his beard and pair of oversized shades. Over the years I'd learned to trust any instinctive feeling I might have after gazing in someone's eyes. The glasses made that impossible. I withdrew the vial from my coat pocket and held it up to the dim light. A few drops shimmered like mercury along the sides.

Jimmi Redding looked up. "Hey mon, Doc has some booty. What it be, THC? You want Jimmy to sprinkle it over the hash?"

I explained that I had found the stuff in one of the call rooms and that Brian thought he might have an idea what it was. Jimmi Redding listened intently.

"Here, mon," he said, grabbing for the vial. I held back, his strong hand wrapping itself around my fist.

"You thinks it's illegal, mon? If so, Rasta Jimmi's tried them all." He gave a deep laugh that reminded me of a pirate. "You have a worried look about you, doc." He stared at me and I felt revealed, naked. I wished I was the one wearing shades.

"Poison, you think somebody poisoned a patient," he said.

I froze. How did he know? I never even told Brian Picolli what I was worried about.

"How...?"

"The eyes, mon."

Let me see yours, you bastard! My grip on the vial loosened.

"Let Rasta Jimmi have a look now." He nudged open my fist, like an officer disarming a felon of his gun. "Ahh, see, you can trust Rasta Jimmi. Picolli be right on the mark."

Jimmi took the vial, held it up to the smoky ceiling light. "First, I give it the old shake test." He turned it side to side.

"Careful."

"Ah hah, just as I thought."

"What?"

"Next I give it the old smell test." Jimmi wafted two fingers of his right hand over the vial toward his nose. "Ah hah!"

"Got something?"

"Need one last test."

"What?"

"Taste test, mon."

"No!" I screamed, lunging toward Jimmi. The six remaining drops splashed with a finality into the back of Jimmi's throat.

"You sonofabitch."

"Hey mon, don't be cussing Rasta Jimmi out. I be trying to help."

"That's not what I had in mind."

Jimmi turned and high-fived his friends. After a moment he turned back. "At least you know it's not poison." He licked his lips.

Then, without warning, Jimmi's neck stiffened. His arms became rigid, turning robotically outward, and saliva began pouring from his mouth like a rabid dog. His eyes rolled back into his head.

Shit! I dove for him.

He let out an guttural moan, then crashed to the floor.

My God, I'd killed him. I jumped to his side, feeling his neck for a pulse. My hand went to his face to tug off his glasses so I could check his pupils. Suddenly Jimmi's hand was on my shoulder.

"Don't be messing with me specs, doc. "Me eyes sensitive to light." Jimmi jumped up to the high-fives and exclamations of "Damn!" and "sheet, motha fucker, you scared the devil from us." I, too, nearly wet my pants.

"You okay?"

Jimmi sat up. "That there is some good shit, doc. Know where I can get me an ounce?"

"Narcotic?"

Jimmi straightened his glasses. "No, doc. Purified fruit extract. Raspberry and pineapple I think. Stuff would be damned good on Rasta Jimmi's Caribbean curry." His friends laughed, and soon turned their attention back toward the glass bong, simmering in the corner. Dejectedly, I turned away. I'd been taken again. Only this time it was worse. I'd lost the only physical evidence I had.

From a distance I heard: "If you need an escort just call."

"1-800- G-A-N-J-A," another said.

Chapter 38 hacklethorpe

When Winston Hacklethorpe III saw me approach, he picked his 7-up can from the bottom of the soda machine, and without collecting his change, scampered off in the other direction. I quickened my pace, catching up to him and his entourage of students just outside the hospital door, where he was perched against the statue of Richard Meese.

He looked at his watch as he turned. "A little late for a flea to be awake."

Winston was one of those surgeons who referred to medicine interns as fleas, insects that flitted about a patient, never quite getting to the source of the problem. I didn't bother with a comeback, knowing my turn would come shortly.

"Got a patient of yours, Amigo," he began. "Came in from Cook County with acute appendicitis."

"Word gets around." I folded my arms. "So?"

"So, what?"

"The laparotomy. What did you find?"

The moon illuminated the tiny beads of sweat on Winston's forehead.

"We found what we expected--a necrotic, ruptured appendix."

"Come on, Winston. You had his records. You knew he was a Munchausen's."

Winston's feet shifted clumsily, as if he were trying to remove himself from a bear trap. "Anybody can get appendicitis. A baby, a ninety year old gomer, and," Winston folded his arms defensively, "it can certainly happen to a Munchausen's patient!"

"Okay, Winston. When I come out of Pathology with a report of a normal appendix, I'm going to paste a copy on every wall of the hospital." It was an empty threat, but Winston didn't know that. Surgeons live for threats; they thrive on them.

Winston sent his students to check on some lab results. When they were out of sight, he moved closer. "See that

191

flagpole?" he whispered. "If my chief finds out I told you this, that's where my scrotum will be hanging."

I put my finger to my lips and shook my head, feigning concern. Winston looked around and lowered his voice even further. "My chief has taken over a hundred people to the OR for acute appendicitis. This was the first time he made a mistake."

"So you took out a normal appendix. It happens to everybody if they operate long enough."

Winston shook his head. "Normal I could deal with. His wasn't even there!"

"What?"

"That's right, dammit. No fucking appendix. Must have been taken out years ago."

"Maybe you could have used one of us 'fleas' buzzing around for a few minutes. Might have saved you a little embarrassment."

"One hundred cases," he lamented. "My chief was bragging how Ingraham's presentation was classic, right out of Cope's *Diagnosis of the Acute Abdomen* --fever, elevated white count, right lower abdominal tenderness; rebound, the whole nine yards. He invited every damn intern and student on the surgery service to see the operation."

I asked what his chief did when they found no appendix.

Winston Hacklethorpe III peered around suspiciously. "He lied. What else could he do? He removed a small piece of bowel. The students couldn't tell the difference. One kid even passed right out in the O.R."

Seeing themselves as infallible, surgeons rarely castigated themselves for their mistakes. When I asked Winston who got the lion's share of the blame for this mistake, he just sneered. "Who do you think? He said I gave him wrong information. Like he didn't do his own history and physical." Winston paused, lost in thought. "I swear to you, if anybody had a hot belly, it was Edward Ingraham. You can't fake a ruptured appendix, you just can't!"

"Did he wake up yet?"

"You kidding? He was asking questions before he got to the recovery room."

Let Eddie ask all the questions he wanted, I thought as I walked the other way. Because when I got to his room, it would be my turn. And he had better have some answers.

Chapter 39 eddie ingraham

Edward Ingraham was sitting up in his bed licking a fudgicle and watching television. His freshly washed hair was brushed evenly to one side, and his caterpillar-like scar looked like it had been buffed with car wax. When he saw me, he smiled, set down the TV remote, and proudly opened his hospital gown, revealing a rectangular betadine-stained bandage, one side oozing a greenish antibiotic ointment. The rest of his abdomen was shaved as clean as an Olympic swimmer's.

When I didn't return the smile, his faded. Winston Hacklethorpe III maybe have been fooled, but Eddie knew that I hadn't.

"Angry?"

I folded my arms across my chest. "Angry doesn't quite capture it, Edward."

"Probably never going to talk to me again, huh? Just close the book on the old war hero?"

"Book, Eddie? Which book is that? The one without the appendix?"

Eddie broke out into a deep laugh, then clutched at his belly, wincing.

"Congrats, Eddie, you faked out the best surgeons here. You could ruin them."

"Sue their asses off, huh?" Eddie checked the doorway, then whispered: "Ever hear of hush money? In return for not suing, all charges against me have been dropped." Eddie admired his belly like it was sculptured by Donatello. "I never hurt Dr. Berger."

"You handcuffed him and threw him into a closet. That doesn't exactly put you in the running for Citizen of the Year."

Eddie straightened. "I wish you could have been at my talk, Danny. You would have been proud."

It was funny the way he said that. Physician interaction with Munchausen patients usually led to confrontation followed by aggressive, defensive behavior. But with me it was different.

195

Eddie really looked up to me. And in a strange way, I was proud of him.

"Anybody can give a lecture, Eddie, especially a boring one. Faking out the surgeons, now that's a feat."

"You're right. Keeping your belly rigid for two hours ain't so easy. Fact of the matter is, I almost soiled my pants twice."

"Spare the details, Eddie," I said, picking up the clipboard from the side of the bed. "I hope you're a better person for the experience."

"It wasn't bad," he mused. "I would have preferred a little less anesthesia though."

I was scanning his vital signs and almost missed his last statement. I looked up. "What do you mean 'a little less anesthesia'? The anesthesiologist knows the correct doses."

Eddie smiled. "Not after I explained how my torture in Chile left me sensitive to fluorothane, and that I had previously suffered two cardiac arrests from half the normal dose. I'd say the dose I got was enough for...let's say a newborn."

"You mean to tell me you were awake during your operation?"

"Groggy is more like it. I could hardly get a good look at my belly being opened."

"You're lying!"

"Ask the poor stooge who was standing in the OR watching them open me. He was blocking my view, and I tried nudging him out of the way. When he looked over at me, I winked. He passed right out!"

Eddie began flipping through the TV stations with his remote. "Do you know when the next anatomy class starts at the medical school?"

"What for?"

"This operation has intrigued me to the point where I'd like to get some first hand experience in anatomical dissection."

"You've already been in trouble for impersonating a medical student. I wouldn't try it again."

Edward looked at me through narrowed eyes. "But I am a medical student!"

"And I'm Mohammed Ali."

"Who said anything about impersonating a medical student, anyway? I'm more interested in impersonating a cadaver."

I ignored him, instead quickly scanning his post-op record. Seeing nothing of concern, I turned to leave. "By the way, thanks for conning me out of that vial I found. I suppose that went into the wastebasket with that coat hanger you punctured your penis with?"

"You only gave me a sample. There's plenty left."

"Tell that to the Rasta in the basement who swallowed the rest."

Eddie shrugged his shoulders. "Didn't hurt him none. Stuff isn't digestible by the oral route."

I looked up. "How do you know that?"

Eddie smiled. "Doing my job. Have you done yours? Been playing Sherlock?"

I wasn't about to tell Eddie about the fifteen people who had met the same fate as Mrs. Garber. Not now at least. "I've been busy, Eddie. You know how many hours an intern works."

"But you're a doctor. Doctors use the library, don't they?"

I nodded suspiciously. I hadn't stepped near the library since internship began. No time. Reading would come next year, as a resident. "What's your point?"

"Poisons, Daniel. I thought you had a personal interest in poisons."

"And I suppose you found something in that vial?"

"Let's just say that progress is being made."

"Like?"

"Eddie helps those who help themselves. If I were you, I'd hit the library. There's information out there about drugs that affect the heart."

"You mean it's really possible that..."

Eddie waved me off. "Check the library, Danny. That's all I want to say for now."

The man sat at his computer, plucking at his keyboard until the files he needed appeared before him. Having worked at Richard Meese Hospital, he knew the exact codes that would allow him access; the private files of that upstart bitch, Wanda

197

Bylevin were no match for his own talents. He scrolled for a minute, then stopped. "I'll be a sonofabitch," he said, beads of sweat beginning to form on his forehead. "How the hell did they come up with that?" He continued his examination. This was not good. Raskin and Bylevin were getting closer than he thought possible. He had already followed that cunt to her car on two different occasions, just to scare her. Things were already too hot after the bungled job on Charles Cantrell to do more than that. Besides, if need be, his friend would take care of Bylevin. As for himself, he'd continue to focus on the one person who already had hurt the cause more than anyone else: Danny Raskin.

Chapter 40 wanda bylevin

Spare time.

I pondered when it was that I had last related to those words. I badly needed some free time, away from patients, responsibilities, and the thoughts of murder and conspiracy. But when fifteen patients die suspiciously, somebody has to act. For me, that meant going through the only data I had--patient charts--looking for clues, grappling for an explanation that might help make sense of things.

Why had Eddie been so sure I'd find something in the library? I'd already checked through the toxicology textbooks in the Department office, even called up the Poison Control Center at Children's Hospital. Nobody knew anything about a drug that could cause an instant heart attack. What more could I expect to find in that dingy old excuse for a library that I hadn't already found?

If I trusted anyone, it was Wanda Bylevin. In fact, I began looking forward to our afternoons together, lurking behind her closed office shades, watching while she hacked away at her computer terminal, looking for clues, chasing down imagined ghosts from the past. Wanda seemed to anticipate these meetings as much as I did, though not at first. For a week or so, I was just a shoulder to lean on. I spent hours comforting her, assuring her that Alex's dismissal of their relationship was not her fault, that in fact, he thought she was beautiful, a great lover. I lied, said whatever I could think of to get her out of her funk. While I resented Alex for what Wanda was going through, a part of me knew he wasn't intentionally trying to hurt her. Had he any inkling of the obsessive behavior he had triggered he never would have slept with her in the first place.

Alex couldn't help the fact that he charmed the masses. He had a way about him, an off the cuff grin with eyes so bright that a woman could easily believe that by looking into them she'd see the reflection of both their souls. And it wasn't just a woman thing either. His boyish, easygoing attitude made attending physicians look the other way when he discharged their patients earlier than planned. Or carried out an order that was against the private physician's wishes. Rather than getting angry with Alex, they more often than not ended up lunching with him at places like the posh Pump Room, downtown.

Wanda had used my shoulder these past two weeks, so it wasn't surprising that as her love-induced depression subsided, I became the object of her transference. I wanted to believe I would have helped anyone in need. But I, too, was needy as hell, had gone without romance for longer than I could remember, and my entire being ached to be softly curled up next to a woman. While I longed for Wanda in a sexual way, I couldn't see myself becoming romantically involved with her. I didn't understand this, since for me, one longing usually didn't come without the other. "It's your feminine side," Alex had remarked. "Love and sex, that's how women want it. For me it's as incompatible as oil and vinegar."

My feminine side wasn't what bothered me. It was the rest of my life. I was too messed up with everything else. To have sex with Wanda under these circumstances seemed a bad idea, maybe even worse than when Alex did it, since he'd had no way of knowing beforehand how emotionally vulnerable she was.

Within a week after I began visiting Wanda, her wardrobe took a sharp turn toward the seductive; blouses open to reveal cleavage, lace chemises provocatively tickling the tops of her breasts, a hemline that scooted up her knees an inch a day. It might have been my DSB acting up again, but I'd swear her perfume took on a distinct sexual essence--like she had discovered the genetic pheromones that drove me crazy.

When in Wanda's office, I kept my lascivious thoughts to myself. Instead, I stood behind her and watched while she gainfully worked at solving my 'other' problem. Computer hackers like Wanda hated unsolved mysteries, and it showed in the way she attacked her keyboard. In a week's time, she cross-checked every imaginable patient variable: city of birth, current address, all medical illnesses. The only link we had was that all fifteen dead patients were Jewish, and considering the number of Jews coming to Richard Meese, it seemed like nothing more than a predictable coincidence.

Late one afternoon, my eyes bloodshot and my body soaked with fatigue from the previous call night, I entered Wanda's office. She lifted her head full of black curls, exposing dewy eyes and a full mouth dressed in lipstick that fluoresced pink under the overhead light. Her blouse was buttoned halfway down, the bottom tied in a loose knot. She swiveled back in her chair and a shadow of forbidden darkness greeted me as she uncrossed her legs. Her office was joined to the next by a large window whose gray shutters lay open.

"Any progress?" I asked, moving close enough to waft under Chanel number something or other. She had called an hour earlier, rousing me from a precious impromptu ten minute nap.

"Shut the shades," she whispered, turning back to her computer. "My colleagues have been asking questions. I don't want the whole world to know I'm chasing down a conspiracy for a paranoid intern." She lowered her glasses, and put her hand on my wrist. "I ran into Alex today."

"I told you to...."

"Never mind, Danny. That's all over between us. In fact, Alex and I talked mostly about you." She kept her lips puckered at the end of the sentence. "He told me about your dreaded semen backup syndrome."

I felt myself flush. "Alex should mind his own damn business," I said. "For all he knows I have a different lover for each night of the week." I cleared my throat. "I have friends," I added.

Wanda's eyes glowed like the neon sign on a motel.

"I thought we had some business to attend to?" I said, trying to change the subject.

"We do." Her face was red. Probably felt like I had slapped it. As accurate as she was about the state of my sexual hormones, the noticeable increase in my heart beat told me I'd better be careful. If I were ever going to have sex with Wanda, it couldn't be here, and not now. We needed to talk first. She needed to know where I was coming from.

Wanda pulled up her on-screen menu and typed in her password. In seconds, a large spreadsheet appeared. I looked over her shoulder as we read the summary, the scent of cologne drawing me to her slightly angled cleavage, as if an open perfume bottle were nestled between her breasts.

Dammit Raskin, lay off.

"Fifteen patients," she said, looking up and catching my averted eyes. "All had heart attacks, none had a history of heart problems. Two were patients of Dr. Emile Horner. All the rest had different doctors."

"Until I came along."

"Alex said that fifteen of fifteen being Jewish is too much to be a coincidence."

I wanted to ask her what the hell she was doing talking to Alex about this stuff. I'd thought it was just between the two of us. Besides, I felt a congestion in my lower abdomen as I glanced at the desk. "Maybe he's right, Wanda. "

"Look here," she said. "Only thirty five percent of patients admitted over the past three years were Jewish."

"Hmm." I'd thought it might have been more. Wanda double checked her figures.

"Don't forget," she said. "Shiksas like me prefer Jewish doctors. And think of all the black patients who rely on this hospital for their health care. You know what the chance is that fifteen dead patients who were all Jewish was just a coincidence?"

I shook my head.

"Over ten thousand to one against."

I swallowed hard. So I had to face it. Jewish patients were being murdered. "What do we do now?"

"What do you mean, 'we'? This is your thing. It's gone a little too far for me."

"Wanda, come on."

Wanda stood and ran her hand against the shades, cutting off the light that escaped from the next room. "Somebody followed me out to the parking lot yesterday."

"Wanda, don't you think you're making something ...."

"I'm not kidding. Never saw the guy before. You may like the sound a baseball bat makes as it cracks into your head. I don't."

Perhaps Wanda was being a bit overly dramatic about this, but if she really was in some sort of danger, it was my fault. And if something ever happened to her...I couldn't finish the thought. I stood up. "We'd better not pursue this any farther, Wanda. You've been a great help. I think I can take it from here."

Wanda grabbed my hand and pulled me back into my seat. "I didn't know there were any gallant men left in this world."

"It has nothing to do with gallantry, Wanda. I just don't want anyone taking any chances on my account."

Wanda shrugged. Maybe I was letting my imagination get the best of me."

"I don't know, Wanda. We should really play this thing safe."

"Let's at least finish what we started, shall we? Where were we?"

I took a breath. "We were trying to find out if there were anything particular about those Jewish patients who were killed."

"All right," she said turning back to me, her skirt hiked twelve inches above her knee. "I'll run a correlation analysis between those fifteen patients and an aged-matched group of other Jewish patients admitted to the hospital over the same time period. But that's it. The rest is up to you. Why don't you see what you can find in the library? Tackle that poison angle. If you ask me, you've got a lot better chance of getting something concrete there."

Wanda swiveled back to her computer, but then appeared to be lost in thought. "You owe me, you know," she beamed and looked me in the eye.

"What do you mean?"

She smiled. "You should know exactly what I mean, Mr. 'dreaded semen backup' king."

I had too much at stake to play games with Wanda. I could hardly afford to lose her valuable assistance and our developing friendship. Then again, I could feel my brain inching its way from inside my head down toward my crotch.

"We should talk about this."

"About what?"

"You know." I couldn't get the words out. My face burned and I felt the tightening of my pants over a developing trouser trout.

"Look Danny, I'm not asking you to marry me. And with your help I learned a lot about myself. I've called a moratorium on boyfriends for awhile. And you've been...well..so nice..and..."

Damn, did she have to look at my crotch?

"Attentive, shall we say." Wanda smiled. Her pupils were a solar system begging for exploration.

"Want to see me disprove the idea that computer hacks are nerds?" Before I could answer, she moved to the desk and with one long stroke of her arm, swept the array of folders, desk accessories and two coffee cups crashing off the table. Through the slits in the shades I thought I could see the outlines of heads turning. Wanda stood before me and removed a barrette from her hair. She then sat on the table, not even noticing that her skirt was hiked up one stop short of never-never land.

"Come here," she said, as if she wouldn't take no for an answer. She grabbed me by the lapels of my coat.

"Take this off."

I obeyed. She loosened my tie, then began unbuttoning my shirt.

"Wanda..."

She nibbled on my ear. "If you're hungry, how about we go to dinner, you know, have a real date?"

Wanda pulled me close and anchored her lips onto mine. Her tongue pulsated to the back of my throat. She smelled of tuna fish and Binaca. I wanted to push away, but slowly my mouth relaxed, tranquilized by the rhythmic movements of her kisses. Wanda's hand went toward my belt. "What's wrong with here on this desk?"

Somehow the thought of having intercourse on a hard desk with the peanut gallery so close struck me as a little risky. "Look, Wanda, how about we go across the street to my place. I could fix up some Ragu and..."

"Why wait?" she whispered, unbuttoning her blouse and unhooking the clasp in the front of her bra. Her breasts seemed to float out, settling two inches from my face. Wanda's hand was on my head pulling my lips to her body. "Let's start with appetizers."

Chapter 41 sex

It was two days before I could walk normally again. My whirl with Wanda had netted me grapefruit sized bruises on both knees, a slalom course of scratch marks on my back, and two hips that made me feel like an arthritic eighty year old.

All things being equal, it was a small price to pay. Just as Alex had said, a fog had miraculously lifted from my body. I could think more clearly, felt more energy, was less nervous. I was human again.

At first I worried about telling Alex what happened, but it turned out he not only knew its most intimate details but actually had encouraged Wanda to make the first move.

"Had a bet, Danny, boy. Ten bucks with Picolli said you'd get it on right there on her desk. Had to make double sure I didn't lose this time."

Alex was at it again, making bets with everyone, and on the most trivial things. How many admissions you'd get on your call night, or what your patient's potassium level would come back at. But this was my love life we were talking about.

"You shouldn't have interfered, Alex. What happened between Wanda and me is personal."

Alex munched on a glazed donut and shrugged. "For Christ's sake, it's just pussy, Danny. Pussy for us and dick-meat for her. Plain and simple."

Alex's attitude bothered me. But that was Alex, everything in his world seemed temporary, a one act play full of climaxes and quick highs. After hearing I had been set up, I wondered whether Wanda felt the same way Alex did. Had she taken me on the desk because Alex wanted her to, perhaps as a perverted way of enticing him back into her life? Or had her own hurt feelings driven her to sex for sex's sake, making me just another notch on her desktop mattress? Her orgasm had been a loud chorus of high pitched yelps, mixed in with guttural raspy incantations that almost made her seem possessed. As for myself, I'd kept some semblance of control; it felt like half the hospital was just out of ear-shot in the next room. Nonetheless the release was cleansing, so much so that at the end, Wanda dutifully removed my condom and held it up to the light. "Alex was right," she said proudly, "you did have DSB to the max. There's enough here to fertilize a third world country."

Chapter 42 an ally

Two days later, at two in the morning, I was down in the ER doing what I hated more than practically anything else. I had the unenviable job of disimpacting one of Dr. Horner's nursing home patients, a ninety-eight year old woman whose last bowel movement had occurred shortly before the start of the Korean War. She screamed every time my finger bulldozed its way back into her rectal vault. Above her screams I could hear snickers coming from Mulroney and his pals camped in the hallway outside her door. During one change of gloves I opened the door and glared.

"Unpacking the fudge truck, huh doc?" Mulroney said, raising his hand to lead his band of uniformed cheerleaders in a high-pitched chorus of screams uncannily similar to the woman's.

Two hours and eight pounds of waste later, I headed to the lounge, tired, frustrated, and in no mood to take a ribbing from Mulroney.

Sedated by a bowl full of brown-sugar custard, Mulroney was repentant. "No offense, doc. They couldn't pay me all the money in the world to do that. If you ask me, they should have just left the poor woman in the nursing home. Let the flies take care of it."

This was the night I planned on taking a look around the medical library, but seeing as the coffee was providing little in the way of stimulation at three in the morning, I decided to forget it. Why waste an opportunity for sleep just to follow up on one of Eddie Ingraham's cock-a-maimie ideas? I set my cup down and walked out. Mulroney jumped up and followed me to the stairs.

"Slow down, Danny. I want to show you something."

I kept walking. I was tired of Mulroney. Tired of a lot of things.

Mulroney pulled out a pouch of chewing tobacco and then a piece of folded newspaper. "Probably don't get time to read the Tribune much, huh?"

"Mulroney, World War III could be going on and I'd be the last to know." Mulroney unfolded his paper and handed it to me. My pupil size doubled as I read.

Arbor Hills, Mich.

The mystery surrounding the death of Charles Cantrell, former Dean of Arbor Hills Medical School, took an unexpected turn yesterday when authorities reported that James Bramwell, Dean of Columbia Medical, was found dead in his Central Park flat. While the victim apparently suffered a heart attack, police report evidence of a scuffle, and say that some personal files may have been taken. Drs. Cantrell • and Bramwell were classmates at Yale Medical School, class of '60, and unnamed sources reveal that both had ties to an ultra right-wing extremist group known as Friends of Tomorrow....

I stood in the hallway outside the ER, my body numb, trying to register what I'd read. Was this another coincidence, or was it proof that Cantrell was involved in something more serious than I had imagined? He and Bramwell--classmates at Yale, 1960. Friends of Tomorrow. Who else were they friends with? Friends of Tannenbaum? Friends of Goldman? *'We want that file,'* Tannenbaum had said. So did the guy who clubbed me at the lake. How badly did they want it? Enough to slit the throat of Randy Jordan? Or kill my patients?

"You okay?"

I looked up, dazed. "Dammit, Mulroney. That fucker, Sol Goldman, is behind this."

Mulroney's eyebrows rose. Goldman was covering something up, I was sure of it. I remembered back to our first meeting--the disparaging way he looked at me when he spoke of how I had gotten Cantrell fired. Goldman went to Yale, didn't he? Said he had run across him from time to time. Was it possible he knew him better than that? A lot better?

Mulroney shrugged. "That might explain the man from the medical board he was with last week. The one who wanted you terminated."

"He didn't know an artery from a vein, Mulroney. He was no doctor."

Mulroney smiled. "Not bad for a rookie, Danny. That man used to be a cop. Jack Hodges."

"You know him?"

"Same precinct for six years. He worked his way up in another, shall we say, more prestigious organization." Mulroney picked tobacco from his teeth. "Ever hear of the Federal Bureau of Investigation?"

I felt the walls closing in, my windpipe constricting. "Does Goldman know?"

Mulroney shook his head. "If your boss is involved in something he shouldn't be, then believe me, he doesn't know. Hodges is a pro."

"You mean the Feds know about this? About Goldman?"

"Be my guess."

An ally, I thought. I finally have an ally.

Chapter 43 the library

The notion that someone else was watching Goldman infused me with a bolus of energy and sent me scampering toward the medical library, where in five minute's time I was tapping on the window of the security office, requesting the key from the sleepy security guard. He rubbed his eyes and looked at his watch, then at me. Just another crazy intern.

I walked down the steps and out the front door of the hospital. Except for the distant sound of the big rigs on the Dan Ryan Expressway, a chilling stillness filled the air. What the hell was I doing going to the library at this hour? Especially on the suggestion of my lunatic patient, Eddie Ingraham.

I unlocked the door and stepped into the darkness, where I fumbled blindly for the light switch. The fluorescent bulbs buzzed overhead. My pulse refused to slow.

The Richard Meese library was steeped in the grandiose tradition of other University archives. Thick, hand-carved oak book shelves built just after World War II rose high up into the vaulted ceilings, sprawling over a room as large as a movie theater. I could hear my own heart as I headed toward the journal rack and I felt as if I were breathing through an atherosclerotic snorkel. I sensed I was being watched, though I knew that was impossible considering the hour and that I had the only key. I felt for my beeper, normally an albatross, now a guardian, even though it would be no help if I encountered trouble. If only I could dial out on the thing. I couldn't of course, and left it next to my stethoscope, which hung loosely in the side pocket of my coat.

I began by perusing those journals which might in some way relate to poisons or to myocardial infarctions. I scanned dozens over the next forty-five minutes, until my vision blurred and my mind drew blanks. The caffeine had crept out of my brain and was now swimming laps in my bladder. I removed my white coat. My scrub top was damp, my armpits sticky. I guess I'd seen too many TV shows, read too many mysteries, I thought, replacing the last journal. It worked for guys like Columbo, slithering around in the middle of the night, always coming up with answers. All I had were paper cuts and the beginnings of a cold. What the hell was Eddie Ingraham talking about? *"There are clues in the library."* What clues? How the hell would he know?

In a final effort to salvage the mission, I sniffed my way over to the current textbook section, removing the most recent edition of the textbook, *Toxicology.* Might as well take it home, I thought. I filled out the withdrawal slip, then located the alphabetized deposit box. Pangs of envy shot through me as I realized some people actually had time to read around here. Maybe next year, when as a resident, I would be less burdened and could catch up on all I had missed.

I thumbed through the stack of slips as if I were shuffling a deck of cards, stopping at the name Malcolm Spool. He had signed out three infectious disease journals, one pathology textbook, and two monographs dealing with something I couldn't pronounce but ended in the letters 'ptyxlyth'. He found the time to read. All he did was read. Of course his patients weren't being killed, at least not by anything other than his offensive bedside manner.

I yawned. I stuck my finger in the cards and flipped them opened again, hoping to find the R's. Instead, I was still in the S's.

There it was. "Goldman, Sol." Why had he filed his card under 'S' and not 'G'? I lifted the card from the box. American Journal of Obstetrics and Gynecology, Volume 43, issues number two and three. Signed out yesterday.

It was half past four in the morning. Anybody with a brain and a full complement of chromosomes would have been in bed, and here I was, suspicious of couple of journals my chief had signed out, periodicals that dealt not with poisoning or heart disease, but with babies and pelvic exams. What in God's name was I doing? I walked toward the exit, leaving the cards scattered like bird seed on the table top. This had gone too far. Poisons....murder....It was time to forget the whole damn thing. Let Mulroney worry about it.

As I reached the exit, I felt my pocket for the key. It was gone, back in my white coat, which I had left at the check-out desk. The coat was lying next to Goldman's checkout slip. American Journal of Obstetrics and Gynecology. It seemed strange. On the other hand, he was the chief of Medicine. He needed to keep up on new developments. But OB-Gyn? It didn't make sense. Forget it, I told myself. Still, it couldn't hurt to check out Current Contents, a weekly journal listing of the table of contents of every major medical journal.

It was sitting on the reference table nearby. And for the hell of it, I flipped to the contents of the issue that Goldman had signed out. Sol was an Endocrinologist, and the lead article was a review on endocrine disorders of pregnancy. The rest of the contents read like Obstetrical hieroglyphics and my eyes began to glaze. Then something at the bottom of the page caught my eye. It was starred in ink.

"Brief report: a fatal myocardial infarction due to postpartum injection of Ergonovine Maleate."

I rubbed my eyes, wondering if I was imagining things. I refocused. Ergonovine maleate. I remembered little about ergonovine, just that it was occasionally used in cases of postpartum hemorrhage. Back to the front desk I pulled out Goldman's card. The other issue of the journal he'd checked out was from the previous month. I dug out that issue of Current Contents, turned to the journal and lasered through the contents until they exploded before me.

"A report of two deaths at Columbia Medical Center resulting from inadvertent administration of intravenous ergonovine Maleate."

I thought back to Mulroney's newspaper clipping. The friend of Cantrell's, Bramwell, the one who'd died under mysterious circumstances, was currently Dean at.... the words rocked me. "Columbia Medical."

A loud clang suddenly echoed to my right. I was enveloped in darkness. Don't panic. You know where the exit is. Power failures happen all the time. Footsteps--near the door. I swaggered, then backed up, bumping into a table. Pain shot through my hip. Closer now. Heavy, like at the swimming pool and-- Oh God--the lake. Icicles of fear plunged into my body. *Keep moving, Raskin, keep moving.* Closer. *Got to get out. Faster, Raskin, faster.* Oh my God, a figure nearby. Can't scream. Can't breathe. Felt something under my hands. Lights? No--too far away. A box--a bar. I pulled the bar down with all the strength I had left. A loud, shrieking alarm filled the room.

Chapter 44 over due

I slept through two wakeup calls the following morning, and by the time Gail pounded on my call room door, it was too late to prepare for morning rounds. Not only that, but as I walked toward my the nursing station, I noticed my stethoscope was missing. I retraced my steps to the call room, and not finding it there, ran down to the E.R. No one had seen my stethoscope. I ran outside, crossed the street and checked the library. Not there, either. A stethoscope is more than a mere object; the two of you grew up together. It was alive; it helped you learn how to listen to hearts; it cooed when you rewarded it with a caress, like patting a horse on its mane. It took a sloppy intern to lose his stethoscope.

After morning rounds, I apologized to Bruce for not being prepared. There were things on my mind, most notably, Wanda Bylevin. I had to tell her what I'd discovered in the library. She needed to know that in large quantities, ergonovine caused heart attacks and that Sol Goldman might just be the world's expert on the subject.

I ambled over to Kaufman Pavilion, the administrative wing of the hospital where Wanda's office was located. I relaxed when the elevator door closed. It would be okay, I thought. Everything would work out. The elevator opened on three. Sol Goldman stood there, ready to enter. I tried jumping out. We bumped hard. The door closed.

"What brings you to Admin?" he asked.

"Picking up an old chart," I said with measured steadiness. I amazed myself at how quickly I could lie if the situation arose. "Eddie Ingraham. Munchausen with a necrotic appendix."

Goldman nodded. "More rotten than the state of Denmark."

I moved toward the exit, Sol's arm came down like a railroad crossing.

"Where's your stethoscope, doctor?"

With every ounce of restraint I could muster I gave a nonchalant shrug. "Lost it last night."

"Where?" His eyes were armor piercing lasers.

I went with a hunch. "The library."

"Go get it."

"Can't."

"Why not?"

"Somebody checked it out."

Goldman stepped back, fingering his coat buttons. "What were you doing in the library at night?" His voice was even, his face devoid of rage. I lurched out. The door began to close.

"Catching up on Obstetrics," I yelled just as the door closed behind me. I saw it though. A slight twitch in his eyes.

I graphically relayed to Wanda the events of the night before, and when I saw my own fright mirrored in her eyes, I thought I might break down and cry. Wanda planted my head on her shoulder. Two minutes passed, with Wanda lightly rubbing my temples with her fingertips. Finally she lifted my head. Wanda would know what to say.

"Let's make love,"she said.

"Huh?"

"I mean it, right here, right now."

I wondered if this sort of come on was second nature for Wanda. She had, after all, been used to doctors coming to her office with adrenalin levels high enough to trigger her own meltdown. On the other hand it might be that she was still trying to regain the sense of self that had been inadvertently trampled on by Alex. Then again, Alex might have put her up to this a second time.

"You and Alex have some sort of deal, going, Wanda? He makes a bet, you help him collect?"

Wanda smiled, then tightened the bun holding her hair and logged onto the computer. "Can you at least rub my shoulders then?" she asked, typing in her password. "I've put in a lot of overtime at this terminal on your behalf." I agreed and pressed my fingertips into the soft flesh above her collarbone. Wanda typed. "Sorry if I put you off."

"It's okay," I replied softly, her perfume taking the fast track from my nose to my pelvic anatomy. "We have to find those toxicology reports, that is if they still exist."

Wanda continued typing. I looked over her sloping shoulders, high at the collar bone, the fleshy tops of her breasts swan-diving into her laced bra. *Forget it, Raskin, forget it. Not here, not now.* Besides, my knees and hips still hurt from the week before.

After a minute she said: "That's strange. Someone is interested in those same reports." She pounded the keyboard. "How the hell...?"

"What?"

A moment later she slammed her fist on the desk. "That's impossible. Somebody stole my security code. Someone broke into my file."

"Who?"

Wanda's fingers tapped nervously. "How should I know? This is the first time it ever happened." Her breaths became long and deep. "I've been fucking violated." She turned around, her face radiating heat, eyes beginning to swell with tears. "This is computer rape."

I put my hands on her shoulders. "It'll be okay, Wanda."

Wanda sniffed, then kept a fixed gaze on me while she undid a third and fourth button on her blouse. She placed her warm hands on mine, and guided them over her cupped breasts. "I hate being violated," she sniveled, pulling me along side her and then sliding her right hand along her upper thigh, anchoring at the top of her nylons. After that there was naked soft flesh. "I really hate it," she repeated, licking her upper lip.

"Wanda, we get on that desk again and the whole office will see."

Wanda's hands went to my trousers and before I knew it, my zipper was down. She pulled me by my manhood down to the floor.

"I hate being violated," she said, exploding in moans. "Hate it!"

Neither of us lasted very long, which was for the best, since the whole damn programming office seemed to be in the vicinity. You could have sold tickets. After I tucked in my shirt, Wanda promised to work on the reports, as well as finding anything else that might tie those fifteen Jewish patients together.

As I walked back to the ward I began to think about what Wanda had said about being followed to her car. Though I hadn't paid much attention at the time, I now had reason to be worried. Someone was watching her. They knew her security code, they knew what kind of car she drove. And worst of all, they had access to the same information we did, knew that we were onto something. If it was the FBI, fine. But what if it wasn't? What if it was someone else, a person or an organization who would do anything to keep us from locating some potentially very damaging information?

Chapter 45 maxine

After work the following day, I joined Brian Picolli and Alex Rosen at Mr. Gee's bar across the street from the hospital. We were sitting in a corner booth finishing off a second pitcher of Guiness, which tasted as smooth as the cold mug of A & W root beer I used to guzzle on sunny days at the beach. I was bragging about Maxine Chu, who had yet to ask for pain or nausea medication since coming into the hospital. No matter how hard I pushed, she would tease: "I'm just your run-of-the-mill perfect patient."

Brian wiped his foam mustache with his tied-dyed sleeve and turned to me with a curt, "Don't flatter yourself, dude."

"I wasn't trying to," I replied. "She's just a great kid. The perfect patient."

Without looking up, Brian said: "How would you know? You've hardly talked to her."

What the hell was he getting at? I'd visited Maxine every day since her admission, sometimes twice. Sure, we didn't have long, involved tear-jerking conversations like we'd had the first time she came into the hospital--but then Maxine no longer needed that kind of counseling. She rarely had any questions, sometimes barely lifting her eyes from the magazine she was reading when I came into her room.

The beer tasted warmer. I looked up. Brian and Alex were conversing with their eyes. Mine were beginning to twitch.

"My patients aren't any of your business, Picolli."

Brian shifted in his seat. "Okay, Danny. Forget the whole thing."

"What whole thing?"

"Never mind, dude."

"Never mind what?"

"Tell him, Brian," urged Alex.

"Tell me what?" Brian looked at Alex. He grabbed the third pitcher and chugged directly from it. When he was finished he let out a loud belch. "Did you ever stop to think that maybe this perfect patient of yours is not so perfect?" Before I could

222

respond, he continued. "Did you ever consider that maybe, just maybe, little Maxine doesn't want to disappoint you?"

"What?"

"Maybe she doesn't want to ruin your image of her, dude."

"Maybe she's not feeling as well as you thought," added Alex.

"Maxine would have told me," I argued. "Besides, if she were feeling sick, she'd be asking for the medication I ordered."

"What if those drugs don't work?"

"She would have told me. I'm her doctor."

"No," said Brian, straightening up. "You're a professional dickweed. Max only wants you to think she doesn't need it. She doesn't want to bother you. Same with her boyfriend, Po."

"That's Lo."

"That is low, dude," said Brian. Let me tell you what happened a few nights ago. Around midnight I was checking on another patient when I hear this retching noise followed by sobbing. I go in and find Max sitting on the bathroom floor, little body hunched over, praying to the porcelain god."

"Huh?"

"Barfing, my friend. She was so white she looked like friggin Casper the ghost! Her wig was laying on the floor next to her. She looked about ninety years old."

"She never told me, Brian."

"Hear me out."

I poured another glass of beer. It tasted viscous, like motor oil.

Brian continued. "I put my arms around Dame Maxine and I say: 'Yo, Max, that's cool. Purging oneself brings balance to the soul. Why don't I order some Compazine for you?'" Brian refilled his glass. "She said it didn't work. Then these bodacious tears start rolling down her face--you could surf on those tears. She says nothing has helped so I ask her: 'How long has this been going on? Dr. Danny boy said things were great.'"

I bit down hard. My knees were locked together in tetanic spasm.

223

Brian continued. "Before she could argue, a giant retch surfaced, and just like before, she bent over for a conversation with the big white phone."

I lowered my eyes. "How long has this been going on?"

"Start of chemo."

"Every day?"

"You could set your watch by it," said Alex. "She told Picolli she didn't want you to think badly of her."

"For Christ's sake, the last thing in the world I would have done is to think badly of her!"

Alex shook his head. "As unintentional as it was, you held up some lofty expectations."

I unglued my knees and stretched. "She believes in me, guys. She's convinced I'm going to cure her."

"Exactly my point," said Brian. "She wouldn't dare burden a relationship with such profound implications."

For the next few minutes, I nursed my beer in silence. Finally I spoke. "Did you give her any medicine?"

No answer. A shrug from Brian. A look from Alex, who then said: "You better tell him."

"Tell me what?"

Picolli said, "I gave her some medicine, dude. Just not the kind one routinely finds in the hospital pharmacy."

"What medicine, Picolli?" I snapped.

"Relax Kimosabe. Maxine didn't want anything on the formulary."

"Why not?"

"Because, my well-meaning student of Hippocrates, she had already tried everything there was. "

"Benadryl?"

"Check."

"Phenergan?"

"Like I said, dude, there was nothing around that could stop Maxine from tossing her fortune cookies."

"Wait a minute, Picolli," I said with some measure of authority. "You got it wrong. Maxine never asks for medicine."

"When you're around, dickweed, she's a friggin Emily Post."

224

"My God."

"When you weren't on call," continued Brian, "we tried them all. Just didn't put it down on the order sheets."

"Why didn't you guys tell me?"

Brian crossed his chest. "She said, 'If you tell Danny, I swear I'll get Dr. Stool to be my doctor.'" Brian laughed. "You taught her that?"

I felt like I'd stepped under a waterfall of Novacaine. I couldn't even lash out at my own stupidity. "What did you give her?"

"Well," said Brian. "She was sitting on the floor holding her stomach and sort of rocking back and forth, moaning. So I say: 'You still got a high barf titer?' She smiled a little, nodding. Anyway, she says she'll probably be up all night. So I run and get a wheel chair."

"In the middle of the night?"

Alex signaled me to relax.

"I load her in, cover her with a blanket, tell her to keep quiet and all, seeing as the nurses might not take kindly to our leave of absence."

"Where were you taking her?"

"To a pharmacy of sorts."

"The nurses didn't see you?"

"Said I was taking her to x-ray."

"Where did you take her?"

"Escort service. Sort of a 24 hour Rastafarian pharmacy."

"Picolli, what the hell are you talking about?"

Brian took a breath. "Ganja, man. Maxine smoked ganja." Brian paused. The ER tunnel--the sight and smells came rushing back like an old girlfriend showing up uninvited to an engagement party.

Brian slapped my shoulder. "I wheel Max over to Jimmi and his friends. 'Jimmi,' I say. 'This here is Senorita Max. She has a bad case of technicolor yawns.' Jimmi's only an escort dude, but when it comes to matters concerning the healing properties of Jamaican ganja, he's practically Albert Schweitzer. He comes up to Maxine, lifts her frail little chicken neck with his hands, pulls her eye-lids down, then takes her pulse. Then he says: 'Blowin' grits, young lady?'"

"Maxine must have been petrified."

"Au contraire," said Brian, smiling. "She sort of lifts up her chin and says: 'Cancer, Jimmi dude. Think your ganja will help?'"

Brian relayed how Jimmi brought out a fishing tackle box, displaying several compartments, each containing a different vial. "I thought I'd died and gone to heaven," said Brian. "He had grass for nausea, grass for sex, grass for about anything." He paused momentarily. "He even had a type that you fish with."

"As bait?"

"Hell no. Makes you so high you could care less that you don't catch nothin." Alex snickered.

"Anyway, Jimmi brings out this cigarette the size of a kosher hot dog and says: 'Smoke this, me lady, and you'll never be talking to those toilet fish again.' Maxine had her first good night's sleep in a month."

I leaned back in my seat. "You expect me to believe all this?"

"Relax, Danny."

"No retching?"

"Nada."

"I'll be one dumb son of a bitch."

"You know," said Alex. "The oncology attendings are trying to get the real stuff, THC, on the formulary for just this type of condition. It works. Studies prove it."

"So she goes back every night for her medication?"

"Except when you're on call. She's into it, Danny. You should see her play the bongo drums. Plus I think she's got a thing for Rasta Jimmi. They talk for hours at a time. He tells her all about his life in Jamaica. Asks her a lot of questions, too. He's a tender guy, Danny. You'd really like him."

There wasn't much else to say, and I sat in silence. I had been duped by Maxine.

Finally, as we began emptying our pockets to pay the bill, I spoke up. "I guess I owe her an apology."

"Don't you dare," said Brian. "I promised to keep quiet."

"Besides," added Alex, "Maxine might feel disgraced. That's too much face for an Asian woman to lose."

"Let her be who she needs to be." Brian smiled as he smacked me on the back. "Even if it is a Chinese- Rastafarian pot-head!"

Chapter 46 eddie

Of all the different physician specialties, it's the surgeons who most despise being sued. Death and medical malpractice are the two things that prove their fallibility. Understanding this, Eddie Ingraham made the most of his excised appendix that was never there to begin with. Kidnapping and assault charges were dropped, and he was given carte blanche at the hospital--he could stay as long as he wanted, eat what he wanted, do what he wanted. The only request they refused was a transfer onto the medical service--my service. It was one of those dirty laundry things the surgeons wouldn't go for. Eddie took care of that, too. He injected himself with the biliary secretions of the patient in the next bed, and two days later, when he developed a raging fever and cultures of his blood revealed numerous colonies of three different species of E-coli, he was transferred back to the medicine service. And to me.

I still hadn't figured out why Eddie had urged me to go to the library. Had he known that Sol Goldman had signed out two reports on Ergonovine-induced myocardial infarctions? Or was it something else?

Eddie's spacious room had a large window and a view of the courtyard garden. In one corner was a nineteenth century, mahogany fold away desk. I heard it had been removed from the Chief of Surgery's office at Eddie's request. It was at this desk that Eddie happily spent his days, digesting his way through Grant's Anatomy Atlas, sketching the human body on his drawing board. His impressions were both artistic and accurate.

"You're a man of many talents, Eddie," I remarked one day while checking his antibiotics. "If you ever get over your Munchausen's, you'd have a lot to offer."

"That's why I'm studying to become a doctor," he said, flashing a smile. He was putting the finishing touches on a picture depicting the blood vessels as they coursed through the pelvic triangle. "I do have a lot to offer. By the way, if someone made an incision over this part of the pelvic area, would they bleed to death?"

228

I remembered Eddie's interest in casting himself as a cadaver in the upcoming anatomy class. "Forget it Eddie. You're not getting any more medical information out of me. Stick to your art. You're damn good at art."

"You ought to see me in the chemistry lab."

"If concentrating a syringe full of Mr. Hildebrand's biliary secretions counts as chemistry, I'd say you were fairly adept."

Eddie smiled. "In chemistry you have to be precise. For instance, when I borrowed some secretions from my neighbor the other day, I first had to calculate the exact number of bacteria I would need to cause a moderate state of sepsis." His thin, sparse eyebrows rose. "Too much and I would have died."

"Where'd you do this?"

"Down in the lab," he answered matter-of-factly. As if it was no crime to impersonate a lab tech or doctor in order to gain access to a high-resolution microscope. "Simple case of first order kinetics, dose-response and benefit versus toxic dose-ratios. It works for just about everything."

I paused for a moment and rubbed my eyes. It had been a hard week. It was going to get harder. Gail Peterson was about to take an unscheduled family leave back in Colorado. I agreed to take her call night as well as mine. That meant two nights out of three without sleep. "Tell me Eddie, this first order kinetic stuff...concentrating something....would it work for a drug like Ergonovine?"

Eddie set his red pencil on top of his drawing. "Are you asking what's the proper dose of Ergonovine for pre-term, labor? You must know that."

I forgot that Eddie had recently impersonated an obstetrician. "I'm talking about *other* effects of Ergonovine, Eddie. Like.... if you were to give too much."

Eddie smiled and nodded. "Ah, you're talking about potential cardiac effects."

Why the hell was I doing over Eddie like he were a Nobel prize winner? "I was just wondering whether that drug could cause a heart attack?"

Eddie paused. "In normal quantities, impossible."

"How much would it take?"

"Probably a pharmacy's entire stock. We're talking at least 100 cc's"

That would take five large syringes. I couldn't imagine someone taking the time to inject five syringes worth of Ergonovine into somebody's IV. And what about the small vial I found under Mrs. Garber's bed? That held five cc's at most. "Guess it would be impossible."

"Unless..."

"Unless what?"

"You manufactured a highly concentrated version." Eddie thought a moment. "It's a derivative of a common Ergot plant species. A good chemist could pull it off, concentrate the stuff down to its barest ingredients. In that case, I'd guess a couple of cc's might do the trick."

"Could concentrated ergonovine constrict a normal artery enough to cause a heart attack?"

"If you're asking me if someone bumped off your patients with Ergonovine, the answer is no way."

My feet scraped the carpet. "What do you mean?"

"People with heart attacks have a lot of pain. They'd be yelling so loud, they would be sure to attract attention. You can't kill someone that way and get away with it. Ergonovine, by itself would never work." Eddie paused. I continued acting disinterested, though I made no move toward the door.

"If I wanted to kill someone with ergonovine," said Eddie, "I would add a non-depolarizing neuromuscular blocking agent-- something short acting and non-traceable like Pavulon. Knocks out the ability to breathe in a matter of seconds. The patient, in essence, suffocates."

"Untraceable?"

"Unless you leave a little glass vial of it hanging around."

The room was quiet. In the distance, nurses chatted, a gurney wheeled by, Jamaican accents. Eddie smiled at my look of shock. "You mean..."

He nodded. "Told you I was a good chemist."

"Why didn't you tell me?"

Eddie laughed. "I told you, Eddie helps those who help themselves. I take it you went to the library?"

I nodded. So it was true. Mrs. Garber had been murdered, probably the other patients as well.

I suddenly had the feeling I shouldn't be talking to a patient about hospital business. Especially murders. Especially to Eddie. For safety's sake, it was time to revert to the 'usual' doctor-patient relationship. I picked up his flow sheet for the day and recorded the values. I then briefly examined Eddie, telling him he was doing well, and turned to leave.

Eddie cleared his voice. "How many is it now?"

"What?"

"I'd heard fifteen."

I was speechless, stopped by a bolt of lightening. Finally Eddie said: "Give a Munchausen a little credit, will you. I told you I was a computer whiz, twice as good as that friend of yours, Wanda."

"How the hell...?"

"Trade secret," said Eddie.

"Wanda said someone had broken her code."

Eddie wasn't smiling. "I wasn't the only one. Someone else was snooping in her files."

"Who?"

Eddie shrugged. "Whoever it is, you better hope they're on your side."

"What about the toxicology reports? Any ideas where they are?"

"I told you, doc, I'm better than Wanda."

"Well?"

Eddie paused. "I can get them but it will take a few days. There are a lot of programming hoops to jump through."

Eddie dipped into a tattered leather briefcase and pulled out a printout. "I did something better though," he said smiling. "I tapped into the hospital payroll. Three year's worth of every employee's work schedule; days, hours, everything."

"And?"

"I ran a parallel analysis of where the murder victims were located, when they were killed, and who was working those shifts." Eddie paused for effect. "The bad news is that there were over a hundred people working during the three deaths of your patients. Doesn't do us much good. However, for the twelve other patients who were killed before you started internship, only one name popped out." Eddie was obviously pleased with himself.

Why hadn't the Feds come up with that, I asked Eddie. After all, if they'd been onto this thing, surely they would have checked work schedules. "Of course," he beamed. He wasn't on the work schedule during several murders."

"Huh?"

"Worked overtime. Never logged it in the computer."

I couldn't believe it. A suspect, looming at he hospital for three years, murdering innocent patients. "What about my patients? Was he working then?"

Eddie shook his head. "He split the year before you started internship."

"Do the Feds know?"

Eddie nodded. "Didn't figure out until he was long gone, though."

"What is his name?"

"What's the difference? You'll never see him again."

"I still want to know."

Eddie balked. "Trade it to you."

"For what?"

"I need some information."

"On what?"

"I want to know the exact time and place the next anatomy class starts over at the medical school."

"We've been through this, Eddie. You can't impersonate a medical student."

"I'm not interested in impersonating a medical student."

It was one thing to have your appendix out with practically no anesthesia, watching as masked strangers explored your belly. But lying on the table, letting students cut out pieces of your anatomy, dissect you down to the bone? Even Eddie wouldn't go through that. It was not humanly possible. "Okay, Eddie. I'll get you the dates tomorrow. Now, the name."

Eddie smiled.

"Thaddeus Anderson."

Chapter 47 women

I was running when I nearly crashed into a patient food cart coming around the corner of Kaufman Pavilion. I didn't care. I had to tell Wanda Bylevin about Thaddeus Anderson. I passed a few interns who asked whether there was a code blue in progress. Thaddeus Anderson was a code blue of sorts. Was he really the one who killed those patients? And if so, where did he go? Did someone find out about him? Is that why he suddenly disappeared the year before I came to Richard Meese? My breath quickened. There hadn't been any killings for a year. Then they started again. Was he back, disguised as somebody else?

Wanda Bylevin's office was locked. I went next door, where a few of her colleagues snickered when they recognized my voice. Wanda had called in sick, they said. I asked for her phone number and every eyebrow in the place lifted.

"Can't even go a day without it," someone said. They told me her number was unlisted and I decided not to press the issue. I'd see her tomorrow. Besides, I had enough to keep me busy. With new resolve, I planned on spending every free moment going through those fifteen charts all over again. If there was any thread that wove those fifteen patients together, I was going to find it. I would present it to Wanda tomorrow along with the name, Thaddeus Anderson.

Wanda would help me. She was smart, cared about her job, seemed to like me, at least physically. But desktop sex for the rest of my life? I'd be in a wheel chair before fifty. On the other hand I was lonely as hell, and even though it was sex for sex's sake, it was better than nothing. Short term, anyway. Long term, though, not a chance. For as good a soul as Wanda had, she could never be my soul mate. Near as I could tell, I never sensed what it took to feel that close to one person. That is until Gail Peterson.

Chapter 48 gail

Three times in a two week period Gail Peterson had been called into Sol Goldman's office and chewed out for disobeying a direct order from a superior. Each time, Gail's response: "I was doing what was best for the patient."

Gloomily, she replayed the latest incident over an afternoon soda in the Deli bar. She had refused an order to push a toxic chemo regimen into a terminally ill eighty two year old man with lung cancer metastatic to every bone in his body. When the oncology attending went to push the stuff himself, Gail put herself between him and the patient, refusing to budge. Once he left, she disconnected the patient's IV. "He was in pain, Danny. He needed morphine, not some worthless poison that would've had him throwing up until he died."

"But was it necessary to shove the chemo syringe in the attending's face and threaten to inject him with it?"

"They're bastards, Danny. You come here with ideals, just simple, basic ones, like doing what's right, and look what happens. People don't give a shit. Either that or there's some other agenda like making as much money as they can."

Gail was right about that. Patients were kept in the hospital longer than necessary by attendings who served to profit by their visits and expensive tests.

"Even the interns are shits," said Gail. "We're supposed to be the new breed. But except for you, Alex, and Picolli, it's unbelievable." She asked if I ever saw Malcolm Spool give a patient a comforting pat on the arm or a word of encouragement. With Malcolm, it was all textbook--diagnosis, treatment, and prognosis, delivered in a caustic style that sent patients teary eyed into their pillows.

"At least the guy's got something on the ball. You can't deny he's an unbelievable diagnostician."

"I would have decked him."

Gail sniffed, then exhaled. "That's what I'm talking about, Danny. I just don't know how long I can take this."

My body tensed. "What do you mean?"

Before she could answer, her beeper sounded. Gail rose to go. "Thanks, Danny. If everyone treated their patients the way you treated Maxine Chu, the world would be a lot better off."

She walked away, then stopped and turned. "And thanks a lot for covering for me while I'm gone. I'll make it up to you."

I sat by myself for a moment, thinking about Gail. I wondered what exactly that 'family emergency' was that had her scurrying home to Colorado, leaving me to take an extra night of call for her. Maybe she really couldn't take it anymore. Maybe she was going home for good. Gail, I decided, was simply too good and too compassionate to be happy in a setting where misery and apathy was the order of the day. Her expectations being so high, she couldn't cope with the fact that not everyone carried the same dedication she did. She needed to learn to accept those things she couldn't change, and just get through the remainder of the year with her sanity intact. *"I just don't know how long I can take this."* Considering how standoffish she'd been all week, I was worried as hell. Several times I found her staring into space, eyes bloodshot and vacant. Allergies, she said, but I wasn't so sure. I told myself I had better spend more time with Gail. She needed someone to talk to and I had to be there for her.

The elevator doors opened on 4 Beyer House. I took a breath. Someone else I had to be there for. Someone I already had let down.

Chapter 49 confronting maxine

Maxine's eyes had held a subversive, far off stare for the past few days. Maybe she knew I'd talked to Brian Picolli. Maybe she sensed my own trepidation at confronting her, admitting that she was something less than perfect. What a dolt I'd been.

I took a cleansing breath of sterile hospital air as I headed toward her room. Nurses with medication carts passed by. Lunch trays were already on the floor; their smell reminded me of junior high cafeteria days. Tact, I told myself. The key here was tact.

I paused outside her door, tucking in my scrub shirt. Maybe I could ask her how she's feeling, then hint about some not yet legal anti-nausea medications. She'd take it from there.

Maxine's door was closed. Okay, Raskin, remember; let her express herself. Don't accuse her. And don't let on that you know about Rastafarian Jimmi. I dabbed my forehead and walked in.

Maxine was seated in bed, painting her fingernails a fluorescent purple. My jaw tightened. My heart kicked. *Keep cool, Danny.*

"Hello, Danny."

"Hey, Max." I stood frozen. "Smoking any pot lately?"

Oh shit.

Maxine recovered first. "Matter of fact, got big plans tonight. Just as soon as you go home."

I couldn't find any words for several minutes. Maxine's IV machine began beeping, so I fiddled with the tubing, flushing saline through the access port. Maxine continued with her nails.

Finally I coughed the frog out of my throat. "You could have told me, Max." Maxine was fanning her nails. The odor of mashed potatoes wafted down the hall. "Marijuana is no big thing; practically lived on it in college. I would have understood."

"Would you? I couldn't even tell you I was getting sick every night. How was I going to tell you about that?"

My weight shifted. "What happened to trusting your doctor?"

"What happened to trusting your patient?"

"I guess I had certain expectations that..."

"Expectations!" Maxine shouted. "Every time one of your friends stopped by, they all said the same thing: 'Dr. Raskin is so proud of you. All he ever talks about is how brave you are, how you're always smiling.'" Maxine bit her lip, hoping to stem the flood of tears welling up. "I don't know which made me sicker, those comments or the chemotherapy. You ordered me a big pair of shoes, Danny. I'm only a size six."

I sat on the edge of her bed, my own size ten permanently affixed in my mouth. "Why didn't you tell me, Max?" I waited, but no response. "You're right about the bragging. But there's another side." I took a breath. "You put me in an awkward position from the start. My first month on the wards, I barely know a thermometer from a blood pressure cuff, and all of a sudden I meet someone faced with a life-threatening disease. Before I know it, this beautiful young woman has me promising that I'll cure her. That's a tall order, even for size tens."

Tears dropped onto Maxine's gown. I swallowed back my own anguish. I wanted to hold Maxine and tell her how sorry I was, tell her that if this were a different time and place, it might have been me and not Lo she was spending her time with.

"So you were a little green," Maxine said through a chorus of sniffles. "I'm only twenty two. Look at the rash of shit I've had to deal with. Starting with my father. Do you know that he sent us to America, and that's the last we saw of him? He stayed in China and started a new family."

"Sorry, Max. I didn't know."

"And when I'm ready to go away to college, mom gets multiple sclerosis. Who's left to take care of her? My older sister is married and raising a family out east. So I put everything on hold. Why do you think I've been taking classes at De Paul? My SAT scores were in the ninety ninth percentile. I was a National Merit finalist."

Maxine summarized two years of taking care of her invalid mother nonstop while working to support both of them and trying to take a class or two at the same time. "The last six months of her life were a nightmare, Danny. She was incoherent, incontinent, and required a full-time nurse. When she died... well it was a blessing."

I nodded.

She paused and blew her nose. "Then, just when it becomes my turn to live my life, look what happens! To me!" I reached toward Maxine but she pulled away. "Please, I don't need any of the life isn't fair routine. I just wanted to get better. I needed one person to believe in, someone who could give me the strength to do the things I need to do even if he couldn't cure me. To live my life the best that I possibly can!" She threw her arms into the air. "For better or for worse, Danny, you're that person!" We wrapped our arms around each other, suspended in time, our chests heaving like Olympic hurdlers crossing the finish line. We held each other until my beeper went off. I hastily pulled away and retreated to the nurses' station.

When I returned, Maxine was gazing into the mirror above the sink. Her eyeliner had run part way down her cheeks, and her hairpiece was angled like a French beret. Without looking back, she asked me if I still thought she was attractive. I put my hands to my mouth and blew her a kiss. "Magnifique," I replied. "Tres magnifique, even for a dope smoking, crazed Chinese hippie!"

Maxine smiled. "That's just how Dr. Picolli put it."

"Speaking of illegal substances, does Lo know what you've been doing?"

Maxine laughed. "It would kill the guy."

"I saw him carting enough Chinese food for the Red Army. That's got to be a good sign as far as your appetite goes."

Maxine's eyes darted like sparrows, and she whispered. "I've been bringing the food down to the basement. We get the munchies."

"Maxine!"

"Don't be judgmental. Smoking marijuana is the first thing I've done that's actually improved my appetite."

Unceremoniously, she untied the top of her flowered chemise and let it fall to her waist. "These boobs of mine have just about disappeared," she said, lightly supporting her breasts.

Maxine smiled as she pulled up her gown. "Then again, at least according to Rastafarian Jimmi, anything more than a mouthful is a waste!"

"Maxine!" Suddenly I felt like Lo, a backward Chinese country bumpkin who could do nothing but stand back and watch his dream girl disappear.

"Relax," she said. "Nothing's happened down there, not yet, anyway."

"Yet?"

"I ought to take Lo down there. Get him to smoke that stuff and he'd be in my pants in a minute."

"Max, give it time."

"Easy for you to say. It's a lot of fun down there. I'm even learning some Jamaican music:" Maxine sang: "Get your momma give you a spankin, I got myself the Bridgeport blues, yeah baby." She grinned sheepishly. "Listen, Danny. Jimmi is the sweetest man I've ever met."

I cringed slightly.

"Under those shades and hair, lies a beautiful person. He likes me for me. Hodgkins and all."

I started to say, I like you Maxine, Hodgkins and all, but held back. "Maxine, there can't be any future with a guy like Jimmi."

"Oh yeah?" she grinned. "He's been accepted at Harvard law school. He deferred a year to write poetry and find himself."

"In the dingy basement of a hospital smoking twelve different kinds of pot. I saw those samples in his fishing tackle box, Maxine. Plus some other stuff. I don't even want to guess what that was."

"He says it's good for the soul, Danny. I really wish you wouldn't judge him until you spend time with him."

"You might say we shared a drink together."

"He told me about the vial, Danny. He was only trying to help. Please, Danny. You have to hear his poetry." She picked up a napkin with scribbling on it. "Listen to this:

Un homme je suis
Une jeune fille vous etes.
Un amite nous avons

Un amour peut etre."

I gave her my 'I don't speak French' look.

"A man I am, a woman you are. A friendship we have, a love perhaps."

It was simple, yet beautiful. *Dammit.* "I get the picture, Max. I'll be happy to hang out with this poet of yours. But I still advise you against going to the basement in the middle of the night."

"Tell that to the six other people I'm bringing down there tonight." Maxine saw my surprise. "I'm in a cancer support group, Danny."

"I didn't know."

"We're making our pilgrimage at midnight." Maxine folded her arms triumphantly across her chest. "For the first time in months I've started to feel alive, like there really is some significance to life. A person can only be nauseous so many hours in the day."

"The nausea won't last forever."

Maxine swallowed. "Neither will I."

"You don't need to talk like that."

"There you go again, trying to shelter me from all the evil." Maxine's hands gracefully reached toward the expansive ceiling. "I can always get Malcolm Stool to be my doctor. Now there's a man who tells it like it is. Bet you a dollar, he'd sign me up for an autopsy before I kicked the bucket."

"Please stop."

"Stop what?"

I was a doctor, for godsakes. I shouldn't be so uneasy around the subject of death. Even Maxine Chu's death.

"There's a time and a place to talk about that sort of stuff."

"And when that time comes?"

"When...if it comes...I'll be there, Max. Count on it."

"Good," she said, opening her bedside drawer and pulling out a copy of Rolling Stone magazine.

"Where did you get that?"

"Lot more interesting than Cosmo." She sat back on the bed. "You better get back to work. Hey, I heard you've been banging some computer whiz."

"Who told you that?"

"You know hospitals. Besides, I don't approve. Gail Peterson is much more your type." I felt myself blush. "I bet she's in the same boat as me--needs one of those hot beef injections!" Maxine repeated herself, and still not believing those words came from her mouth, burst into a laugh filled with youth and hope.

"I'm going to call for a Neuro consult. That reefer has caused brain damage. "

"Just make sure they get here before midnight," she said as I closed the door.

Chapter 50 wanda

Wanda Bylevin's colleagues giggled when I appeared in their doorway the following day. I felt myself blush when I saw their eyes scanning my body like a video camera at a bank. Wanda had called in sick two days ago, they said. She had a cold and thought she might as well take some extra time and clean up her apartment. She'd be back tomorrow.

As I turned to leave a tall woman with cranberry hair, twice the usual amount of lipstick, and a cigarette dangling from her lip, tapped me on the shoulder. "Let's check her office," she said. She followed me in. The desk was orderly, her computer untouched as far as I could tell. The files she had printed the other day were not on the desk where I had last seen them. I assumed she had taken them home in her briefcase, since that was also missing. "She called me at home the other night," she said, staring at the table where we had so furiously copulated in broad daylight. "She sounded worried about something. Said you were coming over to talk to her about it."

"Me? We didn't have any plans."

The woman took a slow drag on her cancer stick and looked at my name tag. "It was you all right."

"What night was that?"

"Monday."

"Couldn't have been me. That was the night I took call for Gail Peterson. She had a family emergency I was knee-deep in patients all night long."

"Beats the hell out of me, then," she said. "Do you have her number?" I shook my head. She scribbled something on a piece of paper and handed it to me. "Here, why don't you try to call her?" she said, and disappeared back into the well of pencil pushers and disc drivers.

I tried Wanda at home several times but got no answer. On the way home I stopped at the Medical School bookstore and bought a new stethoscope, hoping that whoever stole mine found good use for it. When I got home, I called Wanda again. Still no answer. Maybe she had flipped out about her access code being violated. Maybe whoever followed her out to the parking lot last week came back and scared the hell out of her. I felt my chest squeeze inward. I called the ER, asking for Officer Mulroney. If I told him everything, he would help. Mulroney was out on assignment so I left a message. To calm my nerves, I threw down one Strohs, then another, and scraped the green mold off the inside of a half-full container of Ragu, and sat down to watch television. Then, over instant coffee, I spread out the fifteen xeroxed medical records on top of the kitchen table. I taped two pieces of logarithmic paper together and labeled the columns across the top: birthplaces, colleges, type of employment, medical diseases, medications, everything I could think of.

The eleven o'clock news was coming on as I closed the last medical record. I sliced away the rotting part of an apple and began studying my chart. One category after another, I read down the list of patients. Nothing tied them together. There weren't even two patients who attended the same college. All had different occupations, most had different diseases. The only similarity was their religion. And how could that be significant considering that so many other patients who were Jewish left the hospital as good as new? As I stared at the endless columns of figures, dates, and medications, it struck me as interesting that many of them were born in Eastern Europe. But then most Jews over sixty had emigrated from Eastern Europe. I thought back to poor Mrs. Dombrowski, the woman who said that putting in her IV was more torture than all of. *Hmm. Treblinka.* I said it aloud. Then again. I opened her chart, going to her initial history and physical. Social history: Auschwitz- 1943-1944. I grabbed another chart. Buchenwald. Then another--Auschwitz. Then Dachau. Right down the line. All eleven patients over sixty years old had been in concentration camps! My breath was short. I dialed Wanda's number again. No answer. I returned to the charts. What did it all mean? And what about the patients born here? Then it hit me. Mrs. Garber. Goldman's words echoed back. *"Her father in the Warsaw ghetto resistance--he escaped from two different camps."*

Concentration camps. The Holocaust. The Nazi rally. Friends of Tomorrow. I looked at my watch. Eleven pm. I dialed Wanda again. Where was she, dammit? She would know what to do with this. Plus, she could help me find Thaddeus Anderson.

My thoughts were interrupted by a loud knock.

"Raskin, you in there?"

It was Mulroney. Thank God. I unlocked the door. "That's what I like Mulroney, answering my phone calls in person."

Mulroney wasn't smiling. With him were two other men in dark sport coats, white shirts unbuttoned at the top.

"These men want to talk to you, Danny."

"Sure, come on in."

"Not here, down at the station."

"What?"

One of the men stepped forward. "Do you know Wanda Marie Bylevin?"

I felt faint. Sensing what was coming, my body shook. "Is she dead?"

"Strangled in her apartment."

The man paused and looked me in the eye. "With your stethoscope."

Chapter 51 innocent

"Danny, answer their questions! These guys mean business."

James Mulroney scooted his chair closer to mine and peered across the table at the two investigating officers, both of whom resembled sharks swimming toward a meal.

One glanced at the other and scratched his chin. "Don't know, James," he said, "but maybe your doctor pal ought to get himself a lawyer. It don't look too good."

Their cigarette smoke filled my eyes and clouded my vision. "Can you please put that damn thing out?" I asked.

"Then you answer our questions," he snapped, blowing smoke out his nose like a raging bull.

Mulroney put his hand in the air. "Ease off, John. My boy is innocent."

"Then why won't he say nothing?"

Truth was, for a while, I couldn't. I was too numb at the realization that Wanda Bylevin was dead, brutally murdered in her own apartment. I was deadened by the officer's description of the crime scene, the way they found her contorted body swinging from the kitchen ceiling fan, her neck at a grotesque angle, tongue swollen, eyes bulging. My stethoscope anchored her neck to the base of the fan. For a while I felt like I was going to puke. Then, after I got my body under control, I tried to tell them my alibi. But nothing came out. I was frozen by the fact that someone had gone to great lengths to pin the whole thing on me.

On the face of it, the evidence was damning. The cops had already interviewed Wanda's colleagues. They knew about our desk-top sex. "You're an animal," one of the officers said.

"In the middle of the work day," another scorned.

I could deal with that. I wasn't about to blame those on Wanda, not now, not ever. The rest, however, was much worse. There was the co-worker of hers who stated she had received a call from Wanda the day of the murder in which she purportedly told her that I was expected over for dinner. That pinned me to the crime scene. When officers arrived after an anonymous phone call, they found a half-filled bottle of Chardonnay on the kitchen table, a jasmine candle burned down to its wick, and a Gloria Estefan disc on the CD player. Two plates of Risotto Milanase sat uneaten at the sink.

One of the officers reached beneath the table top and pulled out a sealed plastic evidence bag. Inside were two Reese's peanut butter cups plus the wrappers from several others. My jaw dropped. He smiled. "Mulroney says these are a favorite of yours." I turned and saw Mulroney's hands cover his face, surely thinking he had been wrong about me the whole time; that I was, in fact, the reincarnation of Ted Bundy or some other serial killer.

I'd had about enough. "Check for prints," I snapped. "You won't find mine anywhere."

The officer with two zits at the base of his chin looked hard, then gave a guttural snicker. "Truth is, you must be pretty good, Raskin. We didn't find any prints anywhere, even on the victim's body. You'd figure you have sex with someone, you ought to leave prints."

Sex? Somebody had sex with Wanda, then killed her? What was left of my heart went into a tailspin. "She must have been raped."

Mulroney asked the cop for an explanation.

"There was no forced entry, at least not according to the medical examiner at the scene. We'll know more later."

Intercourse. Again made to look like it was a set-up. Wanda had more lovers in a given year than anyone could keep track of. Alex had said she usually ended up sleeping with a high percentage of all the unmarried male interns.

"It looks like someone came over with some wine, she cooked dinner, they fucked, and then he strangled her.

"Stop," I yelled. "No way was this a seduction. Somebody purposely murdered Wanda and wanted me to fry for it."

And fry is just what I would have done had it not been for one thing. The murderer overlooked something, though he had no way of knowing it at the time he orchestrated the crime. I couldn't have killed Wanda Bylevin that night at her house because I was at the hospital, on call. The murderer never figured that. He obviously had access to our standard call schedules and didn't know I'd offered to take Gail Peterson's place when she left town.

I looked at Mulroney when I finished explaining. His arms were folded and he was trying to hold in a grin. The two officers, fidgeted, mumbled, and then started making phone calls. It took two hours to substantiate my story fully, calling the entire night shift at the hospital, my resident, and the doctors down in the emergency room who had been working that night. Mulroney had spent his shift right there next to me, plying me with coffee and precinct donuts, which were an order of magnitude greasier than the ones in our emergency room.

"Okay," the one Mulroney had called Lieutenant, said finally. Without sounding apologetic he said I was free to go-- except for one last thing. "We found a semen sample at the victim's apartment."

Mulroney winced. He knew what was coming.

He handed me a sterile container. "We'll need one from you too, if you don't mind."

"What?"

"You heard me. Whoever did this planned it well. But if it were a true professional he wouldn't have left a calling card on her cervix. Not unless he was a demented piece of crap."

"But it's five-thirty in the morning."

"You should have fessed up sooner."

Mulroney's hand was on my shoulder. "Come on, Danny, there's a private bathroom upstairs. I'll get you a copy of Playboy."

When Mulroney finally pulled his Chrysler into the circular drive of my apartment, the sun was beginning its ascent over the lake. The morning was ice-cold and I felt alone and scared. If they could get to Wanda, they could get to me. Why hadn't they?

Away from the precinct, Mulroney had his own questions. Though he'd never doubted my innocence, he now realized that trouble had a way of following me around. "What the hell is going on?"

Even though I never would have survived the night without Mulroney, I couldn't bring myself to tell him that Wanda was killed because she was on the verge of unlocking a conspiracy to murder holocaust survivors. The black leather Gucci bag she had scooted under her hips that afternoon on top of her office desk, the one she used to carry her printouts to and from work, was missing. This was the work of an angry professional killer.

"Come on, Danny. What gives?"

I just couldn't. Not now. I remembered how Mulroney blew me off that night in the ER when Randy Jordan had his throat slit by Frank Tannenbaum. He didn't believe me then. Why would he believe me now? Especially when I had no substantial evidence to go on. And what if he did believe me and started running around shouting about conspiracies? A loose cannon at this juncture might ruin any chance of getting those toxicology screens and nailing that slimy bastard, Goldman. For now, I would remain mum, much as I knew it hurt my friend, Mulroney.

In my apartment I turned on the kettle and started the shower running. I gazed out my window, watching the sun skate across the lake. Why had I involved Wanda in the first place? Why couldn't I have minded my own damn business? The kettle rattled on the stove. Well, now it was my damn business. Whoever was behind this, Thaddeus Anderson or Frank Tannenbaum or anyone else, had better watch themselves. I was committed to find them. They were close by, they had, apparently, access to my call schedule.

I was going to pay more attention from now on. And it was going to start at the office of the person who seemed to know just about everything--Sol Goldman.

Chapter 52 family

Maxine Chu's words stung. "Your parents were right, Danny. You should have left today."

I winced as I carefully pulled my nose from her icy hospital room window where it had nearly frozen to the glass. The wind was whistling right through the frosty pane, and down below the first snowflakes of the season sprinkled on fallen elm leaves like Parmesan on spaghetti.

I sarcastically thanked Maxine for her show of support. I had rehashed the phone discussion with my parents only to have her blatantly take their side, making me feel exactly the way they had wanted me to feel. They could spread guilt like cream cheese. "Our son, the bagel."

"What do you mean, you don't want us to worry? You're going to drive five, maybe six hours to Detroit Thursday morning, Thanksgiving day? After being up all night? In that car of yours? In this weather?"

They had points in their favor, like the ominous weather report, now coming to fruition outside Maxine's window. But asking another intern to cover the day before Thanksgiving was out of the question. Wednesday was considered a holiday, like New Year's Eve, and it wouldn't be fair to impose on somebody else. Besides, there was another reason for me to stay in Chicago, one I purposely left out of my conversation. A memorial service for Wanda Bylevin was scheduled that afternoon in the Richard Meese chapel.

"I'll be there!" I assured my parents. "No sleep... heavy snow fall... no problem." Not for a grown boy, *their* grown boy-- now a doctor no less, one who despite their vision of me as a third grader, could take care of himself.

"You won't get off duty until God knows when. By the time you get to Detroit, it will be dark and the turkey will be cold." A pause. A few whispers were shared in the background, then: "Maybe you shouldn't come after all. I mean, would it be so hard to switch call nights with one of those gentile boys? Couldn't you offer to cover Christmas instead?"

I wondered what heavenly fortune had blessed me to be the son of the world's biggest Jewish mother? And more importantly, I asked myself, why did my Jewish mother just happen to be my father?

"Look Dad, for the last time, there's no one to switch call with. I'll leave first thing in the morning. Even if I don't get any sleep, it's still only a four-hour drive to Detroit. I can hack it."

At least this time I'd held my ground. I felt great for exactly ten minutes, the time it took for the smell of mom's turkey and cranberry sauce to begin percolating through my cerebral giblets. I imagined myself back home, nestled comfortably on my velveteen afghan by the TV, while family and relatives lavished attention like I was a soldier returning from the front. Everything I'd given my patients these past months now beckoned for a return favor. I thirsted for that glass of punch spiked not with alcohol but with tenderness. Who cared if Mom fumbled over me while I ate, picking turkey pieces off my clothes? So what if Aunt Edna's stories of Latvia were more unbelievable than the year before--the temperature colder, her family poorer, her plight more formidable. It would still be fun to watch my sister Leslie make faces behind her back, pantomiming her every gesture. And so what if the turkey, according to my younger brother Gilbert, was an exploited victim of Western culture that reminded us that the celebration we had gathered for was nothing but a ruse used to placate any Native Americans whom society hadn't yet turned into disenfranchised alcoholics?

So what? It was home. My home. No cockroaches sharing my leftovers, no fungal cultures in the refrigerator, no banshee sirens slicing through my sleep centers, no calls at 4 a.m. for bothersome IV or medication orders. Sleeping in my own bed, cuddling under my twenty-year-old quilt adorned with baseball heroes--my own room, decorated with mementos of past glories: wrestling ribbons, eagle scout badge; ticket stubs from the 1984 world series, my Detroit Tigers versus their San Diego Padres.

Pangs of remorse filtered through my body as I finished recounting the details to Maxine Chu. Calling home had been different this time. A tension was present that wasn't there during college and medical school, when the mere mention of a home-cooked meal and free laundry service was enough to point my car toward the Motor City. Apron string cutting--101 had never been my major. But things had changed. Like a razor sharp scalpel with a deep seeded grudge, the jagged alienation of internship had slashed its way through the first of those apron strings. I was growing up.

Chapter 53 maxine

Maxine looked at herself in the mirror, admiring the caramel cloth turban that had replaced her outlandish hairpiece. She was spending Thanksgiving at "Chez Meese" thanks to a bone marrow which refused to cooperate with the chemotherapy. "If I were you, Danny, I would get someone to cover for you, starting now. It looks like some nasty weather is going to hit. Listen to your father. I would if I still had one."

"If I were you, fur ball, I'd quit worrying about me and concentrate on our fixing your bone marrow." To change the subject I asked if she and her friends were planning on making a Thanksgiving day pilgrimage to Rastafarian Jimmi's basement condo. The other night I passed by Maxine and a group of cancer patients sitting amidst a cloud of smoke thick enough to close O'Hare airport.

Maxine checked the doorway. "The stuff really helps."

I got off the bed and stood in Maxine's reflection.

"I'm sorry I wasn't more tolerant of your needs."

"And I'm sorry I wasn't there to see you running down the tunnel in a towel in the middle of the night."

Mrs. Garber's code blue. The swimming pool. I could taste Christie's lips. "Who told you about...."

"Heard you looked cute running down the hall with your wet butt sticking out. Who was the lucky girl?"

"No lucky girl, Maxine, just an unlucky patient."

Maxine readjusted her turban. "What happened in the swimming pool?"

"This hospital is a cesspool of gossip!"

"Come on, Danny. I may come from an old fashioned family, but at least according to the questionnaire I filled out in Vogue magazine, I'm as healthy as they come." Maxine pointed at the survey on her desk. "I scored an eighty six," she announced proudly, "which means, among other things, I ought to be able to tell when a man is aroused--especially when the physical criteria are so obvious."

"Maxine, I don't believe you!"

256

"I'm sort of surprised myself," she said smiling devilishly.

I felt an uncomfortable wetness under my collar. I suddenly had difficulty breathing, and a heavy pain gnawed at my breast bone. I was either having a heart attack or a panic attack. "Listen, Maxine, I'd appreciate it if we could keep our relationship a little more professional."

I might as well have slapped Maxine in the face, the way she fell backward, face filling in like she just had a blood transfusion.

"Max, I'm sorry, I really didn't mean..."

"Don't apologize, Dr. Raskin."

A left to the jaw. "Come on, Max."

"No, really, I understand. I just hit one of your defense buttons, that's all. I'll be more careful next time."

"You didn't hit anything." The pain in my chest said otherwise.

Maxine moved closer, her nightgown sliding off her shoulders. "You know, I can remember a time not so long ago when I'd catch you taking more than a little look at my body. I though you liked it when I made a comment or two about yours."

It was my turn for red cheeks. "What are you getting at?"

Maxine took a breath. "You used to think I was attractive," she said, turning away and fixing her turban in the mirror. "You used to think I was beautiful. And sexy."

"You are beautiful!"

"Were."

"Are, Maxine. For Christ's sake, you could be right there in that Vogue magazine of yours."

"In the turban section."

"Maxine! I don't get it. Are you feeling sorry for yourself?"

I came over and put my arm around her. Her head rested on my shoulder while she cried for a few moments. When she was done, she looked up.

"Rastafarian Jimmi said my breasts are getting too small!"

"Maxine, you let..."

"I just showed him, Danny. He was curious."

Without hesitation, Maxine slid her nightgown down until the noticeable give in her soft breasts became apparent. Maxine gently cupped them. The pain was back in my chest. My heart raced.

"Maxine, please pull your nightgown up."

"See, I told you I wasn't beautiful anymore."

"Maxine, if someone were to walk in right now..."

Maxine reluctantly replaced her silk nightgown.

We stood looking at each other. I gathered my thoughts. "Maxine Chu, hear me out. You are quite possibly the most beautiful woman I have ever known. I mean that. You always were and you always will be. I think it's critical that you know this because I believe your opinion of yourself is somehow tied into your perception of what I think about you." Maxine rocked from side to side. I continued. "It seems like you've been using me as a manometer of sorts--something to measure your attractiveness by. I think that's okay, but we both have to remember that the logical extension of those feelings is that I prove it in other, more intimate ways."

"Like going for a swim with me naked?"

"We have to make sure nothing like that ever happens. Because sometimes I think.."

"You would sleep with me?" We both swallowed hard.

"Maxine, I couldn't live with myself if that ever happened. Not while you're my patient. Max, we're such good friends..."

"We're more than friends, Danny. You're right. I do measure my attractiveness in your mirror. You're my blood, you're my soul, you're..."

Maxine and I embraced. My chest pain subsided in a flood of tears. Damn this whole fucking world! Why can't this woman just be cured and get on with her life?

"You'll be out of here soon, Maxine," I said as we separated. "Maybe you and Lo can work out some sort of mutually compatible agreement."

With the mention of Lo, Maxine stepped away from the mirror. "Forget Lo," she said, retying the sash on her bathrobe. "He'll never change. "

"Take it from me, Maxine. Sex ain't all it's cracked up to be. And that's from someone who spent half his life hoping to get something published in Penthouse magazine's letter section."

258

Maxine didn't understand, and I wasn't about to explain. "What about tomorrow, Max? Is Lo coming up for dinner?"

"Hah, you must be kidding. He wants to bring over this humongous greasy Peking Duck." Maxine's face contorted with a shiver. "I'd rather get turkey in my IV than sit through another meal with him, especially a holiday meal. I'll deal with Lo when I get out of the hospital. It will be put out or get out time." Maxine took out some facial cream and began massaging her cheeks. "Rastafarian Jimmi and the boys are making a smoked turkey. Guess what they're stuffing it with?"

Chapter 54 memorial service

Sol Goldman was standing outside the chapel. He was dressed in a crisp black suit, and his hair was parted carefully to one side. For a change, his glasses sat where they were supposed to. Though his face was freshly razed of stubble, he wore an after-shave of worry.

"The service is inside," I said as I tried to pass by. The chapel was half-filled already. I spotted some of Wanda's fellow workers. There were several people crying.

"I'm on my way to New York. I just wanted to reassure you that I know you weren't involved in any of this."

I couldn't help myself. "Fuck you."

Sol stared. "I could fire you for that."

"Do it, Sol. And fuck you again, and whoever it was you sent to kill her."

Sol stepped back. Seeing a few passers-by look up, he asked me to whisper.

"Why should I? What do you have to hide?" My voice caused some heads to turn.

"Shh!"

"Sure, Sol, I'll be quiet. We don't want word to get out about Thaddeus Anderson."

A bombshell exploded inside Sol, shrapnel filled his face. "How did you.... I mean who is..."

"Thaddeus Anderson. Friend of yours?"

"This is not the time or the place." Our eyes met in battle. "We have to talk." He did an abrupt about-face and stormed away.

Despite Chagall glass windows depicting the plagues Moses instituted against the Pharaoh, the Richard Meese chapel was considered non-denominational. I remembered Hebrew school and the Passover adage: 'Let my people go'.

The chapel was filled with upwards of seventy people, probably more than in the entire rest of the hospital, considering it was the eve of a holiday. Only a skeleton staff remained to

260

run things. Elective labs and procedures were closed down, and except for the basement coffee shop, no food was available.

I was the only intern in the room, probably one of the few left in the hospital. I sat in the back row. I knew I was going to cry and didn't want anyone else to see, one of those man things, I guess. Up front I saw Wanda's family. I remembered them from a picture on her office wall. Younger sister, older brother, both consoling a distraught mother.

The service was a series of eulogies, delivered by grieving friends and relatives, some of whom could barely deliver a sentence without breaking into sobs. I would never have the courage to do that, I thought. Her brother got up and tearfully told about growing up together in their tree-lined lot in Winnetka, chasing butterflies, playing in their tree house. And how through college, she developed her panache at computers, something that had become her life's blood. My eyes began swelling. Though I alone knew it, that very passion he had described, had drained her blood as well. Who would have gone to the trouble to rape and then strangle Wanda, and then try to pin it on me? How could he have gotten away with it without a struggle unless it was someone she knew, which meant that someone she knew was intricately involved in other patient murders as well. Despite what the police had concluded, that the sperm left at the scene was the earmark of an amateur, I knew better. This act was perpetrated by a trained professional killer who was trying to get to me. *See what we can do. See the damage we can cause.*

I went through my Kleenex supply as well as both shirt sleeves as the eulogies continued. I dreaded being on call that day. I wanted to be home. I wanted to be taken care of. I envisioned my own family at the chapel crying while the the Rabbi spoke of my life, insignificant as it was. If only Danny Raskin had kept his nose clean, Rabbi Klein would bellow, he might still be here today. I saw Mom sobbing, my Dad comforting her. I saw my brother counting up the value of my coin collection; boy did that piss me off. I saw myself laying in the casket, scrub shirt on, buried like the Egyptian kings with my peanut butter cups in one hand, Ragu Sauce in the other.

I stayed seated when the service ended, watching as the mourners shuffled out, feet scraping against the worn carpet. A figure brushed up against me, looked down, then turned his head and darted out. I looked up, catching a glimpse of a black man sporting a well trimmed beard and wearing an English raincoat, broad rimmed hat drawn low over his eyebrows. The eyes. I'd seen those before. My heart nearly burst from my chest. It was him. Tannenbaum! How could he be black? And the beard. No-- *that was Tannenbaum!* The man in the E.R.-the man who threatened me-the man asking about Dean Cantrell! I jumped up, pushed my way through the crowd and out the door into the hallway. I saw a figure rapidly walking toward the exit.

"Hey! Just a minute!" The man quickened his pace and then ran the last twenty steps to the revolving door. My heart pounded.

"Tannenbaum!" I yelled, chasing the fleeing shadow. "You son of a bitch!"

The mourners glared.

"He did it!," I yelled. "He killed Wanda."

Screams dissected the air.

"Call security!" I yelled, struggling to get through the throngs of mourners. I reached the door and nearly pushed my hand through the glass as I forced my way out.

Outside, snow was falling in chunks and a bitter wind sliced at my body. Where the hell was he? Across the street was the parking lot, and across from that, the apartment complex where I lived. I listened, and heard a car engine turning over. In the parking lot were two cars whose hazy exhaust mixed with the snow flakes. One of them had to be Tannenbaum. As I watched, one of the cars, a black Eldorado, screeched out of the lot and raced around the corner. Maybe I could cut him off at the corner. The wind slapped at my face as I ran. I slid across a thin layer of ice hidden buried below the dust of snow until I reached the one exit he had to use to leave the Richard Meese campus. I looked up. Quiet. Maybe it wasn't him. Maybe he didn't even have a car.

I jumped at the sound of an engine, tires like a train, bearing down fast. I froze like an icicle in the middle of the street, watching. Tannenbaum, his eyes focused on me, was bearing down hard, planning to hit me! I begged my legs to move, but they were numb. Seconds away I saw his teeth, grinning daggers, going for the kill. I reached within myself for strength and managed to move my feet upward-- I leapt higher and higher, saw the curb, sprawled out, waited for the impact of his car. I closed my eyes- thought of the mourner's Kadish they said at my grandfather's funeral. Waited for the blackness.

Then nothing.

When I looked up, a trail of dust and rubber had blocked out the snow. I was on the curb, my hands bloodied and laced with icy gravel. "I'll get you, you motherfucker! Whoever you are, I'll get you."

Chapter 55 thanksgiving

The Kaufman Deli was empty except for me, several labor and delivery nurses, and Thorazine Carol, who cackled like a witch when she brought me a piece of pumpkin pie. Her fingers had poked two holes into the center of the pie--"eyes" she said--"so that the pumpkin could see itself being eaten." It didn't matter. My appetite had dwindled shortly after the memorial service and had disappeared altogether since Thanksgiving Day morning when I'd awakened to the weather report. Blizzards had blanketed the Midwest. Interstate 94 was closed all the way to Michigan. There would be no home-cooked meal, no back-to-the-womb comfort care. It was Thorazine Carol, snow-drifts, and me, stuck in this God awful place on the very day after I had seen the reflection of my own mortality in the headlights of an oncoming automobile. I was willing to bet it was driven by the same bastard who had raped and strangled Wanda Bylevin and then had the nerve to attend her memorial service. If only I could have gotten a license plate number. But my panic had been total and I couldn't remember a thing.

I kept telling myself it couldn't have been him. How could Tannenbaum disguise himself as a black man and get away with it? I had heard it could be done with skin dyes, but for what purpose? And what the hell was he doing at the memorial service? I'd assumed that Sol Goldman, standing outside the chapel, had been waiting for me. But maybe he was waiting for the black version of Tannenbaum--a meeting perhaps, or some type of signal.

I flipped Sol Goldman's office key over in my hand. If I was going to be stuck here, I was going to make the most of it. It was the perfect opportunity to break into Sol Goldman's office. The entire Medicine department was off for the holidays, and hospital security seemed as thin as the ice covering the pools of rain collecting in the outside courtyard. Sol's secretary never even knew I had slipped Sol's office key out of her drawer when she went to Xerox a medical certificate for me. No one would find out.

While waiting for Thorazine Carol to bring me a refill of coffee, I weighed my ambivalence. What other choice did I have? Sit by idly while the carnage continued? Pretend nothing was really happening? What was so important about those damn files of Cantrell's? Cantrell and Bramwell, both deans. Both murdered. Both from Yale, class of '60. Both with ties to an ultra-right organization named Friends of Tomorrow.

The Department of Medicine took up three thousand square feet of the first floor of Gardner House Pavilion, beginning with large glass doors adjacent to the east lobby. Dr. Goldman's office sat behind an outer corridor of desks and xerox machines on one side, and a small departmental library on the other.

At ten p.m., camouflaged in olive-green surgical scrubs, I approached the outer foyer. The key sat in my pocket, alongside a contraption consisting of two paper clips and a bobby pin--a device I had concocted back in college while working summers at K-mart. With practice, I had learned the art of opening car doors for patrons who had inadvertently locked their keys inside. The clips and hairpin made a fool-proof pulley and lever system. Dean Cantrell's files had been no match for me. I hoped the same would hold true for Goldman's.

Darkness blanketed the inner corridor as I pushed Sol's office door open, grimacing at the squeaking of hinges. Though the shades were closed, his window faced the circular patient drop-zone in back of the building. Turning on the lights would cast a luminous shadow, and I couldn't afford to take the risk. What kind of detective couldn't even remember to bring a flashlight?

Feeling my way along a wall, I reached Goldman's desk and sat down in his swivel chair, waiting until my eyes adjusted to the darkness. A small tungsten reading light perched at one corner of his desk. I turned it on. Too bright! I grabbed the long cord and thrust the lamp under his desk, out of the glare of the windows. There--just enough of an oaken hue to make out the furniture, bookshelves and wall hangings. The shades were dark. I let out a breath.

The room reminded me of a mausoleum described in a Gothic novel I had once read. High arching walls sloping steeply onto the thick oak bookshelves which were crammed with hard-covered, bound journals, some dating back to 1950. His collection of textbooks included standard internal medicine texts, plus a plethora of Endocrine texts, some of which he had either authored or edited himself. The walls were covered by a potpourri of physician memorabilia- diplomas, certificates, even an anthology of class pictures. A series of three foot high oak cabinets stretched halfway across the room. It didn't take a genius to figure that this was where Dr. Goldman kept his files. I had seen him pull out individual manila folders on a number of occasions. I moved the light from under the desk and plugged it in just under the class pictures. The glare was more than I wanted, but considering that everything seemed quiet, I took the risk.

The first three files contained journal articles; several others contained department and other hospital business. One file was our employment file. I thumbed through the folders, the largest of which was Kurt Mallincroft's, containing over a dozen complaints. The last cabinet contained a personal communication file which contained a list of positions Dr. Goldman had been recruited for during the past three years. Dean of Yale. Chair at the Brigham. The plums of academia. He must have had a strong motivation for turning those jobs down. Murder seemed strong enough to me. I closed that file and scanned the rest of his office. Where were his locked files? Anyone of his stature had to have certain things he wanted kept from everybody, including family and secretary.

Without warning, the outer office door opened. At the sound of a key being inserted in the inner door I lunged for Goldman's desk, diving into the cubby hole beneath his chair just as light flooded the room. Footsteps entered and stopped. From under the desk the polished black wingtips threatened. *Oh shit, the light. I forgot to put out the light!*

I fastened my arms across my curled up body trying to control the shaking as I watched the flashlight beam make its rounds. Footsteps coming closer, toward the desk. Stopping next to me. An odor of onions filled the room. I was afraid to look. A loud click--then another. A gun?

A voice bellowed through the silence: "Sanders, this is Westerfeld. I'm in Goldman's office. Nothing here--no forced entry. Appears Dr. Goldman left a light on. Over."

The man on the other end of the walkie-talkie spoke through the static. "Okay, why don't you head over to Gardner House? They need help restraining a patient in bed 402."

A loud belch, then: "Over." The light switched off and I heard the door close behind him.

Sweat poured from my face. I refused to breathe, lest I cough or sneeze, until several minutes passed. When I was sure there was no one in the vicinity, I moved out of my crouched position. I winced as my left leg spasmed. When I placed my hands on the inner surface of his desk for support, they hit a pair of handles. My hands traced the outline of a drawer-- two drawers--each opening from under the desk.

Sol Goldman had expertly fashioned two file cabinets secured by a latch with a removable panel.

The ends of the two paper clips fit snugly into the slit-like opening of the first file, which was about the size of a generous gap between two teeth. I twisted the attached hair pin counter-clockwise while I gently slid the paper clips into the newly opened space. After twenty seconds, there was a soft click. The latch slid off.

I pulled a file out and set it on his desk: Personnel File: Thaddeus Anderson.

I spent the next fifteen minutes scanning the contents, trembling beneath the weight of its incriminating evidence. First was his employment record, three years down in the housekeeping department. Reason for termination; 'employee disappeared shortly after being questioned about being in the room of a patient who was later found dead'. A police report: In his locker several vials of an unidentified liquid was found. I felt weak, sure it was ergonovine. Damn. Also in the folder was a telephone ledger--several calls to New York, several to New Haven. My breath stopped. He had called the same number at Arbor Hills a dozen times. I'd called that number dozens of times too. It was the admissions office at the Medical School! I breathed deeply as I continued. I read through a police report on a search of his apartment. Nothing except Nazi propaganda, several Aryan magazines. Everything else cleared out. Final summation: 'No trace of Thaddeus Anderson'.

It was too much to comprehend. An employee of the hospital was a murderer. Was he working by himself or for someone else? Why was he killing only certain patients? And why did my chief of medicine, Sol Goldman, have all of this information? Was he launching his own investigation? Or was he keeping tabs on a friend?

I turned my attention to the second file cabinet. Maybe this one held the toxicology reports I needed to nail Goldman. I congratulated myself for being such a sleuth and pictured myself marching into morning report, trailed by the FBI's best, toxicology reports waving high. I'd delight in seeing Sol Goldman humiliated in front of his flock. Watching him try in vain to explain his position. In my excited state, I was too quick with the paper clips, winding them too fast or too many times. The top clip broke off inside the lock, effectively sealing its contents from me and everyone else. "Shit!" I said aloud. For the next ten minutes I tried furiously to fish out those metal fragments. I even chewed a piece of Juicy Fruit gum and attempted to glob it onto the embedded paper clip. It refused to take hold, and left the entire lock looking like the floor of a movie theater after a Saturday matinee. This was a problem. Goldman would know somebody had been here. If he knew I was on to something, he'd have to suspect it was me. I thought about tampering with Kurt Mallincroft's file so that Goldman might blame him. No sense in that, I decided. Besides, let Goldman lose some sleep. Let him suspect it was me--as long as he couldn't prove it, I'd be fine.

I replaced the latches covering the files and began straightening his desk. Nothing of note there, a New England Journal of Medicine, a bunch of drug-company pens. I needed to replace the lamp I'd moved over to the first set of file cabinets. Its light shone on a wall full of photographs, pictures of Goldman dating back to high school in New York city. There he was, winning a Westinghouse award. So that's how he got his start, I mused. He was all smiles back then, his eyes intense yet friendly. Further up the wall was his college picture, Harvard, class of '56, then Medical school. Yale, class of sixty.

It took a second to register. How could I have missed it? There was Goldman, decked out in a white coat. Standing right next to him, was a face I recognized. Charles Cantrell. Colleagues. My God, Goldman had told me he had barely known the man, yet there they were, arm in arm. Weak kneed, I scanned the legend until another name caught my eye. James Bramwell, the now dead Dean from Columbia----just as dead as Charles Cantrell.

Chapter 56 christmas spirit

It was Saturday morning and I couldn't help smiling as I packed up to leave for the day. It had been an incredibly easy call night, and with five hours of sleep behind me (twice as much as any previous call night), I had the entire day free to forage in downtown Chicago. I signed out my service to Kurt Mallincroft, then bounced down the first of six flights of stairs. Gail Peterson was standing in the stairwell. Our eyes met momentarily, but then she quickly dropped her head and began walking.

"Wait up, Gail." My words surprised both of us, considering we had hardly shared a conversation in the past two weeks, although we were working on the same ward. I'd wanted to talk to Gail when she'd returned from Colorado, but was so caught up in Wanda Bylevin's death and my break into Sol Goldman's office, that I'd never found the time.

Gail came back from Colorado even more withdrawn than before. She seemed to have lost her fighting spirit, allowing herself to be dominated by our very uncaring resident, Art Redmon. Yesterday, Alex Rosen had told me he'd heard that Gail Peterson was going to quit.

I caught up to Gail at the bottom of the second flight of stairs, her fur-lined green hood bundled up over loosely braided carrot-colored hair.

"What's your hurry?"

Gail stopped, her amber eyes searching the floor. "Tired, that's all. I need some sleep."

"Sleep?" I protested. "You can't sleep. It's Saturday, and it's beautiful outside. Besides, you weren't even on call last night."

"So?" she questioned, turning just enough to expose half of her face, most of which was covered by her hair.

"So..." I had to think quickly. I couldn't let her slip away. "I'm going Christmas shopping. Why don't you join me?"

Gail looked up, surprised. "I wouldn't be any fun," she said, barely an inflection in her voice.

270

Part of me agreed. She didn't seem very amiable, and I wasn't in the mood for babysitting. Though I felt like saying, "Okay, have it your way," I didn't.

"Who said anything about fun? I hate shopping. If I don't get some female input, I'm likely to buy my mother a pair of cowboy boots."

"What's wrong with cowboy boots for your mother?" Gail wanted to know.

"She doesn't have any legs."

Gail brushed hair from her face, revealing a collage of freckles and a broad, genuine smile.

"Maybe for an hour. I have an appointment with the laundry room."

Gail didn't know it but I had an appointment, too--with her laundry, dirty or not. Before the day was over I intended to find out why this red headed mystery woman was about to throw her life into the hamper.

The howling lakeshore winds swirled down Michigan Avenue, literally thrusting Gail and me into an icy ocean of holiday shoppers. Lofty buildings beckoned us with their glitzy window displays, luring us with things we couldn't afford. The aroma of hot pretzels and mustard mingled with that of evergreen and muddy street slush. Bells dangled from the robotic arms of the Salvation Army volunteers as we passed through the turnstile entrance of Marshall Fields Department Store. Despite my prodding, Gail hardly spoke. This bothered me. How many Saturdays would I have off during a year of internship? At least it should be pleasant.

Gail followed me into the men's clothing section, where a tall brunette sales lady with an hour-glass figure inquired as to whether I needed any help. Help? Me? I rubbed my eyes. Suddenly I was back in the real world. Gone were the nursing uniforms, the beeping IV set ups. People were no longer asking me to help them, they wanted to help me.

This wonderful woman hasn't even been near a bed pan!

Crazy as it sounded, I wanted that saleslady to want me like she never wanted anybody else. It wasn't sexual validation I was after, though if by chance she ripped off her clothes, got down on her hands and knees, and belted out an x-rated version of "Come all ye faithful", I wouldn't have complained. What I needed was a personal and social stamp of approval, like I truly did belong in the real world, and that life did indeed exist outside the confines of Richard Meese hospital.

"It's unbecoming to drool in public," Gail said, nudging me in the shoulder. "I have to find a shirt for my father."

I held up a pair of dress slacks. "Have anything that comes pre-wrinkled?" I pointed at my crumpled corduroys. "I'm trying to match these."

I paused, waiting for the woman to laugh. Instead, her lips wrinkled like prunes and her jaw tightened.

"Hey, Danny," interrupted Gail, "you ought to try on a pair of these pants. They have buttons."

"So what?" I scoffed.

"You won't have to worry about your zipper being open all the time."

The saleslady folded her arms under a tight fitting bodice and sneered, no doubt assuming we were a couple of barbaric street urchins whose line of credit extended no further than the K-mart toy department.

"Anything else?" she asked impatiently, looking a few aisles over, hoping to find a customer who had his American Express Gold card taped to his forehead.

Screw you. "Just one more thing," I shouted as her high heels scuffed the floor in her hasty retreat. "Do you happen to carry a line of shirts that come pre-stained with blood and vomit?"

For the first time, Gail laughed.

We zig-zagged our way throughout Marshall Fields, following the fragrance of Frango mints and cologne, no clear goal in sight.

"When was the last time you simply wandered around with nothing to accomplish?" I asked.

Gail's posture was no longer rigid. "Truthfully," she confessed, "it feels pretty good. Back at the hospital, I'm always on a mission; always some patient or family to talk to, or a consent to get. Some fire to put out."

"And the pattern never alters until the rat dies."

"What?"

"That's a line from an old Simon and Garfunkel song. I agree with you. I'm tired of collecting data sixteen hours a day, seven days a week. I think today we should just...."

"Just what?"

My arm cradled Gail's shoulder. "Today Dr. Peterson, instead of collecting data, let's just be data."

So that's how two insignificant data points in life's schematogram spent the morning wandering aimlessly and happily among the display counters in Marshall Fields. My shopping list was small--couple of books for my brothers, cologne for Alex, a water pipe for Picolli, something for Maxine.

My main agenda was Gail. My own problems dissipated by listening to others, and in Gail's case, I had more than a casual interest. A month ago I would have begged for an opportunity to be out with her. She seemed like someone I could be close to, even fall in love with. But between what was happening to my patients and Wanda's death, I started to feel as if I were poison to be around. Still, I wanted to be back in Gail's life. We needed each other.

Without letting on that I'd heard rumors of her imminent departure, I searched for the one strategic question that would let her know I was interested in what troubled her.

Internship had taught me how to take a good history, ask the right questions. I cleared my voice. Gail looked up, the tranquility in her face giving way to anxiety.

"What's on your mind?"

"You quitting?"

"You don't mince words, do you? Let's keep walking."

As we exited Marshall Fields, the early afternoon sun jackknifed behind a bale of clouds. We crossed Michigan Avenue, turning down trendy Oak Street. Gail pulled on a pair of oversized green mittens and then smothered her freckles with a tightly wrapped matching scarf. My own bare hands dug deep into my parka and I cursed my fate for owning only two gloves, both of which fit the same hand.

"What gives you the idea I'm quitting?"

I rubbed my glasses to clear some of the frost. "Rumor. Plus my observation that you're depressed as hell."

"Miserable is more accurate."

"We're all miserable, Gail. It's written into our contracts."

Tears landed in the folds of her scarf. We paused at a traffic light and I imagined its blinking box flashing: "Cry. Don't Cry".

We crossed the street, barely sidestepping an onrushing taxi. By now the wind had penetrated my parka and was freezing my skeleton, one bone at a time. I pointed out a coffee shop on the corner of Elm and Superior. Gail nodded and we entered.

Music of Bach and the scent of espresso beans filled the air. Besides a counter with half a dozen seats, there were a handful of tables, all but two of which were unoccupied. Two men sat at the counter gazing longingly at each other. Another thumbed through a magazine rack, the titles of which were mostly foreign. A piano was unmanned. We ordered cappuccinos and scones and for ten minutes thawed in silence.

We sipped at first, then gulped our coffees, taking small bites of a raspberry scone, making small bits of conversation. Gail motioned to me to wipe some fruit from my cheek and cringed as I put my sleeve to good use. "It's strange; all the euphemisms in medicine that apply to food: currant jelly stools, nutmeg liver, strawberry tongue," she said, sticking hers out as an exclamation point. I spit the coffee in my mouth back into the container.

"There."

"What was that?"

"Coffee ground emesis." We both laughed.

"There are so many," said Gail. "Blueberry muffin baby, chocolate cyst. It makes me feel like never eating again." She continued pecking at her scone while I worked on my second cappuccino. "Do you realize that this is the first time I've been out with another intern since the beginning of the year?"

"I asked you to do stuff before. You always had an excuse."

"You're different."

274

"There you go again."

"You know what I mean. There aren't even other women interns to pal around with."

"What about the other specialties? O.B.-gyn has a lot of female interns."

"You ever have a meal with the O.B. terns? Try eating turkey while they're talking trichamonas. They had their Christmas party in Chinatown last week, and I heard they were doing pelvic exams on the Peking ducks. I'm sick of O.B. I don't ever want to think about O.B. again."

"You must know somebody."

"Two cousins I used to spend my summers with drove up from St. Louis when they found out I was going to quit."

"So it is true?"

"I get up every morning searching for a reason to continue. I would have moved home three months ago if it weren't for the fact that my dad would have been disappointed in me for wimping out. That's why I went home to Colorado. The family emergency was me. I asked dad if I could quit."

"What did he say?"

"Told me to deal with it. Then called my two cousins I used to be close with. They had been out to see me a few months before."

"You guys grew up together?"

"Our paths diverged after college. They went into the real world of high tech fashion design. I entered the protracted puberty state called medical school. Four more years of student loans, garage sales, living off daddy. The way they judged me when we got together made me feel naked."

"They didn't want to hear about medical school?"

"I tried talking about the cadavers in anatomy lab, or the all-nighters we pulled before tests, they gave me.. well they gave me this look." Gail flashed an expression that reminded me of one my mother gave me in third grade, when she opened my lunch box and found a dead frog laying on top of my peanut butter sandwich.

"Then like nothing happened, they continued with their latest discourse on home accessories, like I wasn't there anymore. They're into china patterns, while I'm into paper plates and twenty hours of studying a day."

"Sounds like medical school created quite a gap."

"Try the continental divide."

Taking large gulps of her coffee, she continued. "Last month, purportedly on their way to Minnesota for a college reunion, they came to town and took me out to dinner. We hadn't seen each other in two years. I'm sure dad was behind the whole thing. Their visit was a disaster, but I guess they served a purpose."

"Which was?"

"Someone at whom to vent my anger." Gail sat up straight. Now that she had more color in her face, and wore a softer expression, she seemed much more life-like, less Raggedy Ann-ish. Gail took a sip and continued.

"There they were, both pregnant, both settled into a routine, comfortable, upper-middle class existence, trying to act concerned, while daintily wrapping their angel hair pasta the required one and a half loops around their forks. Maybe they hoped their feigned interest would be rewarded by titillating stories of heroism under fire, or sexual hedonism in the call room. I mean what else would keep a person in the hospital one hundred hours a week, they asked. I tried my best to explain everything in a way that they might accept and even admire. You know--saving humanity on a daily basis. I even considered making up a story about an incredible affair I was having with the surgical chief resident."

I felt a tinge of jealousy. "Winston Hacklethorpe III?"

Gail brushed the hair from her face. "After a few minutes, my stories of heroism and prowess degenerated into chasing down lab values, checking x-rays, admitting patients, discharging them, dealing with nurses, dealing with med students, dealing with attendings, getting up in the middle of the night to replace an IV, working up someone who's just vomited all over the patient you had just prepped for surgery; let's face it; hardly the stuff heroes and vamps are made of. You should have seen the indifference plastered on their faces. And you know what it was that bothered me the most?"

"They didn't give a shit about what you were really going through."

Gail appeared on the verge of tears. "It was their fingernails, dammit. They had the nerve to sit with their God-damn French manicured fingernails and stare at mine." Gail paused and held up her hands. Now I don't claim to know much about fingernails, but Gail's were bitten down to the nub, some worse than others, cuticles sprouting like crusty patches of weeds. Gail turned up her nose in imitation of her cousin. "'Oh Gail, you used to have the prettiest fingernails; what happened?' And it hit me. Even during medical school, I still took care of things like my fingernails. But now, caring about my fingernails is the furthest thing from my mind. I thank God if I can get an occasional shower." Gail paused, her scraggly curls testimony that personal hygiene had taken a seat in the back of the internship bus, a bus that was driving Gail dangerously close to the precipice. "When they commented on my fingernails," she continued, "I looked them straight in the eyes, comfortably sitting in their Donna Karan sweaters and their Liz Claiborne blouses, and said: 'You go stick your fingers up people's butts all day and see what your fingernails look like.' I said it for the shock value of course. I wanted to remind them, and myself I guess, that we live in different worlds, and while they're free to discuss marriage and china patterns and inquire about my love life, judgments about my fingernails are not acceptable."

Gail's excused herself and went to the bathroom. When she returned, she wiped her mouth and sat forward. "It's a lot harder for a woman to meet someone than it is for a guy. Especially in our position. You have nurses, physical therapists, medical students that are dying for companionship, Christ, all you guys have to do is walk into a bar and start talking doctor talk. I bet Alex does that all the time."

"Hardly. I'm the one who needs the doctor crutch, Gail. Not Alex. That guy could walk into a bar and tell a woman he's a disgruntled postal worker. An hour later they'd be in the sack licking each other's bodies like they were postage stamps."

277

Gail smirked. "If I go to a bar, I don't tell men what I do for a living."

"Why not?"

Gail shrugged. "What normal man would want to spend time with someone who's chronically tired, on call every third night, and is used to calling the shots? I tell them I'm a doctor and I'm immediately labeled: Gail Peterson, M.D.-- ball buster."

Through smudged lenses I watched Gail pick at her pastry, taking measured sips of coffee as if she were recording her own fluid intake. My own worries seemed far away. I knew how to lose myself in other people's problems. Friends used my shoulder like rent-free housing because I was a good listener. And a good dreamer. Listening to other people's problems lessened my own. Or at least the perception. I focused on Gail. She needed me, if not as a boyfriend as I had once hoped, then at least as someone who was there for her.

Gail finally spoke. "I don't even feel feminine anymore. I'm working so hard and spending so little time with other people. I don't have time to go out on dates and don't even get asked...well ..." Gail took a long, deep breath. "It's hard to feel desirable."

"It's hard to feel human."

Gail nodded. "But as an intern, it's much easier to express masculinity than femininity. This sounds stupid, but the only way I can express my femininity these days is by wearing nice underpants. It's all I have." Gale caught her reflection in my glasses and pulled the hair from her face.

Gail looked at her watch. "We better get going."

After bundling ourselves up, we made our way back toward the thinning crowd of shoppers on Michigan Avenue. Gail's nose was like a leaky faucet in the cold air, but at least she had a pair of gloves. "You know," she said. "It's cold enough out here to freeze the balls off a brass monkey."

"Such a mouth!"

"What can I tell you? I used to hang out with guys a lot, and I tend to talk like them. You can say 'fuck it' with males if you feel like it. You can't with some of the prissy little bitches I knew growing up."

Gail's mood had changed. I don't think it was anything I did or said. Maybe just having someone to talk with. We crossed Michigan Avenue and headed toward Water Tower Place, a large, glass-enclosed state-of-the-art shopping mall.

"It's your turn to talk," she said, wrapping her scarf in neat layers around her face.

"My fingernails are fine," I teased.

"Come on. I haven't been the only one down in the dumps. Alex said you and Wanda were good friends."

I nodded.

"I'm sorry. You want to talk about it?"

"Nothing to say."

"Alex said that she was helping you figure out who killed your patients."

"Alex talks too much."

We walked the next block with a strong wind to our backs. After what happened to Wanda, I was afraid of involving anybody else.

"Everybody knows," she declared.

I wiped my nose and kept walking.

Gail appeared momentarily distracted, looking behind her. "Someone's been offing your patients."

"Yeah, me, Gail. It's called being a lousy doctor." Right then I wanted to cry, spill my guts about what had been eating away at my soul. But the vision of Wanda Bylevin hanging from her apartment fan kept me from saying anything. Look what happened when she became involved. Look what happened to Randy Jordan in the E.R. and to crotchety Mrs. Garber. I was a walking communicable disease, and whomever I touched, died.

"I'm sorry, Gail. I don't want to make a big deal about it."

Gail looked behind her as we crossed the street. "You better tell that to Emile Horner. He's been telling people there's a conspiracy around the hospital, that someone is knocking off Jewish patients in order to close the place, to discredit the Jewish community. He's publicly asking Goldman for an investigation."

I felt like choking. I was glad I hadn't told Horner about all the other patients who had died, people, who like himself, had a very personal association with the Holocaust. If Horner went public too soon, it would ruin any chance of getting to the bottom of things, not to mention endangering the life of the little spark of a man.

At the corner of Chestnut Street and Birch, Gail looked over one shoulder and then the other.

"What's the matter--see one of your clinic patients back there?" I teased.

"I know you're going to think that I'm totally paranoid, but I could swear someone's following us."

I stopped breathing. My jaw clenched as I turned. Lots of stores, lots of people. Nothing unusual. "I think you're coming down with frostbite of the brain, Gail." We walked another twenty steps or so and Gail stopped, adjusting her loose fitting hat, scanning the crowd behind her.

"Listen," she said as she stepped forward, picking up the pace. "Just for grins, follow me."

We walked by our intended destination, turning left at Superior Street, then making a quick right onto Grant Avenue, and continuing for two blocks to the third intersection.

"Over there," Gail whispered, as if somebody might be close. "I want you to bend down like you're tying your shoe."

"I'm wearing loafers."

"Come on. Tell me if you see someone in a blue parka, beige ski hat and leather gloves."

Our side of the street was shielded from what little sun remained, lending gray shadows to the icicles on the trees overhead. It took only seconds to locate the person matching Gail's general description, a man who had planted himself at the corner some thirty yards behind us, his head buried in a newspaper. I watched until his periscope-like eyes slowly rose up from the depths of the Tribune. Searching. For a split second, our visual radar collided. I'd seen that man before. It wasn't Tannenbaum, but I'd seen those eyes before. Where? In the hospital? At the Nazi rally?

"Come on Gail, let's go. I'm freezing my ass off."

In silence, Gail followed as we retraced our steps to Water Tower Place.

"Well, did you see him?" Gail inquired as we entered the glass elevator.

"Yeah, but what's the big deal? He probably had the same shopping itinerary we did."

"Danny, that guy was watching us in Marshall Fields this morning."

"And I suppose he was having coffee and croissants with us?"

But I already knew the answer. I remembered a man sitting at the counter, reading. Same man, I was sure of it.

"So why is he following you?"

"Maybe it's you. I hear mashers have a thing for redheads."

"Then why are your hands shaking like you have Parkinsons?" She leaned over and whispered: "Do you know that guy?"

"No," I whispered back. "And after three cups of coffee, I'm sure your hands have the same tremor as mine."

We stepped off the elevator. "Look, Gail. If I had known you were in the mood to play cops and robbers, I wouldn't have bothered shopping with you in the first place. We came to shop, so let's just shop...and don't look back. If someone wants to follow us, let him."

And to drive home the point, for the next two hours I embarked on a shopping spree that would have made the VISA card bosses proud. Two pairs of pants, three shirts-permanent press, ties without stains, all color coordinated thanks to Gail. Every now and then, when Gail wasn't looking, I quickly scanned my surroundings just to make sure. Maybe I had over-reacted. Maybe he hadn't been following us after all.

We stopped at a sporting goods store where Gail picked out a new golf bag to ship to her father. I found a Troy Aikman autographed football for one of my nephews. We next entered the women's department.

"You sure you want to do this?" asked Gail. "She's your patient, not your friend."

I had decided weeks ago to buy Maxine Chu a Christmas present and had spent a long time contemplating exactly what it would be. I had yet to come up with an answer. Gail suggested we check out the sweater section which was around the corner from lingerie. I couldn't help but slow my pace as we passed through the shelves of chemises, slips and some of the more risque' Italian silk negligees. I was glad to have Gail there, since I never was comfortable shopping for lingerie by myself. I always felt like women looked at me like I was a pervert who at any moment might grab a few pairs of pantyhose and go jerk off in the dressing room. And I hated those saleswomen who smiled with that smirky glint in their eyes when they asked whether the pink teddy with the lace and garter belt was the right size. Did she think I was shopping for myself?

Of course I never could buy something like that for Maxine. I had to admit, though, that the few times I'd seen Maxine's frail body wrapped in the sheer elegance of one of those items, seemingly for my pleasure, it sent my blood flowing to certain anatomical regions best left in a low flow state, as least as far as Maxine went.

The sweaters on display were mostly wool and I picked one with blues and reds that said 'hand knit' on the label. I sniffed as I touched it, my allergies reacting like I was holding a cat. But it was beautiful and Maxine was worth every penny. After paying, we headed over to Kroch's and Brentano's. It was my first visit to a book store in six months and my heart pounded with excitement. God, the novels that had climbed and fallen from the best seller list without my knowing they existed. I briefly perused the fiction section, then wandered down the 'healthy living' aisle, which seemed like some sort of porno section.

"Look at this, Gail: How an Orgasm a Day Can Keep the Doctor Away. I haven't seen this in our textbook of medicine yet."

A few minutes later I found a beautiful photography book filled with all of Maxine's favorite models. It was even signed by the author. Why not two presents for Maxine? They may be her only ones. At the checkout counter, Gail cautioned me. "That book is fifty-five dollars. You don't make that kind of money."

I waved her off, fishing through my wallet for rectangular plastic. What else should I spend money on? My meals at home added up to about fifteen dollars a week, two thirds of which was invested in spaghetti sauce and peanut butter cups.

"I only regret not picking up a good mystery for myself."

Gail turned as she zipped up her coat. "There's one over there," she said quietly. "As good a mystery as I've seen in a while."

"Problem is, no time to read."

"It's not a book," she snapped. "It's that guy who's been following us."

A sharp pain zinged through my head, and had I still been a medical student, I would have incorrectly diagnosed myself as having ruptured a cerebral aneurysm. Without looking up I spun around and stepped quickly through Sports and Travel, then circling back around by Cooking. I peered over into Mystery. There he was, a figure right out of the books. Collar turned up, hat drawn down just below his eyebrows. Crooked front teeth. I lurched in front of him. He saw me and jumped, his paper falling away. I grabbed him by the parka, flipping him around, and before I could even think about stopping, I let loose with my right fist. I winced in pain as it found its mark squarely on his jaw. The impact exploded like a cannon as he whirled backward, tumbling over the entire shelf of mysteries. I looked down. He lay still on a bed of John Le Carre paperbacks.

Gail and other customers arrived on the scene moments later, "What the hell happened?" she gasped.

Pain pierced my right hand. I watched as it began swelling.

"Let's get out of here," I said, grabbing her arm with my good hand. We moved quickly into the street and back to the shielded parking lot off of Elm Street.

The ride back down Lakeshore Drive was done in silence for twenty minutes.

"Maybe we should stop and get some ice," Gail said.

"It'll be okay. I just hope that loud crack I heard was his jaw and not my fist."

"So what happened?"

"Keep driving."

The skyline was gray, menacing shadows of buildings loomed. To my right a bundled up couple lingered on the Fullerton beach, mittens locked. "It was a case of mistaken identity."

"Your mistake?"

"Nope. His. Messing with my identity was definitely his mistake."

"You better tell me everything, Danny."

"Forget it, Gail."

"I want to know. I can help."

"Keep your eye on the road and leave me alone."

"I swear to God, I'll drive this car right into Lake Michigan if you don't tell me."

No way was I talking. Not after what happened to Wanda. "Go ahead, Gail. The cold water may help the swelling."

Gail snarled. "You can't escape me. We're working together on 5-Meese."

"Wanna bet?"

"You sound like Alex." She paused. "Yeah, I'll bet."

Chapter 57 meese

"The indigent ward." That's what they called the fifth floor in the central section of Richard Meese Hospital, home to the dispossessed South Siders with no medical insurance. A throwback to the infirmaries of World War II, Meese's bragging rights were limited to the fact that this was the only ward in the hospital where patients actually outnumbered cockroaches. Actually, Meese held two expansive wards, so large that patients often found themselves in the wrong beds, sometimes getting a procedure they didn't bargain for. Like a spinal tap meant for another patient. Or a conjugal visit from somebody else's wife.

You couldn't fault Richard Meese Hospital for its squalid conditions considering the fact that no other private hospital offered anything comparable for people saddled without insurance. We were assured that a new inpatient building with adjoining outpatient and prenatal centers was in the works.

Most interns dreaded their assignment to Meese and with good reason. Substandard conditions, patients without regular checkups who didn't come to the hospital until they were on death's door, and call nights from hell, since most admissions came through the emergency room at ungodly hours.

But none of this bothered Gail and me. Taking care of patients with diseases born of poverty was answering to a higher calling, an affirmation of the Hippocratic oath we had sworn to uphold.

Still, it was tough delivering proper care to the multitude of patients on Meese. The nurse to patient ratio was as low as one to eight. Keeping someone at bed rest was a joke. Monitoring fluid intake and output was impossible. Enforcing no smoking rules was even harder. Patients with pneumonia pulled off their oxygen masks as soon as the nurses left, to inhale from the cigarettes they left smoldering under their beds. One ninety five year old man, a bed-ridden partial vegetable whose oxygen entered his body via a small plastic tracheotomy tube embedded in his neck, was caught smoking. The guy in the next bed placed a lit cigarette into the hole leading to his windpipe, watching with curious amusement as he blew smoke rings out through his Adams' apple.

But mostly, Meese ran surprisingly smoothly, perhaps more so than many of the plush, more private wards in other parts of the hospital. And that success was due mainly to the efforts of one person, someone I would shortly call upon for some very important information.

Chapter 58 gator-aid

Maggie Gator brushed her tightly woven braids from her face, her girlish features making her appear a decade younger than her forty years, especially impressive as she worked full time while raising four children. Gator's medical acumen put many MD's to shame.

"Your patient, Mr. Johnson, was treating himself and half the ward to this stuff." She handed me an empty body of aftershave. "Said it tastes like Tequila and lime."

I studied his flow-sheet. She had started an IV in his thrashing arm, flushed the volatile after-shave from his system, and sedated him with just the right amount of librium. These were the heroic tasks of a battle-weary intern, not a floor nurse. And the funny thing was, Gator was hardly high up on the medical food chain. She was a ward clerk, a job that entailed clerical tasks such as scheduling tests, locating empty beds for new admissions, and calling in for lab values. There was no mention of shoving large bore catheters into stomachs, floating IV's into veins as wiggly as earthworms, or performing entire histories and physical examinations on our resident's patients.

I raised the aftershave bottle to my nose. "Came out smelling good on that one," I said with a wink.

Gator, as we all called her, had a wide smile anchored by high cheek bones. Her carmel-colored face was a backdrop for perfectly sculptured teeth. She grabbed the green bottle. "Hey now. Drinking that stuff can be nasty. I thought I handled things pretty well."

"Except for one thing."

"Oh?"

"Next time have some lemon and salt at the bedside."

Gator punched my shoulder. "Okay, Mr. Bartender. You try putting an IV into a moving target. Next time I'll call you at three in the morning."

"Put away the pout, Gator. Why don't you get your nursing degree and make it official? You'd be head nurse in no time."

Gator flashed a sheepish grin. "You guys need me as ward clerk," she said, rummaging through the papers on her clipboard until she came upon an order sheet in my handwriting. "Who else could put up with these orders of yours, Dr. Danny?" Gator's eye-lids furled in mock distaste as she read down the page:

"<u>Vital signs</u>: make sure patient is breathing.

<u>Activity</u>- poker 4 hours a day max.

<u>Fluids</u>- limit intake of colognes, perfume and antifreeze.

<u>Diet</u>-search room for hidden salt shakers.

<u>Medications</u>- roach motels at bedside."

I tossed the after shave into a garbage bin and prepared for morning rounds. "On second thought, Gator, you ought to be in medical school."

"Like I said, you couldn't get along without me. I may be the most well-connected person at this broken down old place. A good ward clerk needs connections." She smiled.

"Gator, I need a favor."

"Gonna cost you."

"Big time I bet. I need an employment photo of someone who used to work in housekeeping. His name is Thaddeus Anderson."

Chapter 59 gail and me

Ever since we had gone Christmas shopping, things had changed between Gail and me. That night Gail had insisted on getting my hand x-rayed and then accompanied me to my apartment where she packed my hand in ice and poured me a cup of hot tea with a shot of Wild Turkey, every bit the analgesic that codeine was. Tired, drunk, and anesthetized, I told Gail everything. From my Thanksgiving encounter with Tannenbaum, to the break-in at Goldman's office. Now she knew about Cantrell's file that was stolen from my apartment, the charts, the poisons, everything.

Unlike Alex, who laughed off the notion of conspiracy, Gail took me seriously. It was ironic the way Alex, the born-again Judah Maccabee, willing to defend his religion to the death, taunted me, telling me I was getting too paranoid for my own good. If there really was a killer, Alex would of course be more than happy to rip his lungs out. With Alex, life was that simple. Ripping someone's clothes off, or ripping someone's lungs out.

Gail, who'd spent her formative years dodging rulers across the knuckles at our Lady of Sorrows and had been told that the way to tell if someone was Jewish was to look for the horns on his head, listened intently. When I was done, she hugged me and with tears in her eyes, said: "Oh my God."

Gail had two points of contention, the first concerning the black man at Wanda's funeral. The man I said was Tannenbaum in disguise. "Sorry, Danny, but a white man can't just walk around with his face painted and expect to get away with it."

"I know, Gail. But I also know that it was Tannenbaum. The eyes. And the startled look when I called him by his name." I needed to find out if it was possible to change from white to black and then back.

Gail's second disagreement concerned Sol Goldman. I explained how his connection with the now deceased deans, Charles Cantrell and James Bramwell, stretched all the way back to his medical school days. "Goldman knew that patients were being poisoned, Gail. And he knew it was ergonovine that was used to poison them."

"I don't know," she said shaking her head.

"For God's sake, he checked articles out of the library. The missing toxicology reports are locked in that other drawer of his. I'm sure of it."

"At worst, he's obstructing justice. But killing people? I don't think so. Besides, why the hell would he order a toxicology screen on a patient who presumably died of a heart attack? Don't you think that would be the last thing a killer would do?"

That particular point had bothered me for some time. Why would Goldman do something to incriminate himself? "He may not have ordered them, but he sure as hell is suppressing the results."

"I would too, Danny. If word got out, they'd close the place down. Poisoning Jews in a Jewish hospital isn't what I'd call a smart publicity stunt. Besides, there is one other thing you've overlooked." She paused. "Sol Goldman is Jewish. He looks Jewish, he acts Jewish, and I don't know many Catholics who take two days off for Yom Kippur."

This seemingly simple observation caught me by surprise. I'd looked at Sol in many different lights before--Chairman, physician--and lately as a possible killer. But until now the religion thing hadn't been there. A Jew killing Jews? It wasn't possible, was it? Then again, a lot of things didn't seem to be making sense anymore. But she did have a point. "If Goldman didn't order those tests, who did?"

"Don't start talking like some TV show detective. Let's just figure out which leads we can follow."

"What do you mean, 'we'?" I saw Wanda Bylevin hanging from her kitchen rafters. I imagined her taking her last breath, her eyes bulging from their sockets, her urine and bowel contents spilling down her leg.

I felt a nudge in the ribs. "Hey, what's wrong?"

"I don't want you involved."

"Then why did you tell me?"

"Lapse of intelligence."

"Fine. I'll go down to the ER. I'm sure Mulroney would be interested in hearing what I have to say."

"You wouldn't."

"You're damn right I would if I thought it would save your life."

"They'd shut the place down."

"We could go to Northwestern."

"Come on, Gail. This is serious."

"Far as I see it, there is only one lead we really have to work on."

I sulked in silence.

"Thaddeus Anderson," she said. "I've got a feeling he's still working at the hospital. New name, new face, same old Thaddeus."

I remained silent, weighing my options.

"Well?" she pursued, packing another towel with ice. "Am I in or out? I'd appreciate an answer before Mulroney goes off shift."

Gail smiled as surrender filled my eyes. I knew I was going to regret it.

Chapter 60 thaddeus anderson

You'd never guess that Thaddeus Anderson had been employed in the Richard Meese housekeeping department for three years, at least not from the response Gail got that next week as she besieged hospital housekeeping personnel with questions. Thaddeus, it seemed, might as well never have existed, for in those three years, Gail couldn't find a single employee who remembered anything that would give us a bead on the guy or anyone who might have helped him. It appeared that Thaddeus Anderson usually dined alone and took his breaks with a pack of Camels and the hospital newsletter, rarely lifting his head if someone sat down to join him.

He'd disappeared over a year before, the same time the murders had stopped. I wondered whether that vial of highly concentrated Ergonovine found unopened in the back of his locker mentioned in his file in Goldman's office was not a blunder, but rather a deliberate act to taunt: 'Catch me if you can.'

The timing of the murders as well as the vial I found under Mrs. Garber's bed were all the proof I needed. Thaddeus Anderson was back at work.

The killer didn't have to be Thaddeus of course, it might be a clone trained by the same organization. But I still had a strong feeling this was the same person, someone who knew the hospital inside and out, computers, call schedules, hospital routines. It would take a person years to accrue that kind of knowledge. If there were any chance of finding the current Thaddeus, first I had to find out everything I could about the old one.

A few days later, Gail ran up to me, her eyes bulging like a patient with untreated hyperthyroidism. "Come on," she said, dragging me over toward Meyer House Pavilion before I could finish the progress note I was working on. Once there, she led me into a room where an older woman was fastidiously arranging the bedspread and pillows on one of the beds. Her face was a bulbous collection of nasal cartilage and skin folds.

"Eva," Gail said breathlessly. "This is that other doctor I told you about. He has a distant cousin named Thaddeus Anderson."

Distant is right, I thought. From here to Neptune.

Gail's eyes warned me into silence. "Doctor Raskin is very concerned about his cousin. He's been looking for him for over a year, ever since he missed his cousin's Bar Mitzvah. He's trying to find out if it's the same man as the one you used to work with." Gail turned to me, silently chiding me to look concerned. "Eva and Thaddeus worked the same shift for half of the three years he was here. They often grabbed a cigarette together in the stairwell."

"But I thought..."

"Never mind that stuff about Thaddeus being a loner," Gail said. "He and Eva were friends. He seemed to take to Eva." Gail winked. "Maybe it's that Croatian accent of yours."

Eva's eyes twinkled through doughy lids, and her face flushed against her overly starched uniform.

I wasted no time questioning Eva, starting with Thaddeus's appearance. Eva's description was vague. "Sort of regular-- blended in with everyone else. Medium height, brown hair, sometimes came back from vacation with a mustache."

"Do you have any photos of him? You might have taken one at a party or something."

Eva scratched her chin. "Maybe you have one I could look at. That way I could tell you if they were the same person."

My eyes besieged Gail's. "As soon as Dr. Peterson told me you knew a man named Thaddeus, I called home and asked my mother to send me a picture. It won't be here for a few days." I gave her my sincerest look. "That's why I was hoping you might have one."

Eva paused in thought. "Once we asked Thaddeus to pose for a photo at Thelma Radcliff's retirement party. He didn't take too well to cameras."

Damn.

"Where'd he go?"

Eva shrugged. "Had family somewhere in Michigan," Gail and I looked at each other.

"Arbor Hills?" I asked.

"Dunno. But the boss didn't like that goatee of his. He don't like facial hair on employees." I wondered if that included Eva, who had more of a mustache than I grew in four years at college.

"Anything else remarkable about him?" I asked.

"I already asked her," said Gail. *Hey, we all take our own history, don't we?* "Do you remember any scars?"

"Where?"

I fidgeted nervously. "On his face."

Eva shook her head. "Don't recall a scar."

"Hey," I pursued. "One other thing about my cousin, he never wore dress shoes, not even to Bar Mitzvahs and weddings. Always wore boots."

"Every man here wore low shoes with rubber bottoms. Orders from the chief."

"How about any unusual behaviors. My cousin... he ..well... he often made a bit of a fool of himself at parties."

Eva set two neatly folded towels down on the freshly made bed. "I don't think the man I knew is your cousin."

"Why not?"

"This Bar Mitzvah thing," she said," that's for Jewish people, right?" I nodded. "I don't get personal or nothin' with people, but the Thaddeus I knew didn't seem Jewish."

"He's not," I said. "He married into the family."

"Well, I sure couldn't see him goin' to no Bar Mitzvah."

"Why not?"

"One time at lunch, we were talking about my family in Europe. I told him how one of my brothers helped hide a Jewish family from the Nazis. Thaddeus says there's no such thing as no Holocaust. He says it's just made up. Said the Jewish bankers and lawyers started it."

Bingo.

Chapter 61 gator

Margaret Gator stood with her arms folded.

"How do you expect me to get a photo of someone who hasn't worked here in two years?"

"Impossible?"

Gator nodded. "I'm sure it's been trashed."

"Suppose you get me a few photos of people still employed here?" I was hoping Gator wouldn't ask me what I meant by a few. She did. "One hundred and twenty three," I answered. That was the number of employees hired since Thaddeus Anderson had disappeared from the hospital based on a search through back issues of the monthly hospital newsletter. Since Wanda's death, I was going it alone on the research end of things.

If Thaddeus Anderson found it necessary to remain inside the hospital he would need a new identity. One of those photographs was likely to be on his new ID card. One out of one hundred and twenty three. It could be anybody, I mused as I watched Gator's face. Even a woman. But even if I had a chance to peruse those photos, how likely was it that I would be able to pick him out, considering I'd never seen what Thaddeus looked like? It was also possible that Thaddeus Anderson and Frank Tannenbaum were the same person. That I could tell with a close-up picture.

Gator had been tapping me on the shoulder with the eraser side of her pencil. "What's your interest in all this, anyway?" she asked, but then nodded and smiled. "Oh, I see."

I turned around. Gail Peterson was standing there making a fornicating motion with her thumb and index finger of one hand and the middle finger of the other.

"I may do lots of things, but operating a dating service ain't one of them. You want pictures of pretty women, you go out and buy one of them girlie magazines."

"Thanks, Gail."

Gail wrapped her arms around Gator. "We could use your help, Gator. You must know someone in the employment office."

Maggie held her tiny chin in her hand. "Can't you folks just go down and ask?"

"Been there, done that." Private and confidential. They wouldn't release a damn thing, not to a couple of interns. Especially when one of them was me. I had rapidly gained a reputation.

"Come on, Gator. I'll set you up in tacos for life." Those were her favorite.

She shook her head. "Not a good enough reason to risk my neck."

"It's important, Gator. It has to do with...." I swallowed hard.

"Wanda Bylevin," Gail finished.

Gator's smile faded. Though she had never worked closely with Wanda, they knew each other on a first name basis. She was shocked by Wanda's death, crying her heart out that day in the chapel. Gator must have known of my friendship with her, but never mentioned it.

"What's Wanda have to do with..."

My voice was stiff. "Wanda's murderer used to work in the housekeeping department here. We think he may have taken on a new job."

"This is beyond me," said Gator. "Why not go to the police?"

I winced. "Been there, done that, too." For two days I had tried to get Officer Mulroney to obtain the photos of the new employees, only confirming his suspicions that I was holding out on him. When the cops dragged me down to the station after Wanda was killed, Mulroney saved my ass from what could have been a lot of trouble, especially if things had leaked to the press. But he was sure even then that I hadn't told all I knew.

"Come on, Raskin," he'd probed, planting a wad of licorice smelling tobacco into his fleshy cheek. "What gives?"

Something held me back. I didn't want to talk about Thaddeus Anderson. Not to Mulroney. I remembered the argument we'd had in the ER when Randy Jordan had had his throat slit. Mulroney wrote it off as gang revenge, refusing to believe that the murderer was a patient in the next room, alias Frank Tannenbaum, and that the slaying had been a message to me. If I couldn't convince Mulroney of that, even after my apartment had been ransacked, how was I going to convince him it was possible that the same man had been killing patients in the hospital under different disguises for years? He'd either think I'd gone completely insane with paranoia, or worse, he might actually believe me, whereupon he would launch an investigation on his own. Which was exactly what I didn't want to have happen.

I needed a copy of the toxicology reports proving that thirteen patients had been poisoned. Short of that I had to be able to physically identify Thaddeus Anderson, or Tannenbaum or whoever he was before he could kill again. It was Maggie Gator or nothing.

"One other thing, Gator," I said, packing up my clipboard. "Do you think a white man could disguise himself as a black person?"

"What?"

"You know, get away with looking like a black man."

Gator winked at Gail. "Not if he was naked, he couldn't."

Gail burst out laughing. "Come on, Danny, get off it. No way. Right, Gator?"

Gator shrugged. "Beats me."

"Danny thinks the killer had his face painted black. Maybe with a little Halloween makeup."

"It's important, Gail. If Tannenbaum can get away with being black, he can get away with anything. It also means he was waiting for Goldman that day at the chapel."

"Well," said Gator. "I don't think makeup would do it. But I read something in Ebony how ancient Egyptians used to darken their skins. Used some sort of plant dye or something."

"Marry me, Gator."

Chapter 62 skin color

The Laboratory for Medicinal Plant Research was located in Hyde Park adjacent to the large, ivy covered Horticulture building. John Stedmire, associate professor in charge of investigations, an authority on the antioxidant effect of plant phytochemicals, met me inside the largest of the synthesis laboratories. After a five minute discourse on the many discoveries his lab had come up with in the last several years, he asked the purpose of my visit.

"I'm interested in knowing whether there are any plant dyes that can turn the skin black. I heard the ancient Egyptians used them."

Dr. Stedmire, a bean pole of a man, wore slightly crooked wire rims and a shirt untucked in back. He gave me a bewildered look, as if trying to tell where I was coming from. "You mean the Nubians," he finally said. "They were an ancient African tribe that used plant extracts to dye their skin darker."

"That's what I'm looking for, Dr. Stedmire. Dyes that affect skin color."

"Dr. Raskin, this lab focuses it's studies on plants that have therapeutic potential, especially in the field of cancer."

I knew this was going to be a dead end.

"However, in the age of diminishing grant funding, we sometimes find it profitable to ally ourselves with certain industries. A mutual back scratching if you will."

Here comes the part about Halloween makeup, I thought.

"Come on," he said, rising. "Let me show you something that might interest you." He led me to a long lab bench covered with test tube racks, graduated cylinders, a large spectrophotometer. "Ever hear of henna? It's one of the plants the Nubians used to make their dye." He picked up a small jar of what looked like shoe polish. "Our lab spent two years synthesizing a novel paste consisting of Henna root and essence of the juniper berry. That plus an added catalyst, the strength depending on the shade we're aiming for makes the best damn hair dye in the whole world." He smiled proudly.

302

"Does it work on skin?"

"Let me show you." He opened the top of a jar and with a small metal spatula, lifted a dollop of dark paste from the jar. There was a smell of berries and I sniffed twice.

"Juniper," he said. "Unmistakable. Once in the hair, it soon dissipates." He spread a thin layer of paste onto my hand, then wiped away the excess with some cheese cloth.

"My God, it really does look black."

"Lilly Pharmaceutical's dermatology division thinks it will work wonders for patients with the skin disease vitiligo. Turns an albino into a normal looking person."

"How long does this stuff stay on?"

Dr. Stedmire nodded. "Once it's in your hair, it stays until you use an alcohol based rinse to remove it. That's one of the reasons Lady Clairol is so interested in it."

"You sold it to Clairol?"

"Like I said, it pays the bills."

As I readied to leave I asked: "Mind if I take a small sample with me?"

Stedmire looked at me suspiciously. "Sorry. This is all we have left."

"What happened?"

Stedmire paused. "Somebody stole it."

"When?"

"Last July."

Chapter 63 eddie ingraham

When Maggie Gator excitedly slapped my shoulder and whispered, "Guess who's here?" I smiled. Call it a sixth sense, but I'd been feeling it for several days: Eddie Ingraham and I were about to cross paths again. Gail had told Gator everything there was to know about Eddie. I watched as the two of them giggled like pre-pubescent girls when Eddie appeared. He wore a sheepish grin, and the daunting wave of charcoal hair dangled over his eyebrow like an autumn eclipse. It was as if Paul McCartney had walked into the room. Or Elvis.

Eddie nodded at me, and when he reached the nursing station, Gator touched him softly on the arm.

"My, oh my. You be one messed up guy. Tell me you didn't really watch them take out that appendix of yours."

Eddie grinned modestly. "Looked like a big, bloody anchovy," he said, sending Gator's cupped hands to her mouth.

I noticed the hunk of plaster around an arm that was holding several books. "That cast for real, Eddie?"

"Sure is," he smiled, banging on it with his good fist. He moved closer and whispered, "but the break isn't. It's amazing that a little knowledge of anatomy and a couple of pilfered x-rays can fool the most enlightened orthopedic resident."

Gail sneered. "What's the point of a fake cast? I thought people with Munchausen's liked inflicting real harm on themselves."

"Righto," Eddie nodded. "Which is why I'm headed downtown to see an orthopedic surgeon who will hopefully stick a nice fat metal pin right about here." He pointed to the mid-portion of his humerus.

"Yechh!" cried Gator, steadying herself. She turned and hurried away, Gail in tow.

I walked with Eddie to the stairwell. "The elevators are forty years old," he said. "I got stuck in one a few weeks ago. Nobody came for an hour." Eddie handed me an envelope. As I reached out, he stared at my hand. "Looks like your white is coming off. I knew you had the soul of a black man."

"Don't get cute, Eddie. What's in the envelope?"

"Merry Christmas," he said. "I do expect something in return. A small gift will suffice."

The word 'Confidential,' emblazoned the letterhead on the inside of the envelope. Before me was a rough draft of a computer printout of a memo Dr. Emile Horner had addressed to Sol Goldman, copies going to the Chief of Staff as well as the Chicago chapter of the Anti-Defamation League. My legs felt like Jello. Horner was going public, exposing the murders on paper, something sure to ignite all the wrong people, not to mention the press. Meese would be as good as closed, and those responsible for the killings would find the next hospital at which to wreak their havoc. This was my fault, I said aloud, remembering the day at lunch when I'd told Horner about the Nazi rally and the visitor in the ER requesting a file I no longer had, then murdering the patient in the next room. Then two patients on my service died who shouldn't have. None of it meant a hell of a lot at the time, but I remembered how intently Horner had listened, his tattooed arm gripping mine, a man who had survived the century's worst horror, a man who wrote symphonies conducted by Leonard Bernstein, a man, now in the twilight of his life, struggling to eke out a living with what few patients he had left. Back then he was a shoulder, not an ally. I never thought he would pursue this the way he had.

When I finished, I turned angrily toward Eddie, demanding to know where he'd gotten the letter.

Eddie shook his head. "It doesn't matter where I got it. What matters is that if I could get it, so can other people. People who might be less benign than you are."

He was right. If the wrong people got a hold of that memo, Horner's life wouldn't be worth the paper it was written on.

I had a sudden sinking feeling. "Did you tell Horner about the poisonings?" I got close enough to grab him by his flannel shirt.

"Relax, Daniel. Don't you remember? You asked me to help, not the other way around. Believe me, I have better things to do than double cross a friend. Especially a doctor. You should know us Munchausens gravitate toward doctors. That's how we get the love we never got growing up."

That was only the second time I heard Eddie utter the word 'Munchausen'. Maybe he was making some progress. I felt my body relax. It was true. Not only had I told him about the killings, but I was the one who had given him a sample from the glass vial I'd found under Mrs. Garber's bed. I smoothed the tabbed collar of his flannel shirt.

"You better go talk to Horner," said Eddie. "Warn the sonofabitch."

If a final version of Horner's memo had already been completed and circulated, he was in big trouble. I had to find him. If he was being threatened, it was time to fold the cards. Bring what I had and go to the authorities, for Horner's sake. And for mine, since I was responsible for getting him involved.

Maggie Gator reappeared as Eddie was putting on his coat. She anchored the medicine cart against a wall and moved close, watching as he packed his books in a satchel, scrutinizing him the way she might an IV that was backing up. "Is it true young man, that you're going to impersonate a medical student in that anatomy class at the medical school?"

Eddie smiled and Gator puckered up like she had just sucked a lemon. "That be some gnarly stuff, them stinkin' cadavers and all. I'd sooner be stickin' hat pins in my auntie's voodoo doll then be takin apart some dead person."

Eddie flashed a smile, patting his anatomy book. "That's not quite true," he said. "I'm not going to impersonate a medical student."

I smiled, putting my arm loosely around Gator. "He's right, Gator. Eddie's going to impersonate the cadaver."

Chapter 64 emile horner

Dining with Emile Horner was like taking a journey to an old European restaurant nestled in some distant crevice of the Swiss Alps. Remembering a trip up the Matterhorn during a spring break in college, I felt like saying, "I'll have the Jungfrau fondue." Instead, I ordered the Kaufman Deli special of the day, a Reuben sandwich.

Emile Horner stared straight ahead. When his food came, he ate sparingly, insisting his meal be served in three courses, each accompanied by new silverware, a fresh cloth napkin, and a refill of soda water, a new lime garnish required. It took forty minutes to consume our first two courses: gefilte fish and matzoh ball soup.

I looked at my watch, wondering how much longer Gail would be willing to watch my patients. Between eating and dabbing his lips with alternating corners of his napkin, he told me stories. Tales I never wanted to hear. Or believe. Stories that brought him back to Vienna in the late thirties and directly in contact with a faith he had left behind in Poland.

Horner had had it all back then--a two-bedroom flat facing Swartzenplaff Square, a tenured position at the University of Vienna where he taught music and history, and most importantly, he was the number one violinist in the Vienna orchestra, widely considered to be the best in the world. The fact that Horner was Jewish seemed of little consequence, especially considering his University life. His colleagues and friends were almost exclusively gentiles from families who were the financial cream of Vienna. To them, Horner's religion was a minor peccadillo, a quip at a party mentioned only when the conversation dulled.

One day, Emile Horner was summarily dismissed from both the orchestra and the University. Cutbacks he was told, although no one except Jews were fired. The daily news began running editorials about the impure Jewish filth that had plunged Europe to the brink of collapse. Jews were the problem. Hitler had the solution.

Cognizant of the spreading Nazi storm, Horner sold his flat for a paltry twenty percent of what he originally paid, (ostensible infestation of Jewish germs bottoming out Vienna's real estate prices), and made his way back to L'vov, his family's shtetel in central Poland. News there was worse--talk of resettlement, whispers of liquidation. The rumors racked Emile, and he spent the next year trying to get his family to book passage with him to America. His pleas fell on deaf ears. His father was the village Rebbe, the religious and spiritual leader of the four hundred families who eked out the barest of livings, yet lived richly spiritual lives. His older brother Reichel had followed his father's rabbinical footsteps while Emile was allowed to follow his passion for music.

For eighteen months Emile bided his time in L'vov, assisting with the farm animals, handling the family's finances, helping his mother prepare the Sabbath meal. He frequently played violin at their makeshift synagogue, a converted barn house with an emerald-covered arc containing a Torah dating back to the Spanish Muranos.

His favorite pastime was playing with his younger sister Mara. "Such a lovely little girl," he repeated a dozen times. "Such a twig of beauty in a forest of hatred." Mara was six, with wonderful brown curls, soft ruby lips and hazel eyes that sparkled like a mountain spring.

His worst nightmare came to pass. He remembered it perfectly, he said. That day he arose earlier than usual to accompany his father to the makeshift synagogue where daily morning prayer filtered through the town like an April breeze. When sirens suddenly rang out he was brushing Mara's hair. The under-nourished chickens scattered for cover across the dusty road. Colorful leaves rose up from the ground as if carried by a volcanic force. Then a rumbling, far off at first, like a thunderous roll of clouds on an open prairie, then louder and more threatening--metal, dust, and wheels of destruction. The Gestapo unit halted in the central square of the village.

"They shouted through bullhorns in broken Polish. Told us we had thirty minutes to assemble outside with our belongings, one suitcase per family." Emile struggled to ease his family's terror. He found an inner strength, and comforted them while they packed. Then they were outside, assembled in the central plaza which every Friday afternoon, hours before the Shabbat sunset, was a happy, bustling market place.

"Ach schnell Juden!" one commandant ordered, and rudely herded the villagers into the oversized trucks. When his own family reached the front of the loading area, a soldier shouted at his father in German and then ripped the parcel of Jewish texts from his hands, scattering them in the road.

"It surprised the hell out of them when I spoke fluent German, which was a prerequisite at the Vienna Conservatory. One of the Gestapo lieutenants who happened to have been schooled in music in Heidelberg had heard of me. He spoke away from us to the commander of the unit, sometimes shouting. They wanted to take me back to Warsaw headquarters for interrogation. I refused unless my family was also permitted to go. After much debate, my wish was granted."

Emile Horner quickly skipped over the family's resettlement in Warsaw--the near-starvation, the daily brutality. Sixteen months of struggling to survive. All eight of them in one rat-infested room of a three bedroom flat with five other families.

"It was actually a relief," Horner said, "when they finally loaded us onto the trains that would carry us to Auschwitz. We were very proud to have survived as a family. We believed that better times were coming."

At Auschwitz, he and his brother were marched to one line, his parents and five sisters to another.

"I never saw them again," he said, wiping his eyes. "I remember waving to Mara as she marched to the delousing showers, trying to shout that I would talk to the authorities. That everything would be okay."

I could barely watch as Horner spoke. What it would be like watching my own family led to slaughter?

Emile Horner described how he was placed second in command of the Auschwitz symphony orchestra, a group of Jews who were forcibly imported from as far away as Vilna and Crackow. They were kept in separate quarters, well-fed, and well-clothed. They had two duties, one to placate international inspection agencies like the Red Cross, the other, to entertain visiting Gestapo dignitaries.

"Adolf Eichmann drew lots of attention with his Zyklon B ideas. Heinrich Himmler loved to stop by, as did just about everyone of importance in the Third Reich except for the Fuhrer himself. Anybody who slipped up during a Wagner symphony was dispatched to the gas chambers within an hour of the last encore."

Emile was able to smuggle food to his brother, Reichel, who was put in charge of cremating the thousands of people killed in the gas chambers. "He was strong, Reichel was," Emile said. "He died two weeks after we were liberated. Probably a form of refeeding dysentery."

Five minutes of silence. The matzoh ball from my soup sat like a paperweight in my stomach. The rest of my lunch remained uneaten. Considering I had been running from it for so much of my life, I wondered why I was suddenly so touched by this "Jewish stuff"? Growing up Jewish in Farmingdale, Michigan had meant growing up an outcast, an outsider. Christ-killer, the kids whispered. I represented the entire religion. If I was smart, all Jews were smart. I wore glasses, so naturally all Jews had bad eyesight.

Worse yet was having to leave baseball practice early for Hebrew lessons. I cringed when that pint-size yellow bus with the Jewish star painted on both sides pulled up to the backstop. Praying to the very God I was denying that the damn bus, along with its crazy driver Moishe, would just disappear. And if not, at least get rid of the yellow star on top, so I could lie and tell everyone I was being taken to my parole officer, or for a try out with the Detroit Tiger farm system. "See ya, sissy," they razzed. "Have fun at Jew school." Moishe took special delight in my torment. "Vun day you'll understand," he decreed.

And I hated Hebrew school so much that I started to hate myself. Why couldn't I just be normal, which in my town, meant Christmas trees and Easter eggs? My parents were unshaken in their conviction that I have a Jewish education, even if it meant alienation from my classmates and a daily identity crisis for me.

311

Farmingdale was not their choice, my father's job had been relocated. We had no option but to make the best of it.

The springboard to one's manhood, a Bar Mitzvah, should be a happy time, a celebration of hormonal effervescence. In my case it was just the latest in tribal embarrassments. Most of my classmates turned down their invitations, and those who did attend covered their ears when I chanted in Hebrew so as not to be hypnotized into doing something like donating their genitals as a sacrificial gift. My four years of Hebrew school weren't worth a fraction of the three hundred dollars in U.S Saving bonds I'd received, or the grove of trees planted in Israel in my name. Hell, there might be a whole forest of Danny Raskin pines somewhere in Tel Aviv and it still wouldn't make up for the countless hours I could have spent shagging fly balls with my friends or hanging out at the West Bloomfield Star Eight Movie Theatres.

In college I felt more comfortable going to the dorm Christmas party than to the Hanukkah celebration put on by the local Hillel chapter. I pledged a non-Jewish fraternity, whose members, now that I thought about it, looked like a bunch of poster boys for Hitler youth. I was their token Jew, taken to boost their frat g.p.a. and to fill a vacant position at second base on their intramural team.

In medical school there was no time for even thinking about religion, though if God ever took me up on all the deals I'd made in order to pass my midterms and finals, I would have ended up an orthodox rabbi.

None of this begins to explain, however, how I ended up at a predominantly Jewish hospital. Especially when the pearly gates of the Mass General and John's Hopkins had swung open for me. Why had I chosen Meese? Was it guilt ransacking my intestines? An inner yearning to come to terms with who I was? It was as if the Passover angel had stopped at my door and moved right in. I came to Chicago to become a good doctor. What happened? I was drawn into a Nazi rally and found myself throwing rocks with Alex Rosen on national TV. Then my patients began dying. Jewish patients. Murdered. People demanding a file I no longer had. For the very first time, it was

312

personal. Horner's life became a horror movie inside me. The kids who taunted me, dared me to defend a faith I'd cursed being born into. "Jew boy, kike, Christ killer," enough insults to fill a Thesaurus. I looked at Horner. In a different time and place those kids would have worn boots and starched brown uniforms, and I would have worn a yellow Star of David on my arm. Horner's pain triggered a release inside me.

"When was the last time you told anyone that story?" I asked. I knew some kids at college whose parents had survived the Holocaust. Few ever discussed it.

"It's been fifteen years, Daniel. You can understand my reluctance. There's a reason for talking about it now. To you."

Dr. Horner removed a handkerchief and wiped the inside of his wire rimmed glasses. Then he rested his arms on the table.

Horner's words were deliberate. "Danny, there is evil at this hospital."

I felt him scrutinizing my reaction and did my best to keep a straight face. Horner knew that Jewish patients at Richard Meese Hospital were being poisoned.

"How did you find out?" I asked.

"I was the one who ordered the toxicology screens."

Gail had been right. Suspicious from the start, Horner had ordered the tests. The first two came back positive for an Ergonovine-like drug, along with the respiratory depressant, Pavulon. After that the results no longer made it back to the computer. He had gone to Goldman repeatedly, never considering that it was Goldman who was hiding information.

Horner knew nothing of the association between the murder victims and having been a concentration camp survivor or a relative of one. Both groups were part of a declining population of individuals whose lives bore testimony to the true existence of such a horror. If you can't wipe out the Jews, then wipe out the memory of their attempted genocide. The motto of the Jewish people, 'never forget,' was being attacked in a diabolical fashion. Get rid of the witnesses, then change the story.

Horner folded his napkin and set it carefully to the side of his plate. "So eat, Danny boy. You're still growing." He stared into my eyes, sensing I was keeping something from him. I had no intention of telling him this murderer had worked at the hospital and that he might have passed Horner in the hallway on a daily basis, pushing a broom or passing out medications. Horner could be in danger, and I had to warn him without arousing further suspicion on his part.

"Things will die down, Dr. Horner. The crazy sonofabitch will get caught."

"A meshuganah if there ever was one," Horner said, raising his voice and pointing a bony finger.

By withholding information, I felt like I had betrayed Emile Horner and everything he represented. But what choice did I have? If that memo leaked any further than it already had, he would be in great danger.

"We need to keep this quiet, Dr. Horner."

"And go to slaughter like sheep? Feh," he spat. "I went that route once before."

Treading dangerous water, I told myself, shifting uneasily in my seat. "I don't suggest we pretend it's not happening. I just think it's best to keep things quiet while the officials are investigating."

"Officials? Tell me, Danny. Who do you mean? Your Chairman, Sol Goldman?"

He was right. Who the hell was looking into this besides me? "People know what's going on, Dr. Horner, that's all I can tell you. The bastard who killed those patients is going to be caught."

My voice was firm, my eyes focused. He had to believe me.

"Oh, Danny. You're either a poor liar or you feel sorry for me. It's beyond one man. If he's caught, someone will take his place. The force of hatred behind all this won't stop until the damage is irreparable."

"Close the hospital?"

"More than that, Danny."

"Huh?"

It was Emile Horner's turn for silence.

"What could be worse?" I asked. "I remember you telling me how important this hospital was to the Jewish people of this city."

314

Emile Horner sat quietly, thinking.

"What could be worse?" I repeated. My legs bounced with nervous energy under the table. After a minute Horner reached down and brought out his brief case. He pulled out the Chicago Tribune and scanned the second section. "Here," he said. "Read this."

Plans have been finalized for the June 15 visit of Vice President Barrish to Chicago where he will dedicate the opening of Richard Meese Medical Center's state of the art diagnostic cardiovascular center. The former Chicago Congressman, born at Richard Meese Hospital, will lecture on the future of health care delivery, after which he will undergo a cardiac workup, similar to what the new facility will offer.

A sour taste rose to my throat.

Horner looked up. "The first Jewish Vice-President in history is returning to the place where he was born, into a place where Jewish patients are being murdered."

"You don't think..."

"That's the trouble," Horner interrupted. "Nobody is thinking. Something has to be done."

Horner left the table to answer a page, and I tried to convince myself that what he implied was impossible. Not here, even with all that had happened. Vice-President Barrish was one of the best liked politicians in recent memory, a hero to Jews across the country. Political analysts were touting him to be the next President, the first Jewish president. My mother refused to even utter the words, Jewish president, lest an evil eye look down and ruin everything. God forbid if something were to happen to him.....again, I forced the idea from my mind.

When Horner returned he picked up his briefcase and the check. "I'll take this," he said. "I've got a patient waiting to see me."

I remembered the reason I had asked him to lunch in the first place. "Dr. Horner, I need to talk to you about a memo you sent."

"Tomorrow night, at the hospital Christmas party."

"But.."

"No buts, or I'll leave you the bill. Tomorrow will be fine."
He turned around.

"Dr. Horner, whose idea was it to invite Vice President
Barrish to Richard Meese Hospital?"

Horner wasn't smiling as he laid two dollars into the clean
ash tray.

"Sol Goldman's."

Chapter 65 Sol's perspective

Sol Goldman looked up from his desk. Through his window shades, he watched as the wintry moon darted between clouds. How had he let it get so far? Why hadn't he done the safe thing--the right thing? Close the hospital, for Christ's sake. Let the killing move to a different battle front. He was so used to being in charge, yet now stood helpless as the hospital which he had given his life for was unraveling before his eyes. And with Vice-President Barrish coming to town, an event that should be a crowning glory for himself and the medical center to which he had dedicated his life, he realized things had gone past the point of no return.

It wasn't his fault, he told himself. Why should he feel guilty? He brought in help, dammit, the best that was available anywhere. They told him he was doing all that he could. But he knew inside, as any good captain does, that Richard Meese was his ship and his alone, and culpability not withstanding, he saw himself as ultimately responsible for its likely demise.

He opened his desk drawer and pulled out an intern roster, flipping through the biographies until he came to Danny Raskin's. He slugged down the last of the scotch. That Raskin. So innocent, so naive, yet so full of purpose. Didn't he know he needed to get the hell out, to leave things as they were, before it's too late? But much as Sol hated to admit it, Danny was their last chance. It was Danny or nobody. And now Danny sat directly in harm's way. And it was Sol who put him there. The last straw, Sol thought. Even if he could cope with everything else, how could he live with himself for sending Raskin to a likely death?

Sol bit down hard on his lip, looking at the picture of Raskin. The boy was brave, stupid but brave. Sort of like his own son Richard, who'd died four years before in a motorcycle accident. Richard wasn't afraid to stand up for what he believed, for what was right. He had learned that from his dad, dammit. And now Richard was dead. And soon Raskin soon might be, too. And just like Raskin, his son Richard had once hated him. But thankfully they had worked things out before he'd died.

Sol would never have let his son down. How could he let Raskin down? Raskin was doing the right thing and he didn't even know it. And now it was Sol's turn to do the right thing. He touched his finger to his lips and rested it on the picture of Danny. "Thank you," he said.

Chapter 66 preparing for the party

Clinic ended later than expected. I needed time to shower and change into the only clean clothes I owned, so clean that the price tags were still on. I had no idea how much work awaited me on 5-Meese. But the hospital Christmas party was our party, thrown in our honor. I'd better show up.

Maggie Gator folded her hands as she watched me lumber toward the nurses station. She nodded at the wall clock. "You got yourself a party to go to."

"Be lucky if I make it by nine."

Gator moved closer. "Now what you got to do that ain't been done already?"

I looked at my cards. "For starters, rewrite IV orders on six patients."

"Wrote them for you," she said, handing me a stack of papers. "Just sign. What else?"

"Change a few IV's."

"Done."

"Gator, you didn't?"

"What else?" she demanded.

I looked down my patient laundry list. There had to be something Gator hadn't done. "Here we go," I announced. "Draw two sets of surveillance blood cultures on bed four." Gator picked up a sterile bag containing four bottles of blood mixed with culture media.

"Just waiting for the lab to pick them up. Anything else?"

I thought hard. "I have to replace Mr. Lawrence's nasogastric tube. You couldn't have done that, because you didn't know I was going to change it."

Score one for the intern.

Gator's eyes twinkled. "Done."

"Impossible."

"Saw the x-ray report that said it was kinked in the duodenum."

"Maggie Gator, will you marry me?"

320

Gator let out a laugh normally produced by lungs twice her capacity. "And have to clean all them stains off your clothes? Boy, you be crazy! But I do thank you for your Christmas present," she said, shaking her head. The small hoops in her ears played a delicate chorus of Jingle Bells. She handed me an envelope. "Here's something for you."

"It wouldn't by chance be something from the employment office, would it?"

Gator shook her head. "Lord knows I tried getting you those pictures. People up there seemed a bit antsy. Someone from security gave me a call. Wanted to know why I asked for pictures of all the new employees. Asked me if you was in any way involved in the request. Anyway, got you something better."

I held the photo in my hand. I knew from the description I'd heard that I was looking at Thaddeus Anderson. I wrapped my arms around Gator. "Where did you get this?"

"Hortense, the clerk up on Kaplan surgery. Takes photos all the time. Three years ago, there was a hospital picnic. A tornado touched down near by and trashed the place. Hortense was taking some pictures while housekeeping was cleaning up the mess. Eva over in housekeeping helped me pick him out."

I took a closer look. "It's good to finally make your acquaintance, Thaddeus," I said aloud. "Very good, indeed."

Chapter 67 resident complications

Arthur Redmon was the unlucky resident chosen by lottery to spend the night in the hospital instead of going to the Christmas party. That meant covering three floors by himself. The two of us hadn't gotten along from the start, and he seemed to take undo umbrage at my growing friendship with Gail.

Art's mood was worse than usual when he showed up twenty minutes late for my signout. Angry lines traversed his cheek bones as he glared at Gator. "There better not be any admissions tonight," he warned, as if she could control who rolled into the ER.

"Don't you worry yourself none, Dr. Redmon. I take care of things for you. You know that. Remember last week? Told me not to get you out of bed for nothin."

"I didn't mean..."

"And I didn't. Worked up the patient myself. Just like you asked."

"Gator..."

"Wrote your note. Signed your name. Everything."

Gator gleefully noticed Art's discomfort. What difference did it make if Gator admitted Art's patients? He never examined them anyway. Just copied someone else's findings into his own notes.

Art took my signout sheet and placed it on his clipboard with the rest. "Don't drink too much tonight," he said. "I may need to page you at midnight."

I bit my lip. Theoretically, interns on call the night of the party could be called back into the hospital at midnight. But only if it got too busy for the residents to handle things by themselves.

"He doesn't need to come back here, Dr. Redmon. The party's for him. I take care of things around here."

"Who asked you?" barked Art. "Besides," he glared in my direction, "you think I'm going to have fun covering three floors all night while you and that dyke intern friend of yours..."

"Beg your pardon?"

"Peterson. Your buddy. Don't tell me she's not a lesbian. The only woman in your group not married or screwing around."

I wondered whether strangling Arthur Redmon would be considered a mercy killing. "Lay off, Redmon. You don't give a shit about the patients around here. Why concern yourself with the doctors?"

I glanced at Gator who bit back a smile. Art turned. "Remember the memo, Raskin? At midnight you're mine. My discretion."

"You have no discretion." I said as he walked away.

When he disappeared, Gator smiled.

"Whooee, Dr. Danny! You've gone and got yourself in a mess of trouble. Whooee, Cinderella turns back into the pumpkin! That boy be calling you at midnight sure as the sun sets."

"The only way I'm back at this hospital tonight, Gator, is as an in-patient on the alcohol detox service."

Chapter 68 maxine chu

I had one last stop to make before leaving. Maxine Chu's room. Originally Maxine was supposed to go home the next day, her third attempt since Thanksgiving. Each time, she had returned inside a week with a complication, usually an infection caused by organisms whose names I couldn't even pronounce. Thanks to the latest round of chemotherapy, Maxine was medically stable, but barely so. Much more was needed. Scans revealed the continued presence of nodes, no larger than four months ago, but no smaller either. Without regression of her cancerous lymph tissue, her prognosis was dismal.

While waiting for the elevator, I thought back to the tumor board meeting Gail and I attended. We sat in the back of the Grand Pavilion at University of Chicago, listening in disbelief as they threw around four syllable investigational drugs, garbled statistical analysis, and ranted pompous renditions on the state of the art as they knew it. At times it didn't even seem like they were discussing Maxine. She was more like a set of data--ugly bone marrow slides, a liver studded with tumor, a CAT scan plump with lymph tissue, or even worse, a statistic; ten percent response with one treatment; fifteen with another. Why couldn't they see her as I did, a living, breathing woman whose boundless soul was much larger than the sum of her individual organs, diseased or not? Gail watched me shift anxiously in my chair.

"Easy, Danny," she whispered. "They're just trying to be objective."

"I'm fucking sick of objectivity," I replied, causing heads to turn. The discussion continued in sterile fashion. Which drug to try next, what invasive test they could inflict. One of the Mudd-Fudds, an MD and PhD, suggested that to fully and finally understand the aggressive nature of the tumor, an autopsy would be necessary.

My hand shot up. "Excuse me!" I stood up, taking notice as heads turned in unison. Some had that puzzled 'who invited the intern?' look.

"Dr. Raskin, I believe." Dr. Chagris, chief of Oncology service, as cold a man as I'd ever seen, tilted his horn-rimmed glasses over his nose. "Shouldn't you be back at the hospital taking care of patients?"

"I am trying to take care of my patient," I said. Gail tugged at my pant leg. "I'm not well versed in your statistics and technical lingo," I continued. A few nods. Go ahead, dirt ball, they probably were thinking. Make a fool of yourself.

"Maxine Chu is my patient. She is warm, wonderful..." I felt my voice crack.

Chagris had a reputation for rarely talking to interns. "Yes, Dr. Raskin. I'm sure she's sweet. But this is not a popularity contest. What is it you want to say?"

"Sit down," Gail whispered.

"Maxine has had four different chemotherapeutic regimens over the past four months. Along with the laparotomy and radiation they have taken their toll. "

Dr. Chagris looked at his watch. "We have one more case today, so if there's a point to this, make it."

"Chemo's not working."

"Precisely why we're here, young man. To find another regimen that will work."

"None of it works, dammit. Don't you see? The chemo is for shit."

Gail cringed. A loud hush filled the room. Telling an oncologist his chemo is shit is like telling a French chef his souffle tastes like pudding.

Dr. Chagris straightened. "Dr. Raskin, we're dealing with a severe illness. Grossly diseased lymph nodes. Total infiltration of the bone marrow."

"We're dealing with a human being, not some wind-up doll whose string you pull and she smiles and says: give me adriamycin. Give me cytoxan. Watch me puke. Watch my hair fall out. Chemotherapy hasn't worked. It's draining the very life it's supposed to save."

Some snickers.

"Maxine is a young woman who needs a chance to live."

Dr. Chagris rubbed his chin. "You suggest that we give up?" His tone mocked me. Throw in the towel when there was yet another regimen to nauseate the patient? Or to remove that last hair follicle from her head? Oncologists didn't give up. It was just that simple. I'd seen them push intravenous chemotherapy into a 95 year old woman who was already comatose.

"I don't want to give up," I said loudly. "I want to try something else."

"What do you have in mind, Dr. Raskin?" The bastard was smiling. "Why not share your idea with the rest of us."

My tie felt like a noose. The spaghetti sauce stain on my white coat loomed like a gigantic Rorchak. The eyes of intelligence stared skeptically in my direction. I took a deep breath.

"A bone marrow transplant."

Silence filled the room. Heads shook. Talk about long shots. Dr. Chagris cleared his throat. "Perhaps our visiting intern should spend a little less time befriending his patients and a little more time reading his medical journals. Transplants of bone marrow stem cells work for several childhood leukemias, but is not an effective treatment modality for Hodgkin's disease."

"There have been scattered reports of success in some lymphomas." Keeping a straight face, I quoted three different references. Actually, I read them off the sleeve of my white coat. Nevertheless, Gail and the others looked aghast. And for once I was thankful for Malcolm Spool, who first proposed the idea of a bone marrow transplant, and for the past week had been supplying me with case studies. I vowed right then and there never to call him Malformed Stool again.

Dr. Chagris waited for the murmur to die down and for his own color to return. "I'll grant you there has been a smattering of success. But it's too premature for us to be involved with such a procedure. Especially in a case like one four eight."

"Her name is Maxine Chu."

"Right. Besides, here in Chicago, we haven't even done a marrow transplant."

"Maybe you should get off your butts and start!"

Gail pinched my leg.

326

Dr. Chagris had finally had enough. "Young man, I will not tolerate insolence from someone who has yet to complete a year of post-graduate study."

A deep voice in the center of the room rose above the fray. "Dr. Raskin is right. We should get off our butts."

It was Sy Kornfeld, one of the best liked clinical professors at the hospital. He had done the initial consult on Maxine, and even though he was no longer involved in her care, he stopped by now and then just to chat with her. Chagris looked lonely up there, now that he was shadowed by a man whose practice of medicine was shaped by ethical standards.

Sy Kornfield remained standing and nodded appreciatively. "Dr. Raskin knows the patient better then any of us. I think his consideration should be taken seriously."

"Sy, we can't do a marrow transplant."

"Can't or won't, Mort? Sheldon Moskowitz is one of the top oncologists at University of Washington. We all know he's coming here next month for a six month's sabbatical. If anybody could orchestrate a bone marrow transplant, he could."

"But stage-four Hodgkins, Sy? Come on, be realistic."

"You be realistic, Stan. Can you tell me an easier way to get compassionate approval from the Human Subjects Committee? It's a slam-dunk."

Chapter 69 marrow preparation

As I stepped into Maxine's room, packages in one hand, doctor's bag and coat in the other, she smiled. On her bed lay several magazines: Rolling Stone, Mother Jones, and a book of Jamaican poetry. Eyeliner, lipsticks, and an assortment of facial cosmetics littered the room. Maxine's turban rested comfortably on her head, while an open terry cloth bathrobe barely covered a lace nightie. An unfamiliar perfume lingered. I handed her the packages and stepped back as she gracefully removed the wrapping paper. She thumbed through the photograph book, eyes wide. "Tres chic," she said. A minute later she held up the hand-knit wool sweater that still had me wondering whether it was really made of cat hair. "Tres elegant. Merci beaucoup!" She removed her robe and pulled the sweater over her head. I couldn't help but watch the shadow of her breasts bounce lightly with her movements.

"I'll grow into it," she smiled, cuffing the ends of the oversized sleeves. "Hey, you better get outta here. Your party starts in an hour."

"I'm planning my usual fashionably late entrance."

"I wouldn't if I were you. Not if you plan on making it with Gail Peterson tonight." Maxine whistled. "She told me about her outfit. She's going to have those sex-starved surgical residents eating out of her hand."

Maxine had been doing that lately, making assumptions about me and Gail. I won't deny that I blushed when she teased me, especially if Gail happened to be nearby. I found I couldn't keep myself from asking Maxine what she and Gail talked about during their visits, secretly hoping I had come up in the conversation. But Maxine could keep a secret better than I could.

"I'll probably be the only one not drinking, Max." I told her that I might have to return at midnight.

"Don't you dare. This is your night. Besides, I don't want you in my room later." Maxine smiled and threw her head back. "Got big plans."

"You and Lo made up?"

"Hell no!" Maxine sat up at the side of the bed and reached down to pull out a box. Saks Fifth Avenue. Maxine lifted out a sequined black dress, the length of which I calculated to barely cover her thighs.

"Wanna see me in it? It grabs me in all the right places."

"What's the occasion?"

Maxine ignored my question as she looked into her mirror on the bed stand. She opened her mouth and picked at her lower gum. "I have a date with Jimmi tonight." She abruptly stood and walked to the bathroom. "Be right back."

Rasta Jimmi Redding. Much as I hated to admit it, the idea of it sent pangs of jealousy into my chest. I actually had grown to like Jimmi. I often found him in Maxine's room, cuddling her hand in his. Sometimes he would read her poetry. Other times he was strumming an oversized guitar, something between Jimmy Cliff and Bob Dylan. He was very courteous to me, felt I was the one responsible for the medical hope she lived for.

Last week, passing by the escort office at one in the morning on my way back from the ER, I stopped to say hello and ended up playing Caribbean poker with Jimmi and his friends until three a.m. I usually won in poker, but that's because I can tell a bluff by looking in my opponent's eyes. Jimmi and his dark shades cleaned me out of ten dollars.

I heard the toilet flush and the door opened. "Jimmi's bringing me a special Christmas present tonight."

I felt my face redden. It was probably gift-wrapped inside his zipper.

"Do you think it's wise to let Jimmi come up tonight, considering what's happening tomorrow morning?"

The next morning Maxine was to receive the first of the drugs that would irrevocably knock out the stem cells in her bone marrow. Ten days later, she'd get the harvested stem cells from her sister's marrow. If they took, she would live. If not, she would die. It was that simple.

Maxine took out a piece of floss and ran it between her lower teeth. "All the more reason to party tonight. Beside,

Danny, he's up here most nights anyway. She paused. "I told you before, we already went to second base."

"You let him touch....."

"I already told you that."

"You said you showed him, not..."

"Jealous?"

"Yes. I mean no. I mean..you just shouldn't be doing that sort of thing. It leads to... you know..."

Maxine smiled. "That's what I'm hoping."

I held my tongue. What business was if of mine what Maxine did? If it helped her feel good about herself, what the hell? No, this wasn't about Jimmi. I hated to admit it, but it was about me. And my own confused feelings for Maxine.

"Yesterday he said he might be falling in love with me."

Maxine had come a long way from dating a strict Chinese boy to a Rastafarian escort supervisor in his thirties who inhaled enough vegetation to fill a tropical rain forest.

"Isn't he a little old for you?"

"I never really knew my father very well, Danny. I suppose I'm compensating. At least that's what they would have said in Psych class."

Maxine's father had sent Maxine, her mother, and sister to the states fourteen years before from Taiwan. He stayed behind to get his business affairs in order. Six months later the family received a letter saying that he had remarried and his new wife was expecting a child. That was the last anybody ever heard from him.

"Ah, what the hell, Max. If you're happy, go for it. I was only worried about you getting enough rest before your marrow suppression tomorrow."

"If things go the way I expect, I'll sleep as sound as a baby. I'm supposed to smoke a cigarette." Maxine giggled. "You want to hear more?"

"I don't think so."

"And I don't want to tell you."

"No fair."

"You never told me about you and Wanda Bylevin."

Her name erased my smile.

"Sorry about that. After her death you looked like they had buried you too. I figured you two were closer than you let on. I'll give you one hint." Maxine checked the doorway, as if Lo would appear any minute. "Jimmi's going to bring two pairs of soft leather restraints."

"Maxine!"

"I read about it in Cosmo. Bondage. How to double the intensity of orgasm."

I'd thought that Maxine and I already had reached the limits of the doctor-patient relationship. Now I wasn't so sure.

"Besides never having sex, Danny, I've never had an orgasm. I've read all the books, tried all sorts of things." She paused, obviously blushing. "I figured that if this was the one good chance I have to experience one, I might as well make the most of it. Believe me, Jimmi had nothing to do with this. It was my idea. Took Jimmi a week to agree."

"Maxine!"

"Quit being such a prude."

"I'm not."

"Maybe not with Wanda Bylevin. But you are with me." Maxine folded her arms.

"What does that mean?"

"Nothing."

"Max, I'm your doctor."

"You can't even look at me as a woman. I see how you stare lustfully at Gail Peterson, like you're undressing her. With me, it's vital signs and cursory chit-chat. When was the last time you palpated my abdomen?"

I shrugged my shoulders, remembering two weeks ago when during the course of my examination, my palm pressing lightly below her belly button, Maxine pressed her hand on top of mine. "It hurts over here," she said guiding my hand down toward her pubic area.

"Don't get cute, Maxine," I had said, pulling back. "I could get fired." Later, I allowed myself to recognize my rapid heart beat, finding my palms more sweaty and my breathing quicker than I could explain.

"Look Max, I have to get ready for the party. Just wanted to give you your gift and say good luck for tomorrow."

Maxine frowned. "Don't remind me," she said. "But that's another reason for being with Jimmi tonight. Just in case things don't work out so well."

I had given careful thought to this bone marrow transplant before recommending it to Maxine. I read everything I could find, talked to physicians all over the country. I had great hopes. I had to. This was Maxine's one and only chance. Without it, her prognosis was three, maybe four to six months. Maxine needed years. She needed a life.

In the three weeks between the conference and the Christmas party, we located her sister and two cousins, all possible donors. Their blood types and immunologic status were ascertained and forwarded to Dr. Kornfield. Her sister was a near perfect match. Dr. Kornfield and visiting professor, Sheldon Moskowitz met with the Human Subjects committee and compassionate approval was obtained.

I had spent hours talking to Maxine, explaining that a successful bone marrow transplant could mean a complete cure. I hadn't used those words since we had met. "Cure me," I remember her saying over a fortune cookie. Now there was a chance. "I was just getting used to remission," she said. "Cure sounds a lot better."

The drugs Maxine would be getting deserved to be called poisons. Maxine's marrow would respond in one of two ways. They'd either spit out the new cells donated from her sister, or spit out nothing, in which case she would die from overwhelming sepsis or massive bleeding.

"Think positive, furball. The drugs you're going to get tomorrow will kill off those nasty cells being made in your bone marrow. Your sister's cells will then take over."

Maxine smiled. "My sister's not as cute as me. Will my bone marrow make ugly cells? After all is said and done, will I be ugly?"

I couldn't stifle my laugh. " Hardly, Maxine. When this is over with, you'll be the most beautiful woman in the whole world."

Maxine paused in thought. "You know," she said. "Between you and Jimmi I think I have just enough confidence to pull this off."

Chapter 70 frank tannebaum

Frank Tannenbaum, alias Thaddeus Anderson, was sprawled on his tattered, stained couch, oblivious to the six o'clock news blaring from a T.V. perched precariously upon a splintered crate. Two week's worth of Chicago Tribunes, along with several back issues of American Purity lay scattered about his apartment, a small run-down studio located in the far reaches of Chicago's segregated and inconspicuous west side. Well, at least it was affordable to Frank, who at the moment was in a negative cash flow thanks to the lousy wages they paid down at the hospital. But this didn't seem to bother him as he reached over and opened a fishing tackle box. The money would come, it had been promised. Even if it didn't, well, no matter. His was a higher calling.

He removed one of the many small glass vials from its plastic holder, raising it toward the light fixture on the ceiling. With two quick flicks of a fingernail, the cloudy, incandescent solution dissolved into a silvery fluid. Frank was glad he'd finished his third beer just moments before; it flattened the tremor in his hands, allowing him to withdraw 5 cc's from the vial up into his syringe. There we go, just like old times, Frank thought, tapping the upright syringe more out of habit than necessity. After all, he had served his country as a medic in Korea, not like the Jews who bought their way out, and the niggers who belonged on the other side of the battle lines. He knew one end of a syringe from the other, that was for sure. He would have made a great doctor, in a different time and a different place. But the country, his world, had gone to hell. His path had veered far off in another, more important direction. He pushed the plunger forward just enough to remove the excess air, causing half a milliliter of liquid to spurt out onto the wall. He set the syringe down on a cork coaster and held out his hand. Smooth as the scotch his boss had given him during that first meeting. Not even a trace of a tremor. As he picked up the phone and dialed Richard Meese Hospital, he thought about a time when he would drink scotch before every mission, rather than cheap beer. A change in prescription was coming, he thought. It would usher in the day when this country finally became wholesome and pure.

"Hello, this is Dr. James Calloway, calling," he said, his tone confident, authoritarian. He was, after all, very good at imitating dictatorial people, having grown up with a father who meted out justice with a stiff leather belt.

"I wonder if you might tell me whether Dr. Emile Horner is still in the hospital?" While waiting for an answer, he picked up the scrapbook from the rickety coffee table. No matter, he would be moving soon, perhaps to the Mies-Vanderow building right on Lake Shore Drive. Or maybe even to another state. New York maybe; his boss would find plenty of work for him to do there. He began flipping through pages of memorabilia, pausing only when he reached a tattered article, one generated by the Nazi march downtown. He stared at a picture of himself standing behind a young man wearing a Michigan sweatshirt. God, he thought, focusing on the shiny object in the palm of his left hand. If only that cameraman realized that he had accidentally caught on film his stabbing of a troublemaking Jew doctor, a kike who had done enough damage for one lifetime, even if only inadvertently.

On the next page was an obituary of his former employer, Dr. Charles Cantrell, Dean of Admissions at Arbor Hills Medical School. He had purposely positioned it to follow the picture of Daniel Raskin. He wanted to remind himself of the person responsible for the death of a noble leader like Cantrell, one of the founders of the movement. "Sorry, Doctor," he said shaking his head. "You were too vulnerable after Raskin exposed you at that graduation ceremony, too dangerous to be trusted; too visible to be of any further use to the cause. He squeezed the receiver with his clenched fist. It wasn't your fault you were about to sell us out. It's Raskin's fault and he'll pay. Once those files of yours are found, he's finished." Tannenbaum closed his eyes a moment and thought back a few weeks to when he had Raskin in his sights, an easy hit and run, right outside the hospital. If not for his friend on the inside,

Frank would have done it with relish, backing up his car when it was over just to splatter Raskin's guts right out his throat.

His only regret was that the uncanny bastard had picked up on his disguise in the first place. Though all of the organization's top operatives had been trained extensively in the fine points of disguise, even his colleagues grudgingly admitted that Tannenbaum was the master chameleon among them. Nobody picked out Frank Tannenbaum in one of his disguises, especially his black ones. He had the skin color down perfectly, thanks to samples he had stolen from the plant research lab. How could Raskin have spotted him?

Not to worry. When the time came, Raskin would suffer a fate much worse than any of those Jew patients Frank had bumped off, even worse than that whore, Wanda Bylevin. How dare that bitch stick her nose into something that was none of her business?

Still on hold, he toyed with a stethoscope, one that looked fairly similar to the one found around Wanda Bylevin's neck, the one he had taken that night in the library from Raskin. He laughed aloud. Like his colleague on the inside, who had fucked, then strangled that whore, he too would leave a message--a ritual gift wrapping of sorts, for a Jew conspirator.

Frank closed the scrapbook. It didn't matter what others might think of him--he knew he was a professional, polished American hero. Frank knew who he was and for what purpose he was put on earth. Sure he got smacked around a lot as a child, but that was for his own good. Two medals in Korea, then an invitation to join the special forces, serving with dignity deep undercover in jungles of Cambodia. He'd returned home to a changed country, run by traitors who, in a just world, would have been taken out back of the White House and summarily shot. He'd spent a year wandering the country in disgust, drinking himself sick every night, until finally he met up with a group of men just like himself. Frank felt he was the most vocal, the most sincere about his beliefs. One day someone came to talk to him about those beliefs and about how Frank could help to change the country. And the next thing he knew he was in Paris for three years, studying everything from weaponry and explosives, to disguises and history.   Two years in Damascus were followed by a year in Northern Ireland. He came back a new American,a true soldier, a righteous torch carrier for the new order.

The operator returned to the phone.   "Doctor, he didn't answer his beeper, so I assume he signed out. I believe he had plans to attend the hospital Christmas party tonight."

"The one at Morton's?"

"That's right. Would you like the phone number there?"

"No, that will be fine." He paused, hoping his rehearsing would pay off.

"I wonder if you might tell me the location of one of his patients, Mr. Jules Steinberg?"

"What did you say your name was?"

"Calloway, Dr. James Calloway. I'm not actually on the staff at Richard Meese. Mr. Steinberg is my wife's brother." Frank steadied his hand which was now beginning to shake slightly. He hoped this information from his friend on the inside had been correct.

"Let's see," the operator said. "Mr. Jules Steinberg. Hmm that's interesting. There weren't any more beds available in Meyer House. He's in the only private room on 5-Meese, room 507."

Frank thanked the operator and after replacing the receiver, opened another beer. Yes. Great. 5-Meese was perfect. Quiet, dark, no nurses. No security. Just perfect. He looked forward to meeting with Horner, the stupid Jew bastard. Telling those lies about extermination camps. There were no murders, not like Horner talked about. And the sooner his kind were gone, the quicker people would know the real truth.

Frank checked his watch, then went into the bathroom. Looking in the mirror, he removed the residual brown stain with an alcohol pad. For tonight's job he needed to be good and white. Professional. He removed the towel from his head. The gray hair was shiny, very becoming. He opened a box and after scanning its contents removed two, bushy eyebrows, dark blond but with streaks of matching gray. He shaved his brow clean then added toner makeup to cover over the scar under his

337

eyebrow. *Normally, he wore that scar like a saber tooth medal; but tonight, well tonight he had to look the part. He couldn't take any chances, not with that Raskin uncovering information right and left like he was a fucking Colombo or something.*

The new eyebrows attached perfectly with adhesive. He then opened his mouth and inserted a thin metal retainer, specially designed to angle his jaw an extra fifteen degrees. He smiled, hardly recognizing himself. He spent ten more minutes adding wrinkles to his forehead and a slight indentation to his chin.

When he was finished, he brushed off a size 44 white coat and straightened the name tag that read 'James Calloway, MD'. He reassured himself that the care he had given to his plan, though executed to perfection so far, wasn't even necessary. Nobody would catch on, not until it was too late. After he took care of business, he would change back into his work disguise one last time, just long enough to even the score with an old friend. It was a masterful disguise, he told himself, but was glad that this was the last night he would need it. He hated the forty minutes it took each day to apply the makeup, the wig, all the right touches. Fucking Jew, Raskin. He'd be sorry for the day he stepped up to that graduation podium.

As he readied himself to leave, he gazed out the window. The wind had whipped to blustery force. It was going to be a cold trip to and from Richard Meese Hospital tonight, he thought, deciding at the last moment to wear a scarf. He put the filled syringe into his pocket, along with a pair of surgical gloves and his stethoscope. He held out his hands. Steady enough, he thought. He paused at the door, as if the picture that hung from the mantle had beckoned him.

"Heil Hitler," he saluted with his outstretched hand.

Chapter 71 christmas party

Tuxedoed parking attendants, white-gloved doormen, a foyer modeled after the Palace at Versailles. Morton's Restaurant was one of Chicago's finest, the perfect place for a hospital Christmas party. Champagne flowing. The food like nothing I had seen since my cousin's wedding in Yonkers. Gail and I hovered over the lavish buffet like refugees from an Ethiopian famine. The jumbo shrimp resembled baby lobsters. The prime rib was so rare, and sliced so expertly thin that it reminded me of skin grafts I had seen in the burn unit.

At the other end of the room, barely drowning out the banal doctor chit-chat, a twelve piece orchestra belted out Benny Goodman tunes. It was the first time I had traded in my blood-stained whites for a sport coat and tie, an outfit I had been saving for either my wedding or my funeral, whichever came first. Gail's red-sequined cocktail dress reflected light from the crystal chandeliers, giving her the look of a human prism. Her hair, the color of apricots, sparkled in a French twist, and her delicate freckles seemed to dance across her cheek bones.

Gail watched as a Pulmonary attending sauntered by and refilled my glass with Cordon Negri. It was the fourth refill in ten minutes. "Easy buddy," cautioned Gail. "Don't forget when the clock strikes twelve, you turn back into Art Redmon's pumpkin."

"Screw him, Gail." I meant it. By midnight I planned to be just as anesthetized as that slab of prime rib on the cart. I took a long, deep drink, squinting from the effervescence. "I don't care what he says. I am not setting foot in that hospital tonight."

For the next half hour, Gail and I two-stepped our way through the restaurant, smiling at the attendings, making polite conversation. We stopped at the dessert table where Gail licked the confectioner's sugar off the top of a lemon tart. "This is bullshit, Danny. It's a farce. Tomorrow we go back to the same old torture. Lousy hours, lousy pay, no sleep. Treating us like royalty for one night doesn't make up for the abuse we get the rest of the year."

I gulped my champagne. "It's better than nothing."

It's better than nothing. That's exactly what Wanda Bylevin had. Nothing. Had she not tried to help me, she might have been at my side this very moment. I suddenly remembered I needed to speak with Emile Horner about his memo. I spotted him, the white scarf around his neck wafting in the room's ventilation. I would work my way over to him, to tell him that his so called "secret memo" to Sol Goldman was about as secret as a rumor in a sorority house. Horner needed to hear it from me. At all costs, do not trust Sol Goldman. I had to tell him.

With a hand oily from too much finger food, I felt the inside pocket of my sport coat for a napkin. Instead I pulled out the photo of Thaddeus Anderson. Gail grabbed the picture, blotting it with her napkin. "You're something else. Do you know the trouble Gator went through to get this?"

"Do you know how drunk I am?" But I wasn't really that drunk, and in fact I was quite embarrassed. The reason I'd brought the picture to the party was to show it around--see if anyone recognized someone even remotely familiar to the face in the photo. Gail cleaned it off and handed it back. I held it up to the fluorescent light and took another look, not really necessary since I had committed that face to memory the moment Gator placed it in my hand. The hair, bushy and gray and parted so perfectly upon an egg-shaped head. Housekeeping employees didn't have hair like a senator, did they? A rounded chin covered by a trimmed goatee. A tea spout of a nose and slightly up-turned, poker-faced lips, nothing extraordinary about those. In fact, this Thaddeus Anderson was a real melting pot of facial characteristics, a computerized configuration of America's most unwanted--simple, understated, bland. Except for the eyes. Even in black and white those eyes were different. Two penetrating darts of deception. I'd met those eyes. Or imagined I had. The Thanksgiving eve memorial service--the chapel-- Those were his eyes, Tannenbaum and Thaddeus Anderson were the same person--it had come to me the moment I looked at the picture. And I was sure these eyes belonged to someone still working at the hospital. A different department, different name,

341

different appearance. The eyes were the same. I had seen them recently. But where?

Alex Rosen and Brian Picolli were sitting like stalled Chevies at the end of the bar. Alex had a champagne bottle in one hand and a mug of foamy Guiness in the other. Brian was leaning against the bar, bloodshot eyes rolling in their sockets as he air jammed along with the orchestra, oblivious to the fact that they were playing Tommy Dorsey rather than Snoop Doggy Dog. Alex leaned over to pour the remaining drops from his bottle into my glass. Gail resisted, shaking her head. "The boy's had his quota," she said.

Alex waved her off. "His sperm count is backed up all the way to his spinal cord," he said. "Believe me, it's the only way to flush it out."

Alex gave me a patronizing slap on the back. I felt awkward talking about my sex life, or lack thereof with Gail present. Gail rubbed my neck softly, then pulled the price tag off the inside of my shirt collar. "My, aren't we fashionable tonight?" She pinched my neck then changed the subject, asking Alex if he'd ever seen such servile attendings.

"They're treating us like we're in a friggin zoo," he responded.

"Got that right," nodded Picolli. "I'm surprised they don't try to pet us, or something."

Brian was the only man there not wearing a suit and tie, settling instead for a silk Hawaiian shirt and a clean pair of white pants whose strings hung down from his waist. Alex chugged the rest of his bottle and slammed it on the counter top. "Hey Raskin, how 'bout hitting some bars after the party? Rush Street should be hopping."

"As long as I don't have to go back to the hospital."

"What about me?" Gail protested.

Alex looked at Picolli and then at me. "What did you do to this woman?" Alex smiled and turned to Gail. "Love to take you, but...we're sort of on a mission."

"We're after some trim," said Picolli, searching a pocket. "Want to go out back and smoke a doobie?"

"Come on guys," Gail said. "Maybe I'm on my own mission. Maybe I'm looking to stretch some jeans myself."

Our mouths erupted like fountains, two sprays of beer, one of champagne..

"Whoa!" said Brian. "She's talking like a dude."

Alex slurred his words. "Am I going crazy or did I just hear the quiet, timid, conscientious, never-leave-the-hospital Gail Peterson say she wanted to stretch some jeans? Raskin, I thought you said this babe was depressed?"

I winced, then looked at Gail. Her eyes were filled with resolve. "*Was* depressed," she said firmly. "I'm back."

Gail's depression had lifted, and neither of us were sure how. She said it was because of me--my empathy, our talk that day downtown, and her emulation of my just trying to get by.

But I wasn't so sure. More likely, it was due to Gail's realization that it was possible to stick to her ideals during this crazy year, no matter who or what she went up against, and that her superiors didn't have a lock on moral integrity. A week before, Gail admitted a black man whose long-standing hypertension led to a massive cerebellar bleed, a condition necessitating urgent surgical evacuation. But when the chief of neurosurgery, James Weglith, a sixty year old man with an international reputation, staggered into the hospital with alcohol on his breath, Gail refused to let him operate. He screamed at Gail, calling the patient "just black-low life," and began wheeling the patient to the OR himself. Gail barricaded herself in the doorway, and when Weglith left to get security, she wheeled the patient down to the ER, and after pleading with Mulroney for help, transferred the patient by ambulance to University Hospital. When Weglith found Gail in the ER, he grabbed her by the shoulders and began shaking her, vowing she would never practice medicine again. Mulroney jumped on Weglith and pummeled him into submission. The following day Weglith was relieved of his clinical duties. Gail's patient had a successful procedure and was on his way to an uneventful recovery. In the name of decency, Gail had won a big one, and that success, along with some coddling by myself, seemed to have lassoed her back from the abyss.

Gail poked Alex in the mid-chest, but her eyes caught something in the distance. Alex reflexively grabbed her finger, then smiled.

"You're back, then prove it."

Gail waved to somebody in the distance. We turned like spurned lovers, searching for the object of her affection.

"Shit Gail, you don't want Winston Hacklethorpe III coming over here."

But it was too late. That weasel of a surgical chief resident was holding up a bottle, pointing sweetly to its label. On his way over he slapped several attending surgeons on their backs, pinched the butt of one his surgical underlings, and had a smile wet enough to look like he had a terminal case of rabies. When he reached our group, he planted his feet wide apart as if he were straddling a horse. His eyes seemed unfocused, tangential. He casually removed a squeegie of Binaca from an inside pocket, and then just as casually missed his mouth by a mile, spraying his cheek instead. Winston Hacklethorpe III, the quintessential surgeon, every bit as toasted as the rest of us.

"All right, you most beautiful piece of work!" he sang out, slinging his arm over Gail for support, lifting his champagne bottle. "This luscious, lascivious, and..." his voice momentarily trickled to a loud whisper, "I hope lubricated young lady, is in dire need of a refill."

We erupted into a chorus of smirks, at which time Winston threateningly waved his half-empty bottle of Mouton Cadet. "You corn-holing little fleas are just standing around playing with your peckers while this poor woman's glass is empty."

Without waiting for a reply, Winston spilled the champagne into Gail's glass, getting so close that the bubbles zinged off her eyeballs like sparks from a fire. "Now my little princess, why in God's name are you hanging out with these lowly insects when you have me at your side, ready to fulfill your every fantasy, ready to show you why we men of surgery are men of action. Now how about letting this chief resident cauterize those beautiful lips of yours?"

Winston staggered to one side, looking for support as Gail stepped out of the way. She glared at me, then Alex, and taking measure of our thoughts, realized this was a test; one she had no intention of failing.

"Hey, Winston Hacklethorpe III," she smiled, caressing his argentine hair. "Is it true that the three after your name stands for three inches?"

We gasped.

"Gail," I whispered.

"Hardly, my dear. If anything, it's a measure of the number of lovers I have per week. And this week, its only been two." He moved closer. "I'd hate to have to change my name to Winston Hacklethorpe II."

Picolli cleared his throat. "How 'bout Winston Hacklethorpe the dick face?"

Gail shot Brian a dirty look and stepped back." Tell you what, Mr. Surgical Chief Resident. First we make sure you're telling the truth." Gail looked below his belt line. "Suppose we check out just what sort of equipment you're packing down there?"

Winston swallowed hard, then looked around.

"Come on Winston," Gail said rocking back and forth. "If you're everything you say you are, I'll take care of business right here and now!"

We roared with laughter. Faced with the proverbial shit-or-get-off-the-pot scenario, Winston quickly backed off with a wave of his hand. "Interns aren't such hot pieces of ass, anyway." He turned his attention back toward us and a few others joining the group. "Did I tell you guys what happened on the plastics service?" Winston asked loud enough to draw an audience. "How Sophia Loren showed up and asked my opinion about her breasts?"

I gave Gail a modest peck on the cheek and gently pulled her back from the crowd. "That took balls," I whispered.

"Ovaries," she corrected. "Besides, I'm as shit-faced as you are."

Gail and I left Alex and Brian at the bar, and for the next hour we wandered through the party, both of us conscious of the little hand on my watch approaching the eleven. I searched for Emile Horner. Meanwhile, Gail was showing around the picture of Thaddeus Anderson, and when she saw Malcolm Spool talking to a group of post-docs, she excitedly grabbed my shoulder and led me to his corner. I was thankful to Malcolm for turning me onto the idea of Maxine Chu's bone marrow transplant; it was his data that had set me off in the first place. But that was work. This was social. And socially, I wanted nothing to do with Malcolm Spool. The guy was such a germ freak that I could hardly stand to be around him. Lately he had taken to washing his hands every five minutes. Handling a chart, greeting a family member, pressing the damn elevator button; it didn't take much to send Malcolm scurrying to the soap dispenser.

I listened while Malcolm finished discussing the human genome, then halfheartedly extended my hand, which Malcolm summarily rejected, grimacing as if each finger harbored a plague.

"It's only cocktail sauce," I said, licking my fingers.

"Cocktail sauce may contain upwards of three hundred colonies of gram negative E-coli," he said, "especially when it's been sitting out for ninety minutes."

Malcolm set down his glass of port, pulled a small notebook from an ill-fitting gabardine sport coat, and began flipping through the pages. "Ah, just as I thought. Five years ago there was an outbreak of amoebic dysentery triggered by cocktail sauce. You want the reference?"

Gail Peterson laughed out loud. "Oh Malcolm, it's a party! Have some fun! Hey, anybody got an order sheet?" Maybe if I write an order for you to get drunk, you might actually do it."

Malcolm scowled. "Look, Dr. Peterson, I may fit your definition of a nerd, but I'd never insult a surgery chief resident the way you just did. Dr. Hacklethorpe comes from a distinguished and literate academic family. Can you say the same about your lineage?"

"Fuck off, Malcolm!" Malcolm saw the spit fly from Gail's mouth and quickly closed his notebook lest she contaminate that, too.

"Maybe if you had respect for others' feelings, Gail, you'd have a date or two!"

Gail grabbed my drink and launched it into Malcolm's face. "There you go, brain child. That ought to sterilize those germs."

"Leave him alone," said Alex, who had moved onto the jousting platform. He took a long puff from a soggy cigar. "What does Malformed Stool know about dates? He hasn't had one since his French poodle died."

Malcolm dabbed at his suit coat, trying to remain composed. He looked angrily in Alex's direction.

"For your information," he said, "I had a date just last week." He blushed. "A very hot date." He nodded his head in one grand, symphonic gesture and turned to leave. "Ginny is a fine woman."

Gail's hands went to her mouth. "Wait just a minute!" she shouted. "You're not talking about Ginny Cahill, are you?"

Malcolm stammered, his icy glare beginning a slow melt under cross-examination. "What's it matter?" he asked. He turned away.

"Oh my God, Ginny Cahill!" she shrieked, cupping her hands to her mouth. "She was a hot date all right; so hot she ended up in the hospital, with a temp of 103."

We roared with laughter, all except Malcolm.

"And a stiff neck, don't forget," added Malcolm. "I didn't have much choice but to admit her to the hospital."

"Not only did he admit her, he did a pelvic and a spinal tap."

"I did a complete workup, dammit," stormed Malcolm. "I did what was required to make an appropriate diagnosis; nothing more; nothing less."

"You admitted your fucking date to the hospital?" shrieked Brian Picolli. "Awesome!"

"I did what was necessary."

"Sure you did, Malcolm," said Alex, who was puffing cigar smoke like a runaway furnace. "What a great idea. You can't get to first base so you admit her and do a pelvic exam."

"I did a complete physical."

"What did you use to check her gag reflex?" he asked suggestively. With that, Malcolm turned and headed toward the exit.

"Did you make her a no code, do not recussitate special?" Gail called out.

"Can you imagine anyone going out with Malcolm not being DNR?" replied Alex.

I caught up to Malcolm as he was about to enter the bathroom. "Sorry about what happened back there," I said, starting to put my hand on his shoulder. He flinched.

"The pot doesn't stray far from the kettle," he said with a frown, obviously aware of how I had been practically slobbering over Gail's every word, following the bounce of her freckled cleavage with widening pupils, viewing any man who looked twice at Gail as a potential mortal enemy. Any blithering idiot could have figured me out. But even if I hadn't been drunk, even if I'd treated Gail no differently than anyone else, Malcolm would have sensed an energy between us, no matter how hard I tried to hide it. Malcolm's powers of observation were unsurpassed. Whether it be looking at a benign appearing skin lesion and correctly diagnosing malignant melanoma, or picking up a case of fulminant renal failure merely by the frost on a patient's eyebrow, Malcolm was the best.

"Here," I said, thrusting the picture of Thaddeus Anderson in his hand. "What can you tell me about this man?"

Malcolm held it with his fingertips. "Is this clean?" I nodded. Malcolm stepped back under an overhead light. "What do you want to know, what he does for a living?"

That was as close as Malcolm had ever come to being funny. "Good one, Malcolm," I said. I explained that the man he was looking at was an impostor. A man with a disguise. "This picture was taken at a hospital picnic several years ago."

Malcolm's eyes widened like the bullseye on a target. "What's that got to do with you?"

"Nothing. He was... engaged to someone named Gertie, who also works there. Got into her bank account and then split. She thinks he's still working somewhere in the hospital."

348

Malcolm stared at the picture, his face still, his eyes deeply set in concrete gaze. If he hadn't been standing I'd have thought he was dead. He had me follow him over to the coat check room, where he retrieved his briefcase. He removed a magnifying glass and continued studying the picture while I tried to balance myself as alcohol neutralized my last patch of functioning neurons. Malcolm then took out a pen and a three by five note card and began sketching. He handed me the card. The face he had drawn wore a chin sloping like a pencil point. And where there was no scar before, one now took shape under his right eyebrow. But the biggest difference was the hair. There was none.

"So don't believe me," said Malcolm. "But the man in this picture is wearing a toupee. And underneath is the ravaging results of alopecia arreata. His own hair follicles would be seeping through right where this sideburn is supposed to be. But he has none."

"Maybe he shaved his head."

"Those eyebrows are fake too. Someone might shave his head but not his eyebrows. Those were...." he looked once again at the picture and nodded. "Those eyebrows were placed to hide that scar."

I was more than a little curious about the scar. Tannenbaum also had a scar under his eyebrow.

"Look here," he said, holding up the magnifying glass. "Look at the way the skin is furrowed. It's some sort of makeup gel or rubber explant. No dermal hair, no skin pores, nothing. Right below the eyebrow there is a slight retraction of skin, like it was puckered. This is where the scar was. Must have taken a good plastic surgeon to do that."

"Or a makeup artist," I added. I pointed to the picture Malcolm had drawn. "Have you seen anyone who looks like this?"

Malcolm shook his head. "Wouldn't want to, either. He looks like a possible chromosomal abnormality: XYY. You know--the kind that ends up in prison for criminal behavior. All genetically programmed."

From behind a voice slurred. "He sort of looks like you."

Gail hung onto my shoulder for support, then grabbed the photograph. "This man has the same dark pointed eyes as Malcolm. You sure you didn't work in housekeeping during medical school?" Her words were drawn out and slurred.

Malcolm straightened his shoulders. "I was in Baltimore. At Johns Hopkins." Indignantly, he walked away, then traced his steps back. Walking right past us, his eyes looking straight ahead, he entered the bathroom. Gail punched me in the shoulder. "Good news, Danny, it's after midnight. And no page from Redmon, that bastard."

For a moment I was relieved. I felt for my beeper. Gone! I checked the inside of my sport coat. Nothing! Where the hell was it? For all I knew Art could have been paging me for the past hour. All hell could be breaking loose at the hospital.

"Relax," said Gail. "The little monster's probably sitting on some bar stool. If it went off, someone would have heard it."

"I'd better call Art."

"Don't you dare. You call him and you can bet he'll find a reason for you to come back." Gail pecked at my cheek. Her lips lingered for a second longer than I was accustomed to. "Besides," she whispered, "I'm so damn drunk I might let you take advantage of me later."

For the next half hour, I blindly followed Gail Peterson around the party, half-looking for my beeper, half hoping I would never find it again. Gail, in her drunken state, was showing anyone within grabbing distance the picture of Thaddeus Anderson. Her words ran together like wet eggs on a plate, her thoughts just as scrambled. "Did you ever sleep with this person?" she asked a staid female Hematologist. To the head of OB-Gyn: "Do you remember delivering this man when he was a baby?"

When Gail retired to the restroom, I leaned against a wall and squinted through the haze. Brian Picolli was next to the orchestra, gyrating like a groupie at a Grateful Dead concert. Alex Rosen was standing within an inch of a beautiful Pediatrics resident, who looked like she had just met the man of her dreams. I, meanwhile, could no longer see Emile Horner. As I scanned the room, I spotted Sol Goldman, just three feet away; I had kept half an eye on Sol the entire night. Watched him work the crowd like a politician, shaking hands, planting kisses, congratulating interns on making it this far, all the while being dutifully followed by a cadre of servile, butt-sniffing attendings, toilet paper tongues wagging anxiously as they waited for an opportunity to interact with the chief. Paying homage to the boss today could lead to better opportunities tomorrow--cardiac cath privileges, office redecorations; the possibilities were endless.

Sol knew he couldn't prove it was me who had broken into his office, and it really pissed him off. When our eyes locked, he sauntered closer, the odor of his breath suggesting he was every bit as pickled as the salmon he was nibbling. His other hand held a bottle of scotch.

"A little J and B?" he asked.

"I prefer B and E," I said, thinking of my breaking and entering. I bit my lips to stifle a smile.

We stood in awkward silence, Sol eavesdropping as one of his interns made a phone call to her baby sitter. I continued to scan the crowd for Emile Horner.

"Looking for your buddies?"

"Emile Horner. Seen him?"

"Emile left about twenty minutes ago," Sol replied. "He's pushing eighty, you know."

"He has the drive of a forty year old," I replied, looking deep into his eyes. "Too bad he doesn't know how to send a confidential memo."

Sol swallowed his salmon pate as if the fish hook were still present. For a moment he dangled helplessly on the twenty pound test line I had tossed at him.

At that moment, Gail staggered out of the bathroom, her face wet, and the top three buttons of her dress open, freckled cleavage pouring out like a bursting dam. "Hey boss," she said, her arm on Goldman. "Isn't this man a friend of yours?" Before I could stop her she was displaying the picture of Thaddeus Anderson.

"Gail!"

She shoved my shoulder. "Now hold on here. Maybe Sol knows good old Thaddeus. What about it Sol? Danny boy tells me this Thaddeus and you are... you know." Gail crossed her fingers. "Like this."

Sol's face exploded in several shades of crimson. "Let me see that," he said, grabbing the photo from Gail. His jaws clamped down like a vice. "You have no idea what you're doing, Raskin. You haven't the slightest fucking idea."

I looked into his eyes expecting to see flames of hatred pouring out, but instead it was fear, lots of it. There was a clue here, something I should have grasped but couldn't. Was he afraid that I had confirmed his involvement in the murders at Richard Meese? That I had discovered his role in whatever conspiracy was going on? Or was it something else? I tried shaking the alcohol from my brain. I needed to think.

He looked at Gail and frowned.

"Okay," said Gail, raising her hands in surrender. "I can take a hint. I'm outta here." She handed me the picture and staggered away.

Goldman moved closer. "Put that picture away and keep it away."

"Why?"

Goldman paused, weighing his words. "You'll find out soon enough, I promise."

"Yeah, when's that? When I'm lying in the CCU all shot up with ergonovine and pavulon?" What the hell, I thought. Might as well lay it on the table. "What do you have against Jews, Sol?"

"What are you talking about?"

"Why are you killing Jewish patients, Sol? Why are you killing my patients?" My voice was two octaves higher than I had intended. Heads turned.

"This is not the time or the place to..."

"Oh okay, Sol, what do you say we discuss it at the nurse's swimming pool? We can paint swastikas on the wall while we talk. Or better yet, how about we go over to Wanda Bylevin's apartment? Why don't we...you know hang out there for a

352

while?" I tried to control myself. My eyes watered over. Dammit, I was sick of all this.

"One more word and you're under suspension."

"Go ahead, Sol. And this time I'll quit for good." And at the moment I meant every word of it. Who needed this crap? I could be back home in Michigan. Mom could be doing the laundry. My own bed. Safety.

The sound of the overhead loudspeaker made me jump: "Telephone call for Doctor Daniel Raskin."

"Who's that?" asked Sol.

"It's Thaddeus Anderson, Sol." I turned and left.

Alex, Gail, and Brian followed me out to the phone booth.

"I knew I should have called Art," I repeated, trying to steady myself. It was twelve forty five. My beeper was gone. My brain was gone. Any chance of lying naked with Gail Peterson was gone.

Arthur Redmon was about as uncaring as a human being could get. "Don't give me shit about losing your beeper!" he yelled so loud through the receiver that the whole group could hear. "You thought you could get away with not calling me."

His anger sparked my two remaining neurons. "I didn't have to call, Redmon. I was talking to Sol Goldman and...."

"I'm in the ER working up a couple of real sick gomers. You're going to have to come back."

"We're about to head out to some bars on Division Street. I've been drinking all night."

Picolli grabbed the phone. "Listen, dickweed. It's party night for us 'terns. You handle things. Raskin ain't coming back 'til morning."

I grabbed the phone. "Art, it's the Christmas party. We're supposed to get the night off."

"Midnight. That's the rule. After midnight it's up to me. And I need your ass in here."

"Oh yeah? And what if I refuse?"

"Look, you want me to page Sol Goldman? He made the fucking rule."

He said the magic words. I wasn't going to get Goldman involved in this. "Okay, Art. I'll page you once I get to the hospital and slug down some coffee."

Gail pulled at the receiver. "You son of a bitch, Redmon. You're a poor excuse for a resident, not to mention a human being." She slammed down the receiver.

"You didn't have to make things worse, Gail."

"Worse?" said Alex. "It's almost one in the morning. You're as shit-faced as a fly in a horse stable. You're going to get no sleep tonight and tomorrow you'll have the hangover from hell. And all this to bail out that slime ball Redmon, who ten to one will be sound asleep when you get back to the hospital. My friend, it doesn't get any worse."

I fished an ice cube from a stagnant drink sitting by the phone. It stung my neck, but new life traveled down my arms. "Thanks for the support, Alex."

Alex smiled, exhaling fully. "Au contraire, my friend. It is I who is going to bail you out. I'm going to take your place."

It took a minute to register. Alex, taking my place? On call? At the hospital? He was more drunk than I was. Besides, I knew the patients. He didn't.

For the next ten minutes the two of us stood in the lobby, debating the merits of who should go back to the hospital. Alex was insistent, even to the point of yelling, something he rarely did. "I want to do it, Danny. It'll give me a chance to choke Art Redmon." But as much as I could have used the sleep, not to even mention the possibilities that existed with Gail, I couldn't let him do it. It was, after all, my responsibility. One thing I was always accepting was responsibility, even if it took dragging and kicking to do it. I could play the martyr as well as anyone. I wasn't about to blow the chance now.

The three of them escorted me out the door, where the chill sliced through my parka, both reviving me and numbing me from head to foot. "Dump me in a taxi," I muttered to no one in particular.

"Take him to Richard Meese," I heard someone say.

The driver replied in a rough voice. "You don't need a taxi. You need an ambulance."

Through the laughing I heard Gail say. "He's not sick. He's a doctor."

Chapter 72 the return

Through slit-like openings, I watched Zelda Margolis, the all-night waitress at the Richard Meese coffee shop, refill my cup for the fourth time. "You out for some kinda record, Doc?"

"Leave the pot on the table," I muttered, swishing the contents, including a spoon's worth of coffee grounds, down my throat.

"How 'bout some strudel, Doc?"

"How 'bout a large bore IV, Zelda? The quicker this stuff gets in, the better."

The ceiling lights flickered twice, emphasizing the sinewy shadows of rusty pipes and heating elements that decorated the barren basement tunnel just outside the door. Such a dark place, this winding intestine of the hospital, whose single oasis was the coffee shop, now deserted save a small band of Rastafarian escorts intent on indulging their latest case of drug-induced munchies (I counted six pieces of pie and as many shakes among four of them). The odor of marijuana seeped from their bodies and made me feel like puking. I nibbled on a stale raisin bagel, looked at my watch, and fantasized sixteen ways to torture Arthur Redmon. How could I have let him drag me away from my friends on a night specifically designated for interns? Just as Alex had predicted, after screaming my way through an ice-cold shower and downing enough caffeine to awaken a dead person, I'd found him sound asleep in his call room. I wanted to kill the son of a bitch.

The Rastafarian escorts were lip-synching to their ghetto blaster. One escort named Filmore, bandana wrapped around a bushel of golden curls, three gold fillings reflecting into my bloodshot eyes, looked up as I passed his table. "Yo, Doc, how 'bout some seven card stud?"

"Not now, Filmore." I wondered where Jimmi was, then remembered this was the night he was giving Maxine Chu her libidinous surprise. I felt a pang of jealousy, three cups of coffee in the adrenalin department.

There were a number of routes back to the Richard Meese wing of the hospital, the most direct one leading from the tunnel through the ER and across the street. That was out though, lest I run into Officer Mulroney. Knowing him, he probably subject me to a breathalyzer test. Another course had me following the tunnel about a quarter mile to the thirty year old elevator in the basement of Richard Meese. But that elevator gave me the creeps. Reminded me of a sarcophagus. Besides, the phone inside hadn't worked since World War two. I had already been trapped once before behind those wrought-iron gates, and if not for the hospital engineers might still be there, a pile of bones and a beeper.

As a last resort, I chose to climb the seven flights of cold, dark stairs. Seven floors of near total darkness, loose wooden rails covered with spider webs large enough to entrap a rat. Seven floors with a hammer pounding at my head and a gallon of coffee sloshing through my insides. It was two in the morning and I was tired and nauseous. The inside of my mouth had the consistency of fetid oatmeal, and my breath smelled like an old gym bag.

Maggie Gator greeted me with a sympathetic embrace, inquiring whether I needed to be hooked up to a tank of oxygen. Seven floors wasn't that much, I said, pausing to catch my breath. Maggie had heard Art Redmon talking to me on the phone, and she'd tried paging me at the party as soon as he left. She wanted to tell me to stay put, that she would take care of things on her own. But my beeper was missing, probably sitting in the garbage bin at Morton's, swimming amid shrimp tails and empty bottles of single malt scotch.

"I suppose I should get busy," I said. "I have enough orders to write to keep me up the rest of the night."

Gator handed me a paper cup's worth of marshmallow-covered jello. "Took care of that. Signed your name. Started a couple of IV's, did the ECG's which were normal, and went over the chest x-rays with the radiologist on duty. All normal."

The marshmallows reminded me of my pillow, "Gator, I love you. I'm glad it's been quiet."

357

Gator shifted slightly. "Not that quiet." She paused. "We had a death up here a while ago."

I didn't panic. Death on 5-Meese was not unexpected. I looked through the sign-out cards, trying to guess who it was.

"Nobody you'd know," Gator said. "A private patient, believe it or not. They ran out of beds over on Meyer house so they sent one up here." Gator formed a smile. "Teach them a lesson."

I barely heard her. A nest of butterflies exploded in my stomach. "Whose patient?" I asked.

"Dr. Horner's."

"Oh my God, no."

"What's wrong?"

I tried to catch my breath. *Keep it together, Raskin.* "What happened? Was there a code?"

Gator shook her head. "Just found him dead in his bed. Cute little Jewish guy. Cold as a frozen burrito. Must have had a heart attack in his sleep."

"Did you call Redmon?"

"Hell no. I had Dr. Horner paged at the party."

The adrenalin and caffeine had me reeling. Goldman said Horner had left. Gone home.

"He came in, Gator?"

"About an hour ago. Tied up loose ends, paid his respects, stuff like that. The body just went downstairs."

"Where's Horner? Have you seen Horner?"

Gator shrugged her shoulders. "Not for an hour. He probably..."

"Gator! Gator, where's the room?"

"507--the only private one on the floor. Hey, what's the matter?"

"Grab the crash cart and follow me."

It was so fucking clear that I wanted to scream. We raced down the hall, both running, both pushing."Oh God, please," I said aloud, praying that I was wrong.

The door to 507 was closed. I kicked it open. Empty. A few scattered sheets shrouded the empty bed. An IV pole. Ran to the bathroom. Empty. A closet, opposite the window. I opened it.

Gator's blood curdling scream echoed down the hall. There was Emile Horner, his lifeless body hanging from the coat rack, a stethoscope cinched around his neck.

(When we got to the camp, they separated me from my mother and sisters. They went left. I went right. They were gassed. I was spared).

I supported Horner's limp body while Gator slipped the stethoscope off his neck. I then laid him on the bed, ripped open his shirt and buried my head in his chest, listening, praying. Then..."I think he's still breathing, Gator. Check a pulse."

Maggie felt under his neck. "I think I feel something. Maybe."

My turn. A palpable oscillation of life's juices trickled beneath my fingers. Barely. But there. A pulse. This must have happened just minutes before. Maybe there was still time. Maybe.

Just then, the night supervisor, an elderly black man with a wispy mustache, named Oscar, entered the room. "What's going....Oh shit!" he yelled and turned like a revolving door.

"Oscar, wait!" yelled Gator. "Call a code blue. Now!"

"Shit Doc," he exclaimed. He stood motionless.

"Dammit Oscar!" yelled Gator, "call a code."

"No, wait!" I yelled. Margaret looked up, eyes burning with fear and confusion.

"Oscar, listen, just call the ICU. Get the ICU resident. Tell him he's needed up here, stat. And get Dr. Redmon from his call room and have him get his ass up here. And call escort. Tell them I need a gurney and their three strongest guys." Oscar nodded and left.

"Run!" yelled Gator.

With Gator's help, I placed a breathing tube into Horner's windpipe and started two IV's--all in a span of two minutes. But there were blood tests to send, ECGs to do, heart rhythms to monitor.

"It would be a lot easier if we call a code blue, Danny. We could get a lot more help."

"I know this sounds bizarre, Gator, but there's a good chance that whoever did this is still somewhere in the hospital. If he hears a code blue, he could be the first one to come. Let's just stabilize him and get him to the ICU. Quietly."

This whole damn thing is my fault, I told myself. I should have warned Horner. I never should have gotten him involved. If he died, I'd quit. I couldn't take it anymore. I looked at my watch. Where was everybody? I thought of Redmon sleeping soundly. I was going to choke him first chance I got. And the escorts, bonging it up in some smoke filled corridor. They'd get theirs too.

Gator loosened the belt on Horner's pants and emptied his pockets. "What's this?" she asked aloud. She read the number on the beeper and then gasped.

"What's wrong?"

"The beeper." Gator took a breath. "It's yours."

My mind couldn't deal with this. How had my beeper gotten into Horner's pocket? Had he found it at the party? If so, wouldn't he have returned it? Maybe he didn't know it was mine. He could have checked the serial number, or even asked around. No, someone had put it there. I felt faint. My God, the killer had been at the party. I might have even shown him a picture of himself!

My thoughts switched to Emile Horner, whose skin was a hazy gray, the color of dusk, with streaks of red and purple, a sunset slowly sinking before us.

"Gator, what was his last blood pressure?" I asked as I pumped up the cuff, listening for the tiny arterial sounds as I released the lever.

"Only about 70."

"Well it's barely 60 now," I yelled. "We've got to get him to ICU."

Oscar returned by himself.

"Where's the ICU resident?"

Oscar looked ready to cry. "Said he wasn't coming over on just the word of a supervisor."

"Who was it?" snapped Gator.

Oscar stammered. "Whitehurst, I think."

"Shit!" Probably meant to say 'nigger supervisor', knowing him." As she spoke, Gator reached over, handed me the phone, and dialed the ICU. While waiting for Whitehurst, I turned back to Oscar. "Where's Dr. Redmon? Did you get in touch with him?"

"Said he didn't want to be disturbed, doctor. Said to tell you to take some librium."

"Mother fucker."

Whitehurst got on the phone, audibly drowsy. What is this, a fucking pajama party?

"It's Raskin, and I'm about to bring someone over."

"Like hell you are. I approve all ICU transfers, and I don't take orders from interns. Tell your resident to call me back after he's worked up the patient."

"Listen, you son of a bitch," I yelled into the receiver. "Someone's trying to die here, and I'm coming over. Get a bed and a swan-ganz cardiac set up and some Dopamine ready, or I swear to God, I'll pull your fucking eyeballs out with my teeth." I took a breath. "By the way, the patient is Dr. Horner," I said, and slammed down the phone.

"Tactfully done," nodded Gator. "Maybe I will marry you after all." She looked at her watch. "Where's escort?"

"You don't want to know. We'd better start moving."

We secured the bed rails and after tucking Horner's limp arms securely under the bed sheet, headed toward the elevator, Oscar pushing the gurney, Margaret Gator wheeling the crash cart and IV poles, and me rhythmically squeezing the ambu bag. The urgency we felt mingled with the solitude of the late hour, created a surrealistic aura. As we approached the final straight away, I motioned to Oscar to run ahead and ring for the elevator. Oscar looked pale.

"Let's wait for escort," he said. "They have a key to the service elevator. We can't bring this gurney in the regular one. It won't fit."

"Don't have a choice, Oscar."

"Fine by me, Doc," he said. "But this guy looks dead." He turned, and ran down the hall. I felt once more for Horner's pulse, hoping to find a stronger sign of life. No luck.

Oscar unfastened the latch on the antiquated brass elevator door, using all his strength to open the tarnished gate. I looked down at Dr. Horner, felt his tattooed arm screaming silently. "Can you hear me, Emile?" I shouted. "Can you hear me?" From the depths of his body, Dr. Horner made a faint guttural reverberation, and for a moment his eyes almost looked as if they were trying to focus. I imagined myself back on the ER gurney after being hit with a baseball bat; looking down on the events as through a heavy fog, as if I were a curious bystander. Perhaps Horner was in the same boat, looking down on us, trying to figure out an escape route. Or worse, maybe he thought he was back at Auschwitz and I was some hideous reincarnation of his Nazi tormentors.

"Come on," said Gator. "It's a quick ride to the second floor." With that, she gave Oscar a slight nudge with her shoulder and we tripped into the dungeon-like elevator, where we were greeted by a moldy, rancorous odor.

"This elevator don't seem too safe, Doc," grimaced Oscar. "And it smells funny in here, too."

"What do you want me to do, Oscar, call a taxi?" I lifted the back end of the gurney in. The front end abutted the back wall, leaving the rear wheels barely within the confines of the elevator.

"There's no room for the crash cart," said Gator. "Maybe I should run to the ICU and get a smaller transport bed."

"How are you going to get it up here, on your back? The service elevator is locked. Those damn escorts have the only keys. Just leave the crash cart."

I felt suffocated by impatience, especially considering that Horner's pulse was so damn thready. "Come on, let's just go. We'll be there in a minute."

After grabbing a few meds from the emergency cart, Gator closed the elevator door and pressed the second floor button. A loud, mechanical whine serenaded us downward, and momentarily I relaxed. Once in the ICU, Horner had a chance. Hopefully there wouldn't be any brain damage. I couldn't wait to settle scores with Art Redmon as well as those lazy escort bastards. Then...the selfish thought of a long awaited reunion with my pillow surfaced. God, a little sleep would be great. Maybe if I got to lay down for ....

My thoughts were interrupted by a force which threw all of us to the side. Dr. Horner's arm flung against the rail dislodging one of his IV's. Sudden silence. No movement. Nothing but the synchronous pounding of our hearts.

We were stuck.

Claustrophobic gremlins began to awaken within me, and proceeded to feed off my oxygen. "Oscar, hit the second floor button again." Oscar obeyed but nothing happened.

"Oh shit!" he whispered.

"Stay calm," motioned Gator, unhooking the entrance latch. "We'll get out of here in a second." But the latch was stuck firmly to its gridiron position. "Oh shit," echoed Gator. "We're trapped."

"Cut the 'Oh shit', would you?" I yelled. "This thing has jammed on me countless times. It usually starts up again in a minute." Of course that was a lie. The engineers were home sleeping. Like I should be. Horner's lungs were becoming more difficult to ventilate. "I think he's filling up with fluid."

I felt for a pulse.

Gone.

Other arm.

Nothing.

"He's arrested, damn it!" I squeezed the ambu bag. "Gator, get me some epi." I jumped onto the gurney, ignoring the low-lying rusty ceiling pipes. "Oww!" I screamed, as I smacked my head against them. What the hell should I do now? No monitor, a pittance of medications. I felt once again for a pulse--nothing. I slammed my fist into Dr. Horner's chest. A loud crack exploded from his osteoporotic rib cage.

Still no pulse. Horner was turning dark blue.

I tightened the seal of the ambu bag around Horner's trach tube. I began rhythmic chest compressions, one every second. Red-tinged mucous began running out the side of Horner's mouth, reminding me of those late night war movies. When you saw blood come out of someone's mouth, you knew he was dead. And this nightmare of a movie was about to end. Damn it Horner, don't die.

Oscar picked up the telephone. "Hello, Hello! Is anyone there? Help!"

"Oscar, that phone goes to engineering. Nobody's there."

"I'm calling 9-1-1. We got to get help!"

I looked at Gator as I struggled to continue CPR. "Oscar, get a grip. You can't call 9-1-1! That's an internal hospital phone."

"That man is dead!" cried Oscar. "He's gonna have rigor mortis by the time we get out of here."

Five minutes later there was still no pulse. Gator injected our last ampule of epinephrine while I continued CPR. My arms felt like anchors on the Titanic. We were sinking fast.

Suddenly, Oscar fell against the elevator door, his face contorted in agony. He pulled out a bottle of nitroglycerin pills and popped two under his tongue.

"Oscar," Gator said. "Is that heart condition acting up again?"

Oscar nodded feebly, his face dripping like a warm ice cream cone, his color turning chocolate to vanilla.

"Take it easy, Oscar."

I whispered to Gator: "Don't tell me Oscar's going to check out on us too?"

"Don't worry," she answered, looking very worried. "It's just a bad case of angina."

Within minutes of taking the nitroglycerin, Oscar's color returned. He sat up straight and shook his head. "My doctor said to avoid stress. That's why they moved me to nights. No stress." He took out two more nitros.

Suddenly I had an idea.

"Pass me that nitro bottle, Oscar."

I dumped out three pills, then lifted up Emil Horner's purplish upper lip. I set the pills under his tongue, holding them in place with my finger.

"What in God's name? The man already has a big zero for blood pressure."

"Trust me Gator. Dr. Horner might have been poisoned."

"Boy, you still got that alcohol dancing 'round or something? The man's been strangled, clear as the mole on old

Oscar's cheek. The only thing's been poisoned in here is your liver."

I felt for a pulse. Nothing. "No, Gator, if he were just hung, he'd be dead, totally."

"Man ain't about to square dance," said Oscar.

"I think he was given the same drug that killed his patient. It constricts blood flow to the heart. The nitro might just...."

"I think I feel a pulse, Danny!" sang Gator. " Stop CPR."

A second later: "I do feel a God-damn pulse! If this works and Horner lives, Danny, I will marry you," said Gator, "I swear to God."

I'm not sure whether Gator's invocation of some higher power had anything to do with it, but suddenly a generator began rumbling. Come on, I pleaded. We lurched forward.

"We're moving!" said Gator.

"Praise be the Lord!" Oscar made the sign of the cross on his chest, his white smock thoroughly soaked with sweat. He sucked on a nitro like he were taking communion. I jumped back up on the gurney.

"Okay, when that door opens, Gator, you're in charge of the IV poles, and Oscar, you push this damn bed as fast as you can."

I had a strange vision as we flew down the hallway, of Washington crossing the Delaware, of all things. Sailors with a cause, tacking starboard toward the ICU--across the bridge, down the hall. I, the reluctant general, kneeling atop our ship, directing the code with all the splendor and none of the false teeth of George himself. Red Cross representative, Florence Nighten-Gator, pumping the ambu bag, securing the IV's in place. And Sir Oscar, who on the strength of three quarters of his one remaining coronary artery, powered our great vessel single handedly toward its rendezvous with destiny, all the while popping nitros like they were popcorn.

Dr. Horner was eventually stabilized on a nitroglycerin and dopamine drip. He was still critical, but at least he was alive. That in itself was a miracle. A security guard was posted at his bedside. Oscar ended up one bed over from Horner with an evolving myocardial infarction. His ECG demonstrated that a small part of his ventricle had been deprived of oxygen for too long. The red beefy muscle in the area of his inferior wall had been strangulated forever. Wounded in the line of duty, Oscar had received, in the fullest sense of the term, a purple heart.

Chapter 73 revenge

Three a.m. Everyone was stable.

Everyone but me. My work was not yet finished, not by a long-shot. There was the all encompassing matter of revenge. I wheeled the gurney that had carried Horner to the ICU all the way over to Art Redmon's call room, where I shoved it through the door and into his bed so hard that he crashed into the wall, lacerating his head. Fortunately for Arthur, the sight of blood running down his forehead tempered my thirst for any further revenge.

I then retraced my earlier path down into the basement, running in near darkness past the all-night cafeteria. Seeing no escorts there, I headed in the direction of the emergency room. The alcohol had long since burned out of my system. Even at four in the morning my adrenalin was high enough to run a marathon. Near the nurses' pool I saw half a dozen escorts lounging in a dark corner. The air was heavy with smoke. I walked briskly up to Filmore, grabbed the joint from his mouth and tossed it on the floor.

"Hey mon, you be out of your fuckin' gourd, or what?"

I held Filmore by his Dashiki. "Where the hell were you?"

Filmore shrugged, then held up his beeper. "Battery dead."

"I paged you motherfuckers twice. Somebody almost died because of you."

Filmore looked down at me as he removed my hand from his clothes. "Don't be blamin' Filmore for killing one of your patients, mon."

"I am blaming you. Where the hell is Jimmi? He promised me service. Said call anytime. He'd be there. Where is that motherfucker?"

A few of Filmore's accomplices giggled. "If it be any of your business, mon, Jimmi still be with your main woman, Max."

I picked up Jimmi's glass bong and threw it against the wall. The sound of shattering glass exploded through the tunnel.

"Hey, mon," they screamed, but I wasn't listening. I saw

Jimmi's tackle box on the floor next to the gurney and kicked it as hard as I could. Plastic vials of marijuana tumbled like bowling pins.

"Oh, mon, Jimmi gonna shit a brick over this. Nobody supposed to touch that medicine cabinet."

"Where is the fucker?"

"I told you mon, he be with Maxine."

I bit my lip, the anger beginning to dissipate. "You tell him I hope he had fun tonight, 'cause tomorrow he ain't gonna to have a job."

Something began to smell--an odor replacing the marijuana.

"Won't matter none," said Filmore. "This be Rasti Jimmi's last night."

I knelt down next to the tackle box. Among the plastic vials of pot was a glass jar, now broken. A dark paste.

"Don't be touching that, mon! It's Jimmi's special stuff!"

Dark paste. The smell.

Filmore moved closer, starting to panic. "Don't be tellin' no one."

"Telling no one what?"

"'Bout Jimmi. Puttin' that stuff on his skin."

A chill grabbed my body. "What?"

"You know, touch up job. Jimmi ain't as black as the brothers and..."

The smell. Juniper!

Jimmi Redding. Frank Tannenbaum. Two names.

My God. Maxine.

Chapter 74 maxine

I propelled myself through the basement floor runway with a greater sense of purpose than I had ever known. My beloved Maxine. If they wanted to get to me, why not kill me, dammit? If it's the Charles Cantrell file you want, I don't have it, you asshole! Wanda Bylevin. Emile Horner. And now Maxine. My Maxine. A woman braving life's tightrope with such grace-- someone who was about to get another chance.

The four flights of stairs posed an obstacle I barely noticed, and I leapt them three at a time. Think Raskin. He's there. Right now! God knows what Jimmi's doing. Maybe he hasn't injected her yet. I cringed. Two orderlies passed by with equipment, almost knocking me over. I'd never forgive myself if I got there too late. If anything happened to Maxine, I'd find him: Jimmi, Thaddeus, Frank, whatever he wanted to call himself. I'd slit the bastard's throat.

At the top of the stairs I was panting. Dizzy. I felt like passing out. I saw darkness ahead in the hallway. Maxine's room was all the way on the other side of the campus--maybe half a mile. I was going to be too late. I felt it. I had to think fast. Now.

There was one possibility. I had to go for it. I grabbed the telephone, dialing zero.

"Call a code blue, 4 Beyer House room 406!" I yelled. "And keep announcing it over the loud speaker."

I slammed the receiver down and began to run.

"Code blue-Beyer House room 406!
"Code blue-Beyer House room 406!
Yes! Keep going! Each new "Code Blue" announcement was a shot of adrenalin propelling me forward. Maybe it would scare Jimmi from her room. I ran faster. Why hadn't I figured it out? Tannenbaum disguised as a black man at the chapel. I proved it was possible. Jimmi--always with the dark shades, drinking down my vial, making a joke of it while destroying the evidence.

I ran past the ICU team and their crash cart. "Hurry!" I yelled.

Maxine's hallway approached. The nursing station--empty. Turn left. A crowd outside Maxine's room. Lord, don't let it happen.

I pushed through the crowd.

"Out of my way!"

I looked down at Maxine. Her eyes were wide as a wolf's. Tears running down an ashen face. Tears! She was alive!

Her chest heaved forward like a wounded animal's.

"Maxine!" I yelled, running to her bedside and cradling her in my arms. She was sobbing. I was oblivious to everything and everybody.

An anesthesiologist busted through, obviously disturbed at the interruption of his beauty sleep. He shook his head. "Who called the God-damn code blue? It's three in the morning!"

"She's going to have a heart attack," I announced. "And she's going to stop breathing."

I turned toward the two nurses. "Grab an ECG. Quick." To the anesthesiologist: "Get ready to intubate."

He looked at me like I was crazy. "What's your problem? She looks fine." He turned away.

"Listen, you son of a bitch. She's going to stop breathing."

"From what?"

"Pavulon," I answered.

The anesthesiologist shook his head. "You know how quick Pavulon works?" He snapped his fingers as he closed his intubation kit. "Five...ten seconds tops. You just get back from he Christmas party or something?"

I pulled back both her sleeves looking for signs of new puncture wounds. There were none. Her IV was running at its normal rate. I finally felt my heart beat again, drumming against my chest wall. My God! Maxine was alive. I had rousted Jimmi just in time!

As I held Maxine, I felt an arm on my shoulder. The voice was that of the ICU resident, Whitehurst. "Raskin, you bastard, haven't you caused enough trouble for one night?" He turned to the anesthesiologist, who like himself wore scrubs that carried a

371

slept-in look. "Raskin almost killed one of our attendings earlier tonight."

I set Maxine down, leaning her head against her pillow, stroking her hair once. "What did you say?"

"I said you practically killed Horner by getting stuck in that elevator. You wasted valuable time."

My chest was exploding. My breath was on fire. I grabbed Whitehurst by the scrubs. "You son of a bitch. I ought to kill you. Get the hell out of here, all of you!"

The room emptied like a plague had hit. Only Margaret Gator stayed behind. She had run all the way over from 6 Meese to help.

"Should we call the police?" she asked after the room was quiet.

I shook my head. That slippery bastard was gone forever. And who would I report this to? Mulroney? He would never believe me over the ICU resident, Whitehurst, who had refused to buy my story about Horner of near strangulation. Said I was embellishing a simple case of cardiac arrest. And the stretch marks over his throat? Whitehurst told me I ought to practice my CPR technique; that chest compressions were far more effective than neck compressions. Damn him! Damn everybody! I thought about going public. Calling up the Tribune tonight. The truth had to come out. I wanted to watch Sol Goldman's face turn fiery red and then chalky white as I exposed him and his secret organization.

But at that moment I didn't care about anything but Maxine. I went back to her bed where I held her. Gator stood in the background. It was four a.m.

"His eyes," Max finally said when she could talk. "The way they suddenly changed."

Poor Maxine. Jimmi had come to her room an hour before. After they'd shared a glass of wine, Jimmi told her he was leaving the hospital. "He had a cause he was fighting for," she said. But before he left he wanted to make good on the gift he had promised her. He lightly bound Maxine's arms and legs in restraints and tied a bandana over her mouth. Maxine could barely describe it. "He tickled my neck then began kissing me--

from my ear all the way down." She traced a path that ended at a slightly soiled pair of underpants. "I managed to get one of my arms loose and began pulling down his zipper." Maxine bit her lip. "He said I shouldn't do that because I would be shocked at what I found." She sniffed. "I thought it was because he knew I was a virgin, but it wasn't that at all." Maxine stared at the ceiling. "It was white," she exclaimed. "His penis wasn't dark like the rest of him." It was at that point, Maxine said, that his eyes changed. Grew mean, almost demonic. The lines in his face became hard. "I thought it might be a birth defect like an albino or something, and then for the first time I noticed a layer of makeup covering a scar under his right eyebrow. I asked him about it. He got angry. Said the scar was his only imperfection. And in a perfect world there would be no imperfections. That's not just niggers and Jews," Maxine sobbed. "But gooks and chinks, too."

Maxine described the syringe he laid out on the bed. Carefully shaking a small vial and then withdrawing the liquid into his syringe. Gator made her way around the room, looking for evidence of the syringe.

"Jimmi was going to kill me," Maxine said.

I couldn't tell if she was more scared or angry at this point. She touched her wrists, both the color of raw bacon.

"He blindfolded me. Then he touched my vagina. How could he touch me there and then want to kill me?"

She sobbed for a moment and then looked up. "Wasn't I sexy enough? "

Before I could reassure her, Maxine's arms and legs abruptly stiffened. Her face contorted in puzzled agony. She began gasping for breath.

"My God....what's..."

"Look!" yelled Gator. She held up a 5 cc syringe, just removed from the wastebasket.

"Empty." I looked at the IV. It was dripping death into Maxine's veins.

"Oh my God!" yelled Gator. "It's in there. The poison! He must have emptied it into her IV bottle!"

373

I grabbed the tubing and pinched it closed. Gator disconnected the IV bottle.

But it was too late. Maxine's breaths were labored, her face was in spasms, her head covered with cold sweat.

"No, Maxine. No!"

Maxine looked up, an empty gaze across her face. Her eyes closed.

Chapter 75 Sol Goldman

The following Monday morning, Sol Goldman stood quietly and watched as I trashed his outer office. Expensive lamp shades ripped like cardboard from their alabaster pedestals. Limited edition lithographs were separated from their oak frames and stamped with my foot prints. I'd had it with Sol. One way or another, I knew he was responsible for Maxine Chu laying comatose in the intensive care unit.

Finally, when his foyer looked like a hurricane had passed through, I stopped, and said something my kid brother once said after shredding my baseball cards. "There. That's what you get."

Nonchalantly, Sol straightened two sofa cushions and beckoned me to sit down. "We have a lot to talk about," he said.

Chapter 76 the story

For three years, Jewish patients at Richard Meese Hospital had been systematically injected with ergonovine and pavulon. The murders stopped when Thaddeus Anderson disappeared from Richard Meese, a year before my internship began. Their deaths were covered up, Sol told me. "I had no choice. They would have closed the place down."

"Maybe they should have," I responded, "at least until everything was straightened out." Richard Meese wasn't the only hospital involved. An epidemic of myocardial infarctions had occurred at two prominent Jewish hospitals, one in New York City and one in Miami, and until two weeks ago had been attributed to the high fat content of the victims' diets. "Salami emboli to the heart," Sol said. "Jewish Deli disease." But posthumous investigations carried out at off-campus sites revealed traces of ergonovine, and panic had set in at the highest levels.

"We don't know why this is happening. And we certainly don't have a handle on who's to blame. It's not just Jewish patients. A large County hospital in New Orleans had suspicious infarctions in several black patients."

Sol was telling me he was innocent. I couldn't believe it.

"Come on, Danny. Sure I had to cover some things up. But do you think I'd really be capable of killing Jewish patients?"

Sol held out his left hand and rotated his gold wedding band. A Star of David was embossed.

"I know you're Jewish, Sol. But...well...maybe you weren't really Jewish. Maybe it was just a cover. I mean what better cover for a killer of Jews than a Jew, himself?"

Sol thought, then nodded.

"And besides," said Danny. You and Cantrell were classmates at Yale. I saw the picture in your office. You, Cantrell, and Bramwell were all friends."

"Let me explain to you about my friend, Charles Cantrell." Sol rubbed his chin pensively as he told me how he, Cantrell, and a few others, all from well-to-do families back east, hooked up with each other almost immediately. By the middle of the first year, they were inseparable; studying, eating, partying together. They formed a small organization--Friends of Tomorrow--dedicated to the humanistic training of the future leaders of academic medicine. None of us had ever heard of it back then."

"Did you join?"

Sol shook his head. "Cantrell and I were Anatomy partners. Got along splendidly. One day he was bragging about flying down to the Bahamas for a weekend meeting. I asked him about joining. I was, after all, second in my class and had twelve publications to my credit before starting medical school."

"And?"

"Cantrell laughed. Said those decisions weren't up to him."

Sol's secretary opened the door and reminded him that the guests in his inner office were getting anxious. He looked at his watch and told her he'd be ready in a few minutes. "Until recently, Friends of Tomorrow was a carefully guarded secret organization which appears to be networked into other more well known groups, whose doctrines and goals are not so secret."

"Such as?"

"Aryan National Front. Society for a Racially Pure America."

"Why the hell would those fascist groups be interested in a bunch of snooty doctors?"

Sol inched closer. "Think about it. You told me how you caught Cantrell cheating on minority admissions. Holding the acceptance letters until it was too late for the minority students to matriculate."

"Of course. That's what got him fired, for Christ's sake."

"And killed."

My heart jumped. I bit my lip. "I'm not taking credit for that."

Sol shook his head. "He became a threat to the organization."

"Is that what this is all about? I was the innocent victim because I stood up to a corrupt administrator?"

379

"Discrimination is one thing. Murder brings it to a different level."

Sol sat up, brushing his hands over his thinning hair, which was now matted with sweat. "Cantrell was a soldier, Danny. All the members of Friends of Tomorrow are soldiers. And we believe that they're using their positions to recruit other soldiers."

"For what?"

"To train them to be physicians and then send them out into the community."

"For what?"

"Medical assassinations."

"Oh come on, Sol. You mean doctors are killing patients deliberately?" I took a breath. " I thought only interns killed patients."

Sol looked at his watch. "Some men in the other room are waiting to meet you," he said. I nodded. "Two days ago," he continued, "nurses discovered an intern in a New York hospital standing over a patient's bed with a syringe in his hand. The patient was later found dead, his body loaded with Ergonovine and Pavulon."

My throat tightened. "An intern? They caught him? What did he say? Where was he from?"

Sol shook his head. "He disappeared. They think South America. He graduated from Cornell. No other links yet."

"So the Cantrells of the world are recruiting an army of killers?" It was both ingenious and diabolically sinister.

"Think about it. The potential to eliminate public figures without generating the slightest suspicion. Anyone threatening the goals of their organization could be a target."

"Why Richard Meese?"

"That's easy," said Sol. "Richard Meese is the foundation of the entire Jewish medical community of Chicago. Close it and you've crippled the Jews of this city."

"There are other Jewish hospitals, Sol."

Sol paused, weighing his words carefully.

"I'll tell you something even the Feds don't know, so long as you keep it quiet."

I nodded. Sol opened his wallet and removed a picture. "It's Trish, my wife. She used to be engaged to Cantrell."

I held the picture tightly. She was beautiful, possibly worth getting jealous over. "It was messy," Sol continued. "Cantrell was crazy about her. I didn't set out to steal her. We were in a lab together, and later we shared a couple of hospital rotations. By that time she had second thoughts about marrying a man who harbored a secretive side to himself. We announced our engagement a month after she blew him off. Cantrell didn't take it well, especially after he found out that she was planning on converting to Judaism."

Sol took the picture from my hands and gently replaced it.

"You're telling me this is his way of getting back at you? Quite a grudge."

Sol shrugged his shoulders. "Even zealots get distracted by emotion. I don't know," he said, waving me off. "I prefer not to think about it."

A minute passed as our heads cleared. That couldn't be the only explanation. Meese was involved because of something else. I just couldn't figure out what. I asked Sol why they hadn't beefed up security at the hospital. Turn the place into a demilitarized zone if that's what it took. Sol shook his head. "That would bring publicity, and we'd have to shut down in no time. See, they'd win. Besides, it's not that easy. This may go beyond hospitals."

"What do you mean?"

Sol tried changing the subject. He motioned toward his office door. "We'd better go in there now."

"No secrets, Sol. What did you mean, 'beyond hospitals'?"

Sol studied his fingers, fidgeting. Finally, he spoke: "The only reason I'm going to tell you this is to make up for what I've put you through."

"Nothing you can tell me will even the score."

"Justice Seymour Rosenberg died last month. Remember?"

I nodded. Despite having no time to watch the news, I had heard that he died right after taking a treadmill test.

"A thallium treadmill," Sol said. "He died after purportedly receiving an injection of thallium."

381

"Purportedly?"

"The physician performing the test was a man by the name of Jensen. He was a protege of Cantrell's during his chief residency at Columbia."

His words stung like an open ampule of ammonia. "You think that Jensen injected the Judge with ergonovine and pavulon?"

"I don't know. The body's been exhumed, but nobody's talking. Jensen's disappeared, probably for good. Now you know the reason for all the secrecy. We've got to figure this thing out. And fast. Vice President Barrish is due here next week."

"A treadmill, Sol. . Vice President Barrish is supposed to have one as part of his cardiac workup."

Sol's face was anemic. "The treadmill will be done safely. It's getting him here I'm worried about. Unless we stop these killings, the Feds won't let him get near the place. Danny, he's a hero in Chicago's Jewish community. His coming here for the ground breaking means the difference between raising thousands and millions of dollars for the new center. We need that center. It will be the best of its kind in Chicago. Probably the only thing that will halt the migration of our patients north. If that exodus occurs, this place is in deep jeopardy."

Sol's face relaxed. We both stood up and his arm went to my shoulder. "That's where you come in, Danny. You're the only link that we have."

"You still think I'm involved?"

"Of course not. But for the first time these killers are targeting a specific physician. You."

Goldman's eyes lassoed mine, pleading.

"That's why you haven't kicked me out. I'm your fall guy."

"I should have sent you somewhere else a long time ago. Some important people were convinced that you wouldn't be harmed."

"That's big of them."

"The Feds know you stole a set of Dr. Cantrell's files. They think you either have them or know where they are."

"They're the ones who stole them."

"I don't think so."

"What do you mean?"

"We'll explain later."

I thought a moment. "Maybe that explains why I wasn't killed the day before Thanksgiving."

"What?"

I told Sol about the memorial service for Wanda, how I chased Tannenbaum outside the hospital and barely avoided becoming road kill under a mass of screeching metal and rubber.

"Another message," Sol said. "These people like messages. First was the Nazi rally; then the incident in the ER."

The ER-- Tannenbaum in one room, asking about a file. The patient in the next room--found minutes after Tannenbaum left---throat slit like a sheep at slaughter. "You said it was gang warfare."

I felt used, an innocent whose emotional stability meant nothing to the guys pulling the strings. "It scared the living shit out of me."

"What could I say--that there was a crazy fascist loose? Besides, at that time we weren't sure whether they were just nibbling at you or not."

"You mean you had your eye on me the entire time?"

Sol nodded. "The Feds have been watching since your graduation speech. Cantrell was fired afterward, then he was killed. So was Professor Calpern, the one whose son committed suicide after he paid a million dollars to get him into Medical School. We assumed that you yourself were not beyond retribution."

Once again, my anger made my blood rush. "You also knew that baseball bat incident was no random event." My head throbbed like a jackhammer. "Dammit, Sol. You made me look like an idiot. And look at the risk you put me at. You are one son of a bitch! You knew everything!"

"Not everything, Danny. We had no idea that your patients would become targets."

I did everything I could to keep from crying. "But it was just fine that I was one. And then, when you did find out about my patients, you didn't do a damn thing. You let me suffer through the deaths of my patients, of Wanda Bylevin. My colleagues thought I was incompetent."

"I didn't."

"I don't sign my patients out to you, Sol. Some of the interns didn't even want to sign out a blood sugar to me. Shit, Sol, you almost had me believing I was killing those patients. Damn you! I hate this place! I hate you!" My hand curled and I grabbed at Sol. He caught my wrists and squeezed. "Danny, cut it out!"

And with that, I began to sob, giant tremors wracking my shoulders. Sol handed me a Kleenex. I wiped, and blew, and wiped some more. It took me a minute to settle down. Sol left to tell his secretary something. When he returned I was more composed. "So who is this guy, Tannenbaum? Or is it Thaddeus Anderson? Or whatever the hell his real name is?"

Sol shrugged. "The million dollar question. We don't know a lot. He's a true believer. He's very good. They almost caught him twice. Missed by an inch at the Nazi rally."

"He was being followed?"

"No, you were, just in case. They got an anonymous tip that you were targeted. The Feds almost croaked when they saw Tannenbaum. Chased him for three blocks before he gave them the slip. Then, about a month ago, we found out where he lived. Got there minutes too late. Nothing much left-- a bunch of pictures on the wall--Hitler, Mussolini. Couple of Aryan magazines, and a monograph by Fletcher Stevenson--ever hear of him?"

I hadn't. Never wanted to meet anyone named Fletcher.

"He's one of the fathers of revisionism."

"What's that?"

"Holocaust stuff. Apparently this guy is a proponent of the idea that the Holocaust never happened."

My mind was suddenly focused.

"Some people will believe anything. It's the newest manifestation of fascism and anti-Semitism."

"If there were no more survivors, then there'd be no one to bear testimony to the fact that the Holocaust really took place."

Sol looked puzzled. "What's that supposed to mean?"

"I thought you guys had everything figured out," I said. "Did you know that every one of the patients killed in this hospital was in some way related to the Holocaust--either as a survivor or a relative of one? Look at Horner. If you're going to kill Jews, why not kill two birds with one stone?"

"I'll be a son of a bitch." Goldman stared off into space for a moment. "Quite a piece of work, Raskin. The Feds missed that one all together."

For a moment I was proud of my detective work. But not for long. I had other things on my mind, which seemed to be spinning out of control. Fragments of information had just been nudged from deep within my brain. I had to think, sort things out.

"Tannenbaum can't be acting alone, Sol."

"He has to have some help on the inside. How else would they have gotten to Emile Horner, who except for a bruised neck and a cracked sternum, is going to be fine." Goldman lowered his eyes for a moment. "I owe you one for that, Raskin. Horner is my favorite person in this whole place, and if you hadn't put two and two together..."

"It my fault, too," I added. "I was the one who confided in him in the first place."

"Yes, but if I had told you all this earlier, none of this would have happened. Anyway, someone else knew about his memo, knew we were worried about his safety. That person also knew we had several undercover agents planted in both Meyer house and Gardner House Pavilion, pretending to be patients. Somehow, Horner's patient was transferred to the unguarded mass of humanity up on 5-Meese. By the way, how did you get a copy of that memo?"

I wanted to smile but didn't. It made me wonder for the tenth time, though. How did Eddie Ingraham get a copy?

"I have a brain, Sol. Every now and then I use it. But tell me. Out of this whole big secret group, all of these murders, nobody has come up with anything except me?"

Sol looked at his watch and then rose, straightening his tie.

"Come into my office. There are some people in there who've been waiting to meet you. They have a few questions."

As we moved to the door, Sol draped his arm over my shoulder. "I have to tell you something, Raskin. I am thoroughly amazed that you've been able to get all the information you have on your own. You picked up on the murders, the ergonovine, got a copy of Horner's memo and then figured out he was in trouble just in time to save his life. You even broke into my office with very little trouble. Remind me to get you a new i.d. tag: '007, M.D.'"

We passed Sol's secretary. "Bring us a couple of drinks, Jenny." He turned to me. "How 'bout a Coke?"

"Sure," I replied, opening the door. "Shaken, not stirred."

Chapter 77 the good guys

Two men rose as I entered Sol's inner office, while a third remained seated in a leather chair facing the window. I recognized the nearest man as the one who interrogated me following Wanda Bylevin's death. Pudgy, smelly cigar, mid-fifties, supposedly just a member of Chicago's P.D.

"James Huber, Bureau chief, Chicago division, FBI," he said, squeezing my hand.

"Daniel Raskin, FBI decoy, Chicago division, Richard Meese Hospital," I replied.

No smile.

The lanky man to his right wore an evenly parted nest of blond hair, speckled with just enough premature gray to remind me of Peter Graves in *Mission Impossible*. I had seen him before as well. He was the one Goldman had brought with him to Mrs. Garber's autopsy, the one claiming to be from the Medical Board. "Jack Hodges," he said, his handshake firm. "Sorry about our last meeting, Daniel. I know we made you feel lousy."

"Cut the maudlin crap, Hodges," barked Huber.

Hodges removed his hand from mine. "We do appreciate all your efforts, though, especially Phil over here. Turn around Phil," Jack said, holding his smile like a greeting card.

After a moment the black leather chair swiveled around, reminding me of how the TV hosts would reveal the identity of a celebrity game show guest. I cringed. It was the guy who had followed Gail and me down Michigan Avenue, the one I'd punched out in the bookstore. I remembered how much my fist hurt at the time, the only solace being the thought that the other guy had gotten the worst of it. My hunch had proven correct. Phil was a mass of metal and shattered ego, with steel wires protruding from his face like an electric fence. I had broken the jaw of a Fed and had lived to tell about it.

His hand was as cold as the steel lanyard zig-zagging its way between his teeth.

"Sorry."

"No need to apologize," said Huber. "If one of our agents is careless enough to get tagged by an amateur, he deserves what he gets."

"I'm not sure the word amateur is correct," Sol flexed. "My boy Daniel, here, came to the same conclusions we did, and in one tenth the time. The fact that he was able to pick up on your man doesn't surprise me one bit."

Suddenly I was Sol's boy, his fledgling prodigy, a Marlon Brando with a stethoscope.

Chief Investigator Huber spent most of the next hour reciting events as he saw them, covering most of what Sol and I had discussed in his outer office.

When he finished talking, Huber leaned back in his chair, set his size eleven Johnson & Murphy's atop Sol's oak desk, and bit off the end of a cigar, wafting it across his nose as if it were a fine Cabernet. "Cuban," he said. "Friend of mine down at Central Intelligence gets them by the boatload." He took his time lighting up, playing the effect for all it was worth, not realizing that a piece of the cellophane wrapping was stuck to his upper lip. After sucking in a fair ration of carcinogenic fluorocarbons, he continued. "It's your turn, Raskin. Tell us what happened at graduation."

The room suddenly felt hot. I found it hard to breathe. I swallowed twice. Instead, I went over everything they already knew, hoping to squelch their appetites. Told them how Cantrell had kicked me off the admissions committee after I'd discovered that he had sabotaged minority admissions. I repeated the story of how I broke into his office and stole two sets of files. One was unlocked. The other was locked and remained that way. Never got around to returning it and as far as I knew Tannenbaum had stolen it during the break in of my apartment.

"That's all well and good," Huber said. "Nevertheless, we need to know exactly what happened during graduation."

I looked over at Goldman, who gave a slight nod. My belt suddenly became a noose, tightening around the hungry creature within.

Chapter 78 medical school graduation

I gave up smoking pot when I began medical school. It stayed that way for four years.

Until graduation day.

I had returned from a cardiology rotation in Oxford the week before only to discover that I had been selected to address the class at graduation, a small fact inadvertently left out of my perverted roommate's letter. "We have a surprise for you, Mr. Popular Guy," he wrote on the backside of the same postcard I had originally sent to him. All right, people liked me. But choosing me as graduation speaker? And without my consent?

And now, perched atop the upper balcony of Hill Auditorium thirty minutes before the festivities began, I grimaced at the throngs of happy relatives scurrying toward their seats. Through eyes stinging from sweat, I watched as my own family was escorted to reserved seats in the second row, close enough to clearly see their son humiliate himself in front of four thousand people. Grandma began knitting as soon as she sat down and I half-expected a guillotine to appear on the stage. Feeling the previous day's quarter pounder well up into my throat, I retreated to the bathroom stall in the rafters at the top of the auditorium, where I sat on an old, cracked porcelain seat, waiting, praying. Panic was complete, for as hard as I had tried to write a speech on the spur of the moment, I had nothing but a rash of crumpled papers to show for it. A few lines about sharing our dreams, the friends we'd all miss, that sort of banal crap. Most of it I had crossed out. All the good memories had been infiltrated by the bad ones; Cantrell, Calpern, the Admissions committee. How could I give a speech full of pithy nostalgia, when all I wanted to do was to get the hell out of Arbor Hills?

From under my stall I watched a janitor enter, bucket clattering atop rickety wheels, mop dragging along for the ride. Unaware of my presence, he struck a match and a moment later, a loud protracted inhalation filled the room. The tassel over my cap brushed across my eyes like a windshield wiper as I poked my head outside the door. I watched while he cleaned a mirror, humming something from Van Halen. Suddenly he jumped back, the joint flying from his hands into the wet sink.

"Shit, man. You scared the hell out of me."

"Sorry 'bout that."

"Should be, man. You ruined a perfectly good dooby."

He was young, dressed in tattered white overalls, face dusted with dirt and grease. His stringy long hair curiously resembled the mop he held. I discovered that he was a psychology grad student, and he turned out to be a pretty good listener. After hearing my reasons for seeking refuge and perusing my rudimentary speech, he took a plastic baggy out of his pocket and began rolling a pinch of buds into a joint.

"Your parents are going to annul your birth when they hear this," he said, throwing the notes back in my face. "It's crap. If I were giving a speech like this, I'd be scared shitless, too." He struck a match on the grout between the tiles, and passed the lit joint my way. "Go ahead. You need it more than I do."

Taking note of the situation, I balked. Thirty minutes before graduation, a mockery of a speech in one hand, a joint in other. Hardly the time to regress to college dormitory life. Hardly the time for a crutch. I looked at the janitor. Then again, why not? Things couldn't get any worse. So, for the next twenty minutes I inhaled the joint and exhaled my entire four years of medical school. Cantrell and his racist admissions committee, the black candidates I had interviewed who were never accepted, Bobby Calpern's death by suicide; Cantrell kicking me off the admissions committee.

The mop wielding therapist nodded continuously, stroking his chin like he was a reincarnated Sigmund Freud. Before I realized how much time had passed, I was brought to my feet by the sound of the Arbor Hills symphony. "Shit," I coughed. "I better get out of here." As I exited the door, I turned back. "What the fuck am I going to say?"

"Give your speech, man."

"I don't have a speech."

"Sure you do. You just gave it!"

391

I left that part of the story out, of course, when talking to Goldman and the Feds. What good would it have done? It wasn't until I was marching up the aisle that I even realized I was stoned out of my mind. Until then, dancing my way among the wafting black capes, I thought how great it was to be part of some great big Zorro convention.

As we reached the base of the podium, someone asked me a question. My lips couldn't form the words and gibberish poured from my mouth like lumpy oatmeal. My legs were like rubber sausages as I climbed the podium. I stepped in line behind Charles Cantrell who was standing next to our featured speaker, Nobel Laureate Jocelyn Farlow. Reaching into my pocket for the rudimentary speech, hoping it would somehow anchor me into reality, I retrieved nothing but a pack of stale Dentyne and a peanut butter cup wrapper. Apparently I'd left that stupid speech in the upstairs bathroom with the janitor. He'd probably rolled a joint in the damn thing by now. "Shit," I said aloud. Charles Cantrell turned and looked at me. His nostrils flared like a beagle sensing the fox. He inched closer. "That ain't no Chanel aftershave you're wearing."

Our eyes locked in hatred. "As a matter of fact," I snarled, " it's Cannabis number five."

I felt his finger in my chest. His head lowered. "Don't fuck with me," he whispered. "I know you stole those fucking files from my office."

Maybe it was the marijuana. Maybe it was the fact that I had just emptied my venomous feelings about Cantrell onto the janitor. I'm not sure why, but I grabbed his finger and began bending it backwards, watching his face tighten. "In one hour I'll be free of you and this place. And if I see you after this is over, I'll kick your ass all over the campus." I let go of his finger.

Cantrell let out his breath, then clenched his teeth. "An hour's a long time." He leaned closer and whispered in my ear. "Better pray to your Jew God I don't hold your diploma back." With that, he turned and smiled sweetly at our speaker.

After taking my seat, I rubbed my eyes, which itched like someone had rubbed cat fur into them. I scanned the audience, zeroing in on my family. Mom met my gaze and when she tapped Grandma on the shoulder and pointed my way, I felt like I was in a zoo. Grandma was still knitting (the best of times, the worse of times) next to Dad, who sat there, thumbing through Fortune magazine. My brother was scanning the procession of graduates for the women, holding up one to ten fingers depending on how cute he thought they were. Suddenly I was thirteen again and about to read the Torah. Only now it was being played in reverse. Boy becomes man, only to revert to stoned out infantile piece of garbage about to embarrass his family and entire medical school class.

I almost missed my introduction. Come on, Raskin, I implored myself. Get it together. Jeez, they were clapping. The class entertainer, the one with a witty response to everything. Their expectations gripped my chest and I struggled to breathe, for a moment sure I was going to pass out. As I ambled forward, three tiers of humanity quieted before me. I grabbed the microphone, praying for inspiration, some opening statement that might rouse the speech maker within me. I looked over the crowd. They had quieted, anticipating words of inspiration. But nothing was there. My oratory career was short-lived.

" I... I'm glad you all.... came here today.....so ...."

I stopped. Damn, I can't do it. I'm history. "Thanks for coming, everybody. I...uh...hope...,"

Suddenly, from high above the rafters a voice echoed out.

"What about Calpern, Doc? Tell them about Calpern."

I squinted, unable to see the source, but the voice was familiar.

"Who really killed Calpern? Tell em."

The crowd turned as one toward the mysterious voice. My vision focused. There--in the rafters, a shadowy figure with a mop. The janitor! The crazy bastard who smoked my speech. It seemed like weeks ago that I'd been up there talking to him. Oh shit! What had I told him?

"As I stand before you on this..."

"Tell them about Calpern- he ain't standing before anybody. Thanks to Cantrell, the boy's taking a dirt nap."

The audience shuffled restlessly. I looked over at Cantrell. His eyes showed unmistakable terror, his arms folded as tight as his jaw was set. Screw him, I thought. Why protect that smoldering boil of a man? Why not lance the damn thing once and for all? I owed it to my classmates. And to Bobby Calpern.

I adjusted my glasses. "Bob Calpern, someone said. Indeed, let us talk about our poor classmate who, unable to adjust to the rigors of medical school, snuffed out his own life," I turned for just a moment. Cantrell's eyes were fixed stiffly on the first few rows of the crowd.

"Truth is, Calpern's suicide wasn't of his own doing. He was a victim. A victim of hidden forces entrenched at our Medical School. You see, Bob Calpern never should have entered this school. It was just one of the many ways your Dean of Admissions abandoned his duties."

I had descended into an inferno from which there was no turning back. "Despite the warnings of two interviewers, Dr. Cantrell admitted Bob Calpern anyway. He did it outside the system, through his secret organization known as Friends of Tomorrow. "

A few shouts flew in from the crowd, zeroing in on Cantrell. I turned around once again, watching Cantrell dangle like an earthworm, speared by the fishing hook of his misdeeds.

I paused to collect my composure. What now? I didn't have to wait long for an answer. Again, from the rafters: "What about those racist admission policies?"

Oh God, what was happening? I thought of just saying thank you, turning around, and walking back to my seat. That bit of damage control might be enough to save Cantrell his job, not to mention my being chased out of town. But something held me at the podium, a feeling, a voice, maybe Calpern's spirit, seeking reparations for what had happened.

"I would like to take this opportunity to thank Dr. Cantrell for his efforts to make our school a true model for affirmative action." I reached into my pants pocket and removed a set of keys which I waved menacingly above my head.

"This chain contains a key to one of Cantrell's files, which until recently was under the strict purview of our Dean. I used this key to borrow an entire file of secret documents which I xeroxed."

I turned. The look on Cantrell's face was unmistakable. Terror. And he wasn't looking at me, he was looking past me, down into the first few rows of the audience. Two men, one of whom suddenly rose, stared straight at me, then turned and walked out of the auditorium. I'd seen that man somewhere. Cantrell started to stand but was restrained by the Dean of Students.

I continued. "Our Dean of Admissions touts himself as the bastion for equal rights, for higher learning-- especially for those groups deemed oppressed. Yet I have incontrovertible evidence that he did his best to keep students of color from ever attending our school."

The audience buzzed. The Chancellor was looking at Cantrell, very sternly.

"Give it to the prick!" the janitor's voice rang out.

"Our Dean proudly claims to offer fifty minority acceptances a year," I continued, swaying back and forth like an evangelist. "But the reason we've had only four black students graduate this year is because Cantrell never sent out acceptance letters until the week before school started--after he was sure these people already had matriculated elsewhere. I ask you, Dr. Cantrell. Is that your idea of fair play?"

"He's a racist pig!" the janitor yelled.

"Damn right he is," I said.

"What other agenda do you have?" I screamed at the top of my lungs. "What else are you hiding from our class and everybody else?"

I stepped back a foot while a tidal wave of classmates rose in unison, yelling, cheering, hooting. Cantrell sat there like a pile of dog shit that had been baking in the sun all day.

Cantrell wasn't even looking at the Chancellor, whose face was contorted in embarrassment and disgust. He was focused on the front row, on the remaining man. Cantrell's eyes were no longer angry--or terrified. They were pleading. His chest was heaving.

The Nobel laureate came over and shook my hand. "Exceptional job, young man. I never heard such bravery in a speech before."

"And I never heard such stupidity," frowned chief officer Huber as he removed the cellophane wrapper from his cigar. "What were you, stoned or something?"

I gave him a look that said: 'what do you think I am, crazy?'

My cheeks were warm, my palms sticky. I hadn't told anyone about graduation, not even Alex. It brought back too many painful memories. And considering all that had happened since that day, I had to admit that perhaps I had given someone a legitimate reason to target me. But talking about it helped me remember something else. Something about Linda Johnson, the woman with whom I had that brief but utterly satisfying encounter with after graduation. What the hell was it?

Replaying graduation had somehow flipped my cerebral tape recorder to the 'on' position. What was it? Moving...Arbor Hills...Linda Johnson... faint shadows danced above me then faded as I tried to pluck it from the clouds.

"Raskin, wake up." It was Huber. "Tell us again what you think happened to that file you swiped from Cantrell." It was Huber. I tried to focus.

"Like I said, the damn thing is gone. I never opened it. When Tannenbaum broke into my apartment, he stole it."

Huber and Goldman looked at each other. Huber shook his head.

"I'm afraid not."

"What?"

"Tannenbaum didn't break into your apartment. We did."

"Bastards! So you've had it this whole time."

"No, Danny," said Sol. "We never found it. You must have left it in Arbor Hills. Or lost it."

"Try to remember, Raskin. That's why we're going through all this about graduation. We're trying to jog your memory."

396

I studied the faces in the room, wondering if they could sense the beginning of a recollection. I needed to be alone. Needed to think.

"Sorry. I don't have it."

Sol Goldman stepped forward fanning cigar smoke away from his face. "Well it's a good thing someone on the other side thinks you do. That's undoubtedly why your life has been spared."

Huber placed his cigar in the ashtray. "It could break the case, dammit. Think."

"I'm sorry, it's gone. I've checked everywhere." ·

"Let's just hope the killer doesn't know that. Your life wouldn't be worth the paper your driver's license is printed on."

Goldman leaned against his chair. "I think it's time we move Dr. Raskin to a safer place."

I swallowed hard. "What?"

"To another program, a new identity."

"Sol, you can't do that. I'm not leaving Meese."

Huber sat back and wore the smile of a man who held the winning poker hand.

"We have no way to offer him any sort of protection program at another institution."

"You lying son of..."

"Hold on, Goldman. I promised protection if and when he either recovered the file or was able to eventually testify." Huber wafted a thick ring of cigar smoke. "Besides, he's better off here."

"As a guinea pig," said Goldman.

"Call it that if you want," said Huber. But at least we can keep an eye on him. Your boy's going to be working in the intensive care unit in a couple of weeks. Hodges here is taking a crash course in unstable angina."

Hodges clutched his chest with his fist. "Got that Levine sign down pretty good."

Officer Phil Warshinski handed Huber a note. He looked at me, and for the first time, cracked a smile. "He wants to know who's going to protect them from you?"

I was lying on my couch later that evening, a third of a pint of Jack Daniels and four peanut butter cups to the wind, watching an old Jimmy Stewart movie. The file never made it to Chicago, now I was sure of it. I'd always assumed it was sitting in my apartment, unpacked, until Tannenbaum had stolen it. Where was it? Glimpses of my last days in Arbor Hills fluttered through my mind like butterflies. First graduation, then packing up and meeting Linda Johnson. Ahh, what a glorious few days that had been. I could have stayed there another week.

Chapter 79 linda johnson

I'd been struggling to negotiate the removal of my lumpy old mattress from my third floor Arbor Hills apartment to the local dumpster when I heard a southern accent call out, "Y'all not going to throw that out, are you?"

"No," I snapped. "Just thought I'd take a little nap outside." I was in no mood for conversation. After what had happened at graduation, I just wanted to pack up and get the hell out of town. Med school was over. I was leaving--the mattress was not. I lifted the mattress to the top of my head where I balanced it like a Tahitian native carrying a pot of water. As I made my way out the back door of the building, the southern voice and a pair of quiet footsteps followed.

"I wasn't tryin' to be funny. I'm sorry. I thought y'all might be able to help me."

I turned slowly and stared at the woman who stood two steps above me, her hands behind her back. She couldn't have been older than twenty. Long tangles of curls spreading out over a skimpy but amply filled halter top and blue jean cutoffs that she wore three quarters of the way up her butt like a piece of dental floss. Her face was southern tranquility--plain but inviting and a gap between her two front teeth sent my heart fluttering.

"Sorry," I gulped, trying to keep my gaze locked onto her amarretto eyes. "I didn't mean to be rude." But I had, and she was starting her ascent of the stairs.

"Just movin' in and could have used a bed, that's all." She turned away.

"Wait."

She kept walking, her sandals catching the tips of the stairs. I caught up with her at the door to her apartment.

"You really need an old beat up mattress?"

"Not from an asshole."

"I'm not an asshole. I mean I was an asshole a minute ago. But I'm really not an asshole. I'm a doctor."

"Oh, so it's Doctor Asshole?"

"At least it's Doctor Remorseful Asshole."

She smiled, her hair whisking off her soft, voluptuous chest. "And to make up for your indiscretion, your assholiness wishes to offer this southern lady his mattress?"

"Yeah," I answered, trying not to stare.

"How much?"

I shrugged my shoulders.

"Trade it for a beer?" she asked, swaying gently on legs spread farther apart than what seemed customary. "Come on up," she said with a flip of her head. "Bring the mattress."

I smiled. "Southern hospitality at its best."

"Not quite. Southern hospitality would be askin' you to show me how it works."

That was Friday afternoon. I was supposed to be in Detroit that evening for a family dinner of lamb chops, mashed potatoes, and home-made blueberry pie, my favorite meal in the whole world, courtesy of Mom, who would accompany me the following morning to Chicago.

Mom and her lamb chops had to wait.

Three days.

Southern hospitality being what it was, it took that long before I got my clothes back on. I was too tired to pee, barely had the strength to pull the condoms off. And when I finally awoke, I felt rejuvenated, and except for the lingering taste of spermicide, which sure beat the hell out of lamb chops, I had forgotten the circus surrounding graduation. It was a fitting and proper closure to a stage in my life that I preferred to forget.

Linda watched as I packed up the aging Maverick, then smiled her wicked southern smile when the trunk refused to close. Overloaded with textbooks, white coats, and assorted Arbor Hills memorabilia, Linda agreed to store a few things at her place. The return trip to her apartment cost me another half day and a pulled hamstring thanks to a game of nude Twister. A half day from Detroit and Mom and another home cooked meal. I wasn't complaining.

That had been seven months before. I hadn't communicated with Linda Johnson since.

Linda Johnson. I'd carried two boxes of stuff I didn't think I'd need right away back up those stairs. Left them at her place. The files were there. They had to be. I felt my heart race as I dialed the information operator of Arbor Hills. No wonder the Feds couldn't find the thing. I knew I hadn't thrown it out. I never threw anything out, not my two thousand dust-laden baseball cards or my sixth grade poems that never rhymed when they were supposed to.

"I'm sorry, we have no Linda Johnson at 546 Brentwood."

The operator had to be mistaken. Of course Linda Johnson lived there. For God's sake, I lived there.

"I'm sorry," she repeated nasally. "I have seventeen L. Johnsons listed in Arbor Hills. None reside at 546 Brentwood."

Well, she used to live there, I explained. Couldn't she find a listing from back in June?

"I'm sorry. I have no record of a Linda Johnson at 546 Brentwood."

I thought a moment. I was on the top floor, apartment 7. She was one floor lower. It was either apartment 3 or 4.

"Can you give me a phone number from an address?"

"No."

"Why not?"

"Against the law."

In the end, I was given seventeen phone numbers. Every Linda or L. Johnson in Arbor Hills. Turned out there was Loretta, Lionel, two Larrys and the first string half-back of the football team, Levander, who, mistaking me for some unscrupulous agent, asked for twenty grand under the table and a new Lexus as a signing bonus. There were four Lindas and I spoke with each of them. None were southern, none had heard of my Linda Johnson. She had vanished and taken with her any hope of finding the file.

Chapter 80 maxine chu

"I still want Maxine Chu to have the bone marrow transplant."

It was the day after our meeting with the FBI agents, the day after they had convinced me to remain at Meese as a guinea pig. They had gotten their way, now it was my turn to exact a price.

Sol set his pen down on top of the research paper he was proofreading. "Come on, Danny. I care about Maxine, too. But she's in a coma."

There was no denying the gravity of Maxine's illness. Though we were present when she suffered her respiratory and cardiac arrest, she endured an hour of CPR, along with epinephrine and the largest infusion of nitroglycerin I had ever given before we got the heart rhythm and blood pressure back. Her heart was beating fine now, and Maxine was breathing on her own. That was the good news. The bad news was that she would not wake up. Her pupils, once bright and inviting, were set back and widely dilated. Her EEG showed sporadic bursts of brain wave activity consistent with a persistent vegetative state. The likelihood of recovery was, at best, one percent. Sol leaned back in his chair.

"We've never seen anybody wake up after more than a week."

"It could happen," I argued. "Are you willing to say that there's absolutely no chance she'll wake up?"

"Well, there is always a chance, I suppose," said Sol. "We say the same thing every year about the Cubs."

I wasn't backing down. "Maxine's lymphoma is out of control. We agreed that a bone marrow transplant was her only chance. We brought in the technology; we have the personnel. Her sister's marrow cells have been harvested. Maxine will die without a transplant."

Sol stood up, his face reddening. "She'll die with it, Danny. The transplant was experimental in the first place. Human Subjects Committee will never go for it, not when she's in a coma."

In reasonable times, Sol would be right, of course. But these weren't reasonable times, and I no longer gave a damn about protocol and the ethics of experimentation. True, Maxine might die with the transplant, but without trying, I would never know. I'd spend the rest of my life hating myself for allowing Maxine to become a victim of a heinous plot in which I failed to recognize that her suitor was a master of disguise and a murderer. I thought back to when the bastard drank the evidence that I'd found under Mrs. Garber's bed. And to the time when I'd determined that Tannenbaum could indeed get away with disguising himself as a black man. I should have been more alert, should have figured it out.

I moved closer to Sol. I picked up the phone and handed it to him. "Call the Oncologists, Sol. Then call the Human Subjects Committee. You're the most powerful man here."

"I can't bring someone back from the dead, Danny."

"I'll worry about that, Sol. Just call."

"I will not." He grabbed the receiver and slammed it down. "And what gives you the right to storm into my office and start making demands?"

I picked up the receiver. "Then call Agent Huber. Tell him that I'm going public."

"Right."

"I thought that might be your response." I retreated to the door and opened it.

"Come on in Ted."

A burly man, five foot four at most, note pad in hand, sauntered in. Behind him, Sol's secretary was waving her hands in the air. Sol's cheeks were fire-red. "What the hell is going on here?"

"Sol, meet Teddy Korotic. He's a beat writer for the Trib."

Teddy, chewing on some gum, looked at Sol like he were a common criminal. He threw himself in a chair, lifted his size eights onto Sol's polished oak desk, and opened his notebook. "So Doctor, I hear we got some murders going on around here."

Chapter 81 bone marrow

Ten days after our meeting, Maxine Chu, still with no evidence of productive brain wave activity, received an infusion of her sister's cultured bone marrow cells. The arrangements were made personally by Sol Goldman, thanks in no small part to my pretend newspaper reporter, Teddy Korotic, who actually was Sam Feldstein, my clinic patient with a bad case of gout. A former vaudeville entertainer, Sam was more than happy for a chance to show his stuff, never once inquiring whether the murders were, in fact, real.

For the next two weeks I stood outside Maxine's germ free, laminar air flow room, watching as the specialists paraded around in their germ-free, space suit regalia, checking her vital signs, shaking their heads at the lack of response in her bone marrow, staring at me like I was some kind of criminal for having pushed them into performing the transplant in the first place.

Late at night when the doctors and curious onlookers had gone home, when the hallways were empty save the occasional med nurse or pharmacist, I would press my nose to the plexiglass and watch Maxine. She lay there like Sleeping Beauty, except for the IV's, nasogastric tubes, multiple infusion pumps, and ECG electrodes. I longed to see her eyes open, to feel their life-giving penetration. I imagined her laugh, the way her chiseled shoulders shook as she giggled. But there was no Prince Charming in site, at least not for now.

During that first week, Gail Peterson sat vigil both with me and over me; with me during my visits with Maxine, then over me while I slept on the couch in the visitor's lounge. The moment my eyes closed, I felt a blanket softly nuzzle my shoulders, followed by a lingering kiss on the cheek.

Alex Rosen was also around, forcing me out of the hospital for small periods of time. He apologized for thinking I had been paranoid. "I'm not quite ready to buy this Holocaust denial stuff as a motive," he said over a pastrami sandwich and Guiness at Mr. Gee's after a long stint at Maxine's side. "But there's no denying somebody's offing your patients, and if I don't keep a closer eye on you, you may be next."

"Not as long as they think I have that file, Alex." "It's gone, Danny. Any idiot has that figured out by now. I hate to say it, but maybe Sol was right. Maybe you should get into protective custody." Alex gulped down a second glass of Guiness, his eyes wandering toward two off-duty nurses sitting three tables away.

One of the nurses stood up, heels tap dancing across the dated linoleum and approached our table. Almost six feet tall with rusty blond hair and a sweater that seemed painted onto two bouncing breasts, her hand rested on Alex's shoulder. "Aren't you a friend of Sarah Schwartz?" she asked, her thick red lips glistening. As usual when Alex was around, I was about as visible as cigarette smoke in a fog. I excused myself, wanting to check on Maxine once more before heading home. Alex nodded to me, then whispered in my ear. "Can you loan me twenty bucks?"

I left the restaurant, and a chill March breeze took my breath away as I looked up at the starless, lonely sky.

That night I cried myself to sleep, then dreamed I was dancing with Maxine Chu. Laughing, hugging, living.

The next morning Maxine's bone marrow started to work.

Part 4

Spring's eternal unfolding

First they came for the Jews
and I did not speak out
because I was not a Jew.
Then they came for the Communists
and I did not speak out
because I was not a Communist.
Then they came for the trade unionists
and I did not speak out
because I was not a trade unionist.
Then they came for me
and there was no one left
to speak for me.

Pastor Niemoller

Chapter 82 intensive care

Two weeks later, Maxine and I were both transferred to the intensive care unit, I as an intern, Maxine as a patient. Her bone marrow transplant had taken so well that her case was already being touted as nothing short of a miracle. Her blood counts had risen enough to stave off infection, and her platelets were plentiful enough to halt the interminable ooze of blood that had plagued her prior to the surgery. Her vital signs were stable. Her electrolyte values were all normal. Everything was great.

Except for one thing.

Maxine was still in a coma.

The initial excitement of her successful marrow transplant eventually gave way to frustration, particularly on the part of the oncologists. This was an important breakthrough that begged to be written up and published in a major journal. But how could you write it up when she was like this, they would ask sarcastically. What would you say? Miraculous bone marrow transplant cures disseminated Hodgkins disease. Patient, however, cannot be reached for comment. She's on extended leave in a vegetable patch.

Their anger focused on Sol Goldman. How could the Chief of Medicine have permitted an experimental procedure to be done on a cerebral corpse, leaving the hospital exposed to the scrutiny of the entire medical community, not to mention the media? Every local affiliate had cameras parked in the lobby of Gardner House pavilion, and word was out that CNN was sending a crew.

"We're proud of our team, and feel we've made a breakthrough in Hodgkins disease," Sol announced before the lights and cameras, a sweaty hospital president and a baggy eyed chief of staff standing beside him. "Of course we expect the bone marrow recipient to come out of her coma," he answered repeatedly. After the reporters were gone, he would sigh heavily, and if I happened to be in the area, would shake his head at me.

He called me into his office one day, just to vent his frustration. His desk was uncharacteristically littered with legal briefs, books on coma, old coffee cups.

"Do you know what this is doing to me?" he asked, trying to clear a space for his notebook. "The hospital board wants my ass." He paused, leafing through a stack of envelopes. "And look at this," he said, holding out a letter with the White House frank on it. "It's from Vice President Barrish's office reconfirming his attendance at next month's cardiac center ground breaking. What am I supposed to do about this?"

"You can't risk having Barrish come to Meese, not the way things are right now. There's a killer on the loose with a penchant for people wearing the big 'J' on their chest."

It wasn't what Sol wanted to hear.

"Look Raskin, you'd better just worry about Maxine. Get her to wake the hell up. And don't get yourself killed."

To help guarantee my safety, Agent Jack Hodges was admitted to the Unit under the name Seymour Chenowith, his diagnosis being unstable angina, rule out myocardial infarction. I was the only one who knew the fictitious nature of his symptoms, which made me appear cold and irreverent whenever the nurses caught me giggling at his nitroglycerin-induced headaches or his alternating constipation and diarrhea. I guess it was my way of denying that agent Jack Hodges was there to protect me, denying that I might actually need that kind of protection. I pictured myself lying on the road looking up at Tannenbaum bearing down at me in his New Yorker, swerving away in a cloud of dust at the last moment. Then lying on the shores of Lake Michigan, seeing large boots, then watching a Louisville Slugger come crashing down on my skull. Painful as the memories were, they reminded me of how important that missing file must be to those guys. It was my one and only life insurance policy.

I was also sure about something else. Linda Johnson had that missing file, and I didn't know where the hell she was. The Arbor Hills registry office refused to provide any information, but would pass along a letter addressed to her care of the school. I just didn't have time for that. I was sure Sol Goldman or potbellied FBI agent Huber could have gotten her address from the school in a minute, but my instincts told me to leave them out of it, at least for now. I'd already lost Wanda Bylevin by involving her, and I didn't want to take a chance on something happening to Linda. I hardly knew who I could trust anymore. Someone at the hospital was helping Tannenbaum. Someone with the authority to have transferred Emile Horner's patient to the secluded area of 5-Meese where no undercover agents were stationed. And how did my beeper end up in Horner's pocket when I found him? Someone had to have taken it from me at the party.

Coming up with a suspect was impossible. Someone close to Goldman, perhaps someone with access to his files. Maybe a mole out of Huber's FBI office. That I couldn't control. What I could control, though, was my own surroundings. The list of people at Meese who might be in a position to pass along information about patients and doctors was huge. From now on, I had to be careful with virtually everyone.

And if I was going to find Linda Johnson, I'd need help. I decided I'd raise the least amount of suspicion with Officer Mulroney. I told him that Linda Johnson was my girlfriend from Arbor Hills who had suddenly disappeared, and that in light of what had happened to Wanda Bylevin and now Maxine Chu, I needed to know she was okay. Mulroney said he would see what he could do.

·

Chapter 83 menage

"Are you happy?" We were sitting at the telemetry station in the intensive care unit, Gail watching me eat cashew chicken out of a paper container with my ECG calipers, a habit for which I had earned something of a reputation. Surrounded by hemodynamic tracings on one side and stacks of ECG rhythm strips on the other, Gail's question caused me to pause. Are you happy? Did that mean she knew I was falling in love with her?

"What do you mean, am I happy?"

"Two birds with one stone this month, Danny. You get to keep a close eye on Maxine."

"And the other?"

"Hearts," she said. "You've always wanted to take care of people's hearts."

"Only certain hearts, Gail." Though the telemetry module was in the center of the Unit, I couldn't resist the impulse to kiss Gail. I leaned over but at the last second she pushed me away with her index finger and smiled sheepishly.

"I'm not talking about me, Danny. Cardiology. You've always wanted to be a cardiologist."

"Not really, Gail."

"Oh yeah. You just never realized it."

Gail laughed, then reached over and brushed a black mushroom from my cheek. "I wouldn't be surprised if your umbilical cord had been made out of stethoscope tubing."

Thinking about it, I suppose hearts had been my passion of mine, both sentimentally and anatomically, beginning with a frog dissection in sixth grade. I remembered being mesmerized as that tiny cardiac metronome danced rhythmically in the palm of my hand like a Mexican jumping bean. Life's most hidden secrets pulsated in that heart, each beat a rhythmic whisper, a clue to the mysteries of the universe. From frogs I graduated to turkeys--dissected ours Thanksgiving day. I showed Aunt Hannah what a turkey coronary artery looked like--she showed me what barfing into her stuffing looked like.

414

The cardiac theme continued into the onset of puberty. My first public erection occurred on Valentine's Day when sixth grader Mindy Parks--that facial map of freckles--handed me that special "secret" valentine with 'I love you' scribbled in one corner. When you got right down to it, hearts had a way of running my life. Forget oysters--I lost my virginity after eating a hearts of palm salad with Sheila Moskowitz.

During those early years of medical school when most of my classmates still thought the atrium was part of a new shopping mall, I was busy running to the library looking up anything and everything concerning cardiology. While other third year students spent their time palpating boggy prostates or pregnant bellies, I became one with my stethoscope. Every patient, a cardiac disaster waiting to happen; every friend, relative, and even our Labrador retriever, Noodles, a potential murmur (to this day I'm convinced I diagnosed his fatal case of heart worms). I learned to discern the clicks and the whooshes and kerplunks better than most of my friends, who began asking for personal consultations on the patients they were following. For me, a Saturday night date became a clinical opportunity. "Never mind whether or not I scored, you should have heard how that second heart sound split." Multiple orgasms were nothing compared to multiple murmurs.

I looked over at Gail, and even though it bothered me that she was constantly brushing crumbs from my face, I was happy we were paired together again. Our relationship had taken on a new closeness, a palpating, throbbing excitement that I could feel whenever we were in the same room.

After Maxine was poisoned, I had stayed awake for some sixty hours, finally collapsing in Gail's bed while she was in the kitchen fixing pasta primavera. I awoke at four in the morning in unfamiliar darkness, turning over, my arm on Gail's back. Then we were kissing, but the memory is incomplete. Her hand groped gently at my body, which except for gym shorts was naked. Then a subtle separation, a gentle push by Gail back down into the recesses of her bed, her hand running through my hair, then nothing. The next morning I asked what had happened and she smiled, saying I tried one of those "man things" on her.

415

"You sure you didn't try one of those 'man things' on me?" I asked, trying to remember. Gail laughed at the time. The same laugh I heard now as we sat at the nurse's station. I needed Gail——needed her and wanted her. It was a desire I hadn't felt for anyone in a very long time. Yet, as I sat at the nursing module fingering my rhythm strips and sorting out the CCU admit orders, I sensed a slight uneasiness in Gail. Especially when Alex was around. I was hoping it was my imagination.

I was used to the fact that Alex was the local Lothario, the most handsome, suavest, most desirable bachelor in the whole hospital, if not the entire Western Hemisphere. Women quivered like Jello in his presence. Unfortunately, they were often women with the I.Q. of Jello. So why did I get the feeling that the reason Alex switched a cushy renal elective with Brian Picolli was not so much to watch out for my safety as he had claimed, but rather to spend more time with Gail? Come on, I told myself. Not Gail. She embodied everything in a woman that Alex didn't want. Her Raggedy Ann looks were pleasant, but not Miss Illinois appealing, not like the vamps that kept Alex's glands working overtime. And Gail's intelligence put Alex's bimbos to shame.

Of course I wasn't about to discuss any of this with Alex. He would deny it and then act insulted. But because my radar had picked up something, I didn't want him in the ICU with us. I told him I had all the protection I needed. I even told him about Jack Hodges. But Alex finally had bought into my conclusion that Holocaust survivors were being systematically eliminated. "That's my territory," he said. "Don't you remember how we met in the first place?" Alex gestured like he was launching a rock. It felt like so long ago. So he remained resolute about sticking around wherever I was.

Alex had completed an application to the Weitzman Institute in Israel. He had decided on transferring there the following year to do research, followed by completion of his residency at Hadassah Hospital. "After that," he announced proudly, "I have a chance for the Israeli Air Force. Danny, I need to do something to help the cause. I've done nothing all this year."

I'd miss Alex, the whole hospital would. The man could do no wrong. Any mistake he made was considered minor by his

416

residents. Nurses went out of their way to provide care for his patients. Attendings often invited him for lunch, many tried fixing him up with their daughters. His list of sexual conquests read like the Who's Who of hospital beauties. Alex had them all.

One day Alex took me to the call room in the back of the ICU and closed the door. He opened his doctor's bag and took out a gun.

"Jesus, Alex!" I yelled, backing away. "What the hell are you doing with that?"

"Relax, it's not loaded."

"It's a gun, it's loaded." I had as big an aversion to guns as I had to snakes. I didn't want to see one, touch one, or be anywhere near one.

"Protection," he said. "For you." He paused, then looked toward the floor. "And for me, I'm afraid."

"What happened?"

"My bookie. He was killed."

"No offense, Alex, but I don't get it. He placed bets for you. And hundreds of others. What do you have to worry about?"

Alex shrugged nervously.

"Are you in trouble, Alex?"

"Not really," he said, avoiding eye contact. "It's just that maybe somebody was sending me a message, that's all."

For the very first time since we met, Alex looked scared. "What message, Alex?"

Alex suddenly caught himself and shook his head. "Shit, Danny. You're right. What am I thinking? It was his own fault, probably got in over his head, maybe skimmed off the top a little." A big smile crossed his face. He held his doctor's bag in the air and turned it over. "This is also for my protection," he said. I watched as a reflex hammer, an otoscope and dozens of individually wrapped condoms dropped onto the bedspread. Enough rubber to make a Goodyear radial.

"Jeez, Alex. How many can you use in a night?"

"It's not the number, it's the variety," he said, shuffling the assortment like a deck of cards. "Some women like these," he said, holding up a multicolor monstrosity.

417

"That's something Bozo would use." Alex laughed, picking up a ribbed one. "Remember Wanda Bylevin? I had to hang one of these babies at half-mast after she died."

Alex had used the same oak mattress I did. For a moment I relived both the pain and pleasure that that desk had offered, then imagined my stethoscope dangling around her neck. "I don't have a problem with condoms, Alex. Just guns."

Alex set his gun on the bottom of his bag and began replacing the condoms and other hardware. He stopped and held up a green condom. "Fluorescent," he said. "Glows in the dark. You heard of the big green monster at Fenway Park? Try this on at night. Here, keep this one for Gail."

My breath stopped.

"What?"

"Bet she likes green rubbers." Alex looked up with a smile. "Just kidding," he said.

I was more paranoid then ever. No way would those two... no, she wasn't Alex's type. Or was she?

Chapter 84 agent hodges

"Damn you, Raskin. How can I do my job if everyone knows my identity?" FBI agent Jack Hodges, alias Seymour Chenowith, sat up in bed and picked at the tape anchoring the IV to his arm.

"Sorry, Jack."

"Quit calling me Jack."

"Okay, Seymour. Hey, why don't you try speaking with a Yiddish accent? Remember, your parents were from the old country. They're survivors of Auschwitz."

Even in his oversized hospital gown, black and blue marks dancing down his arms, oxygen cannulated into his nose, Jack Hodges still looked far more like a preppie WASP then a Polish-Jewish emigrant.

Jack set the Tribune aside and ran his fingers through his dyed hair. "What do you want me to do, dance the horah? If Huber finds out that Rosen and Peterson know my identity, I'll be on laundry detail in Quantico. Besides, I can't be sure of anybody right now."

"Well, you can be sure of them, Jack. I've seen the killer. I've seen him as Tannenbaum and as Jimmi Redding. You have nothing to worry about."

"I have everything to worry about. Remember what Huber said. Medical assassins may already be in place."

"Get real, Jack."

"I'm not talking about Rosen and Peterson. They're okay. We've done extensive background checks on both of them."

"What?"

"I'm here to protect you, Danny. But I have to watch my own back, too. I don't want someone offing me when I'm not looking."

I put my hand on Jack's shoulder. "If you weren't masquerading as the son of a Holocaust survivor you wouldn't have to worry."

Jack Hodges couldn't quite hide a smile. "It's my job, Danny."

Chapter 85 juan gonzalez

The virus was a seamstress, weaving her DNA throughout the gray matter of Juan Gonzalez's brain. His four hundred pounds lay awkwardly, draped over an ICU bed like a series of bulging innertubes. Responding only to deep pain, he spent his days uttering nonsensical answers to basic questions. "Do you know where you are, Mr. Gonzalez?"

"Ar....ling......ton race track," the former stable hand muttered. The President of the United States was George Foreman one day and Freddy Fender the next. But there were also flashes of unaccountable brilliance, like when out of the blue he sang 'Sur La Pont, D'avignon'. Perfect French, even the accent.

"A migrant worker with no education," I said to Alex. "Explain it."

Later that evening Mr. Gonzalez belted out a chorus of the opera The Barber of Seville, his hands waving in the air, moguls of porcupine-like hairs dotting each of his three chins. An hour after that, he sputtered in what I swear was Olde English. "Beowulf," I told Alex.

Mr. Gonzalez had two sons, both in their late teens, who stood vigil at their father's bedside. With each utterance their father made, the sons buried their noses in the Tribune's sports section. Occasionally, they shouted animated in Spanish and ran out of his room, disappearing on the other side of the MICU. Whenever I asked what they were so excited about, one of them would shrug his shoulders and say: "No hablo ingles."

Both sons were present the next day while I performed my daily neuro exam on their father. They wore cheap polyester suits and muddied Italian loafers that were once pointed at the tips.

"Who's the president?"

I repeated the question several times before Mr. Gonzalez lifted his thick folded lids.

In a deep throaty monotone, he said, "Car...los San.....tana." Both sons scanned the paper.

"Where are we, Mr. Gonzalez?"

"Tia....juana." A moment later he sat bolt-upright, with such force that his IV pulled out of his arm.

"Voila! Hayburner! C'est la Hayburner!" His sons buried their faces in the Tribune and a moment later shrieked in unison, then hugged their papa. "Thanks, dad," the older one said. "We'll be back later."

Thanks dad. We'll be back later. Those guys spoke English? But before I could stop them, they were gone, muddy footprints marking their exit. I picked up the Tribune. It was open to a list of that day's racing entrants at Arlington Park.

Chapter 86 mulroney

On my way out of the hospital that evening, I stopped by the ER where I found Officer Mulroney spooning yogurt into his mouth. He was thinner, one of his many chins having disappeared.

"What gives, Mulroney? Run out of twinkies?"

Mulroney patted his paunch, then eyed me with murderous resentment as I shoved a peanut butter cup into my mouth. "Flunked my cholesterol test. From now on, it's yogurt and carrot sticks."

He spoke convincingly but his eyes never left my second peanut butter cup. Fixed on its course from wrapper to my mouth, his head involuntarily bobbed as I chewed.

"Think of the money you'll save, Mulroney."

Mulroney pulled a few bills from his front pocket. He thought of himself as a big spender, often picking up the late night pizza delivery tab that fed the midnight crew.

"Saved two hundred bucks this month. Blew the whole thing this afternoon on one damn horse race." He shook his head. "A sure bet," he mumbled, fishing out a racing stub from his coat pocket. "Lost at the god-damn wire by some filly I ain't ever heard of. Hayburner."

The name sounded vaguely familiar.

I hesitated asking Mulroney about the Arbor Hills registrar's office, but when I did, he snapped, "I can't poke around other peoples' business. Especially out of my jurisdiction." He swabbed the empty yogurt container with his finger and made a face like he was eating castor oil. "Even if I could find out what happened to your friend, why the hell should I?"

It wasn't just the diet and loss at the race track that bothered Mulroney. He was still in grudge mode over Wanda Bylevin's death. I had left him out of the details and he knew it. Same with Maxine Chu's near fatality. "You ask me for stuff but what do I get from you? I know you met with Goldman and the Feds. I know someone tried to murder Maxine. I know about that escort geek, Rasta-fart face Jimmi." Mulroney's placid face turned hard. "Hell, I'm part of the security force at this hospital."

Mulroney had helped me a hell of a lot this past year and I liked the guy too. But in FBI agent Huber's eyes, Mulroney was just a cop whose beat happened to be Richard Meese.

"The less he knows, the less chance he'll have of blowing our operation," Huber had said.

Out of respect for Mulroney, I played the innocent victim. "They won't tell me anything, Mulroney. Honest. If they did, I'd tell you."

Mulroney's face relaxed.

"Mulroney, I really need that information from Arbor Hills. I need to find out what happened to Linda Johnson."

Mulroney patted the inside of his jacket pocket. A smile formed on his lips. "These are phone numbers of some people I know in Detroit." He shook his head. "But I don't know, Raskin. Something about you. Everything you touch is trouble. Lots of it. Remember that day I stopped you for speeding?" I nodded meekly. "You seemed like such a wide-eyed, innocent little intern back then. What the hell happened?"

After he walked away, I felt tears well up. I remembered that drive, my mother sitting next to me. I was ready to conquer the world back then, sure that nothing would keep me from becoming a great doctor. How did life get so turned around? Since then I had been threatened repeatedly, both physically and emotionally. Other people I cared about had been killed or hurt. It wasn't enough just to treat patients anymore. The first hard realization that someone could hate, even kill, because of a religion had stunned me, making it impossible to take my own heritage for granted ever again. Sure, I wanted revenge. But I wanted to make sense of all this, too. Learning to be a good doctor was important, but I had another mission at the moment, more important than anything I'd ever been involved in before.

Chapter 87 gonzalez

Mr. Gonzalez thrashed about so wildly the next day that he ripped right through his cloth restraints. He plucked his ECG's wires from his chest, and tore the IV's out of both arms. It took a bunch of nurses, hospital security, and a good chunk of the hospital stock of Valium to calm him. When he finally slumped back into his bed, locked securely in new leather restraints, frothy green bile spilled from his mouth. "Ich me knee, san che. Ich me knee, san che," he repeated in satanic cadence.

"We need a twenty four hour babysitter," announced Brenda, the MICU charge nurse.

"Hell with that, Brenda. We need an exorcist."

Later, the oldest son, Ceasar, rubbed his hands through his father's forest of hair, while the younger son, Augusto, tore rapaciously through the Tribune's sport section. Both wore freshly pressed dark-pinstripe suits and clean oxfords with dark socks. The new duds must have set them back seven hundred dollars each.

When the Valium began to wear off, I filled the syringe with a dose of the longer acting sedative, Ativan, and when I attempted to attach it to his IV tubing, I felt a firm grip on my wrist.

"Momento, por favor." I twisted my wrist free, the syringe dropping to the floor.

"Oh, Jeez, now look what you've done!"

Ceasar shrugged his shoulder. "No conprendo, doctor."

"Yeah, and I suppose that's the Spanish edition of the Chicago Tribune you're reading? Don't give me that crap. I know you guys speak English. And I want to know what the hell's going on. Your father yells something, you run out of here, and the next day you're better dressed than the day before. And now, you're interfering with medical treatment." I slammed the door to the room shut. "What the hell is going on?"

The two sons eyed each other, shoulders slouched in resignation. Ceasar stepped forward. "Keep a secret, amigo?" I folded my arms. Augusto nudged his brother. "Go ahead, tell him." Ceasar picked up the sports page. It was opened to the day's entrants at Arlington race track. "Pop's been picking the winning horses."

"Big winners," added Augusto, his new Oxfords dancing from side to side.

I adjusted the flow rate on Mr. Gonzalez's IV. "No offense, but your father is in critical condition. A virus has destroyed most of his brain. Some circuitry may have gotten crossed in the meltdown. His speech is mostly nonsensical gibberish."

"He's picked two long shots in a row."

"That's impossible. He's babbling." Then a thought. "Who was that longshot yesterday?"

"Hayburner," Augusto replied. "Papa called it. You were there."

That was the horse that cost Mulroney a week's salary. I'd heard stories of clairvoyant behavior emerging as a result of brain dysfunction, even watched a documentary on it during my neurology rotation. But picking winners at the race track? These poor kids, I thought. Maybe this was their way of holding onto something they shared with their old man--after all, he used to work at Arlington Park as a stable hand.

"Okay, guys, show me."

Smiles broke out. I watched as Augusto read down the list of that day's horses. Oblivious to his sons, Mr. Gonzalez was shaking his head like a metronome, singing a rendition of the French national anthem. He made no unusual movements as his son read through the sixty horses running that day. Augusto was on this third read through, when I stepped forward. "I think that's enough. He doesn't even know you're here. He's off somewhere on the East Bank of Paris." I refilled the syringe with Ativan. He began singing Freres Jacques. "Sorry guys, time for pops to get a little 'dormez-vous'." I smiled and aspirated the syringe. The singing suddenly stopped and Mr. Gonzalez's extremities stiffened. Green bile seeped from his mouth a la Linda Blair. He eyes became sharp, focusing on his sons.

"Ooh la la, Patisserie" he repeated over and over, like a mantra. "Ooh la la, Patisserie."

"Look!" yelled Augusto, his quivering fingers pointing to the fifth race. "Here it is! Pastry--going off at 40 to one!" Ceasar confirmed his brother's finding. They pecked their father on his slimy green cheek and opened the door to the room. "Post time two o'clock, doc. Want some action?" I paused only a second then, "Adios, doc," and they were gone.

Who were they kidding? I stuck the syringe into his IV port and injected the Ativan. "How 'bout a little sedative with your pastry, Mr. Gonzalez?"

Mr. Gonzalez's speech pattern steadied slowly as the medication took effect. I picked up his vital sign sheet and began perusing yesterday's blood pressures.

"Tannenbaum. Oh Tannenbaum."

I looked up. Mr. Gonzalez's lids were like heavy curtains, yet his eyes peeped out the bottom like those of a lurking Everglades reptile. "Tannenbaum, Tannenbaum."

A chill electrified my body, sending spasms to my heart. I went to his bedside. "What did you say?"

"Tannenbaum, Tannenbaum."

"What are you talking about!?" I shook him.

"Tannenbaum, Tannenbaum." He let out a sleepy laugh.

"Mr. Gonzalez, please."

The curtains over his eyes closed.

428

Chapter 88 intensive care

"For Christ's sake, Danny, don't be so paranoid!" Gail laughed. "He was singing a Christmas song, 'Oh Tannenbaum, oh Tannenbaum'," she said, waving her ECG calipers through the air like a baton. She smiled but I detected an edge to her voice. I think she was afraid that paranoia was getting the best of me.

We were sitting at the central nursing console in the ICU, reviewing ECG strips and writing orders amid a cacophony of beeping arrhythmia monitors. An x-ray tech was yelling for everyone who wanted to keep their gonads intact to get the hell out of the way, and several patients were crying out for pain meds or stool softeners.

Alex handed an order sheet to a waiting nurse. "You sure he wasn't singing, 'Oh Thaddeus, Oh Thaddeus'?

"Did you ask him if he knows Rastafarian Jimmi?" Gail added, slapping Alex a high-five. I buried my head in a set of ECG strips. I felt vulnerable, alone. Maybe I was paranoid, but damn, after all that had happened, I had a right.

A hand began massaging my neck. "How about I make dinner tomorrow?" Gail's breath was warm and therapeutic.

"What's on the menu?"

"Name it."

"Peanut butter cup casserole."

Gail pinched my arm. "It's been a few days since we've talked."

"You've been too busy with Alex," I replied, instantly regretting it.

"If that's true, it's only because you've been spending every second here in the unit. Watching over Maxine."

I gave Gail my standard, what-the-hell-am-I-supposed-to-do look.

"Danny, she's on autopilot. She's off the ventilator. Her kidneys are peeing up a storm. Her heart, thanks to you, suffered only minor damage and is pumping· like a hydraulic engine. Also, thanks to you, her blood cell count is near normal. That crazy idea of yours worked." Gail looked at me, pupils wide. "It's a miracle."

Miracles had happy endings, didn't they? Then why wouldn't Maxine wake up from her coma? I had fine-tuned her like a musician preparing to play Carnegie Hall. Every lab value perfect, every day's input of fluids matched the output minus the insensible losses that occurred through evaporation. And if I was off by even a decimal point, Malcolm Spool was right there, looking over my shoulder and offering up a corrective course of action.

These daily mini-victories with Maxine were met with snickers by my fellow interns and residents. To them, my heroic efforts were the product of a warped mind, and behind my back they began the vegetable game. "How's the broccoli coming along?" I might hear someone whisper to a colleague. "Watering the cabbage today?" They knew better, of course, than to say those things to my face. Besides, Maxine was my responsibility, and if they wanted to call her a vegetable, then at least she would be the healthiest vegetable in my garden.

When all the work on Maxine was done, the sun had gone behind the clouds and the day shift had gone home, I would sit at Maxine's bedside, holding her hand, talking to her about my day, or hers, explaining my worries to her. I asked her rhetorically about Linda Johnson, whom I had just about given up locating. I spoke to her knowing, or at least hoping, that somewhere within that sleeping brain, a synapse or two might know someone was watching out for her, waiting for her to come back into this world and into my life. Maxine's hair had begun growing back, though patchy in spots and not to the shoulder length span it once was, its silkiness was every bit as inviting as it was the first time we'd met. Thanks to the nutrition she received through a large intravenous line, her face and skin had regained their earthy tone and smooth contours. I thought of Lo, the food he used to bring into her room, how his ancient ways had driven a permanent spike into their relationship. I imagined him here now, begging Maxine to allow him to grind his Peking duck into a gooey pulp so he could pour it down Maxine's NG tube. But Lo had vacated the scene, selling his Moon Palace restaurant in Chinatown and moving out to Los Angeles to be with his brother and nurse his broken heart. Maxine's sister had spent a few days in Chicago and then returned to New York and her family.

I closed my eyes and whispered: "Please wake up, Maxine."

"Wake up, yourself, Doctor R."

I jumped. It was Officer Mulroney. Holding a half-finished piece of pizza loaded with Italian sausage.

"New yogurt flavor, Mulroney? Dannon's double cheese with sausage?"

Mulroney's color resembled Roma tomatoes. "I'd rather die at fifty than eat alfalfa sprouts for the rest of my life." He looked us over and in a low voice asked, "What room is Jack Hodges in?"

"There's no Jack Hodges here," I answered, knowing Mulroney knew the true identity of patient, Seymour Chenowith. After all, the two had gone to school together.

"Don't get cute, doc. I want to see how badly you've been treating him. Yesterday he couldn't even talk on the phone. Said you gave him so much stool softener you may as well have super-glued his ass to the toilet seat."

"He's a cardiac patient, Mulroney," I whispered. "Remember? All cardiac patients receive stool softeners."

"Yeah, well I have another reason. I also want to find out what's going on around here, especially since you ain't doing any talking."

I reluctantly told Mulroney the room number of Agent Hodges, after which he stuffed the remaining pizza into his mouth and began walking down the corridor. I caught up with him.

"How about it, Mulroney?"

"How about what?" he mumbled, a piece of crust protruding from his mouth like a dorsal fin.

"Linda Johnson. Did you call Arbor Hills?"

Mulroney looked toward the ceiling. "When you gonna learn, Raskin? Scratch Mulroney's back, he scratches yours."

"I told you everything I know."

"Have it your way," he said, turning his back.

"How about a tip?"

"What?"

"Arlington Park. Fifth race. Pastry."

"What?"

"Pastry. Like what you stuff into your face every morning."

Mulroney pondered my words, then pulled out a pouch of tobacco and thrust a thumb's worth inside his cheek. "That horse couldn't run if you shoved a hot poker up his ass." A nurse walking by gave us a dirty look. "Besides, she's running 40 to one. And the jockey's three pounds overweight."

"Probably on the same diet as you're on."

Mulroney frowned. "Who gave you the tip?"

"Never mind."

Mulroney's tone shifted. "Come on, doc. I can't afford any more negative cash flow."

"Let's just say an unnamed source."

"But it's reliable? I mean a healthy day at the track and you might just find yourself with some information about your old girlfriend in Arbor Hills."

I measured his words. What had this world come to when my only chance to retrieve an important file depended on a name shouted by a demented Mexican who carried enough virus to start a colony?

"Well? Is it reliable?"

I looked Mulroney square in his dolphin shaped eyes. It was my last chance.

"Damn right it's reliable."

Chapter 89 call night

My call night had been so quiet that I was almost happy to see Malcolm Spool when he dropped by for his regular 10 pm visit. Despite his reputation of being an arrogant, obsessive-compulsive creep, without Malcolm's help, I would never have been able to convince the oncologists to replace Maxine's bone marrow. And during the past two weeks, when one consult team after another concluded that Maxine Chu would never regain consciousness and that the only humane action left was to withdraw life support, Malcolm Spool was the only one who stood next to me in her defense. While I was armed with a resolute emotional bond--Maxine was my patient, my friend-- Malcolm was armed with a persuasive knowledge. When a professor of Ethics and the Human condition stated that the chance of survival after three weeks of coma was next to nothing, Malcolm quoted a half dozen studies where complete recovery did indeed follow a prolonged vegetative state. With his command of neuro-integrative pathways, he was able to convince even the most wary neurologists that under certain conditions, neurons might be able to regenerate themselves and function at normal capacity. "They just need the right care," he would say, implying of course, that he and only he could supply that kind of care. That I couldn't agree to. I was Maxine's doctor. Forever.

It took Malcolm a while to get used to the concept that I was as capable of taking care of Maxine as he was. Yet for the last several weeks, he seemed to accept it. He started coming by, looking carefully at Maxine's chart and offering suggestions for her care, sound ideas that I usually pursued.

Malcolm appeared worried as he perused Maxine's lab values. For thirty minutes his eyes were glued to the reams of paper, never once glancing at Maxine. Maxine was never a person to Malcolm, merely a difficult case the success of which depended on his ability to correct every abnormal test, anticipating any dangerous trends and then nipping them in their embryonic stages. Malcolm set Maxine's clipboard next to the

434

sink in her room and turned on the water. "Do me a favor," he said without looking up. "Run out and get me some betadine. The soap they give you in this hospital only covers seventy eight percent of the nosocomial bacteria floating around. That leaves approximately two million organisms per centimeter of air space left to wander as they please."

I wasn't quite ready to call out the National Guard on the basis of Malcolm's bacteriological paranoia. I got him his disinfectant, then watched while he scrubbed at his hands with all the vigor of someone cleaning a raw potato. After he finished, he took a package from his black bag and opened it, removing a sterile towel. "I'm worried about your patient, Daniel. Her urinary output is too high."

"That's the idea, Malcolm." Good urine output was like getting the most mileage per gallon of gasoline. It usually meant everything was running properly.

Malcolm took a step back and wiped his forehead with a Kleenex. "She's making too much urine for what she's taking in. I'm worried she has diabetes insipidus."

"What?" I knew very well what diabetes insipidus was, something in the body that triggered massive fluid losses. "What's causing it?"

"Brain edema."

I swallowed hard. How could he make that kind of diagnosis? He hadn't even examined Maxine. "Her neuro exam is normal, Malcolm. No focal defects and no evidence of papilledema." Papilledema was swelling of the optic nerve because of increased pressure on the brain.

"Maybe I should stay here tonight," he said. "Give you a hand if there's any trouble." Malcolm spit out the word 'trouble' with pompous contempt, as if without his input, trouble was a foregone conclusion.

"No thanks, Malcolm. Besides. There's a guy in the next bed over who was admitted with a raging pneumonia. He's coughing all over the place."

Malcolm's jaw clenched before he saw me smile. "I know very well who is in the next bed over," he said, packing up his bag.

I struggled to swallow. How could he know about Hodges?

"Seymour Chenowith. He's taking up valuable space.."

My heart settled down. "He has intractable angina, Malcolm, not that it's any of your business."

"Cutting costs is everyone's business. Mr. Chenowith's ECG and cardiac enzymes have all been normal. I think he's faking it."

An hour after Malcolm left, Maxine's urine output tripled. An hour later, she began to seize. An emergency CT scan showed that massive edema had begun to compress her brain matter. The neurosurgeons rushed in and relieved the pressure by drilling a small hole in Maxine's skull. They finished at 4 am. Just as I was ready to lie down, she began having cardiac arrhythmias. V-tach. V fib. V-tach again. Lidocaine, Bretylium. Shock after shock- Maxine's body arching into the air like a spawning salmon, until finally, after her potassium losses into the urine had been corrected, her rhythm returned to normal.

"You look like shit." Alex handed me a cup of coffee and Gail broke off a piece of her cinnamon roll. Alex patted me on the back. "We heard about Maxine. You okay?" I nodded, holding back tears that hadn't had a chance to fall for the past six hours.

"Don't you think enough is enough?" asked Gail, who suddenly seemed preoccupied by her morning responsibilities. I rubbed the crust from my eyes. "What are you talking about?"

"Why did you shock her, Danny? What were you bringing her back to? She's not going to get better!" Gail's words ripped at me. That wasn't like her. How could she say that? Alex sipped his coffee, and we paused as an arrhythmia alarm went off. The nurses didn't look worried and that was a good sign.

Alex moved closer to me and motioned toward Gail. "Ignore her. She has PMS."

"Fuck you Alex," Gail snapped. "I never should have told you." She turned to me. "Sorry, Danny. You still planning on having dinner with me tonight?"

I nodded.

"What about me?" said Alex.

Gail shoved him. "Quit being greedy. We just had pizza last night."

My eyes shifted from Gail to Alex, then back to Gail. Those jealous gremlins began clawing at my insides.

During rounds, Gail was definitely not herself. First, she had harsh words for a nurse who had inadvertently forgotten to record a lab value. Then she told our resident that if she wanted his input on a case, she'd ask. Sensing her volatility, Alex and I stayed toward the back of the group. "I told you so," he whispered. "But PMS makes them horny, Danny. Very horny." Gail was yelling at a student for not ordering an EKG. I asked Alex to recount his pizza dinner with Gail. At the end I clenched my jaw. "Alex, you and she didn't.... you know." I looked at Gail posturing on one foot. For a moment I imagined her standing naked, her, long apricot hair swaying over her breasts, her thighs inviting.

"What if we did? It's only sex."

Alex's answer caught me by surprise. "You did?"

"Did what?"

"Come on, Alex."

"No, you come on. Did what?"

"Sleep with Gail."

"No, I didn't sleep with Gail. But I could have."

My cheeks felt hot. "She wanted to sleep with you?"

"Who doesn't?" Alex wasn't boasting, just stating the facts. "But I didn't, partner," he said. "She's hot for you."

"That's a funny way to show it."

"Not at all," said Alex, pausing to watch Gail and the resident argue over some orders. "She's afraid of getting emotionally involved with you, just like you are with her. I think it's called..." Alex put his fingers in quotation marks: "love." And then he laughed.

"What's wrong with it?" I asked a few minutes later when we were in another patient's room. This time Gail was yelling at her patient for hiding cigarettes in his shirt pocket.

"What's 'it'?"

"Love. What's wrong with love?"

Alex looked around and smiled.

437

"Do you know what love is?" He grabbed at his crotch.

"Wrong organ, Alex. It comes from the heart."

"Damn right it does. In fact, love is an abscess of the heart."

"What?"

"A temporary abscess of the heart. An abscess that just happens to drain via the penis."

After rounds I showered and tossed down a Denver omelette, a stack of blueberry pancakes and a half-pound of undercooked bacon. The day proceeded smoothly until two in the afternoon when the alarm sounded in bed 4. One of Gail's patients, admitted an hour before with unstable chest pain, had a cardiac arrest while Gail was performing a rectal examination. Gail stood in the back of the room, still gloved, while Alex and I resuscitated the patient with two lightening bolts of electricity. Afterwards, Gail was inconsolable. "I nearly killed him," she cried. "Offed him with a finger up the butt."

"You were only being your usual conscientious self," we reassured her.

But Gail wasn't buying. "The rectal exam should have waited," she moaned.

I spent the rest of the afternoon working on Maxine Chu and comforting Gail. At three pm I was at the nurse's station when an open fist slammed into my back. The coffee cup I was holding flooded Maxine's notes.

"Damn it," I said, turning. Before me stood Officer Mulroney. His eyes were wide, his teeth clenched, reminding me of our encounter the day I drove into Chicago.

"Forty six to one," he said, barely opening his mouth. "How could I have bet on a forty six to one long shot?" I searched for some towels. My entire four page note on Maxine was a blue rorshach on paper.

"Sorry, Mulroney. I never should have...."

"Horse came out of the paddock and damn near threw the jockey. I took one look and said, 'who the hell did Raskin get that tip from, one of his demented patients'?"

I swallowed. "You didn't have to bet, you know."

Mulroney threw his hands in the air. "That horse took a dump right there on the track."

"I thought that was good."

"I asked myself that same question as I laid down a hundred to win."

"A hundred bucks?" *Forget about any favors from Mulroney. Forget about Linda Johnson.*

"Tell me about it. When that horse got out of the gate late, I saw myself eating Spam for the next ten years. You should have seen it. Coming into the final stretch Pastry was running eight in a field of nine. My eyes were closed."

"Hey, sorry, Mulroney."

He cupped his hands over his mouth: "Pastry is coming up strong on the outside. Pastry is passing Beaurevoir and Thunder. It's Pastry on the outside coming fast. They're approaching the wire. Pastry now neck and neck with Kentucky Woman. They're at the wire..."

"Pastry won?"

Mulroney's smile was big enough to slide a frisbee through. "Photo finish, doc. I almost shit."

"He won? Pastry won?" Mulroney had bet only to win. Second place was not good enough. Mulroney opened his billfold and slapped me on the back. "Forty-six hundred smackers!" he said fanning a two inch wad of bills. "Ha Ha! The bastard won." He pounded my back. "Thanks, Raskin. You've been one helpful sonofabitch."

"Watch the language in here." The head nurse winced. "And keep your voices down."

I was truly happy for Mulroney but of course had no idea how Mr. Gonzalez had called the right horse. Maybe he wasn't so sick after all. He had worked at the track, knew the horses. But EEG's and brain scans don't lie--severe inflammation leading to brain wave patterns incompatible with intelligence. But in a billion to one chance, his cerebral wires had fused and began firing off signals.

"This is for you," Mulroney said, fingering his billfold and handing me a note scratched on official Chicago police stationery. "I got the information you wanted."

My heart somersaulted.

"Wasn't easy. Had to call a precinct in Detroit. Got someone there to help me."

I anxiously read the note:

"Linda Johnson left school October 26, due to family illness. Current address unknown."

"Is that all?"

"Afraid so."

"Address unknown?"

"Well, I did find which city, but what difference would that make? Do you know how many Johnsons there are in Atlanta, Georgia?"

Chapter 90 the library

"Guys just don't understand," Gail Peterson said, brushing her hair from her eyes. She hit the blinker in her VW in preparation for exiting Lake Shore Drive. Of course I couldn't understand the ramifications of PMS. But the relationship between hormones and doing a rectal exam on Mr. Zimbrowski, causing a near fatal arrhythmia, totally escaped me. I checked the AAA road map. "Next exit, I think."

"Premenstrual compulsiveness," Gail repeated over and over. "Thank God you and Alex shocked him out of it. I would have died if those paddles hadn't worked."

"No reason they shouldn't have. We coated them with Preparation H." Gail slapped my knee, then swerved to the left, barely missing a dented Oldsmobile with one tail light. Darkness had ushered in the waning minutes of rush hour. A light rain garnished the windshield. Going to the public library after being up all night wasn't my idea of a good time, especially considering that the lure of Gail's apartment lingered in the chilled air. But I had to locate a telephone book from Atlanta, Georgia. Had to find out if Linda Johnson, my Linda Johnson, still had something of great value in her possession.

Gail sniffed back tears. "Happens every time," she said. "Just before my period I become obsessive-compulsive."

"Quit obsessing about it."

Gail hit me again, harder. "My histories and physicals take an hour longer than usual. I draw blood on the same patient twice in a day just to re-check what I got earlier that morning. I sometimes do rectal exams two or three times on the same person."

"Yech."

"Can't help it," she sniffed. "I keep thinking I might have missed a tumor."

Gail pulled onto Superior Street and several blocks later, turned left onto Michigan Avenue. The library stood out like a Roman amphitheater at night, tall spotlights shadowing high arches, with enough stairs to train on for the Olympics. After parking in the underground garage, we headed to the lobby where we were directed to the third floor reference area. A cinch, I thought, climbing the marble staircase. But the reference area was large enough to hold ten of my apartments. Books on census, almanacs, stacks worth of thick, dusty books. Gail and I separated, each covering half the area. I found myself engrossed in an exhibit on the history of the Chicago Cubs, original team photos, score books from back in the thirties, baseball gloves that looked like oven mittens.

"Over here!" yelled Gail after ten minutes. She was on the other side of the room, knee deep in a section of phone books for the southeast United States. It took two hands for her to hold up the Atlanta directory.

"Way to go, Gail." Her eyes were turned down. "What's the matter?"

Gail's finger held her place toward the middle of the book. "There are on average three hundred and forty four listings on each page," she said. "That means that there are over eight thousand listings for Johnson. Twenty six pages."

"Don't worry. We can do it."

"No we can't." She opened the book. "They're gone! All twenty six pages have been ripped out."

I picked up the book and saw only jagged edges where the Johnsons should have been. "Why? I... I mean who?"

"It gets worse," she said, pointing to two other books. "Greater Atlanta area. Not a single Johnson left there, either."

"Dammit, Gail. Somebody beat us to the punch."

"Might be a coincidence, "Gail offered. "I don't think you can conclude anything."

But I could. As we headed back to the car I concluded that Linda Johnson was in great danger.

Chapter 91 gail's place

A man standing over me, hands outstretched--noticeable tremor as he held an open phone book, laughing as worms and maggots spilled out over my prone body. The man's hair was Rastafarian Jimmi's, his smooth face, Frank Tannenbaum's. His nose was not unlike Thaddeus Anderson's. "Looking for Linda Johnson?" he sneered through broken teeth. He turned the page and blood poured out followed by loops of intestines, then two large eye balls, followed by Linda Johnson's head.

I sat up and screamed.

Warm arms quickly surrounded me, holding me tight, wiping the sweat from my forehead. Where was I? It wasn't my bed. Nor my apartment. I struggled into wakefulness.

"It's me, Gail."

"How did I...I mean what..."

"You fell asleep on my couch, silly."

I couldn't remember a thing. Only that I was drinking a beer and...

"You were up all night the night before," she said caressing my hair. "You fell asleep right in the middle of a Gilligan's Island rerun."

"What time is it?"

"Almost four."

I lifted the cover. Only my underwear had remained in place. "How did..."

"I undressed you," she said in the darkness. A car horn beeped far away. A soft wind blew through her window. Through a shadow of light I saw her smile. "Loved every minute of it."

"You didn't take advantage of the situation, did you?"

"You mean sex?"

It was my turn to smile. "No, a rectal exam."

Gail laughed and hugged me. Her warm breath had the hair above my ear dancing like a cobra. "If I'm not careful, I could fall for a guy like you."

"Over Alex?"

Gail frowned. "He's not my type," she said. "I take it he told you I was a bit on the horny side the other night?" I didn't respond. Gail's fingers went to my chest. "I fall for the innocent type. Someone who always seems to be in a heap of trouble without even trying." Her hands traced a path to my belly button. "I like the vulnerable victim-turned hero type."

"I'm no hero, Gail." I suppose I was no innocent victim either. I could have minded my own damn business and walked away from that admissions committee. I felt tears welling up again. I looked at Gail. "I could have prevented the death of Wanda Bylevin. I didn't want..." I couldn't finish the sentence. Tears spilled like rain sliding off a spring leaf. I found myself rocking in Gail's arms, back to my childhood, snug in my quilt during those midwestern rain storms.

"I need that phone book, Gail," I sniffled. "I need those missing pages."

Gail rocked me gently. Slowly, tenderly. "I love you, Danny. I really love you," I heard her say as I closed my eyes.

Chapter 92 eddie ingraham

I never thanked Eddie Ingraham for the memo that helped save Emile Horner's life. The last time I'd seen him he'd been studying to be a cadaver in the upcoming anatomy class over at the medical school. He'd been carrying a thick, somewhat outdated textbook on Obstetrics. "Never know when you might need to deliver a baby," he had said.

Now I knew. A code green security alert was called early that next morning in the labor and delivery suites. An hour later, our resident, Charles O'Bannon was paged to the area.

"Eddie Ingraham," he said when he returned, and we all knew what had happened. A crowd gathered as he spoke. After all, Eddie was a legend by now. "He bound and gagged an OB attending," said O'Bannon. "He performed the entire delivery, including an episiotomy. The medical student said it was the best he'd seen." Gail and I giggled, feeling pride mixed with disgust. Charles flashed anger. "He wouldn't have gotten caught except for the episiotomy repair. He sewed the vagina completely shut." Gail winced. "This is going to be one hell of a law suit."

"Au contraire. The woman said she was happy with the results. Said it was the best way she knew to keep her animal of a husband away. Said he tried to jump her the same day she'd had her last baby."

Alex smiled. "A gentleman always waits until the placenta is removed." Gail kicked him. Of course none of this explained why Eddie was on his way up to the ICU rather than to Cook County holding area. But it wasn't hard to figure. "Don't tell me," I said. "He suddenly developed a severe case of chest pain. Rule out M.I. Admit to the Coronary Care Unit."

Charles O'Bannon shrugged. Though a senior resident with a solid reputation, he was burned out on medicine and was planning a second stint in Dermatology. "What else could I do?"

The security guards escorting Eddie into the ICU watched dispassionately as he writhed on his gurney, screaming out, his shackled fists clutching at that part of his chest where little

446

mounds of shaven hair anchored onto ECG leads. "Please," he yelled as he entered. "I need an emergency bypass. I'll die without a bypass."

"Hi Eddie."

Eddie looked up. And suddenly smiled. "Danny boy, it's you. How the hell are you?" He reached for my hand. "Sorry I missed my last clinic appointment."

I stopped by Eddie's room after morning rounds. He was lying comfortably in bed with an IV infusion of nitrates in his vein, nose plugs connecting him up to a wall-unit of oxygen, and a monitor above his bed that spat out a pitter-patter of heart beats. He had charmed the nurses into removing his hand-cuffs. The ECG lying on his bedside table was totally normal.

"Why'd you do it, Eddie?" I asked looking at his vital sign sheet. Eddie sat up, his face composed.

"Beats jail, wouldn't you say?"

"Not that, Eddie. The delivery. You know that's against the law."

Six months ago Eddie would have told me he was a certified obstetrician working undercover for the CIA. We'd gotten past that now.

"I always wanted to do one," he said. "And since you've kept me from matriculating into medical school, I was stuck with my own wish list of things to accomplish, like delivering a baby, or being an anatomy cadaver."

We had sent photos of Eddie to every medical school admissions office in the country. We heard back from places like Harvard and Yale and Columbia. Eddie had visited them all.

"Did you pose as a cadaver?"

Eddie was fingering his ECG electrodes, tracing the connection from his hairless chest to the flashing monitor above him. I repeated the question. "It brings on chest pain just talking about it," he moaned.

"Sorry Eddie, wouldn't want to raise those cardiac enzymes. You brought it up."

"It was a terrible experiment."

"You did it?"

He nodded.

"At the med school?"

Another nod.

"Come on, Eddie. How?"

"Simple. Just broke into the lab on the morning of their first class and locked one of the stiffs in a stall in the men's room. I laid down on the dissection table underneath the plastic covering and waited until class."

"And they cut you?"

"Yep."

"No anesthesia?" that was a silly question. Eddie had been awake during his appendectomy.

"That wasn't the problem. It was that damn woman in the group. First day of class and she decides she's going to cut off my dick before they do anything else."

"What?"

"The little bitch said her therapist told her it would help her work out her feelings of aggression towards men."

"Sounds plausible. What happened?"

Eddie paused, then blushed. "It got big."

"It?"

Eddie pointed to his groin. "That's when I made my mistake. I leaned over and said to her, 'Don't worry. It's just rigor mortis'."

"But cadavers don't..."

"Talk. Small point, right? I forgot. She screamed. When she fainted, her scalpel landed in her left eye socket and partially detached her retina. It was a bloody mess."

If anyone else had told me that story I'd have called him a liar and walked away. Anybody but Eddie. Fake seizures, coat hangers up the urethra, appendectomy sans anesthesia. All part of the Munchausen persona, all vintage Eddie. "Once your cardiac enzymes come back negative, Eddie, you're outta here. People will know you're faking."

"I was sort of hoping to stick around, Danny boy. My sources tell me you need more help."

"What help?"

"Solving those murders. It's amazing what you can do with computers. Tapping into other people's business often brings good results."

"You helped me with the Horner memo, I'll give you that. But there is nothing else you can do. Not anymore."

Eddie reached back and turned down the nitro drip.

"You can't do that," I announced.

"It's giving me a headache."

I grabbed his hand. "This isn't a spa, Eddie."

"Linda Johnson."

My grip released.

"What?"

Eddie smiled. "Linda Johnson. You're trying to find her."

"How the..."

"I told you. The computer. I've had a link established to the local FBI office for three years. They still haven't figured it out. I tapped into some files owned by one James Huber, FBI. A file with your name on it. And inside was the name Linda Johnson with big question marks next to it."

"I never mentioned her name to them."

"Phone tap," said Eddie. "Your apartment."

"Get out."

"I saw the transcripts."

I couldn't believe it. If it was true, they must have heard my conversation with the Arbor Hills University registrar's office. They knew that I wanted to talk to Linda. But they didn't know why. That meant they might not know it concerned the whereabouts of the missing file. My mind flashed to the phone book, all the Johnsons in Atlanta ripped out. What the hell was going on?

"Eddie you know where I can get an Atlanta phone book?"

"Sure, but it's not going to help. You going to call up all eight thousand Johnsons?"

"If I have to. Or maybe I'll just start with the ones that begin with 'L'".

"Come on. She probably lived with her folks, listed as another first name, probably her father's. Know his name?"

"If I did, would I be talking to you? Linda left Arbor Hills because of a family illness. That's all I know."

"Well if you give me a chance, you know, let me stick around here a while, I can help you out."

"Sorry, Eddie. Barring an unexpected complication, you're outta here in the morning."

Chapter 93 jack hodges

Sol Goldman knew it was Eddie Ingraham who had given me a copy of the memo sent by Emile Horner. He knew because I told him. And if Sol knew, so did Jack Hodges, which probably explained why he had been watching Eddie through the window in his room from the moment Eddie was wheeled in. "Did you bug his phone, too?" I asked Jack that afternoon. No answer. "Jack, why did they bug my phone?"

"Can't talk about it," he said. "You know how it is. But I do want you to tell me more about Eddie."

"Sorry, Jack. Doctor-patient relationship. You know how it is."

I opened his door and called out. "Brenda, can we up Mr. Chenowith's nitro drip?"

"Hey!" yelled Jack. "Don't do that. My head's been killing me for three days. It's torture."

"Probably reminds you of your stint in El Salvador," I said, writing the order.

"Okay, so we tapped your phone. Nothing personal."

"Hah. You only listened in on everything I said."

"You were never home."

"Why, Jack?"

"Because when this all started we weren't exactly sure which side you were on."

"And now?"

"You're okay with me, Danny. But chief Huber thinks you still know more than you're letting on."

That Huber was one smart son of a bitch. How much did he know about my Arbor Hills friend? "Linda Johnson. Ring any bells?"

Jack shook his head, then put his hand up. "My head's hurting already."

"Be honest. Linda Johnson."

"Nothing."

"No information on Linda Johnson?"

"Should there be?"

"No."

At that moment, Alex burst through the door. "Hi Jack, catch any killers lately?"

Jack Hodges frowned. "Quit calling me Jack. My name is Seymour Chenowith. I'm an insurance salesman from Winnetka. I have unstable angina and thanks to those friggin nitrates, my head feels like it's about to explode."

Alex looked irritated. "Fine, Jack. It won't happen again." Then, to me: "Danny, it's Gonzalez. He's spewing out his crazy stuff all over the place."

I looked at Jack. "Gonzalez--bed 4. The guy who was yelling 'Tannenbaum'."

Alex grabbed me by the coat sleeve. "Come on, we have to check this out. Mulroney made a killing at the track the other day."

Outside of Jack Hodges's room Alex said, "That guy Hodges is a loser."

"He's a Fed, Alex. He knows what's going on."

"If he ain't Jewish, he don't understand."

"He's here to protect me."

"I'll protect you," said Alex patting his doctor's bag. " Me and my two friends, Smith and Wesson."

Chapter 94 to the races

Ceasar and Augusto Gonzalez jumped when Alex bolted unannounced into their room. Ceasar wore a fur trimmed leather jacket that smelled like it had come from a recently skinned animal. The younger brother wore a new but wrinkled suit; Armani, I guessed. Alex stepped within an inch of Ceasar's face. "Visiting hours begin an hour from now. You boys shouldn't be here."

Ceasar's eyes burned and he straightened up so that he was at eye level with Alex. "Business with our papa, doctor. Private business. So if you don't mind..."

Alex was on him in a second, Ceasar's adam apple pinched between Alex's two fingers. Augusto coughed out, "Please, Senor."

"Like, I said; one hour."

Ceasar nodded weakly and Alex released his grip. Alex grabbed the paper from Augusto as the two sons scurried out the door, muttering in Spanish. "If I were you," yelled Alex, leaning out the door. "I'd stay away from the track today. I heard they're checking for green cards."

Alex shut the door and began laughing.

"What's gotten into you, Alex? First you start packing a gun, then you treat those kids like dirt. Their father is dying, for Christ's sake."

Alex mopped his brow, trying to collect himself. "Sorry about that. Not sure what got into me."

"It's the gambling, Alex. Something about gambling sets you off."

Alex shuffled his feet, then held the paper out. "Go ahead, Danny. Take the paper and rip it up and never mention gambling again."

I liked the idea and would have done just that, but Mr. Gonzalez suddenly began quoting from Macbeth. "Out damn spot!" he sang. We watched in amazement. Then, his demeanor abruptly changed. He took a deep breath, rolled his head from side to side, and opened his eyes wider than I imagined possible.

"Come on, Lana Turner. Come on Lana Turner!" he yelled. His head bobbed up and down like a jockey atop a tough steed. "Come on, Lana Turner. Come on, Lana Turner."

Alex and I looked at each other and then fought for the paper. "No way, Alex," I said, as he beat me to it and quickly scanned the racing section. "I seriously doubt there's a horse named Lana Turner."

A moment later he shouted: "This must be it! Land O'Turf. Third race--thirty to one. Land O'Turf." Alex eyed his watch. "Listen. About that gambling problem. It's really not as bad as I implied." He handed me his beeper.

"What's this for?"

"Track opens in twenty minutes."

"What?"

"I'll be back in an hour." Alex paused. "My bookie's dead. Remember?"

He slammed me in the back and opened the door. "Got a good feeling about this," he said and handed me his doctor's bag. "Here. They don't allow guns at the track unless you're the guy who starts the races."

I stepped back, holding the bag in front of me like it was a dirty diaper.

Chapter 95 alex rosen

Alex returned four hours later. He had left me with three sick patients and no sign out sheet. I was already having enough trouble taking care of my own patients, particularly Maxine Chu, who after receiving a burr hole to release the buildup of intracranial pressure, had finally realized a normal urine output. That meant checking labs, both blood and urine, every hour and adjusting her fluid replacement accordingly.

"Should have placed my bet and just walked out," he said, head bowed, upon his return."I'm really sorry. At least I won a few bucks in the last race. Can I buy you dinner?"

Over a plate of Smokie's spare ribs, beef for Alex, pork for me, Alex told me the story. Turns out I was right about Lana Turner not being Land O'Turf. But the winner of the race? A horse named Betty Grable.

"You've got to be kidding," I said, spitting out a piece of charred pork. I hated burnt ribs. I'd rather live on the sultry edge of trichinosis than to eat ribs charred to the bone. The rib joint, the most popular place of it's kind in Lincoln Park, was carved out of an old bookstore. Table room enough for twenty. The noise around us came from the line of customers waiting to get in.

Alex poured himself another Heinekin. "That Hispanic blubber ball has something going. But damn if I know what it is."

"Malcolm Spool says there's a scientific explanation. Synaptic connections melting together as they're destroyed."

Alex wiped his mouth with a terry cloth towel that had a pig insignia on it. "Malcolm Spool is full of shit, hence his nickname." It was easy to see why most people didn't take well to Malcolm. Arrogant, rigid, obsessive, always had to be right. But for Alex, Malcolm was a source of true disdain. Over the past few weeks, Alex would taunt him whenever he got the chance. "Watch out Malcolm, the bacteria count in this hallway hasn't been checked today." Or Alex might have him paged over the hospital intercom: "Dr. Spool, please report to the infectious disease suite. Dr. E. Coli is waiting for you." I asked Alex why all the animosity.

"Do you remember the night Horner was almost killed?"

That was a silly question. I'd retain the sight of Horner dangling from the closet coat rack, as long as I lived.

"Do you know who was the only other intern to come back to the hospital besides you that night?"

"Malcolm Spool?"

"And who's been prowling around the unit constantly checking on Maxine..."

"She's just a case to him, Alex. Malcolm lives for difficult cases."

"Yeah, but why has he been going through the chart of agent Jack Hodges?"

"He's a snoop. He thinks every patient in the hospital is his responsibility. He'll make a great chief resident. Besides, his only interest in Jack Hodges is his doubt in his own diagnosis. He's right on that count."

Alex shook a rib at me. "I can smell it. He's rotten, Danny. I think he knows more about those murders than he's letting on."

"Alex, please."

"Maybe he's a recruited assassin, Danny. Like Goldman said. Specifically trained at medical schools like the one you were at."

"Your school, too, Alex." There had been a report of an intern from NYU, who disappeared after being accused of injecting ergonovine into a patient. "You don't really believe all that, do you? Bringing trained assassins into medical schools?"

"There is a conspiracy, Danny. This hospital. Other Jewish hospitals. You were right. They're hunting down Holocaust survivors. Going to kill them all. Then..." Alex reached for one of my uneaten ribs, then remembered they were pork. "Then you'll see those Holocaust naysayers come out of the woodwork, Danny. Look at what's going on with the attempted reconstruction of Auschwitz. People saying they're only building the crematoriums because they were never there in the first place. That nobody was gassed at all. It's starting, Danny. Talk shows, radio, everything."

457

"No one believes those guys."

"That's because there are still witnesses around. Guys like Horner with their numerical tattoos can get in front of a TV camera and say: 'Look what happened to me.' The people at the Nazi rally we went to were all bearing personal witness to the atrocities." Alex flung a rib onto his plate. "Don't you see, Danny? Once the survivors are gone, and their children are either killed off or become too intimidated to come forward, that's when the real war starts." Alex's eyes were fireballs. "What kind of world do we live in when just forty years after the largest massacre in the history of the planet, people were denying it ever happened? These were not just fringe lunatics, but professors at universities, people in the Austrian government. And it's still happening."

The spare ribs laid heavily in my gut. My kosher grandfather used to grimace in horror watching me eat milk and meat together in the form of a cheeseburger. I was never a practicing Jew, not really. My family never kept kosher, never lit the Sabbath candles. I used to wonder about students my age walking around wearing yarmulkes. How could they stand the looks they got, the audible whispers? People would know they were Jewish. Why would you want to display your Judaism so overtly? When people asked if I was Jewish I thought for sure they could see some scarlet 'J' on my chest. I hated myself for being embarrassed about my religion, and for even considering denying who and what I was. Growing up as the only Jewish kid in my neighborhood, I'd learned to run. Learned to hide. Wasn't it time to stand up? The thirty relatives I lost to the gas chambers never ran. Never had the chance.

I felt as if I was being tested in some way. I had to step forward, and I feared what I might uncover in the days to follow. Tested. It sounded Biblical. Tested by whom? God? I wanted to laugh. I hadn't invoked God's name since I was five years old when I promised always to say my prayers if he'd only make Noodles, our pet Labrador, better. Noodles died and I'd been an agnostic ever since.

We finished our meal in silence. I was more motivated than ever to find Linda Johnson. I had to find out if she held the key to the organization that could be multiplying like algae on a culture plate. I hoped Gail had gotten hold of the Atlanta phone book. No other library in the Chicago area had one. She'd found a friend who had moved from Atlanta to Kenosha, Wisconsin and had kept her phone directory from the year before. Gail was making the three hour drive today, to pick it up in person.

I ordered coffee and Alex ordered another beer. "Maybe I have been too hard on Malcolm," Alex said. "But if there's a killer around, we damn well better find out before Vice President Barrish comes to town."

"Amen. Can you imagine what would happen if..."

"Don't even say it. If a terrorist organization ever wanted a coming out party, this would be an excellent invitation. Jewish hospital. Jewish Veep. By the way, Goldman asked if you and I wanted to stand by during the treadmill examination."

"You're kidding? What about Gail?"

"I'll ask. They need a few doctors on standby. God forbid something did go wrong, we could handle it. He'd prefer us over the old codgers heading the departments who always want to be around. They couldn't perform CPR if their lives depended on it. Besides, he can trust us. Did you know, you and Gail and I are the only ones who have received a full security clearance?" Alex laughed. "Besides, would you want Malcolm Stool injecting thallium into Vice President Barrish? Would you?"

I thought a moment. "At least you could be sure the solution would be sterile."

Chapter 96 johnson

Gail and I split up the Johnsons. Eight thousand Johnsons in the greater Atlanta area. I couldn't believe it. I thought people in Atlanta had last names like O'Hara or Butler. Adding insult to injury were the additional six hundred names spelled J-o-h-n-s-t-o-n-e. I had no clue to how Linda spelled her last name. That night we began by calling every Johnson with a first name beginning with an "L", about 250 between us. I only got though 40 before collapsing. Lucius, Levi, and Larry; no one could identify a person matching my description of the Linda Johnson I was seeking. I called Gail. She'd gotten through sixty calls with no luck. We figured this could take up to two months and about a year's worth of our salary. And the worse part was that we had no evidence Linda Johnson even lived in Atlanta. My mind flashed to Eddie Ingraham. *"I can help you find her."* Was this another typical Eddie Ingraham manipulation? Something to keep him from jail? Or did he know something that I didn't? Could Eddie be a suspect? I'd gone over that possibility in my mind before and concluded that there was simply no way. The only atrocities Eddie ever committed were against himself. And those had been well documented for years. No, Eddie was not a suspect. But he had an agenda, that was for sure. I just didn't know what it was.

Chapter 97 eddie

When I arrived at the intensive care unit the next morning, the place looked like a hurricane had hit. Reams of ECG strips strewn about like confetti, ampules of used medicine decorating table tops. Maxine, I thought. My God, what happened to Maxine? I held my breath and peered into her room. She was as I had left her--tubes running into her head, stomach, and urethra, and veins in both arms and the left side of the neck.

Malcolm was sitting at the central module, working on a progress note. I moved within his infection control area of two feet. His hair was ungroomed, scrub shirt torn and stained with blood, his face ripe with fatigue.

"You sure those aren't my scrubs you're wearing?"

"Eddie Ingraham," he said shaking his head. "Never seen anything like it." Malcolm pointed to the yards of ECG rhythm strips. "Shocked him out of V-fib a dozen times."

He had to be kidding. Eddie in V-fib?

"Faking chest pain is one thing," said Malcolm. "Making your heart fibrillate is something else."

Putting something over on Malcolm would be extremely difficult.

"I tried three drugs," Malcolm continued. "Then added potassium, magnesium and bicarbonate."

Brenda, the head nurse stepped forward. "Poor boy has paddle burns all over his chest."

"Those burns are medals of honor for Eddie," I said.

Brenda tisked. "You guys are too hard on Eddie. He's a perfect gentleman. Each time we defibrillated him, he thanked us for saving his life. Said he'd someday dedicate a medical school to the coronary care nurses."

"If not a medical school, Brenda, then some swamp land in Chile."

While Brenda touched up her purple lip gloss, Malcolm showed me the rhythm strips. "Sure looks like V-fib," he said. "What do you think?"

462

"You're asking me?" It was the first time I'd ever been asked for help by Malcolm.

"You're the wanna-be cardiologist."

The rhythm certainly appeared to be V-fib. Worm-like squiggles of electrical impulses--the signature of a malfunctioning and dying heart. "He had no blood pressure or vital signs with this?"

"Who do you think you're dealing with, Raskin? Believe me, he was dead as a pneumococcus on a culture plate full of penicillin."

I wanted to believe Malcolm, wanted to accept the fact that Eddie had indeed contracted a true electrical abnormality of his heart. He'd been through enough surgeries, had his share of self-induced infections. Maybe it had finally taken its toll. But I knew Eddie Ingraham better than anyone. I'd seen him in action. His seizures were textbook, his chest pain could fool the best cardiology had to offer. And Eddie seemed willing to go to any lengths to avoid going to jail.

Eddie proudly displayed his chest full of circular burns on morning rounds. "Hey, Danny, how you doing?"

Our resident held a bitter look. "Mr. Ingraham, this is Dr. Raskin."

"It's okay, Charles. Eddie and I go back a while."

Charles looked at the strips while I applied lotion to Eddie's chest. "Guess I won't be going anywhere now, huh, Danny?"

"Don't count on it, Eddie."

Eddie smiled. "Relax, Danny. I may have something for you. I'm waiting for a printout to come in."

Printout? When did Eddie have time to get to a computer? When I asked, he smiled.

"Last night."

"You had a dozen cardiac arrests last night."

"In between. I snuck out of bed and over to the computer terminal in the admissions area."

"Impossible. You had two IV lines and a million electrodes attached to your body."

"Just call me Houdini. Anyway, I'm hoping I can locate Linda Johnson for you."

Before I could say anything else, Charles looked up. "Munchausen's or not, these rhythm strips are real, that's for sure." Alex nodded his head. "You can't fake these."

"I'm not so sure," I said, stepping out of Eddie's range of hearing. I turned to Brenda. "Tell the day shift to call me next time he has one of these episodes. Don't shock him until I get there."

"Against the rules," said Brenda. "V-tach and V-fib are immediately cardioverted by whatever personnel is present.

"I'm his doctor, Brenda, and I'm asking you to wait. Please."

"We wait too long and the patient has brain damage."

"Eddie already has brain damage," I said with a straight face, then smiled.

Chapter 98 fibrillation

Later that morning, Mr. Gonzalez, with a blood pressure falling by the hour, sang a repertoire of songs from *My Fair Lady*. That afternoon, Alex Rosen went to the race track and won six hundred dollars on a horse named *Rain in Spain*. When he returned, Mr. Gonzalez was near death. His blood pressure and heart rate both hovered around fifty and his skin had taken on a sallow, empty color. Though Gail had the overall responsibility for his care, Alex ordered blood transfusions, steroids, and an injection of an experimental anti-viral agent. "Open the dopamine all the way up," he told the nurses. "I want that BP up to 80."

"He's my patient," said Gail.

"Oh, come on," cajoled Alex. "Let me handle his case for a few days." Alex lightly rubbed Gail's shoulders until she agreed. Alex stationed a full time nurse in Mr. Gonzalez's room, with orders to have him paged the moment Mr. Gonzalez verbalized even a syllable.

Throughout the day, Eddie Ingraham seemed unduly concerned with my coming and going. Where and when was I having lunch? When was I going home? At five o'clock I told Eddie I was heading off to dinner, then made sure he could see me exit the ICU. I waited on the other side of the door and looked at my watch. Less than a minute later an alarm sounded. I opened the door and heard: "It's Ingraham. V-fib!"

I ran down the hall and burst through the mob scene at his door way. The day nurse, Sophie, had just greased the paddles and was placing them on Eddie's chest.

"Hold it!" I yelled. Sophie looked up.

"Huh?"

"Don't shock him. He's my patient." I took quick note of the situation. The monitor above Eddie's head fluoresced with green electrical squiggles characteristic of V-fib. Eddie lay motionless. The charge nurse, Brenda, burst in. She was on the back side of a double shift and in no mood to compromise.

"Shock that man!"

"No!" I stepped forward, grabbing the paddles from Sophie.

"We need an airway!" someone shouted. "He's turning blue."

"Dammit Raskin," yelled Brenda. "You're going to kill him."

My mind raced. There had to be something. I felt for Eddie's pulse. Not palpable. But he had told me he could autoregulate his blood pressure and heart beat down to almost nothing. There must be proof. My hand went under his bed sheet, searching.

Malcolm Spool grabbed my arm. "Shock him, you fool!" Suddenly Alex was grabbing Malcolm by the throat and pushing him away. "Let the man do his thing, creep."

My hand moved down the side of one leg, then the other. Nothing. I slid it under his back starting at his shoulders. Right at the small of his back I found it--a small box, barely noticeable. It was metal and had a clip-on cover. I pulled it out and found it connected to Eddie's chest electrodes. Inside the box was a tangled mess, five wires twisting around one another. I jiggled the first one. The monitor went flat line.

"You killed him!" Malcolm yelled through the mask he was wearing.

"Shut up." I jiggled the second wire and looked up to the screen.

"He's in v-fib again."

I put my face next to Eddie's, then shook him by the shoulders. "It's over Eddie. I figured it out." Eddie remained motionless. In the back of the box were two AA batteries which I removed. His rhythm went flat line. I traced the wire that exited the back of the box under the covers where it looped twice and ended in a tightly wrapped gauze pack that was attached to his chest lead. I removed the dressing and pulled out the wire connecting the box to Eddie. The rhythms on the screen reverted to a normal sinus.

Alex slapped my back. "A cardiology giant."

Malcolm slumped. " I'll be a..."

"Nice trick, Eddie. Very original. Made those seizures seem like puppy love."

Eddie suddenly grimaced and he opened his eyes. He took a long breath. "Damn you, Raskin."

Chapter 99 next day

"Hurry up." Alex tried to pull me away from my progress notes. I had just finished checking on Maxine and had made final arrangements for Eddie Ingraham's transfer to Cook County Jail. "Come on," he said, tugging at my coat. "It's Gonzalez. He's talking again."

Having given up Mr. Gonzalez for dead, the ICU nurses subtly back off their daily care plan, which explained why his room smelled like a locker room after a wrestling match. "Damn nurses," muttered Alex as we winced from the smell. "I never made him a no-code."

"Everybody thinks you've gone too far, Alex." Ignoring me, he went toward Mr. Gonzalez, who was humming something I couldn't make out.

"*Little town of Bethlehem*," said Alex. He pointed to the Tribune. "Seventh race. Read it and weep." My eyes caught the selection immediately. "*Three Wise Men*."

"Come on, Alex." His beeper was already in my hand.

"Be back in an hour. I promise." Alex folded the paper and opened the door.

"Alex, it's none of my business, but I think you need help."

Alex's eyes became pointed and cold. He moved closer. For a moment I thought he might hit me. Then his hand rested softly on my shoulder.

"My father had a gambling problem, Danny. I don't."

"Prove it. Stay here."

Alex laughed. "Nothing wrong with trying to get out of debt, Danny. That's all this is about."

"What would the Israeli Air Force think?"

Alex grew quiet, then pointed a stiff finger toward me. "Even if I had a problem, the Israeli Air Force doesn't need to find out." Alex turned to leave.

Suddenly Mr. Gonzalez stopped, opened his eyes and sang: "Tannenbaum, Tannenbaum."

"Alex, wait. Listen. Tannenbaum. I told you he said Tannenbaum."

"It's a Christmas song, stupid. He's confirming the tip on "Three Wise Men." Besides, you never heard him sing 'O' Thaddeus, O' Thaddeus', did you?"

Mr. Gonzalez blinked twice and looked toward the ceiling. "O Thaddeus, O Thaddeus," he muttered.

Alex laughed. "Echolalia. He's in that stage of decompensation where he repeats whatever has been said. Ask your buddy Malcolm about it." Alex closed the door behind him. I heard him yelling at a nurse to bathe Mr. Gonzalez as soon as possible.

"Malcolm, Malcolm, Malcolm." Then: "Malcolm Spool."

I stopped. He repeated himself. "Malcolm Spool."

Wait a minute. Alex never mentioned Malcolm's last name. How did he..."Mr. Gonzalez. Do you know..."

"Malcolm Spool," he whined. "Malcolm Spool. Tannenbaum. Oh Tannenbaum."

Jack Hodges was sitting in the chair in his room, staring directly across the unit through his open shades into Eddie Ingraham's room. "Poor little bugger," Jack remarked as I checked his IV infusion rate and pondered his vital sign trends. One had to keep up appearances, after all.

"Malcolm Spool," I said. Hodges kept his gaze on Eddie's room. "What's the bugger doing now?"

"Talk to me, Jack!"

Jack's eyes glared out the window. "What about him?"

"You know. I mean... is there any way that Malcolm Spool... might be involved?" I swallowed hard, felt like I was betraying a friend.

Jack scratched his chin. "Why do you ask?" Then a second later. "Oh shit!"

Suddenly the arrhythmia alarm sounded. I ran to the door and slammed it open. "It's Eddie Ingraham!" someone shouted. "V-fib."

I poked my head out the door. "Forget it" I yelled. "Just disconnect his alarm system."

"I'd get over there if I were you."

"Thank you, Jack. What medical school did you say you graduated from?" Jack was standing now, looking intently through the glass at Eddie. "So, Jack, about Malcolm?"

Jack's voice was hard. "We're watching him. Now, would you please go check on your friend?"

"What do you mean, you're watching him? Is he a suspect? You can't be serious?"

Jack turned and faced me, his face drained of color."Would you please go and check on that kid?"

"Why? Eddie puts his little finger in that box of his and he has instant arrest. No telling what he's tried this time."

"This time he stuck his finger somewhere else."

"Like where?"

"Try the light-socket!"

Chapter 100 eddie reborn

Had it not been for Jack Hodges keen observation of Eddie dissecting the wall socket behind his bed and then delivering a lightening bolt of electricity to himself, Eddie would have died without anyone doing a damn thing about it. As it was, it took an even larger jolt of energy, courtesy of Illinois Bell and Electric, to bring Eddie's heart beat back in syncopy with the rest of the world's. I remained at Eddie's bedside for an hour afterward, titrating the Lidocaine drip and following his vital signs while he slowly regained consciousness. When he awoke fully, Eddie refused to talk.

"You okay, Eddie?" I repeated a dozen times. Eddie remained silent, staring out his window into the Gardner House courtyard. I tried again just before leaving for the evening. Nothing.

I went home and called forty four more numbers in Atlanta, none of which netted the slightest bit of information, although one Abigail Johnson said she'd love to talk to a real doctor, especially an unmarried one. Around midnight I tried sleeping, but I couldn't get Eddie out of my mind. Finally, I dressed and went back to the hospital, just to check on him.

"At least he's up and around," said Brenda. "The boy won't listen to no one. He disconnected his leads and took a shower. Then around ten pm disappeared for an hour. Had security looking all over for him. When he returned, he refused to tell us anything."

"Where'd he go?"

"Who knows? We didn't even know he was missing until half an hour after he left. He rigged his monitor to keep beeping out his heart beat. The guy's a genius."

"The guy's a psycho."

Eddie was sitting in bed staring out the window into blackness. His eyes, usually small spheres of anticipation, were wide as the Venice canal. The lines in his face seemed less distinct, his cheekbones less pronounced than I remembered. I sat in a chair facing him, waiting for him to say something, wondering whether the progress I had made with him had gone to waste. We were probably back to square one, Eddie trusting nobody, manipulating everybody. I closed my eyes, leaned my head back. Sleep came quickly.

"I have something for you."

I jumped. Looking around trying to remember where I was, I glanced at my watch. One-thirty in the morning. I looked up. Eddie was in the same position I'd last seen him, about two dreams ago.

"I have something for you. It's in an envelope on the dresser."

I rubbed my eyes. "How do you feel, Eddie?"

Eddie pondered the question as if asked by a biblical sage. "I really faced death this time," he finally said. I looked at the envelope on his desk, wondering what it contained. Eddie sniffed once. Then again. And for the first time since I'd known him, he started to cry. "I was in a dream having a conversation with my brother."

"What was so significant about talking to your brother?"

"He's been dead for twelve years."

For Eddie, the floodgates opened and tears poured out, enough for a salt mine, stored for decades in caverns of fear. I moved to his bed, sat down next to him.

"My brother and I...." Suddenly Eddie was no longer the self-flagellating, sociopathic, doctor-impersonator that I had come to know and love. He was... well he was...Eddie, a younger, innocent version.

"We were sitting on a swing in the back yard with our dog, Schnowzie," he continued. "Talking about the times our father would come in the room. Mom was sleeping. He was drunk. He would rape us."

"Oh Ed!"

Eddie searched for words. Then: "He killed him. He killed poor Bobby because Bobby told my mother what he was doing to us." He flung his arms around me. "Then he killed Mommy." Eddie sobbed in my arms. "Hold me, mommy." He rocked back and forth."Don't let go, Mommy. Please don't let go. Daddy will hurt me like he hurt you and Bobby."

475

"She won't let go, Eddie," I said feeling his heart beating painfully, mournfully against my chest.

"Don't let go, Mommy."

I rocked him for an hour. Finally his sobs abated and a welcome sleep overcame him.

Chapter 101 linda johnson

Lying on my apartment couch, I re-read for the third time, the paper Eddie had given me:

Atlanta Constitution November 16. Obituary section.

Xavier Cleophus Johnson passed away yesterday morning. Services will be held at Greenpasture Chapel on 114th Genessee Friday at 9:30 am. Mr. Johnson is survived by his wife Isabella and daughters Linda and Sophie.

I laid the letter next to the envelope Eddie had placed it in. Why hadn't I thought of that? Looking for the obituary related to Linda Johnson's departure from Arbor Hills to Atlanta. I opened the Atlanta phone book and found a single listing for one Xavier C. Johnson, 419 Pembroke Lane. I copied the phone number onto a piece of scratch paper, wondering how many months it would have taken to reach the X's in the phone book, not to mention the expense. I picked up the phone. Four in the morning. I hung up the receiver. Picked it up again and dialed. Please be her. Please. I counted the rings with my breathing. Five, six, seven. Come on. Come on.

Eight, nine.

Then, a sleepy "hello."

"Linda?" I whispered, swallowing hard to keep my heart from jumping out of my throat.

"Who is...is that you Ted? I told you never to call me...."

"Linda, it's Danny Raskin. I'm calling from Chicago."

A pause. Some ruffling. Then: "Danny Raskin? From Arbor Hills?"

"One and the same."

Her voice softened. "Been a long time."

"Sorry about your dad, Linda."

"Thanks. Had a bad stroke. Only lasted three days. Doctors said he would have been a vegetable." A pause. "It's four in the morning."

"Linda, do you remember the day I left Arbor Hills for Chicago?"

"Two days later than you planned." A pause, then: "That was one nice week, come to think of it. You involved with anyone?"

"Yes, I mean no... that's not why I called. Remember how I couldn't fit all my stuff in the back of my car? You offered to hold onto a couple of boxes for me?" *Please Linda. Please.*

"I remember."

My pulse quickened. "Still got them?"

A pause. "No."

My body went numb except for a sharp pain on the left side of my head. "What happened?"

"Couldn't fit your stuff in with all of mine. I had to drive back to Atlanta in a Pinto. I went through the boxes but it mostly seemed like junk. So I trashed it."

I felt as if an ulcer had just perforated through my belly. My one chance. My only chance. Trashed.

"I think there might have been one thing I took with me. Looked like some sort of metal strongbox. Since it was locked, I figured it contained some of your legal documents."

My heart danced. "Still have it?"

"Just a minute. Let me check."

It was the longest minute of my life.

"It's sitting in the back of the hall closet."

"Oh Linda, I love you. If it weren't for this phone, I'd....." Oh shit. Like a thunderclap it hit me. My phone. It was bugged.

"Linda. Don't move. I'll call you back in three minutes."

After slamming down the receiver, I kicked the phone as hard as I could across the room. Fueled by fear, I ran across the street, masses of jumbled thoughts causing a traffic jam in my mind's expressway. She had the file. It was actually there. It had to be important. My God, they killed for it. How could I have been so stupid? At least it was the Feds. But then again, how did I know? How did I know anything anymore? Who was on what side? I just knew I needed that file in my hand.

I used the pay phone outside Mr. Gee's, dialed and gave my father's credit card number. The moon was playing hide and seek behind the clouds. There were two flood lights outside the otherwise darkened store front. The circular red light of an ambulance flashed from the ER parking light across the street.

"Danny?"

"It's me."

"Did you call a minute ago and then hang up?"

"No."

My throat tightened.

"Well somebody did."

"Oh shit."

"What's wrong, Danny?"

I took a deep breath. I had been hoping to make this a pleasant call, not to scare or upset her in any way. That was no longer possible. "Is your mother home?"

"Mom's visiting her sister in Nashville. I'm here alone."

"Listen, Linda. Listen very carefully. I think you could be in great danger. I know this sounds strange but you have to take that file and get out of your house now."

"It's four in the morning. Are you on drugs?"

"No, Linda. I'll explain it tomorrow. Just find a hotel room for tonight. I'll pay you back." The plan came quickly, like it had been there all along. "I want you to meet me tomorrow at the Delta airline ticket office at the airport in Atlanta. Say about noon."

"You're comin' to Atlanta? Tomorrow? Can we do lunch?"

"Linda. You're not listening. Some very evil people want that file. They will do anything to get it. I think they might know you have it. Do you understand, Linda? Get out of your house. Now. I'll explain everything at the airport. Noon tomorrow. Delta ticket counter."

"I think so," she said meekly.

Sweat poured from my face. I felt like I had just finished a run in the early morning chill. "Linda. One other thing. If you see anybody suspicious at the airport, or anybody following you, get the hell out. And don't bring the file back to your house. It won't be safe to go home with the file. Do you understand?"

"What should I do with it?"

I couldn't think. *Damn.* "I don't know, Linda. Give it to a cop maybe. Or lock it in a locker. Just don't bring it home. They might kill you for it."

Chapter 102 air travel

I pushed back my seat recliner, let loose a deep cleansing breath, and watched Chicago disappear below. Sears Tower, Lake Shore Drive, the beginnings of rush hour. An early morning sun reflected off the lake.

"Flying time to Atlanta will be three hours and twelve minutes."

I suddenly wished I was going somewhere else. Anywhere else. At the airport I had passed departure gates for St. Thomas, Jamaica, even London. God, to get away from all this, I thought. Maybe Gail was right. I'd called her three hours before and told her that I was going to Atlanta to get my long lost file from Linda Johnson and would be back by dinner.

"It's too much Danny. Don't do this by yourself." After she realized there was no talking me out of it: "Please be careful. I want you back in one piece." She paused. "I need you in my life."

Leaning back in my seat, fumbling with the paper with Linda's address and phone number on it, I wondered whether I should have called the Feds. Too late now. Linda would have been gone by the time they got there. And since someone had called Linda and then hung up, I knew my phone was still bugged. There was no telling who might show up at Linda's house.

I closed my eyes and thought about what had happened to the women in my life this year. Wanda Bylevin dead. Maxine Chu- comatose. I'd probably never again hear her giggly laugh, never be able to watch her hair fly to one side as she tilted her head with that provocative smile of hers. Gail Peterson- thank God, nobody except for Alex knew about us. She had been left alone.

And now Linda Johnson. I thought about how just two nights with her had turned her into a marked woman. Hopefully things would go well, though. My plan after all was simple, maybe too simple, I wondered, having concocted it more by gut instinct than by rational thought. I would land in Atlanta at

11:30 in the morning, meet Linda at the Delta ticket counter at noon, and get the file and hop on the 1:20 plane back to Chicago. With Linda. I had purchased her a one way ticket on the spur of the moment, a final gesture as I handed the Delta agent my VISA card. I barely had enough credit to pay. But after what happened to Wanda Bylevin, I didn't want to take any chances with Linda. She would be safe in Chicago with Agent Huber and his boys looking after her. She didn't know she would be leaving, and I thought it was better that way. On the way home I would break the lock and look at the file. If the information inside was as significant as I imagined, I would call Goldman from O'Hare. Have the feds give us a lift home. That would be that.

A stewardess presented a breakfast cart, but I took a pass. A cheese omelette in a stomach already doing flip-flops would likely pay a return visit to the air sickness bag. Instead I settled for black coffee and a bloody Mary mix. I downed one after the other, trying to imagine what secrets that file held, what information could be important enough to kill for. So important, I thought, that just the possibility of my recovering it may have been the single thing that had kept me alive.

I imagined Dean Cantrell at the top of this organization's food chain. Why else would he have the one file with contents that might threaten the grass-roots of the organization he founded? Who in their wildest dreams would have suspected that a locked file in the personal possession of a respected Dean at a top notch medical school would be anything but safe? I imagined the file might also depict the identities of foot soldiers like Tannenbaum. I wondered what he looked like without his disguises. And suppose there really was a cadre of students being trained as killers? I imagined their deans conferring the extra degree at graduation-- MD and MA--Medical Assassin. That's what we were talking about, weren't we? Doctors, trained to heal, committing murder at a moment's notice. What if I found a picture of one of my Arbor Hills classmates? Or an intern who worked at Richard Meese? What if I discovered a picture of Malcolm Spool?

My eyelids grew heavy. As my level of consciousness slipped, an amusing thought occurred. What if I was able to break up this ring of terror? Would I be a hero? Pictures in the paper, interviews, the Oprah show? Now, as my chance was approaching, being a hero was the furthest thing from my mind. I wanted this whole thing to end. I wanted to get back to work and do what I came to Chicago for. I wanted to get on with my life. Sleep saturated my pores as my body relaxed. God, please let me get that file. Just for once, let things go right.

Chapter 103 tannenbaum

While Frank Tannenbaum never heard of Eddie Ingraham, he certainly shared Eddie's aspiration of getting himself admitted to the ICU. Like Eddie, he had done his homework, not practicing how to fake the symptoms of a heart attack like Eddie had, although he did consider himself to be an actor of unquestionable talent, having successfully impersonated a number of physicians, a housekeeper, and even a Rastafarian pot head. This time though, he would need to go a step further. This time he had to succeed at all costs. No more screw ups like what happened with Maxine Chu. God, he wished he had stayed in her room and watched that little Chink die. Raskin the bastard, ruined the moment, as usual. He smiled through capped teeth as he thought about making Raskin suffer. The bastard deserved as much pain as possible.

Nestled safely in his apartment, he smiled as he lifted a beaker filled with two inches worth of silvery-red liquid. His hand trembled as he lightly shook the container. This was unusual; his tremor only surfaced when he was afraid--and that was a rare occurrence. But this was new, using himself as a testing ground for his own chemical concoction. He had every reason to expect there would be no problems, that the medication would do exactly what he had intended it to do. He had, after all, spent two years at the Marie Curie Institute in Paris, and another eighteen months in Damascus in preparation for such a day. After injecting himself with a pre-measured amount of this solution, one of his coronary arteries would go into temporary spasm, thereby denying the myocardium its needed blood supply. His symptoms would be real: chest pressure, sweats, the ECG changes. More than enough to get himself admitted to the Unit without arousing suspicion. The thought of tampering with his cardiac circulation bothered him, of course, but it was the only way. That asshole FBI agent, Hodges, would be carefully watching everyone who entered. Any suspicion on the part of Hodges and he'd be a goner. His superiors had warned him about Hodges. Then he laughed. The son of a bitch. His inside friend had been itching to take him out. Said Hodges might be onto him. But no, that couldn't be done, not yet. Hodges and Raskin, they would meet their maker holding hands. A clean sweep and then on to bigger and better things.

He smiled as he swirled the beaker like a glass of vintage Bordeaux. He picked up a sterile syringe and sucked up two cc's of fluid from the beaker. He hoped to God he hadn't miscalculated. There was an urgency this time. His superiors were sending someone to have a chat with Linda Johnson. If she had the file they wanted, great. She could be persuaded to turn it over.

Either way, Raskin had run out of time. Once he was dead, the message to Goldman would be clear. The file is gone. We won't kill any more patients at Richard Meese. Goldman would mourn his favorite intern of course, but in the end would be relieved that the worse was over. The Vice President would still make his trip, his dedication of the cardiac center a lock. All was safe. That kike, Barrish. He couldn't wait. Barrish's death would be a real coming out party for Friends of Tomorrow. No reason to not take responsibility for the murder. People--white people--would begin to listen. They would see that it was time to take back their country from the niggers and Jews and the spics and all those goons who smelled like curry and had little red dots in the middle of their foreheads. The Holocaust would be exposed as a sham. If everything went according to plan, in less than eighteen months the last Holocaust survivor in this country would be dead. No more living witnesses. Then the real fun would begin.

Frank moistened the ECG electrodes with Vaseline and attached them to his chest, admiring the contours of his body in the cracked full length mirror next to the bed. He would have made a fine German soldier, he thought, flexing his pecs. He slipped one end of a tourniquet between his teeth and wrapped the other end above the elbow. He slapped at his forearm and a worm-like vein stood at attention. He took a chug from his beer can, hoping to steady his tremor, and injected the contents of the syringe. He watched the blips on the monitor. What he wouldn't do for the cause. Frank Tannenbaum, hero of the new order. He imagined his kids, not the spic kid Fernando, that was supposedly his, living somewhere in New Mexico with that whore of a mother; no, some new kids made from sperm and egg of real Americans, they would see his pictures in the history books. Right up there with Herman Goering. Adolf Eichmann. The good soldiers.

A minute later it began.

First the pressure build up--a vice of sorts--encircling his chest. A large bubble of gas that he could not belch away. He felt the perspiration bead across his forehead. Good, he thought, this is working perfectly. He felt like he wanted to throw up. The monitor beeped faster. The ECG segments arched upward like tombstones. He'd done it, damn it! Real honest to goodness home-grown angina pectoris. He smiled and couldn't help but think that in another time and place he could have been a scientist of great renown.

His thoughts were suddenly interrupted. The pressure across his chest was stronger now. It reminded him of that boa constrictor he had worked with years ago in the jungles of South America. He looked at his watch. Five minutes had passed. The pain should have let up at four. He took a breath, felt as if his windpipe was being squeezed. He felt dizzy, leaned over and puked into a basin. The heart monitor was beating wildly. Shit, he hadn't expected this to happen. It was too strong, damn it! Too strong! His trembling, sweaty hands clutched the bottle of nitroglycerin and he dumped the entire contents into his mouth. His pulse was racing, his respirations shallow. Things around him turned a hazy gray. Barely conscious, he crawled desperately toward the phone. As his hand touched the receiver, he felt himself passing out.

Chapter 104 atlanta

"Please keep your seat belts fastened until the plane has come to a complete stop at the gate."

I opened my eyes, rubbing away the remnants of two hours of sleep. It was 11:40, which meant I had twenty minutes to make my way to the ticket counter. Once off the plane, I walked slowly toward the Delta terminal. I felt surprisingly calm, like I was in some way meant to be there. I took it as a good omen. I dawdled at a newsstand, picking up a pack of peanut butter cups and scanning the magazine rack. The front page of the Atlanta Constitution caught my eye. "Six term State Senator Bernie Kornblum died today while undergoing a series of undisclosed tests at Emory University Hospital." I read on for a few sentences then came to: "a survivor of Bergen Belsen concentration camp..."

The rest was blurred. God, it really was happening, not just at Richard Meese, but all over. I put down the paper, paid for the candy, and exited past security, nearly tripping over a toddler camped out at the end of the down escalator. I parked myself adjacent to the long row of counters housing the Delta ticket agents. A minute before noon. Several dozen people were waiting in line, others milled around, looking for gates, catching a snack, saying good-bye, some with baggage, some with kids.

Twelve o'clock. Where was she?

My feet shifted nervously. Maybe it's the parking. Hard to find parking at an airport.

For the next twenty minutes I paced, I died, I paced some more. Where the hell was she? My heart raced, my mind played nervous games of paranoia. I noticed a man at the concession stand across from the counter. He had been looking at the same paper for ten minutes, hadn't turned the page. Maybe he was watching me. A second man in his mid-forties had given up his place in the ticket line at least six times in twenty minutes, saying his wife had the ticket and was parking the car.

At 12:50 I was in full panic. The TV monitor flashed my impending departure back to Chicago. I went to a pay phone and dialed Linda's home number. No answer. I took one more look around then headed toward the gate. I waited until the last minute. "Last call for flight 459 to Chicago."

I lifted my boarding pass, and tucked Linda's back in my pocket. Attached was the address, 419 Pembroke Lane.

"Your ticket sir." I hesitated. Oh God.

"Your ticket, sir."

I turned and ran, bumping into a stewardess, then two men turning a corner. I wasn't thinking clearly. I stopped at the Delta counter. No Linda. I ran outside, inhaled bus fumes, and scurried across the drop-off parking lane to a free cab. "419 Pembroke Lane," I said. "By the way, do you take plastic?"

Chapter 105 linda's house

Linda Johnson lived twenty minutes east of downtown Atlanta, or so I calculated from the high-sprawling skyscrapers outside the taxi's window. Her house, a one story soft brick structure, was recessed in the back end of a cul-de-sac. Two large sycamore trees stood guard at the entrance. Her front yard was impeccably landscaped with pods of lilacs and daffodils nestling against the house. A large cement birdbath lay empty except for a few twigs. A blue volvo sat in the driveway. It seemed particularly humid for spring and my shirt was already stuck to my armpits. Two humongous orange butterflies swiped at me as I climbed the porch and I wondered if they'd escaped from my stomach.

A screen door was half-open.

"Anybody home?" I yelled nervously. There was no answer so I stepped into an oak foyer at least one hundred years old. Above me hung a dilapidated painting of two horses in a field of lilies. "Hello? Linda?" The house had a musty odor. I passed through a large dining area with a long wooden table, covered with a candelabra so large it could have lit my entire apartment. Swinging doors rustled slightly. I imagined servants bringing large trays of foie gras through these doors, and peach melbas proudly displayed for dessert. A strong scent of coffee grounds in the kitchen. Recent. Something else, too, almost hospital like. I opened the doors.

It took me only a second to spot Linda. Sitting in a vinyl chair at a small breakfast nook, her head was grotesquely bent backward, her eyes glazed. Her neck was opened from one end to the other. Her right carotid artery had been cleanly dissected away from the neck and then severed and knotted like a shoelace. Droplets of blood plopped into large pools of more blood. I screamed and looked again, then threw up in the sink.

"No, Damn it! No!"

I ran for the phone, slipping in the puddle, falling against Linda and knocking her off the chair and right on top of me. Her eyes were wide open displays of innocent death. As I lifted her off me, I saw the blood splattered note pinned to her bosom. "Better luck next time."

"You sons of bitches!" I yelled. "You've got your damn file, now leave me alone." I set Linda gently into the chair, resting her head on the table, closing her eyes. Why hadn't she listened? Why didn't she get the hell out of her house like I told her? I began tearing apart the kitchen, appliances, foodstuffs, everything went flying. Inadvertently, I knocked over her open purse, its contents spilling on the floor. "Damn it, Linda why didn't you leave?" I sat down on the couch and cried.

When I had partially regained my composure, I began cleaning up the mess I'd made. I bent down in attempt to replace things that had fallen from her purse. They'd be needed for identification. Lipstick, wallet, car keys. Couple of grocery receipts. Then I saw it. A parking ticket receipt. Atlanta international airport. Short term parking. Time in: 11:04 am. Time out: 11:32 a.m. Then I remembered *If you smell any trouble, get the hell out of the airport. Don't bring the file back home.*

I picked up the phone and dialed Richard Meese. "Get me Dr. Sol Goldman. Tell him Dr. Raskin is calling, long distance."

Chapter 106 back home

"Of course they have it," snapped James Huber, exhaling cigar smoke into the limousine we were taking from the airport. I had landed at 8 pm and was greeted by Huber, Goldman, and a team of plain-clothed agents. I was promptly hustled into the waiting car.

Huber puffed hard, then lifted a side panel. He pulled out a fifth of Johnny Walker. "Why the hell didn't you tell us, Raskin?"

"Leave him alone,"said Sol. "If it weren't for Raskin, that file would never have even been an issue. He was the one who stole it in the first place. For God's sake, Huber. He just found his friend murdered."

"All his friends seem to end up like that."

I picked up a shot glass, wanting to throw it. *Throw the rock, dammit, throw the rock.*

Huber saw my rage and softened. "Sorry about that,"he said, delicately lifting the glass from my hand. "Let me fill that for you."

We drank silently. Huber removed the cellophane from a new cigar and bit off the end. "On the other hand it could have been a set up. Our men could have been ambushed."

I drank a second glassful, the gold liquid calming my nerves, slowing my heart. The limo pulled off the Dan Ryan Expressway and a moment later we were in the parking lot across from Goldman's office.

"Well, it's over," said Huber. "They have the file. Maybe now they'll stop the killings at Meese."

"What about the Vice President?" Goldman wanted to know.

"I'm briefing the VP's advance team on Monday. If we haven't caught Tannenbaum by then, it's off."

Desperation filled Sol's voice. "Come on Jim. We have plenty of security. Nobody will be allowed into his treadmill test unless I authorize it." Huber finished off his scotch, then dumped cigar ashes into the moist bottom of the glass. "Sol, I'd say you're worrying about the wrong person." His head tilted in my direction. "He's the problem right now. He's gotta go."

"Forget it, Huber. I've got two months of internship left. I'm not leaving."

Huber smiled. "They've got the file, kid. In case you didn't realize it, that was your life line. If you stay, you're dead meat."

"Maybe they don't have it. Maybe Linda Johnson hid it somewhere."

"Unlikely, Danny. Huber's agents tore that place apart. And even if they don't have it, they know you don't either."

Sol's hand was on my shoulder. "You gotta bail, son," he said softly. He looked at Huber. "I want that protection for Danny that you promised. New name, new location, round the clock surveillance."

"Forever?" I queried.

Huber shook his head. "Just until we crack this case."

"Look, let me finish out my week in the Unit."

"No way," said Sol."

" Jack Hodges is there."

"Yeah, and thanks to you," said Huber, "Jack Hodges has headaches and a case of diarrhea that just won't quit. He wants out."

I looked at Sol. "One more week. I owe it to Maxine."

Sol looked at Huber, who lifted his shot glass. "All right, Danny, one more week. Let's drink on it."

Chapter 107 Sol's office

Sol turned on the light in his office and walked toward a small oak cabinet. I scanned the wall, looking at his infamous class picture. Goldman, Cantrell, and Bramwell. I remembered how convinced I once was that Sol was the enemy. It made me wonder now. Could I be wrong about something else? Was there something I was missing?

"Scotch?" said Sol, rising from his knees, where he had been fishing around in the cabinet. "Glenlivet. Single malt. I hate being just half-drunk." He poured. We drank in silence, Sol's fingers restlessly beating against a manila folder. An ambulance wailed in the distance, the noise closed in until we saw the reflection of the red light against his window.

"And to think, we almost stopped it," he said, picking up the folder.

"Guess I blew it."

"No, Danny. You're the one who practically broke the thing. You supplied us with the link between the murders and the Holocaust victims." He opened the folders and began sorting through a stack of news clippings.

"I read about the state senator from Atlanta."

Goldman nodded. "In the past two months, three new periodicals have been published, two in Europe, one here, their sole purpose to discredit the Holocaust. Try and prove it never happened. Last month there were twelve regional talk shows featuring people denying the existence of the Holocaust. These guys are getting air time. Some even have credentials. One guy teaches Revisionist history at Northwestern"

"Teaching that there never was a Holocaust?"

"Denying that six million Jews were killed. Denying that concentration camps were death camps. Denying that Zyklon B was ever used to gas Jews at Auschwitz. One of the tenets around which Friends of Tomorrow was founded, no doubt. I'm afraid Friends of Tomorrow is the elite medical branch of a much larger army. It's one thing to bomb synagogues or get yourself on a talk show, but how do you protect yourself against trained doctors? Assassins in white coats who have unlimited access to the human condition? God only knows where this will end. Do you know what would happen if the full scope of this got out to the press?" Sol threw his hands in the air. "Would you ever go to a doctor again?"

"Especially if you were Jewish."

"What's next? Old people? Democrats?"

"Maybe we'll get lucky. Lawyers."

"At least we've rooted out Tannenbaum's latest disguise. We have a hiring freeze. That should make it safe if VP Barrish shows up."

"You really think so?"

Sol scratched his head. "I hope so, Danny. I really hope so."

Chapter 108 back to the ICU

Gail was waiting for me outside the intensive care unit the next morning. Without saying a word, she tugged at my sleeve, and lead me down the back corridor to the ICU call rooms. After closing the door behind us, she threw her arms around me, and brought her lips to mine. "I'm so sorry about your friend, Linda," she said, gasping for a breath. "I was so..." She didn't finish her sentence, didn't have to, our lips pressed together, our bodies one heart beat, loud and marching.

"I missed you," Gail whispered.

"It's time for rounds," I whispered back.

Gail's tongue did figure eights inside my mouth. "I was so worried when you didn't show up on the 1:20 plane."

"We'd better finish this later."

"I can take call for you tonight. Better, yet, I'll get Alex to cover."

I felt like I was being pitied. "We'd better go, Gail. It's my call day. I don't want anyone doing my work." My words came out colder than I had intended but I couldn't help myself. I didn't want to think about Linda or Gail or anything. I just wanted to throw myself into my work. I grabbed Gail by her slumping shoulders. "Tell me about my patients. What did I miss?"

Gail looked despondent. "For one thing, Alex set a new world record for the longest code blue in history."

"Mr. Gonzalez?"

Gail nodded. "Alex refused to call it off. Almost five hours."

I'd never heard of CPR lasting longer than an hour. "Must have emptied the entire pharmacy."

"Don't forget pacemakers and cardiac needles. Alex used about ten of those. The Chief resident finally interceded and brought it to a halt. Alex would have killed him if it weren't for the fact that one of the nurses thought she heard Mr. Gonzalez say 'Vista vous' as they pulled out the trach tube. Alex checked the Tribune and then ran to the race track to bet on a horse named Vicaroo. He left me to cover the entire unit by myself."

498

"Did he win?"

Gail couldn't hide a smile. "Vicaroo finished dead last. And it turns out that 'vista vous' is French for 'fuck you'".

We were right outside the doors to the ICU. "Listen Gail, it's time for rounds, I'll hear about..."

Gail threw her arms around me. "Tomorrow's Saturday. We both get off early. Let's spend the day..."

"Let's see how my night goes. I slept two hours last night; none the night before. I feel lousy right now." I looked at Gail. Her eyes were red. I felt like such a bastard. "I'm sorry, Gail."

"It's okay," she responded, eyes to the floor. "Maybe you'll have an easy day."

Famous last words. Three critically ill admissions rolled through the door before we had even finished rounds. Two more by noon. At four o'clock Alex sauntered over. "Gail's picking up another BFI," he said. BFI was short for 'big fucking infarct', and at the moment the unit was full of them. "There's a guy in the ER with terrible angina. I'm on my way down to pick him up."

Normally, the interns who were not on call that day only took admissions until twelve o'clock. "It's my patient, Alex."

"I'll take him. You're getting killed."

"Is that figuratively or literally?"

Alex smiled. "Figuratively I hope. I got it."

"It's after 4 pm. You'll never get out of here."

"Good. That way I can keep an eye on you." Alex patted his doctor's bag. Put bullets in this morning."

"Alex."

"Don't Alex me, Danny. Hodges told me what happened. If I were you, I'd think seriously about packing it in. Now."

The way things were going, there was little time to check in on my regular patients. In my absence, Gail found herself fending off two members of the hospital ethics committee, who, after failing to convince Gail to change Maxine's status to 'no code, comfort care', threatened to write the orders themselves. "Over my dead body," she had told them. Although she held to her belief that Maxine had no chance of recovering, she nevertheless defended my position while I was gone.

At the other end of the spectrum was Eddie Ingraham. Eddie's electrocution had spelled a rebirth; a miracle of sorts, a Munchausen patient with insight into the origins of his disease. Eddie hadn't stopped talking since he awoke after falling asleep in my arms. The shrinks were so amazed, they called their boss, the head shrink, who after examining Eddie, gathered all the other shrinks together to discuss their options. They decided that a breakthrough of this magnitude, one of the first of its kind, could, if presented appropriately, bring good publicity heaping down not only on the hospital, but on their own floundering psychoanalytic institute as well. Who knew--if Sol Goldman could raise money for a new cardiac center, Edward Ingraham might prove to be their academic meal ticket for a refurbished institute. The head shrink met with the PR department of the hospital. A call was made to a friend at WGN TV. At 5 o'clock the news cameras rolled into the coronary care unit and into Eddie Ingraham's room. On live TV, his team of psychiatrists standing at his side, Eddie revealed the macabre events of his life; the abuse, the rapes, his father's murder of his brother and mother. He spoke also of his self-inflicted injuries, displaying his scars under the bright lights. When he saw me outside his door, he tried waving me in, but I shook him off. I listened a moment while he recounted his day at the anatomy lab and saw newscaster, Carol Larue, nearly faint. His psychiatrists interrupted frequently, taking credit for Eddie's psychiatric breakthrough. They refused to reveal the specific details, but did allude to a new form of electric shock therapy.

Gail signed her patients out at 7 pm, pleading with me to get some rest. Alex stayed later. When he handed me his sign out sheet at 9, he looked worried. "Don't know if I should leave you tonight, pal."

"Quit looking at me like that Alex. Nothing's going to happen to me. Besides, Hodges is here. And there's a security guard posted outside."

Alex took deep breaths and told me everyone on his team was stable except for Mr. Cummings, his latest admission. He

500

showed me his ECG. The guy's ST segments were low enough to trip over.

"Maybe he needs an angiogram," I volunteered.

Alex nodded. "Ori Ben Gazi, the cardiology attending, knows all about him. If he gets any pain tonight, up his nitrates and heparin. If the pain is too severe, call Ben Gazi. He's sleeping in the Gardner House call rooms. He'll cath him tonight." Alex took off his doctor's coat and pulled a knit sweater over his head, his eyes full of friendly concern. "Try to get some sleep. You look like hell."

It sounded like a good idea until I remembered that in the aftermath of my trip to Atlanta, I'd forgotten to pack an overnight bag for call. I asked Alex to stay just five minutes while I ran across the street to get my stuff.

"It's dark, Danny. No way you're going over there by yourself. Come on, I'll go with you."

"Somebody's got to cover."

Alex picked up the phone and paged Malcolm Spool to the unit. Five minutes later he showed up.

"You on call for Gardner House?"

Malcolm shook his head. "I'm not on call for anything. Just finishing up some work."

"Can you cover the unit for thirty minutes?"

"Sure."

We each gave Malcolm a sign-out sheet. I thanked him. Alex flashed him a stern look. "Don't touch a single thing on any of my patients."

"If you're treating them properly, I won't have to."

Alex pushed up against Malcolm, who recoiled, not from the possibility of getting punched, but rather the fear that Alex's spit might accidentally come in contact with his face.

"Listen, motherfucker. Touch one of my patients and when I get back I'll do such a number on you that they'll write you up as case report in one of those obscure pathology journals you read. Capice?"

Malcolm nodded, his hand shielding his face. "Capice."

Chapter 109 the message

"The guy's a sleeze, Danny. He's up to no good."

"You didn't have to threaten the guy, Alex."

Alex saw Mr. Gee closing up his store and persuaded him to lay a bottle of Beck's Dark on him, which he'd chugged down by the time we got to my apartment. Leaning against my door was a Federal Express envelope with a note attached from Gertie in the building office saying she'd signed for it. I grabbed it and unlocked the door, Alex scooting in front of me and darting to the bathroom. I opened the envelope to find a single piece of paper inside.

Danny

At airport. Got to hurry. Someone scary following me. Leaving quickly. Mailing file to an old friend in Chicago. Don't even know if he still lives there. If he does, he'll get the file with instructions to get it to you when it's safe. I'm terrified, Danny.

Linda

I read it through twice, then handed it to Alex. He read silently. When he finished, his lip was bleeding. "Danny, I don't think you should go back to the hospital tonight."

"Alex, the file may still be out there. It may still come to me."

Alex grabbed my shoulders. "Don't you see, Danny? If Tannenbaum and his cronies don't have the file, they're going to make damn sure you don't get it either." He shook me. "This ain't no fucking game anymore, Danny. You're at the top of their most wanted list."

I'd never seen Alex like this. Usually he was Mr. Cool, the intern Rock of Gilbralter. I grabbed my toothbrush, pulled a peanut butter cup from the freezer and opened the front door. "It'll be okay, Alex."

As we walked back across the parking lot, I thought about Linda. There was no way to know where she'd sent the file. If her friend had moved, the file probably would be sent back to whatever return address she'd listed, maybe even a fictitious one. Smart thinking, Linda.

In the fifteen minutes we were gone, Malcolm had rewritten at least a half-dozen orders. Alex gritted his teeth. "I ought to kick your ass."

Malcolm brushed his hair back to one side with arrogance. "I was trying to save Daniel time so he can get some sleep." He turned to me. "You look tired from your journey."

"How do you know about..."

"I told you he was a ferret," interrupted Alex. We asked Malcolm to enlighten us about his new orders. Most, it turned out, concerned Alex's patient, Mr. Cummings. "Look at this ECG," he said. "The ST segments dropped two millimeters with his last episode of chest pain. I gave him a bolus of heparin and upped his nitro."

Alex turned to Brenda. "Give me a syringe of Valium." When she returned with it a minute later Alex went into Mr. Cumming's room.

"How much did you give?" asked Malcolm when Alex came back.

"Ten milligrams, not that it's any of your business."

"Ten milligrams?" we both repeated. "That'll put the guy in a coma," I said.

"And how will you know he's having chest pain if he's asleep?" added Malcolm.

"Same way you'd know a bear shit in the woods if no one was there to see it. We'd smell it in the morning."

Malcolm reddened. I suppressed a smile.

"Look," said Alex. "Sleep lowers the oxygen requirement of the heart. He sleeps. You sleep."

Around midnight, finding no prospective admission down in the emergency room, my resident, Charles O'Bannon, left the hospital for the night. The Unit was quiet and dark, save a few IV alarms buzzing and flashing, and the computer spitting out ECG strips. I sat at the nursing module finishing up progress notes and eating left over pineapple chicken. I felt a pair of hands on my shoulders, immediately knowing they belonged to Brenda, the charge nurse on nights.

"Get some shut-eye while you have the chance. My girls and I can handle everything."

If I had been in a more playful mood I might have remarked about whether or not that included shocking Eddie Ingraham out of the v-fib he never had. I held my tongue. The nurses here were good, maybe the best in the hospital. Eddie had fooled practically everyone.

"Everybody's asleep," she said.

"How can you tell, with the TV cameras on the blink?" Normally you could sit at the central nursing module and watch each patient via a series of overhead monitors. The feed from each patient's camera into the central hook-up had broken earlier that afternoon.

Brenda reached for a fortune cookie. "We do make our evening vital signs check, Dr. Raskin. Believe me, all is quiet. Even Mr. Cummings hasn't stirred since Dr. Rosen gave him that near-lethal dose of Valium."

"He needs his sleep, Brenda. He'll probably go for a coronary angiogram first thing in the morning."

On my way to the call room, I stopped by Jack Hodges's room. I hadn't had a chance to see him privately since my return from Atlanta, and considering what had gone on, I was sure he thought I was purposely avoiding him. Jack Hodges lay in bed, his head elevated to forty five degrees. His eyes were lightly shut. "Jack," I whispered, touching his shoulder.

He jumped, his hand instinctively reaching behind his pillow.

"Don't shoot. You'll ruin it for the bad guys." Jack rubbed the sleep from his eyes. I sat down next to him on the bed. "I take it you heard about my great vacation to Atlanta?"

"Look on the bright side. All those frequent flyer miles."

"You wouldn't be joking if you'd ridden home from the airport with me and your boss. He wanted to kill me."

Jack ran his hand through his silky hair, still groomed to perfection. The room reeked of aftershave. "If you ask me, what you did took a lot of courage."

"Stupidity is more like it."

"Courage, Danny. In all my years with my sector, I've never met a civilian willing to put his life on the line the way you have. Anybody else would have been out of here. Or out of his mind by now."

"Now that works for me."

"Cut it out, Danny. No matter what happens, you've done everything you could. You even sucker punched that shit of an agent, Phil Warshinski."

"So what happens now, Jack?"

He shrugged. "Guess you go and finish off at some no-name hospital under an assume identity and federal protection. At least until you're out of danger."

"And when is that?"

"They'll crack this case sooner or later."

"And what about you, Jack?"

"I'm leaving."

"What?"

"Got me a great job in LA. Head of the second largest security firm in the city. Double the salary, great bennies. And it's mostly office work."

"I thought you liked the shoot 'em up stuff."

Jack reached behind him and turned on a night light. He opened the side drawer and pulled out a picture. "Just had our third kid, " he said proudly. "Forty three years old and a new father again. Jennie wants me to take better care of myself. I agree."

"I'll miss giving you nitro headaches and loose bowel movements. I think for a going away present I'll order you an enema."

"I'll miss you, too, Danny."

Chapter 110 messenger of death

"Danny!"

I shifted on my mattress. My dream had me far away on a nude beach with Gail, making love in the rolling waves.

"Danny!"

I turned over and looked right into the whites of someone's eyes. "Huh?"

"It's me, Brenda."

I turned over, peeking under the covers just to make sure Gail was only a dream. The fluorescent clock said 3:15 a.m. "What's wrong?"

"Mr. Cummings. Dr. Rosen's patient. Chest pain. Big time." She turned on the lamp next to my bed.

"Hey!" My eyes burned.

"Look at this ECG."

My mind wasn't working. Three hours of rest after two almost sleepless nights had thrown me off. I felt my eyes shutting.

"Danny! Didn't you hear me? He has chest pain."

"Uh... uh.. How about an enema?"

Brenda turned on the overhead light.

"Ouch!"

"Danny. Listen to me. Mr. Cummings is in trouble."

I looked at the ECG. Severe ischemia.

"We've given him three nitros and I started a Lidocaine drip," Brenda said.

"Let's go."

"Leave the light off, "Brenda said as we walked into his room. "The light really bothers him."

"Glad to see you're suddenly so considerate," I said, still seeing white spots. The heart monitor above Mr. Cumming's bed flashed premature ventricular beats, many occurring in salvos of three and four. I asked for and received a 50 milligram syringe of Lidocaine and pushed it into his IV port.

"We better start another IV, Brenda."

"Already did," she replied, lifting the sheet off his other arm. "Lot of dirt under the alcohol swab."

"Mr. Cummings," I said. "I'm Dr. Raskin. Are you having chest pain?" Through the darkness, I made out a man who was suffering. Lots of unkempt hair, scraggly mustache. Long, outdated sideburns. A weak, almost inaudible whisper.

"Death is here, Doc." He clutched his chest.

"Shit," I said under my breath. I hated patient premonitions. They always seemed to be right. I took his hand in mine. It was limp and cold. "Nonsense, Mr. Cummings. We'll have this under control in no time."

"It's too late," he gasped.

Just then his monitor showed a seven beat run of V-tach. "Brenda, call the cardiology attending, stat."

"I already did. Ben Gazi's not answering his page."

"He's sleeping in the four Gardner House call suites. You better run up and get him."

Brenda hurried from the room.

I felt a chill. The room was so dark, the heart monitor so ominously green that the shadow of Mr. Cumming's face made him look like a Martian. "Everything will be okay," I said applying some nitroglycerin ointment to his chest. He had the outlines of a tattoo on one arm but I couldn't make it out.

"Hear my confession," Mr. Cummings whispered. Again, he clutched his chest. "Death is so close. Can't you feel it?" I swear I could. I moved closer. If he wanted a confession, I'd better take it. Just in case. I leaned over him, trying to see into the poor man's eyes, but they were closed. "Please, time for a confession," he said, barely audible.

"Sure," I said. "But I promise you're not going to die."

"It's not me I'm talking about," he said. His eyes opened wide and before I had time to be afraid, two hands were around my throat. Those eyes. *Lots of dirt came off with the alcohol swab.* Tannenbaum! I struggled. The grip tightened.

"Time to die, Jewboy! Scum of the earth. All of you." His arms were vices. I clawed, scratched, tried to scream. Nothing worked. My foot went for an IV pole, just missing. I sucked for breath. None came. Nothing. Dizzy. Room spinning, hazy. Saw

507

my father, my mother. Tiger Stadium. Felt myself beginning to relax. Life draining through my bones. A light.

An explosion rocked the room.

I felt myself falling. I was dead. Blown to pieces. Wait. A breath. A taste of air. Arms releasing me. Wetness-- my face, my arms. A light. I turned. Alex. Standing two feet away holding a gun. I looked down. Tannenbaum lay there, gray eyes bulging out. The left half of his face was gone, only bone and bloody pulp remaining. I rubbed the wetness from my own cheek, looking down at my arms. Brain tissue. Blood. I fell backward off the bed, passing out on the floor.

Chapter 111 aftermath

I came to an hour later. I was lying in the only vacant bed in the unit. Cold compresses hugged my neck. Alex was there. So were Sol Goldman and James Huber.

Huber was sucking the end of an unlit cigar. "You can thank your friend Alex here. You owe him big time." But Huber wasn't smiling.

"Thanks Alex. But how did you..."

"Couldn't sleep," he answered. "Just had this feeling," he said sheepishly. "It's hard to explain."

I scooted up in the bed. "It was Tannenbaum, wasn't it?"

"The one and only," said Huber solemnly. He and Sol both looked grave.

"What's wrong?"

Huber bit at his cigar. "We arrested Malcolm Spool."

"What?"

"I told you," said Alex.

"We think he's the inside operative who's been helping Tannenbaum."

"Impossible." I turned my head. A pain shot up the left side of my face.

"We're not positive," said Sol. "But our computer analysis puts him in the hospital during each of the murders over the past ten months."

"He tripped up tonight," said Huber. "We found him a few minutes ago hiding out in the library."

"Malcolm doesn't hide in libraries. He lives there. He didn't do anything. He certainly didn't try to kill me."

Huber moved closer. "Dr. Spool had a different agenda."

"What? Who?" But as I spoke, I realized who was missing.

"Where's Jack Hodges?"

Goldman and Huber looked at each other as if in a mental game of drawing straws. Huber put a hand on my shoulder. "We believe that sometime in the past two hours, Malcolm Spool piggy backed an ampule of concentrated ergonovine and pavulon into Jack Hodges normal IV solution. Nobody noticed anything until he suffered cardiac and respiratory arrest twenty minutes ago."

I closed my eyes. "Is he dead?"

"Afraid so."

"Oh God," I said. And then, hero that I was, I started to cry.

Chapter 112 gail peterson

I took a week's vacation.

At Gail Peterson's apartment.

We made love on hardwood linoleum, on fluffy sofa cushions, in bouquets of strawberry bath bubbles in which I lightly caressed her sudsy breasts. We kissed while we ate pizza and drank Merlot; we groped each other as we ripped through the Tribune's funny pages spread across her bed. We made up for months of denying our most instinctive feelings for fear of losing the friendship we had. At times we made love vigorously, almost with a vengeance, as if to expunge the demons. Gail climaxed the hardest, her cheekbones tense, her freckles alive, her screams as if awakening from a nightmare that kept coming and coming. At times we were like two gumbies flexing at every joint, reinventing Kama Sutra, discovering erogenous zones we never knew we had. As morning broke, our kisses were soft and light, our caresses gentle, we held each other like babies, fell asleep within each other, merged into one body and soul, then awakened to a gentle rhythmic movement, like a metronome, with no real beginning. A rhythm that gradually peaked to allegro; gymnastics before breakfast. I had always prided myself on knowing the difference between sex with and without love, preferring the former. But never before had I realized the power of mixing love, danger, death, and rebirth. With Gail I was reborn, the ugly demons exorcised forever from within. A new soul emerged, a soul with a partner, a soul mate---a term with real meaning for me now.

Chapter 113 vice president barrish

A thunderous ovation rose from the overflowing crowd in Richard Meese auditorium as Vice-President Harold Barrish spoke of his ties to the city and hospital. On stage with him sat three secret service agents, straight faced, though certainly less nervous than they would have been if Tannenbaum were still on the loose. Also on stage was a smiling Sol Goldman, his white coat so clean it looked like it had been given an intravenous infusion of starch. James Huber, FBI, sat next to Sol, a place of honor I supposed, twiddling a plastic wrapped cigar in his hands. On the other side of Sol sat Emile Horner, neck still in a brace, teak cane across his lap, smiling triumphantly.

I sat in the third row of the audience next to Gail, our hands clasped so tightly that the electricity traveled right into my groin, causing a stirring which was not lost on Gail. "You're an animal," she whispered then ran her index finger quickly down my leg.

The Vice-President had come, finally. Goldman had said I should take great pride in knowing I had played a part in his appearance. But I didn't. I still felt uncomfortable about Barrish being there. Was it really over like everyone said? Had it really ended with the death of Frank Tannenbaum and the arrest of Malcolm Spool? I would have thought not, but in fact, everything seemed back to normal.

Goldman said it wasn't only Meese that suddenly had gone quiet. Suspicious deaths in hospitals across the country had ceased. Tannenbaum must have been a key national operative, so big that his generals had called a temporary moratorium in order to assess the damage. Huber thought they were scared, watching with trepidation to see where the trail of Tannenbaum's death led.

Frank Tannenbaum's real name was Gregory Jardine. Through finger prints and dental records his life unfolded into the saga of a hero gone wrong. Three medals in Korea. Special forces in Vietnam. A year after the war, two years in Paris, one in Damascus, and then nothing for six years. One arrest record in

New York city for assault. A move to Chicago. Employment as housekeeper Thaddeus Anderson right around the time the murders began at Richard Meese. Then as escort Jimmi Redding. Also through his fingerprints, we reconfirmed Tannenbaum's personal interest in my case. Prints were all over the baseball bat that felled me that summer night jogging on the lake front. The only thing he couldn't be tied to was Linda Johnson's death.

All this went in and out of my mind as Barrish spoke about how lucky he had been as a lower middle class Jewish kid who fought the odds and became Vice President. I felt lucky just to be sitting there listening to him. But what about the others-- Wanda, Linda, Jack Hodges? How could I ever wash away their memories?

Without looking at me, Gail instinctively squeezed my hand. Even though I was back at work, our personal vacation had continued. We were together night and day, both inside and outside the confines of Richard Meese. We made love in the call room, groped each other in the solitude of an empty radiology suite. We took walks at lunch time, visited the lake, drank Chablis while we watched Eddie Ingraham on the Oprah Winfrey show. Eddie had a book contract and offers were in the works for a TV movie based on his life. Eddie, true to form, wanted to play himself.

Our love-making sessions continued to be of marathon length and intensity, and I noticed I had lost three pounds since our aerobics had begun. But mostly Gail kept me afloat, holding me in the middle of the night when I woke up screaming hysterically, either about murder and blood and torture, or when I saw myself being filleted with a sharp razor by Tannenbaum, or when a pair of hands around my neck made me gasp for breath, unable for a moment to separate dreams from reality.

There were still loose ends in the case, perhaps they'd never be closed. The infamous file never had materialized. Two weeks had passed since Linda Johnson's Fed Ex. I assumed that neither I nor anyone else would ever see the file again. Perhaps it was better that way. Maybe the Friends of Tomorrow had gotten the message.

Then there was Malcolm Spool. Since his arrest, even Mulroney came out of the woodwork saying he knew it was Malcolm Spool all along. In fact, far as I could tell, I was a lone voice in his support. I knew Malcolm better than most, had gotten used to his pecadillos, even seeing some of them as an advantage. He was brilliant and arrogant, obsessive and compulsive. But a killer? Despite the death of Hodges and the fact that Malcolm had been in the vicinity at the time, despite the fact that computers had placed him in the hospital during each of the murders during the past year, I still couldn't believe it. I couldn't help but think that murder was just too messy for Malcolm Spool.

Gail went with me when I visited him at a high-security lock up downtown. He was slumped at a table, his head resting in his hands when we walked in, not even looking up, thinking it was just another FBI interrogator coming to see him. When he realized who it was, he forced his lips into a weak smile. "How's Maxine?" he asked.

"Same," I nodded. We sat with Malcolm in silence. His hair was greasy, his face an unkempt garden of stubble, and his body smelled of a three day hygienic sabbatical. Malcolm was a mess.

"I can't take it much longer, Danny. My father refuses to talk to me. My family's written me off. The Feds think I'm worse than Benedict Arnold. Nobody believes me."

My hand touched the glass barrier in an effort to comfort him. "I believe you, Malcolm."

Malcolm placed his hand up to the glass, silhouetting mine. A large tear rolled down his face. "Thanks. But it doesn't matter. They got me at the hospital during each of the murders. Circumstantial evidence is going to send me away forever."

"They don't know you like I do, Malcolm. Killing is a dirty business. You're too obsessed with cleanliness to be a killer."

"Thanks," he said, managing a smile. "If I don't see you again...."

"Don't you dare," said Gail.

"Not that," said Malcolm. "They're transferring me to some place in Kentucky. They're going to offer me a deal. Testify about everything I know in exchange for immunity."

"Sounds good."

"But I don't know anything. I didn't do anything. I can't even speculate, Danny. You know me. Just the facts."

The sound of clapping caught my attention. Harold Barrish was saying how important it was to not abandon the embattled south side of Chicago and that poor people, those disenfranchised from society, needed hospitals like Richard Meese to be their shining star in an otherwise ominous sky.

"Wake up, Danny," Gail whispered.

Gail was right. It was time to wake up, to forget the past. In one week, a brand new set of interns would be showing up, clean white coats and cheerful looks of anticipation. We would turn in our short-range beepers in exchange for long-range models. We were no longer interns, the neophytes of the profession. We were on our way to becoming residents. Authorities. Despite all that had happened during the year, I was ready to be a resident. I was ready to leave this year behind--with one exception.

Maxine Chu.

Maxine was still as comatose as the day after her cardiac and respiratory arrest. The next day, by way of edict from the hospital ethics committee, she was being transferred out of the Unit and into the Logan Pines nursing facility on the adjacent property. There would be no further medical care offered; no IV hydration, no medicine, no charting. At best, Maxine would last three days. The worst part was that from an oncologic point, Maxine was free of Hodgkins disease. Like the old joke, the operation was a success, but the patient died.

I had let her down. Some nine months before, a fortune cookie, three wishes. The last: *'cure me'*. I could never forget Maxine, never forgive myself.

The audience rose in one giant wave of applause. Sol Goldman shook the Vice President's hand and asked everyone to move to the large tent set up adjacent to Gardner House Pavilion, where the ground would be broken for the new cardiac

517

center. Following this, the Vice President would be escorted into the outdated Ida and Sol Bloom Cardiac Center. Goldman had kept his word about allowing me, Alex, and Gail to accompany the cardiologist and two secret service agents while Barrish performed his thallium-treadmill test. Then, assuming Barrish passed all his tests, we would join the invited dignitaries on a makeshift terrace in the gardens in back of Gardner House Pavilion, where a five course lunch would be served.

The bulldozers had cleared an area adjacent to Gardner House Pavilion where the new cardiac center would be constructed. A podium up front, two rows of chairs for the dignitaries, and a wide red and blue ribbon hung across what was to be the front entrance. The sun was bright and warm, and a grove of lilacs scented the fresh air. I yawned during the speeches, yet the butterflies in my stomach reminded me of the anxiety I had about the Vice President's treadmill. What if he got chest pain during the test? What if, God forbid, he suffered a cardiac arrest? And worst of all, what if by some chance the killer was still out there? What if he found a way to get into the cardiac suite while the Vice President was running half-naked on a treadmill? Why the hell wasn't there more security?

As I was contemplating how I would resuscitate the Vice President, my beeper sounded.

"Call the Unit, stat!"

I looked at Gail.

The beeper sounded again and I took off for one of the wall phones.

Brenda answered. "Come quick. It's Maxine."

Chapter 114 maxine chu

I fought back tears as I ran the quarter mile to the ICU, leaving Gail well behind. From a distance, I could see Brenda just outside the unit, yelling, waving her hands. When I reached her, she grabbed my shoulders.

"She's dead?"

Brenda grinned and shook her head. "Maxine just opened her eyes!"

When I got to Maxine's room, the commotion was beyond belief. Wall to wall bodies filled the room, even blocking the doorway. Neurologists, members of the medical ethics team, nurses, chaplains. At the door, someone said my name and there was a sudden hush. The crowd parted like the Red Sea. I ran to her bedside. Maxine's eyes were open and gazing at the ceiling, roving back and forth like radar. Her body was still.

"Maxine, can you hear me?"

"She's not responding," a neuro attending offered. "She may stay like this forever. It's called a 'locked-in-syndrome'."

"No way," I snapped. I'd about had it with neurologic predictions. I knelt down, patting her hand. "Maxine, can you hear me?" No response. The neurologist folded his arms across his chest, his smug look making me want to slap him. I rested my palm on hers, leaned over and whispered, "Squeeze my hand, Maxine. Please. Squeeze my hand."

"I don't think that she..."

"Shut up!" I yelled. Several nurses nodded nervously. I stroked her palm with my fingers, ran my other hand over her forehead. "Please Maxine. If you can hear me...if you understand, squeeze my hand."

Nothing. As I was about to let go. I felt something. A slight flexing of her palm just barely touching mine. "Maxine."

And then the impossible happened. With twenty onlookers holding their breaths, Maxine's hand slowly cupped its way over mine, squeezing it like a warm hug. I looked at her, clearly seeing her lips curl into a small smile. Applause broke out from every corner. My cheeks were hot with tears, my eyes a total mist. I continued to clutch her hand. Brenda tapped Maxine's feet together. "There's no place like home, Maxine Chu. There's no place like home."

"Damndest thing I've ever seen," said the attending neurologist, who had joined his cocky senior resident. "Makes a great case report."

I stood up and hugged all the nurses, especially Brenda. I saw Gail run in. "Oh my God!" she yelled. "It's a miracle."

And as we hugged each other, crying, I did something I hadn't done since I was a school kid. I said a prayer of thanks.

Chapter 115 treadmill

Standing at the back of the Cardiology suite along with Gail and Chief Huber, I watched with anticipation as the treadmill machine simultaneously increased its speed and degree of incline. Harold Barrish gripped the side rails with resolute determination, his triceps bulging through the sleeves of his Chicago Bears tee shirt.

"Not bad for a guy who eats corned beef twice a week," he panted, picking up his pace.

Dr. Ori Ben Gazi, Cardiology attending, nodded approvingly as the state of the art computer destined for the new facility spat out an integrated analysis of the ST segments from his ECG as well as his blood pressure and heart rate responses. "Half-way there, Mr. Vice President." He nodded at Alex, who leaned over and checked the patency of the Vice-President's heparin lock, which had been taped securely over his forearm and directly over the vein it had been inserted into. Alex attached a small syringe filled with saline and pulled back until he aspirated a flec of blood into his syringe.

"Works fine," Alex said, smiling broadly. "You have great veins, Mr. Vice President, if you don't mind my saying so."

The heparin lock would be used to inject the radioisotope, thallium, at the peak of exercise, where it would circulate into the coronary system. Any obstruction in the arteries supplying the heart muscles would be picked up as a 'cold spot' by the nuclear scanner that Vice President Barrish would be placed under immediately following exercise.

James Huber nudged me with his shoulder. "Nice little party, huh?"

That was an understatement. Not only was I in the same room as the Vice President of the United States, but just an hour before, Maxine Chu, against all conceivable odds, had awakened from her coma. I tried thinking of a better, more rewarding day in my whole life, and the only thing that came close was the day I won our little league world series game with a last inning homer fifteen years before.

I watched as sweat dripped down the Vice President's neck. Life wasn't so bad after all, I thought. Internship just about over, residency with its more humane call schedules just around the corner. Gail Peterson. Maxine. Just as I was about to slip into a peaceful comfort zone, I was overcome by a pounding anxiety. Things were just too perfect, too quiet. The Vice President was here, in the same hospital where just weeks before, murders had taken place. Until Tannenbaum was killed and Malcolm Spool was arrested, the V.P.'s trip had been dangerously close to being canceled.

I looked over at the agent guarding the door. The only other entrance had been sealed off and triple bolted. There was just one guard, plus Huber, who for all I knew hadn't fired a weapon since Korea. Huber himself seemed a picture of relaxation, which really bothered me. He was leaning against the wall, shirt collar loosened, sleeves rolled to the elbow, chewing the end of an unlit cigar--acting like he was a spectator at some damn sporting event. He had, in fact, placed a five dollar bet with Alex that Barrish wouldn't reach his peak heart rate.

As far as Huber was concerned, the murders at Richard Meese Hospital were as good as closed. Tannenbaum was dead, Malcolm Spool in lock-up at Cook County jail. Huber could play pass the popcorn and enjoy the horse race, all the while knowing there was a promotion looming in his future, a good chance he'd be kicked up the ladder all the way to D.C. as an assistant to the big cheese himself.

But what if Huber was wrong?

What if Malcolm Spool was innocent?

"Quit playing detective," Huber would snap each time I brought up the subject, and I was starting to think that perhaps he was right. I suppose I should have spent more time playing intern, at least it was something I was trained to do, rather than trying to solve crimes that had begun long before I came to Chicago. And besides, the murders had stopped since Malcolm had been removed from the hospital. That had to mean something, didn't it?

Gail flashed a sheepish look as I reached past the guard and once again checked to make sure the door was securely locked.

The guard, a burly man in his forties, eyed me suspiciously. My neck felt damp under my collar. I yearned to take off my white coat which had been starched into cardboard. The treadmill sped up and Barrish began to jog. I looked up at the monitor, watching his heart rate climb past one hundred and forty.

"One minute left," called Dr. Ben Gazi. He turned to Alex, who handed him the premixed syringe of saline and thallium. Once the Vice-President reached ninety percent of his maximum predicted heart rate, Ben Gazi would inject the solution into the heparin lock which emptied into a forearm vein. Thirty seconds later, the treadmill would stop and the VP would be hustled into the nuclear imager, which would assess the thallium uptake into his coronary arteries. Normal counts meant good blood flow and normal coronary arteries.

Vice President Barrish wiped the sweat from his eyes. "A minute's about all the gas I have left. At this rate I'm going to be too tired for that lunch."

I looked around the room, my eyes settling on Alex. Me and Alex, there for each other since that Nazi rally at Daley Plaza, so long ago. I turned and looked at Gail, now perhaps the most important person in my life. Next to her was Huber, a pithy, pungent character, almost more Central Casting than real FBI agent. I was sure Huber saw himself that way, too, a classic cigar smoking tough guy destined for bigger and better things. The agency was his life, he absorbed it like oxygen. But something had always troubled me about Huber and I never quite understood it. According to Eddie Ingraham, Huber had tapped my home telephone, which meant he might have overheard my initial conversation with Linda Johnson. Consequently, he might have known she'd had Cantrell's missing file, and possibly even of my plan to fly down and meet her. Obviously someone besides me had gotten that information, perhaps the same person who ripped all the Johnson listings out of the Atlanta phone book. Huber was the most obvious possibility, and he was even capable of tapping into my airline reservations to Atlanta. I looked over at Huber, suddenly feeling the kind of unnerving chill you'd experience scraping your nails on a chalk board. Huber's eyes found mine, his pupils wide and intense.

"Is it you, Huber?" My heart skipped a beat.

Huber continued his stare. "You know, you're a damn good detective, Raskin," he whispered. "It would take someone with a special talent to pick up the scent of a subtle fart and then be able to trace it back to the asshole it originated from." Huber laughed so loud that the VP momentarily turned.

"Sorry to disturb you, Mr. Vice President," he said, then shot me a look that said he was sorry I was ever born.

Come on Raskin, I told myself. Stop letting paranoia get the best of you. Huber was Fed all the way.

I looked up as Dr. Ben-Gazi raised his syringe into the air and squirted out the excess air, a small bit of liquid escaping in the process. Ori Ben-Gazi, I thought. Mid-east accent, deep set, almost hypnotic dark marble eyes, emigrated from Israel. Obviously he wouldn't be here if there was any question of his..... My thoughts were intercepted by a smell, not coming from Huber; something else, a recognizable odor. I sniffed again, then turned to Huber. "You smell something?" Huber waved me off with his hand and an angry stare.

Almonds. Mrs. Garber's vial. Ergonovine and pavulon. Almonds! Then newspaper headlines: *Chief Justice Rosenberg died of a heart attack after an apparently normal thallium test.*

My God, there was ergonovine in the thallium! I ran toward Ben Gazi just as his needle penetrated the rubber opening of the heparin lock, and as his finger pushed forward on the syringe, I launched myself into the air, over the treadmill, and with outstretched arms knocked Ben-Gazi off his feet, the syringe flying from his grip and smashing into the wall. Huber was there a second later, gun drawn, as if suddenly awakened from a deep slumber. Ben-Gazi rolled out from under me, horror on his face.

"What the hell is going on?" he screamed, looking at Huber.

"It's him!" I yelled, putting my hands on Ben-Gazi's shoulders, keeping him down on the floor. "He's the killer. It's not Malcolm Spool, it's him! And that thallium is laced with ergonovine!"

Huber grabbed me by my white coat and lifted me off of Ben-Gazi. "You're a fool, Raskin! Ori is working with us."

What?

"He's been here for over a year, on FBI payroll. He's on leave from the Mossad!"

I got to my feet and straightened my coat. Ben Gazi? An Israeli agent? Here with us. I felt like an idiot. All eyes were on me, including the Vice President's. I sniffed again, a slight scent of almonds lingering in the air. I looked at Huber defiantly. "How do you know that thallium doesn't contain ergonovine and pavulon?" I asked.

Alex put his arm around my shoulder. "Because we made it ourselves, Danny." Alex saw the embarrassment creep across my face. He turned toward the Vice-President. "Dr. Raskin's intentions are good, I assure you."

Vice President Barrish's breathing had returned to normal, but the sweat continued to accumulate. Huber handed him a towel. He wiped his face, then under his arms. "What will it take to finish the test?"

Huber looked at Alex and Ori Ben Gazi. "Can we get some more of that stuff?"

"It will take about ten minutes to prepare," answered Ben Gazi.

"We keep a supply in the minus twenty freezer," said Alex.

Vice President Barrish wiped his forehead. "I can't go another fifteen minutes," he said wearily.

"What about five minutes?" asked Ben Gazi. "We could probably do it with an additional five minutes of treadmill time."

Barrish nodded. "All right then." He stood up and looked me in the eye. "Young man, I hope you at least had the decency to vote Democratic in the last election," he said and smiled.

"I'm really sorry, Mr. Vice President."

"No apology required," said Barrish. "I've heard some good things about you from Sol Goldman."

"I was only trying to help."

"That's what we have security for." Huber turned toward the V.P. "This intern beat the crap out of one of our best agents, now he wrestles down an elite veteran of the Mossad. Maybe we ought to bring him into the fold."

Before I could register whether or not Huber had just thrown a compliment my way, my beeper sounded.

"Would you answer that?" said Gail. "It's the third time it's gone off." Obviously I'd been too absorbed trying to protect the Vice-President to hear it before. She came over to my side. "Never mind. I'll do it. You've had enough for one day." Gail went into the adjoining room and a minute later returned. "It's Gertie Katz, your apartment supervisor. She says it can't wait."

I left the room and picked up the phone. "Gertie, you know you're not supposed to call me here unless it's an emergency."

"Some guy is standing here who insists on talking to you. Wouldn't leave unless I found you."

There was a pause on the line.

"Dr. Raskin?" The voice was heavy.

"Speaking."

"I have something for you."

"What might that be?" I asked sarcastically.

"A small metal file. Courtesy of Linda Johnson."

Chapter 116 the file

I ran faster than I ever remembered, dodging cars, challenging red lights. I'd refused to tell anyone what was important enough for me to part company temporarily with the Vice President, mainly because I thought it had to be a joke. Or worse, I thought while running, a set-up.

Before entering Gertie's office, I peered inside through half-open shades. A blonde-haired kid in his twenties, wearing cutoffs and topsiders was standing there, hands in his pockets. On the desk next to him was the pewter colored strongbox I had taken from Charles Cantrell.

For a moment, as I opened the office door, I thought I was going to pass out.

"You okay?" asked Gertie, looking concerned.

The young man walked over and handed me the file. "Sorry it took so long. Linda sent it to my old address. Somebody signed for it thinking they could find me. I've moved twice since then. How's Linda doing, anyway?"

Chapter 117 discovery

I was amazed that the file's lock jimmied open so easily with only a twist of my name tag pin. Then again, why would Charles Cantrell ever have worried that someone would steal this from inside a locked cabinet in his office? I lifted open the metal fastener just as the traffic light turned green, letting me cross the street. On the first page I lifted out the words 'Friends of Tomorrow' were emblazoned in gold. Two swastikas and a burning cross were painted across the bottom. I took two steps into the street then backed up to the curb. I was trembling as I began turning the pages. I had before me a dossier, a roster of operatives. No wonder they wanted this thing so badly. Complete biographies on their members, including training, accomplishments, awards. Charles Cantrell was listed on the first page--Secretary General of Friends of Tomorrow. On the next page, I recognized another dean, James Bramwell from Sol Goldman's photos. There were more, many more. Deans. Professors of medicine. Even if I didn't recognize the faces, the names of many were familiar. Among them were medical giants, some having written their own textbooks. Some authors of classic papers about classic diseases.

Suddenly I realized that I was supposed to be back at the V.P.'s treadmill. I quickened my pace but re-opened the book to the second tab, beginning a new section, entitled, "Soldiers of the Fourth Reich." I flipped a couple of pages then spotted him. Frank Tannenbaum. There he was, the bastard. Specialties: poison, explosives, impersonation.

I kept reading, a feeling of dread enveloping my body. One tab was left. I lifted it open as I crossed into the ER parking lot. The top page tore at my soul.

Agenda: Friends of Tomorrow.
Item 1 Assassination of Vice President of the United States, Harold T. Barrish.

I looked at the date at the bottom of the page: June 15th. Today.

I ran across the parking lot and into the emergency room. "Where's Officer Mulroney?" Someone looked up and said: "I think he's off shift."

"No," said one of the nurses. " He just brought in a drunk from a two car accident."

I ran across the hall and saw him standing above a gurney. I grabbed him by the collar. "Mulroney, Mulroney! Help. They're going to kill him!" I could barely get the words out. I could barely get my breath. "The Vice President, Mulroney! They're going to kill the Vice President."

Mulroney shot me a look, like I was some stoned out street kid looking for a fix. He looked at his watch. "Aren't you supposed to be doing a treadmill?"

"Friends of Tomorrow, Mulroney. I got the missing file. I found the file!"

It still didn't register with Mulroney. I opened the book to the third tab and ripped out a fistful of pages. "Here, dammit!" I shoved them into his hands. "Look at these, then get some help. Call the Feds and get them to the treadmill room before its too late."

I took off running. At the end of the hallway, I turned back. Mulroney was still filling out his report on the drunk, ignoring me completely.

Chapter 118 confrontation

It seemed like I pounded forever on the door of the Cardiology suite before the guard finally opened the door. I pushed past him into the middle of the room. Vice President Barrish, looking very tired, turned around.

"Stop the treadmill!" I sprinted to the machine, but Huber grabbed for me. Alex blocked my way. "Not again," said Huber.

"Cool it, Danny," advised Alex.

Huber pulled me to a chair. "Sit your ass down. And stay there."

I could hardly catch my breath. "I got the file. I found Cantrell's missing file!"

Gail stood up, eyes wide. Huber took a step toward me.

Only Alex remained calm and in place. "We'll be done in a minute." He handed the syringe to Ben Gazi.

Vice President Barrish turned around. "What file?"

Huber slipped behind me and said softly: "Good work, Raskin. But we don't need to bore the Vice-President with extraneous details..."

"It's a plot!" Tannenbaum, Cantrell. Everybody's in there and there's a plot to..."

"Shut up!" yelled Huber.

But I wouldn't. "There's a plot to kill the Vice President. Today. June Fifteenth. It's right here!" I slammed down the book.

Barrish turned and stared as Ben Gazi checked the treadmill readings.

"Don't let them inject that thallium, Mr. Vice President. It's poisoned!"

Harold Barrish stepped off the treadmill-sweat pouring from his face. Huber was furious. "Keep your mouth shut, Raskin. If your book is so important why don't you see what you can find out about your buddy, Malcolm Spool?"

Huber had a point. If Malcolm wasn't in the book that meant he couldn't have been the inside operative who'd killed Jack Hodges. Which meant someone else was still out there. I turned to where I had ripped out the third tab and began working backward in the second section.

"Twenty more seconds, Mr. Vice President." Ben Gazi was readying his syringe. I looked up. Alex's eyes were stern, preoccupied.. I found the S's: Stalbach then, one more page Rosenstein.. I let out a breath. It wasn't there! Malcolm Spool's name wasn't there. "He's not one of them, Huber! Spool's not in here!" I flipped back one more page.

Stalbach...Rosenstein....Rosen. I lifted my head but it was too late.

Alex Rosen had already ripped his revolver out from under the med cart and aimed it at the guard by the door. It spit softly, and the guard clutched at his face where his left eye had been. Blood pulsed out between his limp fingers as he slid to the floor. A second later I heard another sound and turned. Huber was leaning against the wall, his hand reaching inside his sport coat. A small hole instantly appeared in the middle of his forehead. Huber appeared wide-eyed, disbelieving. A trickle of blood slid down his face as his bladder relaxed and he fell into a heap on the floor. Alex quickly reached around and caught Ori Ben-Gazi by the neck. There was a sharp jerking movement followed by a loud popping sound. Ori Ben-Gazi slumped to the floor, dead.

Alex had hardly broken a sweat and now looked over at the Vice President, then at Gail, and finally at me.

"So, Danny boy. You were about to read something in that file. Something about an agent code-named Alex Rosen?" He looked at his watch and smiled. "Take heart my friend. I have something special in mind for you and your other acquaintances."

Chapter 119 Jonathan Pentarsky

Alex Rosen was really Jonathan Pentarsky of Portland, Oregon. At the age of six, while at a children's coop, it was discovered that his intelligence, manual dexterity, and ability at sports was three years ahead of everyone else. His parents, father a machinist, mother a secretary, were visited by several agents, reportedly from the U.S. government, who convinced them to allow Alex to undergo a series of tests. Following skeletal muscle fiber analysis, several brain biopsies, and a bevy of advanced intelligence tests, Alex's parents were told that their son qualified for an elite tract of education and training that would prepare him for a powerful, secretive branch of government service known only as K-41-B. Both parents, staunch anti-Communists, eagerly consented, especially when presented with a promise of a yearly stipend of forty thousand dollars.

Alex attended the top prep schools in both the United States and Europe. He also received a second education, the teaching of which took place in outposts like Ulster, Beirut, and Saudi Arabia, all before he was eighteen years old. At that time he was brought back and educated at Harvard then NYU med.

I paused as Alex signaled me to turn the page. I couldn't believe any of us were still alive. Why not just kill us all? Now. Why was he insisting I keep reading his bio?

Alex appeared confident as ever. Security outside this cubicle was nil. Alex knew rescue was highly unlikely, at least for awhile. If Mulroney had read the papers I'd thrown at him and understood their meaning, he would have been here by now. Damn that Mulroney! Damn me for not keeping him involved in the first place.

Alex had secured the Vice President onto the scanning table, making sure his intravenous access was still in place. Gail sat motionless in the corner, inert with shock. It was down to me. I had to get the gun out of Alex's hands. I needed him away from the Vice President and close to me.

"Damn you, Alex," I blurted out as things began to fall in place. "Our meeting at the Nazi rally. That was no accident."

"You were my assignment," said Alex coldly. "I came to Richard Meese at the last minute just to keep an eye on you..." He smiled. "And hopefully find that little file of yours."

"Fuck you, Alex."

Alex smiled and picked up the syringe of thallium from the floor. Holding it in his left hand, he squirted a little into the air. "Ahh, the sweet almond smell of ergonovine and pavulon." The VP's eyes, filled with terror, looked helplessly in my direction.

"You saved my life two weeks ago, Alex. Why?"

For a moment I felt the splattered brains of Tannenbaum running down my face.

"Just business," he replied flatly, keeping the gun he held in his right hand pointed between my eyes. "Tannenbaum was supposed to kill you. When you got the message that the file had been sent to Chicago, I needed you alive, but didn't have the authority to call off the hit."

"That's why you gave Tannenbaum all that Valium when we got back to the hospital."

"Tannenbaum had outlived his usefulness. He wasn't in the future plans."

Think, Raskin. If nothing else, I had to stall for time, hoping that Mulroney might show up with help.

"Alex, we were friends," I swallowed. "Best friends."

"You were my project, Raskin. The reason I came to Richard Meese."

Then it hit me. "You killed Wanda Bylevin, you sonofabitch. Who else would she have invited over for a romantic evening if not me?"

"Little late on the hunches, Sherlock. I needed her out of the picture. She'd been a little too clever with the computer. Needed to see what was in that case of hers. Same with your buddy, Jack Hodges. He was noticing too much, getting in my way." Alex laughed softly. "And even you must agree that Malcolm Spool deserves to hang. The guy's such a dweeb."

Anger welled up. Something inside me was beginning to snap. I started moving forward. I heard the click of his gun and stopped.

"Look," said Alex, "I've got nothing personally against you. In a funny sort of way I think I like you." Alex paused, as if he didn't quite understand where that bit of emotion came from. "I'm a soldier. I follow orders. Jews, niggers, spics. They're my sworn enemies. And someday I'll be in the position to set policy. Friends of Tomorrow, Danny," he said, eyes bright with pride. "I'm in line to take Cantrell's place. Next Secretary-General of Friends of Tomorrow. In a funny way, you did me a favor, getting rid of Cantrell like you did."

I took a breath and somehow found the energy to manufacture a loud laugh. "No way, Alex. Not you."

Alex shook his head. "What do you think I've been training for all these years? I'm the perfect person to lead the new order."

"Not quite, Alex."

"What do you mean, not quite?"

"Fatal flaw, Alex."

His eyes widened.

"I read your bio Alex." I paused and leaped in. I could be dead in several seconds. "Pretty good assets."

I think that meant a lot to him. He'd flushed slightly.

"But I haven't read aloud what the file said about your liabilities."

Alex steadied the syringe, his eye twitching slightly. "What liabilities?"

Go for it, Raskin. I remembered the look in Alex's eyes when his bookie had been killed. That killing was a message to Alex. That was why, for the first time all year, I had seen him scared.

"Gambling, Alex."

"What?"

"I know it, you know it, and guess what my friend?" I tapped the book, laying on the table next to me. "They know it."

Alex stood up, seeming to stumble a moment, his eyes filled with hatred and disbelief. "I don't believe you."

I looked at the folder and pretended to read. ...."Significant compulsion toward gambling, the etiology of which is a genetic predisposition. Behavior has been manifested by unauthorized activities while in service of the Reich. Number one--while in Saudi Arabia..."

Alex moved toward me, charging like an angry bull. "I don't believe..."

"Furthermore," I continued. "It is the ruling of the tribunal executives that this defect is too severe to allow this said soldier to take his designated position as Secretary General of Friends of Tomorrow.."

"Let me see that!" yelled Alex, saliva pooling at the corners of his mouth. I waited until his hands were on the book, then sprung up and knocked the gun across the room. We tumbled onto the ground, grabbing, pinching. We rolled on the floor, smashing into a chair, then over Huber's body. I grabbed at Alex's eyes, then balked. They were smiling at me, smiling in hate. I landed a grazing blow to his cheek, then kneed him in the groin. I tried standing, but he kicked out my knees. I landed on my back, feeling something snap. Then he was on me, his strength overpowering. With his first punch, I heard my jaw crack as pain shot up my head. The second wallop sent me reeling against the wall, and the world seemed like a giant jigsaw puzzle breaking up before me. With the third blow my eyes closed.

Chapter 120 alex

When I awoke, I found myself laying on the gurney next to the treadmill, my arms secured tightly behind my back, my legs tied like a roped calf. I felt a pain at my side and looked in horror at an IV bag hanging above my arm. Across the room in one corner on the floor, Gail too, was tied up, terror in her eyes.

"You and Gail will die peacefully," Alex sneered. "Better than if Tannenbaum had his way." He laughed. "That bastard was a loose cannon. We'll have to be more careful with our recruiting efforts from now on." He looked over at Vice President Barrish. "I'm afraid it's not going to be pretty for you, Mr. Vice President. Had to be a hero 'til the end, huh?"

During my struggle with Alex, it seemed that Barrish had managed to dislodge the IV from his arm. Barrish now lay on his back, secured on top of the scanner, his chest still covered with ECG electrodes. Alex stepped onto the treadmill and reached upward toward the crash cart. He removed a six inch cardiac needle, then attached it to a 10 cc syringe and drew up the mixture of thallium and ergonovine and pavulon. I knew he was planning on injecting it directly into Barrish's heart. I kicked hard trying to loosen the ropes binding my feet. "Why, Alex? Just shoot us, for Christ's sake."

"Orders, Danny." He smiled, then checked to make sure I was securely tied. "Don't you get it? The new soldiers of the Fourth Reich are doctors. It's time the world knows of our capabilities."

"It's not going to work, Alex."

Alex laughed. "You seem to know a lot about my gambling history, Danny. Care to make a wager?"

"Yeah, Alex, this time I will."

"I thought I taught you something about making bad bets, Danny?"

"Oh yeah? Unless you leave right now, I guarantee you, this is one bet you're going to lose."

"What makes you so sure?"

"I saw Mulroney on the way over here. Look at your Nazi yearbook over there. I ripped out some pages, and gave them to Mulroney."

Alex looked over at the file, saw the shredded corners of missing pages. He froze momentarily. Then looked at his watch. "That was over fifteen minutes ago." Alex laughed. "Mulroney never figured anything out before. Why should he start now?"

"Leave, Alex. Now!"

"In good time, Danny," he said checking the attachment of the needle. He looked at the Vice President, then at me. "Want to watch history being made, Danny?"

"I'm not bluffing, Alex. You stay, you lose."

Alex looked at his watch. "In thirty minutes I'll be at the airport, catching a plane to Buenos Aires. I'll need a complete make-over, thanks to you, but I'll be back within six months."

"You're crazy."

Alex laughed as he uncapped the syringe. He leaned against the rails of the treadmill, the ceiling lights reflected off the six inch cardiac needle. Horror filled the eyes of the Vice President.

A loud knock sounded at the door. Alex lurched sideways. I felt the ropes loosening around my ankles.

My God, let it be Mulroney.

Alex looked at Gail. "You're next, sweetie. Sorry we never got it on. You missed something special."

Voices outside and more pounding on the door drowned out Alex's voice. He jumped, then stumbled backward. Suddenly Alex looked like a trapped wolf.

I glared at him. "Alex, you don't know a sucker bet if it's in your face."

Alex was suddenly gray, the life pumping out of him.

The pounding was louder, more frantic. "Open up!" Someone kicked at the door.

"Give it up, Alex."

Alex's eyes reddened.

"I can't, Danny. I've gone too far."

"You can, Alex. Please."

Alex lifted the syringe. The Vice President struggled.

"They'll go easy on you if you help them out. You couldn't resist. You were brainwashed as a child, when you were too young to understand. I read it, Alex. This wasn't your fault! You were brainwashed."

Gun shots exploded outside. Pieces of wood splintered across the room.

"Alex, please. They'll be here in seconds."

"Can't, Danny."

"Alex, there's another door on the other side, where they store the fluoro equipment. Use it."

Alex looked up. "You want to help me?"

"Leave Barrish alone, Alex. Just get the hell out. I won't tell them where you've gone."

Another explosion, wood fragments flying, shadows of people through the fractured door. Alex was trapped, caught in a moment of indecision. Which way to go. Would he surrender? My right leg jerked free.

"Please, Alex."

Another moment of hesitation. For a moment the pensive look of the old Alex. Then he changed. A mean wolf-like look filled his face. He snarled at the Vice president. The door began exploding under the gunfire. Alex stood on the treadmill, his throne, his syringe lifted high in the air. "Here's a bet, Danny boy. I'm going to kill Barrish before the door opens." He laughed.

"Bet not." With that I threw my body toward the treadmill, my free leg catapulting the rail. It landed square on the start switch. With a sudden whirl, the treadmill began spinning. Alex was thrown forward, into the air. He landed on the floor, on his chest, face down. He groaned as he turned over. The needle lay buried in his chest, the contents of the syringe empty.

Alex stared at me momentarily, his eyes filled with confusion and a boyish vulnerability.

"Alex!"

"Danny, I'm..."

His eyes rolled back and he fell to the floor.

Chapter 121 loose ends

Over the next twenty four hours, the Feds rounded up ninety five operatives from the Friends of Tomorrow. Their horde included no less than twelve deans, thirty five professors of medicine, and seventeen medical interns and residents, already scattered throughout various medical centers around the country. The missing file also contained the organization's charter, which, after a rambling, misanthropic preamble with roots in Germany in the thirties, stated its goals and objectives. First and foremost on the agenda labeled: "Final solution number two: To kill every person claiming to have witnessed or survived the Holocaust." Their time table and statistics were as cold and calculating as Adolf Eichmann's had been some forty years before. Names, locations, addresses, projected "innocent deaths per month that could be performed without arousing speculation." The document detailed how fourteen newly trained medical killers were to be absorbed into the staffs of clinics serving the medical needs of large Jewish communities where Holocaust survivors would likely be found... Los Angeles, New York , Florida.

Second on their agenda was a massive revision of the history of World War II, proving beyond any shadow of a doubt that the murder of six million Jews was a fabrication. That few, if any, Jews were killed as enemies of the State. And that concentration camps were nothing but work camps. Zyklon B had been used only as a camp insecticide.

There was much to learn about the extent of the conspiracy, and it would take years before everything could be sorted out. But for now, the threat was over. The FBI director called a news conference, and with the President and Vice President at his side, revealed that they had exposed a murderous group of assassins who had infiltrated the deepest recesses of the medical community. He revealed their basic charter, named a few of the most prominent physicians involved, but purposely left most of the other details vague. Richard Meese Hospital was never mentioned, and under prior agreement, never would be.

Alex Rosen, alias Jonathan Pentarsky, had indeed been next in line for the position of Secretary-General of Friends of Tomorrow. Fuhrer of the Fourth Reich. Despite what happened, I couldn't hold back my tears as they covered him with a death cloth, wheeling his young body away on a gurney. I lifted the sheet and touched his forehead, a cold, almost rubbery texture, and thought of the good times we'd had--the fishing expeditions to Fullerton Harbor, the shared night call, the talking... the memories hurt too damn much. I paused to look at his face, hoping that in death the innocence of youth had returned at last. He had been robbed of that innocence and manufactured into a monster who was controlled and programmed for a new world order. Hopefully, that order was now dead.

I was flown to Washington DC to attend a private reception with both the President and Vice President of the United States. Also in attendance were the directors of the FBI, Secret Service, and the Simon Wiesenthal Institute for Nazi crimes. Because she had witnessed the entire episode, and because her life also had been directly threatened by Alex, Gail was invited too. In exchange, we both promised never to speak to anyone concerning the events that had transpired at Richard Meese.

I was thrown a few compliments during the reception for helping my country, my religion, for being a patriot. Simon Wiesenthal himself hugged me and said a prayer. We were given a wonderful lunch followed by a personal tour of the White House by the First Lady.

Gail and I stayed on in D.C. for a few days, courtesy of Uncle Sam. We took in the Aerospace museum, meandered around a half-dozen monuments, got teary eyed at Arlington, ate chocolate souffles in Georgetown. We might have lingered forever, had it not been time to head back to Chicago where we would undergo the ritual of changing out of our short white coats of internship into freshly laundered, white coats that hung at our knees.

And of course there was Maxine Chu.

Chapter 122 maxine chu

"Hey there, furball." I stood at the doorway with a bag of fortune cookies from Moon Palace. Maxine lifted herself off the bed and took short, unsteady steps into my arms.

"Welcome back, Mr. Hero," she said kissing my cheek.

"Hey, keep that hero stuff to yourself." Of all people, it was Sol Goldman who had briefed Maxine with a basic sketch of the events. Maxine wore a white robe and had her hair in a bow behind her head.

"I'm going home in a few days." She lumbered to her desk and handed me a sheaf of lab tests and scans. "All clear," she smiled. "No evidence of Hodgkins."

"I know, furball. But you need close follow-up. Medical miracles are not to be taken lightly." There would be the usual battery of surveillance testing, plus careful observation for potential side-effects from the immunosuppressive treatment to keep her marrow from rejecting the transplant. But nothing in the foreseeable future would keep her from living the way she and I had dreamed of ever since that August day when we shared our first fortune cookies.

"Giving up fashion?" I asked, spying a tableful of college catalogues where Vogue and Marie Clair used to be.

"As of today, I am pre-med." Maxine smiled. "I'm hoping U of C will take a medical miracle into their class in two years. My goal is to haunt you wherever you go. "

"You've already attained that goal, Maxine Chu."

"I want to be your medical student, maybe even your resident. Who knows, one of these days it could be me and you, partners in crime."

"Forget it Maxine. I'm out of the crime and terror business."

"Don't count on it," a gruff voice said behind me. Officer Mulroney had two donuts on a plate and a glass of fruit punch in hand. "Your reputation's gotten around. Wouldn't surprise me if the boys downtown consulted you from time to time, you know, forensic sort of stuff. There's money to be made on consultations," he said smiling.

544

I waved him off, telling him I'd think about it. He patted me on the back, whispering how proud he was of me before lumbering off.

"See," said Maxine after he left. "Like I said, me and you, partners in crime."

The thought of it made me erupt in laughter. Imagine. Me and Maxine running around playing medical detectives? Then again, who knew?

"You'll never get rid of me, Daniel Raskin. I owe you my life."

Chapter 123 epilogue

It was a gorgeous sunny day in June. A smooth, almost Caribbean breeze wafted across the American flag hanging outside Richard Meese Hospital. We greeted the new interns, handing them their i.d. badges, and telling them what an exciting year they were in for. They looked so young, I remarked to Malcolm Spool, who was sizing up his new long white coat in the reflection of the window.

Malcolm smiled. "I already lectured my students on washing their hands. "

Gail and I laughed.

"But," he said, blushing, "I also told them that if I'm too hard on them, they can call me Malformed Stool. As long as they do it behind my back."

In the corner, Brian Picolli had the undivided attention of Susan Fleming, an intern from Brian's alma mater, UCLA, and former U.S. National women's surfing champion. When he saw me, he came over, his hand on my shoulder.

"Good work, my man."

"You too, Brian. You saved my relationship with Maxine. I never got to thank you."

"No charge. Besides, I'm taking Maxine for her first surfing lesson next week."

I had picked up two new interns earlier that morning, Sheila Cohn and Robert Zendowski. They looked like kids, and I wondered how I had aged so much in one year. The two of them stood anxiously when I approached. Robert held out a nervous hand. "Don't mind my asking, but there's a rumor going around that you saved the life of the Vice President of the United States."

I smiled. "Take out your pen and peripheral brain," I said. "Rule number one. Do not believe any rumor you hear in this or any hospital. Only believe what your residents tell you. They're the only ones you can trust."

I introduced them to the patients they would be handling. They looked scared and tentative. "How do you learn everything?" they asked at the end. "There's so much."

I smiled. "Look. Let me tell you what happened my first call night. I thought someone was dead. I smashed my fist into his chest. He was only sleeping."

Sheila giggled." Really?"

"Crushed two ribs of a sleeping patient in for a diarrhea workup."

"How will we be able to tell the difference?"

"That's what you're here for, Sheila."

At 11:30 a.m. Gail and I hopped on the shuttle bus to U of C hospital. Sol Goldman was giving grand rounds on hyperthyroidism, his area of expertise. As we walked down the hallway toward the auditorium, Gail suddenly kissed me on the cheek. "You sure you want to move in together?" she asked. "I mean, let's make sure we never interfere with each other's life style. Let's always communicate."

"As long as it's not just by talking."

"Hey, let's go hear some blues tonight. There's a great band over at Murphy's on Division."

I shook my head. "Sorry, Gail. Plans."

"Going out behind my back already?"

"Yep. Friday night services at Beth Teresh Synagogue in Hyde Park. Thought I'd check it out." We walked another ten yards. "In fact, with the extra free time this year, I'm thinking of signing up for a some basic Hebrew lessons. Interested?"

"You learn Hebrew. I'll learn Kama Sutra."

Two minutes later we were outside the auditorium, ten minutes late, which was okay considering Sol Goldman, pioneer in thyroid research, was one of the most boring lecturers at the medical center. As we opened the door, I heard a muffled sound, coming from the janitor's closet behind us. For a moment my heart stopped. I opened the door to find Sol Goldman bound to the coat rack and gagged with adhesive tape. I peeled away the tape.

"He did it," he gasped, pointing toward the auditorium.

"Who?"

"Take a look."

We peeked through the small window in the auditorium door. There was Eddie Ingraham, disguised with a new hairpiece that reached down to his shoulders, a full beard, and horn-rimmed glasses perched on the bridge of his nose. We stood in the open doorway, amazed, listening to Eddie lecture. He certainly seemed to know what he was talking about, punctuating his scientific talk with humorous and obviously fabricated anecdotes. Eddie looked over, and saw me standing there. He smiled and waved. I winked.

Back outside the closet, I looked at Sol, then at Gail. "It sounds like a great lecture, Gail. I don't want to miss a word of it."

"Yeah, let's grab a seat," she said, grinning.

"Hey!" yelled Sol. "Get me out of here!"

I started to slip the tape back over his mouth. "Sorry, Sol. Remember how you told us that as residents we have the responsibility of looking out for the best interests of our interns?"

Sol's eyes burned. I reached up, sealing off his mouth. "We'll pick you up after the talk, Sol. Let's do lunch."

I locked my arm through Gail's and entered the auditorium. It was going to be a great day.

ABOUT THE AUTHOR

Alan Maisel attended medical school at University of Michigan, and did his internal medicine residency in Chicago. He was trained in cardiology at the University of California, San Diego, where he currently is a Professor of Medicine and Director of the Coronary Care Unit at the VA hospital. Besides patient care, Dr. Maisel has an active research program and has published nearly 100 scientific articles. He is also the recipient of many medical student and resident teaching awards. He is married to a dentist to whom he dedicates this book, and has 5 children. He is at work on his second novel.